Wizardream

Book 11

Of Wizardry and War

Wizardream

BOOK II

Of Wizardry and War

Bruce Chatfield

Press

Published by 99% Press,
an imprint of Lasavia Publishing Ltd.
Auckland, New Zealand
www.lasaviapublishing.com

Copyright ©Bruce Chatfield, 2023
Illustrations by Bruce Chatfield
Marbling by Bruce Chatfield
Edited by Rowan Sylva
Designed by Daniela Gast

ISBN: 978-1-99-118983-7

To Joanne

Foreword

In Book Two of Wizardream the depth of the trilogy starts to pay off. While editing, I considered moving Chapter Three back, so that the book would begin with a harrowing chase. I decided against it, keeping the book exactly as Chatfield had it. The lore and its riddles, therefore, come first. And as the fragments come together, their importance to the plot becomes more intriguing and apparent.

Book Two has its share of excitement, epic battles, greedy villains, difficult escapes and gruelling journeys. Yet, it also invites us to puzzle over it. Just as Flindas and Triss must solve the riddle of the Place of Puzzles, so the reader tries to decode the role of the Black Wizard, Manzanee, the actions of Rishtan Sta, the identity of Chelesta and the fate of the high and Low Wizards. What happened in the Wizard's Wars? What is the Wizards Way, and how does this effect the strange fate of the Maradass family?

Book Two contains some brilliantly imagined wizards. And more than the other two books, explores the indigenous element to the fantasy, their history, their present, and of course, Manzanee. Finally it tickled me that the heroic Elbrand warriors subsist on oats and dried fruit. A hearty bowl of porridge, being the ultimate in wholesome fantasy fare.

Rowan Sylva

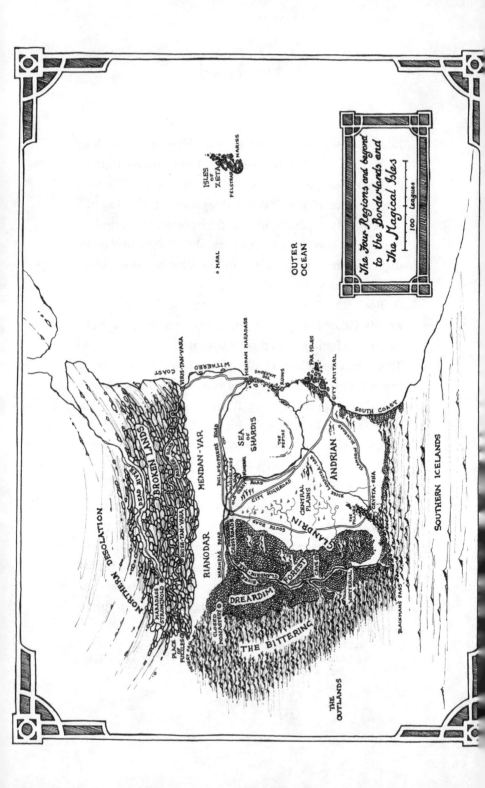

The Four Regions and beyond to the Borderlands and The Magical Isles

100 Leagues

ISLES OF ZETA
FELSTRAND NARISS

MARL

OUTER OCEAN

VIRIS-TAN-VARA COAST

WITHERED

MENDAN MARADASS

THE MARROWS

RUINS

FAR ISLES

CITY AMITARL

SOUTH COAST

NORTHERN DESOLATION

BROKEN LANDS

THE OLD RIVER

MARADASS STRONGHOLD

PLACE OF PILGRIMAGE

DESERT ROAD

SHISTURANI-VARA

MENDAN-VAR

RIANODAR

PHILOSOPHER'S ROAD

SEA OF SHARDIS

THE DEPTHS

CITY HIGHROAD

OLD COAST ROAD

MARINAL ROAD

CROSSROADS

SOUTH ROAD

GLANDRIN

CENTRAL PLAINS

VANGORA RIVER

GLANDRIN RIVER

CRYSTA-SHA

ANDRIAN

THE PALACE

CLOSED MONASTERY

DREARDIM

FOREST OF GLANDRIN

BLACKMAN'S PASS

THE BITTERING

THE OUTLANDS

SOUTHERN ICELANDS

Contents

The Young Hero

After the departure of Flindas and the Elbrand warriors Kerran
spent much time during the day exploring the Green City, and
wandering the many pathways in the surrounding countryside.
Most evenings he spent with Tolth and Verardian, learning
many important and fascinating things. There were more
books on Zeta than Kerran had thought possible. So many
thoughts, deeds, and histories of the Regions and beyond were
told between their covers. Though Kerran had never learned
to read he was given an excellent teacher in Nup, and soon he
began to understand what in the past had been but marks on
parchment, or on shop fronts in his village. He learned quickly
and studied with a passion. A moon passed and part of another
and there was no word from the Elbrand or Flindas. Tolth
became worried, for the ship had not returned. The sharp
bite of winter departed slowly and spring came softly to the
Magical Isles.

Kerran wondered about the family Amitarl. He had been
reading a short history of them that was a simple book for
the early reader. He picked it up again, for he found that he
needed to read things at least twice before they were held in
his memory.

The Seacrest Ma-Zurin-Bidar had been divided at the Crossroads, and the four pieces passed to the families Amitarl and Maradass. Barthol Amitarl had carried the fragment that was concerned with the future until he was more than two hundred years old. He made his home on the coast of Andrian, not far south of the present city which still retained his family name. At his death the piece, that he had tried so hard to master, was passed on to his only son, Faras.

Narinda the daughter of Barthol, who had been present at the dividing, had received the piece that was concerned with the past. For almost a century Narinda had delved into the mysteries surrounding the gift, and during this time she made her home in the place that was known then as the Mountains of the Moon. Here she gathered together a following, and then at the death of her father Barthol, she had passed her fragment on to Arana, the only daughter of Faras, and then she had disappeared from the lands. Though some sought her amongst the three tall pillar-like cliffs of the Closed Monastery which she had founded, none could say where she had gone. There were some who searched and did not return, and others who came back telling of a powerful magic which surrounded the high mountains.

Peace reigned in this time and there was much travel and trade between the Four Regions. Arana, like Narinda before her, did not marry. The fragment of the Seacrest which she carried had filled her life with wonder and adventure. She drew great powers of healing from it, and much of these skills were passed down unchanged through the following centuries. She had also found a deep understanding of the very distant past which no other has ever been able to do. Mardred, her eldest brother, was next to receive Barthol's piece. Lindris his wife bore three children. There was Erindas who founded the City Amitarl, Driadana who helped her brother in the venture, and Mandrin who married his cousin Naral and produced a family of girls.

The House of Amitarl flourished for almost four centuries, but without many offspring. They were long lived, though by now it was seen by all that the women of the family were not inclined towards marriage. Something in the fragment, which influenced their lives deeply, led them into other pursuits, often dangerous, though it was also seen that a protection lay upon them and they prospered in whatever paths they chose to follow. The daughter of Erindas, Noria, explored into the dangers of the Northern Desolation and returned, bringing with her a great wealth of gold and gems. Taras her brother, married a woman of Glandrin who gave birth to the famed Celisor, builder of the castle, and defender of Andrian from the darkness that would come from the north.

Rardana, his sister, was one of the few women of Amitarl to come to an untimely end. She was visiting her mother's home city of Crysta-Sha when Zard Maradass, the benevolent governor of Glandrin, was slain by his mad brother's hand. The city of Crysta-Sha fell into ruins, and Rardana was amongst those who did not survive. It was on the news of her death that Jarla, her young niece, had told her family that Rardana had chosen not to carry her Seacrest fragment to Crysta-Sha and had left it in her own safe keeping.

War raged through the lands. First it was Celisor who led the Southlanders against the Mad One's armies. He was a powerful man, even though well past his hundredth year, and would have continued the fight but for a wound which almost ended his life, and had caused him to step aside. Rubon, his gallant and much loved son, had grown to manhood and commanded in his father's stead. With him went Taras his eldest son and also his cousins, Erindas the second, the twins Faldamar and Randarl and lastly Zy, who fought amongst the men though she was slightly built and could bear little armour.

The war continued for almost two centuries until the Seacrest fragment, which Zard the Black One had borne, was found by Amitarl upon the battlefield. It was the turning of fate, and eventually the dark armies were driven from the Regions and into the barren lands to the north. Though the war had been won, it was at a great cost to the House of Amitarl. Celisor had died of old age earlier, and did not know of the great sadness which was to come. Of those in his family who had gone to war only Zy returned. Rubon, his son Taras, and his three cousins had all died during the last savage battles, and so once again the family Amitarl existed by one slender branch.

Though Glendar was the eldest Amitarl woman, and most revered, she chose not to lead the people into the peace that had been won. Instead she chose in her sadness to seek out the Closed Monastery and she was never seen in the lands again. Celisor the Second, her decadent younger brother, now governed the Four Regions. Glendar's piece of the Seacrest which had been Narinda's, was passed to Nartalin her brother's daughter. Celisor the Second now had two pieces at his command, that of the Future and that of Life. He lived a long and wicked life, and when his younger brother Nerris died in a strange accident, there were many who whispered of jealousy within the family. Celisor the Second would have his way in all things. Brarn, his only son, was an old man himself by the time his father died, and he did not outlive his parent by more than a year, and he left behind but one child to carry the name Amitarl into the future.

Celisor the Third was a kindly man, and the evil, which his grandfather had wrought, he worked hard to undo. The people of the lands had themselves turned to corrupt ways and he knew that it would take generations to recover what had been lost. The golden age, before the Mad One had come, was like a dream of paradise to the old man. When he died, the Regions were a dangerous place still, though stability was still held by the councils of the City Amitarl and Mendan-Maradass.

On the death of his father, Celisor the Second, Darna, his unmarried son, had a dream. He saw the Magical Isles of Zeta across the vast ocean, and when he woke he was gripped by a burning desire to go in search of the mythical green isles. With his sister Anrin who held Narinda's fragment, he prepared a small fleet of ships, and with many followers they left the Regions and sailed into the east, never to return.

With the power in the combined fragments of the Seacrest, and the help of Ni, an Elveren maid who had fallen in love with Darna, they finally reached the fabled shores of Zeta. What they found was a scorched and broken wilderness. Maradass the Mad had found the Isles centuries before, and his own dark magic lay upon their shores still. Few creatures and little of the forest had survived his scourge, and it was a long time before the followers of Darna and Anrin came to truly love their new found home. Darna and Ni had but one child; Tolth was the first Amitarl of Zeta. Kerran wondered if Tolth was just old or very old. Nup entered carrying a lamp.

"Will you eat Kerran?" he asked.

One day Tolth came to Kerran holding a small scroll of paper in his hand.

"A letter for you Kerran," said the old Amitarl.

"A letter?" said Kerran in surprise, he had never received one in his life before, and in wonder he took it from Tolth's hand and stared at it in wonder.

"Well open it!" said Tolth in a teasing voice. "It may be important."

Kerran unrolled the paper, but as yet he did not have the knowledge to understand it all.

"Will you read it for me Tolth?" he asked. "I do not know some of the words, not the big ones."

Tolth took back the paper and read it aloud. "To Kerran the Young Hero, in care of Tolth Amitarl, Nariss. Dear Kerran, I am coming to the city soon and I thought that you may be kind enough to join me for a day and tell me your tale. The Regions fascinate me greatly, and I have never met anyone who actually came from there."

She gave details of when she and her parents would arrive, and where they would be staying in the city, it was signed Piata Wespal in a strong flowing hand.

"Well, well," said Tolth. "It appears that you have a reputation now. Young hero indeed." Tolth smiled. "I remember this young woman from the games," he said. "Strong and valiant. I think a day off from your instruction will do you no harm."

Kerran met Piata at a small eating house near the ocean, not far from the Council Buildings. For a while he felt confused and embarrassed. In his village he had avoided girls, and had led an isolated life even from the boys. He found Piata quite disarming, and thought her the most enchanting young woman he had ever met. Her easy manner helped him to relax, and it was not long before he was repeating his story for her. She was intrigued by much of what he said and the day slipped by as they talked and laughed together.

"My father is a fisherman on Shoalwater," said Piata. "It is a large harbour but not very deep. There are many smaller craft that are used to fish there. Kerran, I was wondering if you would like to come to Felstrar and stay for a while. We can go fishing with my father and brothers, and go walking in the mountains. It is a beautiful and interesting place.

"I would like that," said Kerran. "Nariss is very pleasant, but I miss the countryside. I do not think I am made to be a scholar. I will see what Tolth thinks of it. It seems to be important that I stay on Zeta for now, and I think the lessons are mostly a way of keeping me occupied, though I do enjoy most of them. It can be hard work fighting my way through some of the language at times, though I do like reading and learning history."

"There is no shortage of books at our home," said Piata.

Kerran approached Tolth on the proposed visit to Piata's home, and Tolth agreed with a smile that it would be a good idea.

"You will get to see some more of our country, and that is an education in itself," he told Kerran. "It is a beautiful area that you go to. You will enjoy it I think, and you will also enjoy the young lady's company no doubt."

Kerran felt his face begin to flush.

It was arranged that Kerran would leave with Piata and her parents for Felstrar in two days, Rark would also go as Kerran felt he could not leave the dog behind. Piata's parents welcomed Kerran and Rark aboard their wagon, which was drawn by two large, well matched horses. It had been a supply trip to the Green City for them and the wagon was loaded with goods needed for their village and for themselves.

Piata's father, Amus, had been a scholar in the city for some years, but when he had met his wife, Sharee, they had decided that they preferred a quieter country life. Amus enjoyed fishing, and after more than twenty years in Felstrar, they had found a balance and happiness that was ever present in their light hearted lives.

The country was quite different from the hills that Kerran had passed through in the south and east of the island. A flat plain spread out before them, green and cultivated. The forest became more broken but still ran in wide belts, dividing the land. It was an area where people farmed and grew fruit trees of various kinds. There were many villages and small towns in this part of Zeta, and Kerran had not realised that the population was so large. Rarely did Nariss seem to be overcrowded, and the traffic on the roads was never congested. Without appearing to be well organised the systems on Zeta worked very well.

That night they spent in a wayside hostel, and by the next afternoon they arrived at the village of Felstrar. Beyond lay Shoalwater, the vast harbour that Kerran took to be the open sea at first, until he was told the nature of the great enclosed bay. After unloading much of their supplies in the town, Amus urged the team on, and they began to travel a narrow road that hugged the southern coastline of the harbour. Kerran began to have a feeling that he knew this place. The mountains beyond were stark and familiar in his mind, though he could not remember how he may have seen them before; perhaps in a book of pictures in Tolth's library, though he could not remember when. After a time he shrugged it off, maybe in the south of Zeta he had seen similar mountains and forest.

They were a league or more beyond Felstrar when Amus turned the wagon onto a narrow side road and they began to ascend. Soon they were passing through a flat open field at the top of the small hill. A house lay ahead, nestled into the edge of the forest and with a magnificent view of Shoalwater to the north.

"What a wonderful house," said Kerran leaping down from the wagon.

Rark followed, and gambolled about like a puppy, stretching his stiff legs. He had run beside the wagon for some of their journey, but during the afternoon he had tired and so rode with Kerran amongst the supplies. Smoke rose from the chimney, and soon Kerran saw two almost identical young men coming down from the front door. Both gazed in awe at the great dog that had suddenly appeared in their front yard.

"What is that?" one asked incredulously.

"That, my sons, is Rark, a rare mountain dog," said Amus. "And this is Kerran from the Regions. We are fortunate to have with us the young hero that all Zeta is talking about."

Kerran whispered to Piata. "I wish people would stop calling me that," and he went to greet the brothers.

"These are Carn and Raylard, our sons," said Amus in introduction.

"Welcome to Zeta and our home," said Carn, the older brother. "We have heard your story a number of times second hand, and each time it changes. We would be much pleased to hear it again, and this time without the possibility of other people's variations."

Raylard went to Rark and scratched the great beast's shoulders. "This is one part of the story that lives up to the telling," he said.

The family ate supper on the porch, the sun sending long streaks of light across the harbour and shoreline. Kerran told his story once again, sometimes it seemed like a dream, or an adventure that had happened to someone else. He told of the stranger in the wide brimmed hat who nursed him back from the edge of death, the dangers of the Sea of Shardis, and beyond. He shuddered as once again he felt the knife in his hand on the mysterious wooded island of Marl. The night grew cool and he continued the telling sitting indoors by a large log fire.

"We go fishing early," said Amus to his sons as he left the fireside for bed. "Do not keep our guest up talking too late or we shall miss the tide."

Kerran was speaking of his first sighting of Zeta, when a yawn that he could not stop told the others that their guest was tired.

"Excuse us," said Carn. "It has been a long day for you. We must also get to sleep for father will wake us early. Goodnight Kerran and sleep well."

With that the two brothers left Piata to show Kerran his

bedroom. He had the luxury of a small cabin detached from the rest of the house, built amongst the trees behind the main building. Piata lit a lamp and showed him the way along the narrow shell strewn path. Sharee had made up his bed and a large bowl and pitcher of water stood on the wash stand, Piata placed the lamp by his bedside and turned toward the door.

"Thank you Kerran," she said before she left him. "I think it the most exciting adventure I have ever heard, except perhaps for Elfhand's journeys." For a moment she stood by the door, her hand on the latch. "Good night, young hero," she said with a smile. "Sleep well."

She closed the door and was gone. Almost immediately there was a scratching and snuffling at the door. Kerran opened it to find Rark asking to be let in. He too seemed lonely. Flindas was far away on the Borders or beyond. Kerran let Rark in and he settled down on a thick rug beside the bed. Kerran gave the dog one last scratch behind the ears, stripped off his clothes and crawled beneath the warm blankets. Then he lay in the darkness and was unable to sleep. The talk of the evening had stirred up many memories and thoughts of his young life.

He wished to be home with his mother, but there was more to be done here it seemed. Tolth was wise and understood much. Kerran knew that he would not leave Zeta until the time was right, and that time was not yet. His eyes closed against the darkness and he wandered through the forest of his home. Slowly his thoughts stilled and he fell into a deep sleep, and he dreamed.

Kerran sat before a small fire, and all else was dark. He felt as if paralysed, staring into the blackness that was beyond the fire, which crackled and spat the occasional spark. Into the firelight came the dark face of Manzanee, the one who Tolth had once called the Black Wizard. His eyes were wide and he wore a broad gleeful smile. His large white teeth seemed to sparkle in the firelight.

"Welcome Kerran," he said quietly. There was a long silence as Manzanee carefully studied the young face before him. "You are not happy, I see this," the Black Wizard said.

Kerran could not move, much less reply.

"You have needs that cannot be filled by those around you. This I also see. Let me take you somewhere and it may ease this sadness, then again it may not. It is in your hands."

Kerran felt a strange sensation pass through his body. It was as if he had lost all feeling. Where he had touched the earth floor of the cave, and the warmth of the fire, he now felt nothing. Slowly the fire died, becoming mere sparks, until all the light was gone. He was suspended in the darkness with no sensation of body. It was not unpleasant, and for a while he felt no need for anything else to happen. It was blissful after a time and his mind ceased to wander. He became one with the darkness, even his own identity slipping from his memory.

"Come Kerran," said the disembodied voice of Manzanee. "Come into the light."

There was a small flickering far off. It seemed like a huge distance away, as if he was watching a single star in the black night sky. Without feeling or thought Kerran moved toward the light, or the light moved toward him, there seemed no difference. It grew until it filled his whole vision. Kerran passed into the light and then he recognised where he was. His body had not returned, and he floated joyfully down the path that led to his mother's door. He passed through the gate to his front yard and there, tending the garden, was his mother, looking just as he had left her. He called to her but she did not respond. He moved to her side, and then found that he could not reach out and touch her. The voice of Manzanee came into his mind.

"Do not try to make contact Kerran. If you could you would break the connection that holds you to your living body on Zeta. You would become a ghost, and your part in these great times would be at an end. This I cannot allow, for I would have caused it, and that is not my part to play. Observe Kerran, watch carefully and perhaps you will learn something of interest to you." Manzanee's voice receded and was gone.

From the doorway of the house his mother's best friend from the village came out with a pitcher of apple juice and freshly baked biscuits. Even without his body Kerran could smell them. The familiarity of that smell almost made him weep, though he knew that his physical eyes were far away on an island in the vast Outer Ocean.

"Come and rest Ondwa," said the woman at the door.

His mother straightened from her work, pushing her hands into the small of her back. She gave herself a stretch and walked to the wooden table and two chairs that stood near the side of the house. Kerran moved closer to the two women. He could see every detail, every small wrinkle at the corner of his mother's eyes.

"You dreamed again last night," said the friend to his mother.

"Yes, and again it was so real that I just know it must be true," his mother replied. "I saw him, Kerran that is. He was travelling in a wagon drawn by two large horses, with a man and woman riding up front. There was a girl and that great dog I told you of. They rode in the back. I still do not know what these dreams mean except that I believe Kerran still lives, and is somewhere safe. That was all I saw this time. They travelled on the wagon through green fields and forests unlike any I have ever seen."

She was silent for a time, her friend pouring them both a tumbler of juice. They nibbled biscuits and seemed at peace. Kerran felt himself being drawn backward away from the scene, back into darkness.

"No," he called out. "I do not want to go yet."

"You cannot stay," said the voice of Manzanee. "Time and distance does not allow it."

Kerran's consciousness returned to the darkness, and then once again he sat before the fire. His body now returned, and yet at the same time he knew that this was not his real body, that it still slept in a warm bed on Zeta. The face of Manzanee glowed in the light of the small fire.

"You see now Kerran," said Manzanee. "That is the way it is and your mother does not fret for you. Do not struggle against your situation and your fate. You are chosen to play a part in this game that all around you, others call the present. You have touched on the past with the aid of the Seacrest, perhaps you would now like to see a little of the future?"

A gleeful grin spread across the Black Wizard's face, and then Manzanee was silent for a time looking deep into the fire. Kerran looked also, and there seemed to be an unusual pulsating at its very heart, something dark was moving there. Manzanee leant forward, and bringing his two hands slowly into the flames, he scooped up the dark moving thing from the fire. His hands remained above the flames, palms open. Kerran looked closely at what he held. It began to grow, there were small human figures which moved around on the palms of the old black man's hands. Slowly they grew, until the entire cave seemed filled with floating spectres, unreal wraithlike figures that floated across the cave's open space, he recognised some of them.

There was the tall black figure of Zard, and beside him a wizened, old man, who must be his father, Maradass. Others floated through in this parade of ghostlike figures. There was one who could have been Mindis, and a radiantly beautiful woman who he did not know. A baby lay hovering in space, a boy child, not long born. Then Kerran saw that he too was among them, dressed in strange clothes, he had not recognised himself at first.

The interplay of people was impossible to decipher. They spoke, but no sound came to Kerran's ears. He watched it all closely, unable to take his eyes away, if he blinked he did not notice. All movement was slowed. Simple hand gestures seemed to take a long time. Then Kerran felt the confrontation between those gathered, and there was anger and hatred. Death hovered as a cloud above them all. Suddenly Kerran realised that the phantom that was Zard had turned to his own spectre and had slowly held out his hand to him. The ghostlike figure that was Kerran moved across the cave and deliberately put something into the Black Knight's hand. There was a sudden flash of bright light. It filled the cave and then was gone, taking with it all of the apparitions.

Again Kerran sat before the fire, confusion and fear rushing through his mind, the face of Manzanee looking at him from across the flames, a playful smile flickering across his lips.

"Tolth will not understand this one either," he said. "Though a time will come when you will all know. You are so close to the answer, yet you know not the nature of the riddle. By accident you almost know the play of the game, but not now, not yet. That is all, go back to sleep, go to sleep... Remember, there are no accidents."

Kerran woke late, the memory of the night strong in his mind. The door stood open and Rark was nowhere in sight. On the cabinet beside his bed he found a large glass of milk and a plate of eggs and toasted bread. They were quite cold but Kerran ate them down all the same. He was hungry and they were delicious. He washed his face, the cold water invigorating him, and then he dressed. He felt as if during the night a great weight had been taken from him, and he smiled at himself in the mirror, then laughed at the smile.

"Do all young heroes laugh at themselves in mirrors?" came the voice of Piata from the doorway.

Kerran swung around in embarrassment, almost knocking the pitcher from the stand, but managing to catch it before it fell to the floor. "Good morning," he said weakly, and replaced the jug on the cabinet.

"To be able to laugh at yourself is a wonderful thing," she said. "So it is written in our ancient Book of Truths." She smiled. "Come Kerran, I see you have eaten, so let us go exploring. There was once a town and castle on the hills above us. They are old, very old, before the coming of Amitarl. Perhaps Rishtan-Sta built it, but no one knows. let us go and see."

She had packed a little food and drink, Kerran slipped on his boots and they were soon walking up a trail that led into the hills above. There had been no sign of Rark or the two family dogs. Piata told him that they seemed to have left early on an adventure of their own. The day was clear and warm and Kerran was soon puffing as the climb became steeper.

"So our young hero is out of condition," said Piata teasingly. "That is city life for you." She smiled back at him.

"I wish you would not call me that," he said with a note of displeasure in his voice. "It was an accident that I even came on this journey."

"Excuse me Kerran," she said. "I will not call you that again if it really displeases you, but as the Book of Truths says, 'There are no accidents.'"

"What is this Book of Truths?" asked Kerran. "Tolth has never mentioned it."

"It is a small book, almost a work for children," she replied. "There are quotations from many famous and not so famous people of the past, little wise sayings that have been collected over the centuries and gathered into a book. It is added to and reprinted occasionally. Probably every home on Zeta has a copy lying around somewhere." Piata turned and looked up the trail. "Come, let us climb," she said. "It is not so far to the first ruins now."

They came to a flat open space. Old cut stones were tumbled in heaps in every direction, shrubs and small trees growing through the old fortifications.

"This is the small ruin," said Piata as they walked around what once must have been a courtyard. "Few people come here," she said as she stood high on a ruined wall balancing on one leg. "The occasional scholar comes to poke and prod, but they all go away shaking their heads. It seems that the stonework is unlike any other on Zeta, or even in the Regions. They say that the stones themselves were not quarried here on Zeta. Why would anyone bring stone all the way from somewhere else to build a castle here I cannot guess; there are mountains of the stuff right here?" She waved her arms towards the towering peaks to the south.

They wandered further into the ruins where there were many dark places to explore, for which Piata had brought a small lamp. They came to a shaft that seemed to go directly down for a long way.

"I think this was an escape tunnel," she said secretively. "It leads all the way to the main castle over there."

She pointed to a nearby hill, much higher than the place where they now stood. "It is possible to go this way if you like," she said. "Only the beginning is difficult."

Kerran looked into the hole. It seemed very deep, the bottom lost in darkness. "It does not look easy," said Kerran continuing to peer into the depths.

"Not too dangerous for our young ...." and she stopped. "Excuse me Kerran, one day my mouth will turn around and bite me. That also comes from the Book of Truths."

She laughed again, the sound so full of delight that Kerran had to smile. "Look," she said pointing to the side of the hole. "There are even hand and foot holds that go all the way to the bottom."

Kerran had not noticed them before but there they were small holds at regular distances that disappeared into the darkness.

"Here, I will go first," said Piata.

Holding the lamp in her teeth she swung her legs over the side and was soon moving quickly down the shaft. Kerran tentatively slipped over the edge and followed. The descent was a lot further than he had first thought. He moved by touch, the light of the lamp and the sky above becoming useless after a time. Finally from below he heard Piata call up to him.

"I am down. Tis not so far to go."

It was a surprise when his feet finally came to the stone floor of the shaft. He looked up, and far above was a tiny square of light. Piata stood at the beginning of a tunnel that was cut into the side of the shaft and went steeply downward.

"This part is easy," she said to him. "You have to duck your head at the beginning, but then we can move quite fast along it. There are no steps or obstructions, just straight down until we reach the lower levels of the castle."

She turned, and with the lamp held so that Kerran received some of its light, she entered the side tunnel. Kerran had never been so deep underground before. The knowledge of all that rock and earth above gave him an uneasy feeling in the pit of his stomach, and he followed Piata closely. The descent took much longer than the shaft. The walls became damp, and slimy, small creatures of the dark scuttled away from the light before they could be seen. Kerran felt his skin begin to crawl and he longed for the daylight. A bat rushed by his face and flew further up the tunnel. He almost called out in fright.

"Here we are," said Piata, and she stepped out into a large room.

Her lamp illuminated the roughly hewn stone. It was no longer damp in this part of the underground system, and Piata explained that they had passed beneath a small stream further back up the tunnel. There was nothing in the room except that at its centre stood a large smooth rectangular stone. It stood as high as Kerran's waist and was almost as long as he was tall. It reminded him a little of the sacrificial stone on Marl, though the workmanship here was of a different standard. He ran his hand over the surface. It was as smooth as the best quality glass.

"I wonder what this was?" he asked "It is like the stone on Marl, but only if they sacrificed short people, a grown person's feet would hang well over the end."

Piata laughed at the image as Kerran again ran his hand over the stone. It was completely smooth on all sides. The corners and edges had been shaped slightly to soften it. He studied a while and then sat on it. Immediately he knew that something had changed. The room was still there, and he could see Piata as she walked around looking at the walls. He did not know what was different. It was a slight feeling of concern and anxiety, nothing more. He slipped off the stone and the feeling left him. Without telling Piata why, he asked if she would come and sit on the stone herself. "Do you feel anything?" he asked after awhile.

She laughed. "I feel the cold coming through my breeches if that is what you mean," she told him.

"No, do you feel anything else?" he said. "Does it trouble you to sit there?"

"No Kerran," she replied. "I feel nothing. What is it? What did you feel?"

"I am not sure," he replied. "It bothered me. It did not feel good. I will see if it happens again."

He sat on the stone once more and the feelings were again there in his mind, steady and unshakeable. He explained them to Piata who stood with the lamp held aloft and observed his face.

"It is a feeling as if something will entrap us here, or perhaps that others were trapped here," he said. "It has something to do with the Seacrest I think. It is not unbearable, but is certainly uncomfortable. Wait... it is changing. It is soothing, soft... sleepy... I must sleep."

To Piata, Kerran's voice seemed to drift off into the darkness. His eyes began to glaze and close. In fright she grabbed his arm and dragged him from the stone, he stumbled across the floor and was immediately himself again.

"What was that?" asked Piata in fright. "You looked like you were going off with the little folk and had no intention of coming back?"

"I do not know," said Kerran, rubbing the palms of his hands hard into his eye sockets. "Something told me to sleep. It was comforting, but I knew it was not right, that it was dangerous. I have had enough of these dark places. Please let us go where it is light."

"Come, enough of this dark place," she said with a note of concern in her voice, and she led the way to another doorway in the far wall.

They began to climb ancient, well worn steps. The stones were deeply indented where thousands of feet must have trodden before them. The climb was hard on Kerran's leg muscles. City life had reduced his fitness indeed. Sunlight began to shine down into the spiralling tunnel and soon Piata was able to extinguish the lamp. They eventually came out from the side of a ruined wall into what had once been a large room. Kerran realised that the castle must have been huge, its ruined ramparts spreading over the entire hilltop and down its far side. Piata was troubled for him but he shrugged it off.

"So many strange things have happened to me that strange is becoming quite normal," he smiled.

He told her then of his dream from the night before. There were few who he had actually told of his dreams and visions, while he had spoken to many of his adventures. Tolth knew of them, and would show great interest in these recent experiences, but to most he had remained silent. They sat in the warm sunshine eating bread and cheese and looked out over the ocean, now far below. Kerran watched as many small sail boats came towards Felstrar from the far distance.

"The men will be home soon," said Piata. "The tide

determines the best times to fish. They will unload their catch, and by this time tomorrow someone in the Green City will be eating what my family has caught today, while we will be eating the grain that someone on the eastern plains has grown." Pride showed in her voice.

"*There are no accidents*," said the voice of Manzanee, suddenly loud in Kerran's ears.

Before he could swallow Kerran choked on the bread. He spluttered, his distress soon obvious to Piata as he managed to cough. His eyes watered and he gasped several times.

"What was that?!" she exclaimed as he finally gathered his breath.

"Manzanee," he coughed again. "From my dreams. He spoke to me. His voice was as clear as yours."

"I heard nothing," she said, a worried look on her face.

"No," said Kerran and gulped again. "I doubt that you would. He said 'There are no accidents.' Then I choked." Kerran laughed a little.

"There are no accidents," repeated Piata. "'Tis very strange being around you Kerran Shalastar."

"Sometimes 'tis strange for me to be around me," he chuckled.

They investigated the ruins for most of the afternoon, and from the highest point of tumbled stones Kerran and Piata stood and took in the surrounding country. To the east were plains and forests, and to the north was the great bay of Shoalwater. Gulls flew far below them, and the roof of Piata's house could be seen on the edge of the forest far below. To the west lay the foothills of the mountains, and far beyond was the ocean. They turned finally to face the south. Here stood the tall, craggy peaks of Zeta's high mountains.

"It is the northern end of the Southern Range," said Piata. "It has always been thought of as a place of ancient sanctuary, and there are caves and secret places. 'Tis also said that there is something up there still to be found, some great mystery."

Kerran looked at the details of the high mountains, here, very strongly, he knew something was familiar, a feeling that hovered on the edge of a dream. The mountains rose abruptly from the forested foothills, with a deep valley disappearing between the last two peaks.

"Where does that valley go?" asked Kerran.

"It just goes deeper into the mountains," Piata replied. "No one lives there because it get little sun: a river comes down to the ocean, it flows below that line of foothills." She pointed to their right, where the sun was beginning to lower toward the horizon. "We should return now," she said. "It is a difficult climb down in the dark. I had to do it once when I went to sleep up here. I woke up cold with the sun disappearing, not again if possible."

They began their descent and were home with the last light. They did not have to rise early and so they sat up late, talking about everything that came into their heads. Kerran had never met anyone like Piata, though a natural shyness kept him from speaking many of his deeper thoughts. They stood beneath the stars for a time until it became too cold, and then decided it was time to go to their beds. They whispered goodnight at the back door and just as Kerran turned to go, Piata took his hand and squeezed it, then she was gone. Kerran thought about the touch of her soft hand for a long time before he could sleep.

The next morning they had a good breakfast and went into the garden to work. They were weeding on their knees when their hands again touched. Kerran looked into Piata's eyes and she looked back with a steady open gaze. They did not say a word. With embarrassed smiles they went back to work. Their talk did not flow, and for much of the day they worked silently near each other. By evening they were talking casually again, and were keeping a more than respectful distance, it was after supper in the darkness of the porch that their hands came together again, and this time they held. Then unexpectedly they kissed softly, once, awkwardly, then they held each other and looked at the night sky.

"I will be going back to the city in a few days," said Kerran. "I shall miss you."

"And I you," she said squeezing him closer.

"I will write," said Kerran. "It will be good practice."

She chuckled. "Be sure that your spelling improves."

They kissed again in the darkness, and held each other for a long time.

The next day was spent fishing on the calm water of the harbour though Kerran felt ill at ease, and could not explain why. That night he dreamed but remembered little. All that came to him were a few words from Manzanee.

"There is danger for you in these mountains," was all that the Black Wizard had whispered.

The next morning dawned grey and blustery. They had planned yet another walk in the hills but it turned to rain. All of the family spent the day indoors by the fire, telling stories and playing games of chance and skill. The next day it was time for Kerran to return to the city. Amus was going as far as a nearby town where Kerran would catch a passenger wagon that went to Nariss every few days. Piata and Kerran went for a short walk in the forest before he was to leave. A mist settled on their clothes as they walked. They would meet again soon, they both said. Perhaps Piata would come to the city and stay with her aunt for a time. Amus called to them and soon Kerran and Rark were in the wagon and bouncing down the road, waving a last goodbye to the figures that softened, and then disappeared into the mist. Kerran tightly held a copy of the Book of Truths that Piata had thrust into his hand at the last moment.

Chelasta

It was a long trip on the lumbering wagon. Kerran eventually arrived in the city as dawn was breaking out across the bay. He returned to the upstairs room in the Amitarl household that he had been given and found it prepared for him. He slept for much of the day and woke to the smell of Verardian's wonderful soup that Nup had brought him. Tolth greeted him like a favourite son and wanted to know all about his time away. When Kerran told of Manzanee's words the old Amitarl found them fascinating, intriguing.

"You are so close to the answer," repeated Tolth. "Yet you know not the nature of the riddle. You almost know the play of the game." He gazed into space, absorbing the strangeness of it all. "Those are every word?" Tolth asked Kerran. "Nothing is missing?"

"Yes," said Kerran. "I believe that is what he said." Then he paused, remembering. "No, it is not quite right," he said finally. "It is 'by accident' that I almost know the play of the game, that was it. The strangest thing is that much later the next day his voice came in the daylight while I was fully awake. He then said that there were 'no accidents.'"

Tolth leaned back thoughtfully in his chair, a hand to his

chin. "There is something that is almost making sense," he said quietly. His eyes gazed into the air for a time, as if seeking an answer. "I think we must write this down," he said, and went to a corner cabinet where he had papers and pen.

Mindis sat near the cabinet and Kerran realised that he had not thought of this son of Tolth for a long time. The boy was always in the corner on his chair, or else he had been led away by Verardian to lie still, eyes open, until he was given food in the morning. There was no one that Kerran had known before who was anything like Mindis. He was looking at the strange young man when suddenly, and only for a moment, their eyes met. Kerran saw the pain in the depths of those strange black eyes. It happened so quickly that Kerran could not say if it had really happened or not. A flicker of the eyes, a blink, he did not know. Tolth returned with the paper and began to write.

> You are so close to the answer,
> Yet you know not the nature of the riddle.
> By accident you almost know the play of the game.
> There are no accidents.

"You are close to the answer," said Tolth thoughtfully. "The answer to the riddle. What is the nature of the riddle? This can only be guessed at. What is the nature of the answer? Being close, being close to what?" Tolth shook his head. "Confound it!" he said with an amused smile and another shake of his head. "That went nowhere. Let me try again. Being close... does he mean that you almost know the answer?"

"If I do," said Kerran, "I wish someone would tell me the question."

"No," said Tolth tapping his bearded chin with his pen. "Did he mean that you were perhaps physically close to the answer? Physically close," he mused. "You were at Felstrar with the old castle far above. Near to the answer? Is the answer in the old ruined castle? I have been there a number of times. I have studied it for many days and have read of other people's findings, or lack of them really. If the answer is there, the nature of the riddle may simply be the castle itself or somewhere amongst the rubble, but a search would take years and what would we be looking for anyway? Confound that Black Wizard. Could he not make things a bit simpler?" Tolth paused, obviously frustrated, though still smiling a little. "Manzanee!" he called suddenly. "Why do you not explain anything?!"

"Because that would spoil my fun," the words of the old Black Wizard came loud and laughing into the room.

Both Tolth and Kerran exclaimed loudly, which brought Verardian and Nup rushing from the kitchen.

"What happened?" Verardian asked with concern.

"A voice from nowhere," said Tolth, not smiling now. "Manzanee, the old fiend and tormentor. He is laughing at us. He plays games while the great evil of Maradass is about to come down upon the lands. He may be living forever and seeing everything, but he has a terrible sense of humour."

He paused as Verardian and Nup returned to the kitchen. "So where were we?" he said, and then continued. "Now let us assume for a moment that you were physically close to the answer. I am bothered by Manzanee, but I do believe that he knows what is important to the lands, to our success and the end of Maradass. 'There are no accidents,' this is an old saying, and of course very true. If it was no accident that you were there, then you are perhaps meant to find some sort of answer there, though it does seem to go around in circles. Was there anything else in the time you were there Kerran, something that was strange or unusual?"

"I kept thinking that I had been there before," replied Kerran. "The feeling was very odd. When Piata took me down into the underground passages there was a place with a very smooth slab of stone, when I sat on it I felt strange, a sort of fear that I cannot explain."

"The true origins of the older parts of that castle are not known," said Tolth, finding it easier to talk of history rather than Manzanee's riddles. "Some thought that it was made by one of the High Wizards other than Rishtan-Sta. It is probable that he spent some time there as he is known to have been on Zeta on occasion, but that does not mean he lived here for long." Tolth turned back to Manzanee's words and was silent for a while.

Kerran's mind drifted back to Felstrar and Piata, and he dwelt on her memory for a time. He saw them both as they had walked up the hill toward the castle, and had entered the depths of the ruins. He pictured them both as they studied the magnificent views. Kerran had turned until he had faced the mountains to the south. He pictured the foothills in his mind, and then he understood where his memories had truly come from, the hill on the left with a cut away cliff and rocky outcrop that looked like a face. It was the face he had seen before when he had dreamed of the Seacrest in the mountains, and had climbed the stairs inside the rock. He told Tolth of his realisation and then wondered why it had not come to him when he was there. Perhaps Piata had been too much of a distraction.

Tolth did not speak for some time, finally he nodded slowly. "Kerran, it may be that a secret remains hidden there from the time of the wizards," he said. "There have been strange stories coming out of those mountains for centuries. Some day I would like to go there with you if time allows, but for now it must remain a mystery as it could just be a fool's errand. Manzanee's words could mean something entirely different. After all he does like his games."

"There is something else that has puzzled me greatly," Tolth continued. "Your affinity with the Seacrest is beyond any coincidence, or accident. Leana had not the experiences that you have had, and Manzanee has spoken to no one else that I know of except myself, and never while I was awake until just now. It is as if you were meant to carry Leana's piece. There are indeed no accidents. Can you tell me of anything in your past which may have chosen you for this quest? Maybe there is something in your family history? A happening that may not seem significant, or something a little strange perhaps? "

Kerran thought for a while, his mind going back over the years. He thought of his father and the way that he had died, killed by the falling tree in the forest. There was something about that time that he could not quite remember, a memory on the very edge of a dream.

"Can I help?" said Tolth. "I can try and return you to that time and that dream if you wish."

"Yes," replied Kerran quietly. "I would like to see my father again."

He lay back on the soft couch and Tolth took him gently into his past.

Kerran watched himself from above and saw the seven-year-old boy he had once been. The young Kerran walked in the forest and he was not alone for his father walked beside him. The scene became blurred and darkened. Hunting, fiery-blue eyes gleamed from the shadows of the trees. In fright Kerran saw the face of an evil dog as it moved closer, a savage leer on its face, a dog that was thinking with malevolent intent. The dream shifted again. He now walked beside his father and looked from the eyes of his seven year old self. A darting shadow caught his eye. He looked again and saw a huge black dog slink into the dense forest. It was gone before he could speak. He shook his father's hand and pointed, but his father saw nothing and had only smiled. Kerran remembered now that at that time in the forest he had known that his father had indeed seen the beast, but had chosen to ignore it. The young Kerran had remembered it for a long time. It had been remembered as an omen. The very next day his father had been alone in the forest and had not returned. The memory had eventually faded and had been replaced, as it was soon after that Storm had entered his life.

In his mind Kerran wished to end the dream so as to tell of his understanding to Tolth, but the dream continued. Darkness came, except that it was lit by a glowing fire. Kerran as a child sat close by the family hearth with both his parents nearby. His father told him wonderful stories, histories of ancient times, the names returning now as distant memories. He had been told something of his own family, one that was deeply rooted in the past, the history of which his father planned to expand upon as Kerran grew older. The family name of Shalastar had been in the lands for many centuries, and Kerran again heard his father speaking of a family set apart, living in this isolated corner of the Four Regions for a great many years, then slowly his father's voice faded into silence. For a time Kerran saw and felt nothing. His mind became still on its own, while behind his eyelids a light grew slowly. He blinked his eyes and as they cleared he looked up at Tolth's enquiring face.

"I do not know if this will help but they are memories I had forgotten," he said, and began to tell Tolth of his dream vision.

"Tell me Kerran," said Tolth after he had heard the story. "Did you dream about the dog, or was it actually from your living memory?"

Kerran thought for a moment. "It was something that was real I think," he said. "Although at the time of my father's death all my memories seem to have been like a dream, or a nightmare."

"I wonder at it," said Tolth, pacing the room. "What you describe is no doubt a marauder. If it is a true memory, then Maradass must have been looking in the forest for something even then, and if the object of the search was human it may have been you or your father that he sought. Marauders were very rare in the Regions ten years ago. I know of just one other appearance and that was far to the north. Zard did not ride south until recently I believe, and only the occasional spy of Maradass was abroad at that time. It may be that the marauder sought something other than your family, but your home is so isolated that it seems more than so called chance, or accident that the creature was there. Your ability to use the Seacrest as you have makes me think that in some way there must be a connection, though I cannot see it, not yet. There are no accidents indeed."

He paced the room again, going to the balcony window and looking at the sky, his right hand buried in the pouch at his belt. Then he turned and looked with piercing eyes directly into Kerran's own. "Your family name, Shalastar," he said thoughtfully. "There is something about that name or one like it that touches at the edges of an old memory in my own mind. Why have I not noted it before?" he asked himself quietly.

Kerran watched his old friend as Tolth began to pace the room once again.

"Family names are used so rarely on Zeta," Tolth added,

almost in a whisper; and then he thought for a while in silence. "I can almost taste it,' said the old Amitarl looking at Kerran. "Now on the edge of my own memory there is a name which is one I feel I should know, and yet cannot find it. I have read it in the library and I think now that I know where." Tolth smiled then and clapped his hands just once. "Ha!" he cried. "I will go immediately and get it!"

Tolth had said this in a rush and then he was gone, striding quickly down the long hallway and out of the house. It felt strange to Kerran. Tolth seemed to believe that there may be more to his simple family than he had first thought. What was Tolth going to unearth in the library, he wondered. Suddenly Kerran felt desperately tired. He lay down on the long couch and in moments he slept, and he dreamed.

The face of Manzanee sprang at him from across a small fire that suddenly burst into life. "The answers are only as good as the questions asked," said the Black Wizard rapidly, looking into Kerran's eyes.

"What does that mean?" Kerran asked back, surprised to find that in this dream he had a voice.

Manzanee was also visibly startled and sat back quickly, the fire flaring up again between them. Kerran waited as the fire died to embers.

"You can speak with me now," said Manzanee thoughtfully. "That I did not expect. You must be respectful with your questions." His eyes flashed in the firelight. "You are young," continued Manzanee. "And I am as old as forever and will live longer than time, but I will answer this one question out of my own respect for you."

He paused, the light continuing to catch the humour in his eyes as he looked at Kerran. "You have asked me why answers are only as good as the questions asked," said Manzanee. "The answer to that is; if you ask the correct question, the true answer to that question will give you all of the answers that you wish for; that is the true answer."

Kerran was speechless, and he knew not if it came from Manzanee or his own lack of understanding. "You speak in riddles," Kerran said across the fire. "May I not have an answer

37

that I can understand?"

"You are being disrespectful," said the Black Wizard, his voice low, almost threatening. "And that is another question you ask. That is not our bargain. Did you know that I can make you vanish and never appear again, anywhere, any time?" He said this with a malicious grin and then continued. "Or with a mere nod of my head I can turn you into a fat green lizard," he said. "Would you like to see what that feels like?"

"No," said Kerran before Manzanee could nod.

The old wizard sat back and looked into Kerran's eyes. "No more questions," said Manzanee. "Remember that and we will get on well young Shalastar."

Kerran nodded, he found that if he were to speak, his voice could not help but ask questions.

"Good," Manzanee smiled. "Let me tell you some things Kerran that you do not yet know. Though I am unable to enter directly into the conflicts that will soon come to the Regions, and though I must not obstruct or assist the happenings of these times, I am truly hopeful for the success of Amitarl." His teeth showed in a gleaming smile. "I favour the good over the evil and that is all you need to know at this time," he continued.

All was silent. The fire burned low. Expectation hung in the air.

"Listen to Tolth now," said Manzanee quietly. "That is all I can say for now, young Shalastar. Listen to Tolth, for he returns with a most interesting book, perhaps the second most interesting book in all the lands. May you learn much in the time that is given. Keep an open mind, young Shalastar, eyes and ears open."

Kerran's eyes blinked open as Tolth entered the house carrying a large well bound tome.

"This is it," he said. "It is a book I read many years ago, *The First History and Folklore of the Ancient Wizards*. It is a copy of course. The original has long since turned to dust. It is difficult to read as it too is ancient, though I did manage to decipher parts of it some years ago." Tolth began to pore over the book.

"I fell asleep just now and Manzanee was in my dream," said Kerran.

Tolth looked up into his eyes, questioning.

"I was able to talk to him this time and it surprised him," continued Kerran. "His answer to my one question was a riddle in itself. 'Answers are only as good as the questions asked, because if the correct question is asked, the true answer will give you all answers wish for.' I think that was it, though he always seems to speak in strange confusing riddles."

"We have so many riddles and not many answers," said the old Amitarl and shook his head. "Perhaps the next time you meet with Manzanee you could have a question ready to ask him, something he may be willing to answer. At this time I think I will not continue to try and decipher that strange wizard's puzzles. One puzzle at a time is enough. I will do a little silent study now and see if I can refresh this old mind of mine."

Tolth went to the large outer room which he sometimes used as a study, and here he began to pore over the old book. Kerran could see him at a desk in the darkening room, a smokeless flame lighting his face. For a long time Kerran sat gazing into the flames of the fire, his body tingling with strange mysterious feelings. He was far from sleep now. He felt that something exceptional was about to happen.

"I have it!" Tolth called eventually. "It is here, or at least I believe it may be so."

Kerran joined him quickly and Tolth pointed to what looked to Kerran like an indecipherable mixture of shapes and bent lines. The common language was difficult enough. This looked impossible to read.

"What does it say?" he asked as he sat in the chair beside Tolth.

"These figures and marks are of the early languages of the lands when wizards still lived," Tolth replied. "It is most difficult to read, as there were several spoken languages in the time of the wizards and this book is a rather confused mixture of them all. Partly it tells of how to truly speak these languages, how the words should actually sound." Tolth pointed to a vertical line of letters, lines and shapes. "Right here is what I believe to be a name that is close to your own, it is said if I am not mistaken as Chelasta. 'Chel' is a short form of 'Chellan' which probably meant dawn or morning. The name should more properly be said 'Chel-a-Sta'. It is a very ancient name Kerran and Shalastar is not so different, is it not?"

Kerran had strong doubts.

Tolth looked at his young friend for a moment and then continued. "Of course it may be that I am fooling myself in this," he said with a smile. "But if we do not ask questions we will get no answers at all. The 'a' which breaks the name, is 'of' or 'is', and the 'Sta' is well known by scholars to have been lengthened in these later times; these days we add a long sound to it and it becomes 'star'. 'Star of the Morning' or 'Morning Star' perhaps."

Tolth paused and gazed at nothing, as if remembering some lost thought. "I have studied much that concerns the wizards of that distant time," he said finally. "There were almost certainly just six high wizards who reached these shores, according to most histories. With them were also a number of lesser wizards, perhaps fourteen of them, although that number is not without some flexibility shall we say. Chelasta I believe is probably the name of one of those Lesser Wizards, though a very obscure one. It is also thought that there were others amongst those that came to these lands who were not true wizards at all, but certainly carried varying degrees of power."

There was a touch of excitement in his voice. "It has always been understood that many of the wizards took their names from different phenomena in nature," continued Tolth. "Sometimes from stars for example, sometimes from natural features of the lands, mountains, moon, sky, trees, many such things. Each wizard also seems to have had any number of different names, and at times would drop one in favour of another. The White Wizard, Rishtan-Sta, was White Winged Star amongst other names. There were certainly numerous other wizards back in the time long before they even reached these southern lands, and they too were of greater and lesser power. From my earlier studies, when I was much younger, I now remember that I discovered that this Morning Star was a most minor wizard, and not one of the strong or powerful.

When I read this book long ago there was much that I did not understand, and only now I am remembering this passage. Chel-a-Sta is only mentioned once I think, in all that I managed to decipher during those early studies of this book. I admit I tired of the struggle to find the actual truth in this book, and the few others of its kind that have come down to us through the ages. There is something that I do recall now, a remembrance that was written into another book many years after the events that led to the destruction of the wizards. It is a simple yet difficult passage to understand, unclear and mystifying in its simplicity. It is a book connected to those times and yet not so old. I could go and find it but I do not think I need to."

Tolth sat looking at the book before him with a puzzled frown on his brow, remembering. "Wizard's Bane," he finally said, and then became silent again. The words *unite* and *bring together* came quietly to his lips from his absorbed mind. "I am close," he said turning to Kerran. "Though no closer than I was so many years ago. I should probably go and find the book for I cannot remember it clearly."

There was another long pause and Tolth did not move. "Yes," he finally said. "I think I may have it all now. I remember it because it speaks of Chel-a-Sta, which I believe may be the only other reference to this wizard in all of the many books of wizards that I have ever studied. So this is what I have remembered, without the need to rush back to the library."

Tolth smiled, and then wrote quickly with a firm hand on a piece of paper: *Chel-a-Sta... Bloodline... Unite ... Wizard's Bane* "Let us try this," said Tolth and began to write again. *One of Chelasta Blood may Unite the Wizard's Bane.* "That may make sense, though it seems too simple in some way," he said. "The words do not suggest a true answer as yet. I remember now that there were other words that I cannot recall." Tolth chuckled to himself then continued. "There is still something here I cannot see, cannot recollect, something I cannot make sense of without the library again."

It was late in the evening but Tolth left without a thought for time. He returned after midnight with a sheet of paper and found Kerran dozing on the soft couch. *In a Time to come one of*

Chel-a-Sta bloodline may unite the Wizards' Bane

"Tis as close as I can judge, though I have filled in a few gaps that seem to need filling," said Tolth and showed it Kerran, not noticing that his young friend wished most of all to return to his sleep. "I have made some assumptions which could be incorrect," continued Tolth. "In these old languages, sometimes the words do not run in the order that one would expect. There is one thing that I feel certain of, the 'Wizards' Bane' must be the Seacrest, Ma-Zurin-Bidar, though strangely these words were written an age before the Seacrest was divided."

Tolth was excited, and for a time did not notice his young companion's drooping eyelids. "I missed the first part," he said pointing to the page of the book he had brought from the library. "The words 'Time to come' or perhaps 'Future Time' were on the previous line and I did not notice the connection all those years ago, the impetuousness of youth. Do you not see?"

Kerran showed little enthusiasm and could not stifle a yawn.

Tolth looked at him and then stood. "Tomorrow Kerran," he said softly. "You are tired. May you sleep well."

Kerran stumbled up the stairs to his room and it was late morning when he woke, but Nup seemed to have an uncanny way of knowing when he awakened and his little face popped around the corner of the door.

"Hungry Kerran?" he asked.

"Yes Nup, I am very hungry," he replied, and the face disappeared.

After a breakfast of duck eggs, fresh baked bread and goat's milk, Kerran spent much of the day reading another history of the family Amitarl. He sat in the sunshine and wrote to Piata, slowly, choosing each word carefully. For a time he watched the harbour and a group of tall ships that moved slowly out of the bay. There had been a meeting of the Council and it had been decided to send an armed force to a secret harbour of the Far Isles, there to await the main force which was soon to follow. Tolth came to him that afternoon carrying several books and scrolls with him. He sat on a bench by Kerran, his face showing excitement and something else that Kerran could not name. Rark looked up lazily, and then dropped his head again as Tolth brought forth the paper he had been writing on the night before.

> In a Time to come a child of Chel-a-Sta blood may unite the Wizards' Bane

"Some of this may be unbelievable to you Kerran Shalastar," said Tolth excitedly and continued speaking rapidly as though the words might vanish before they had been said. "Though I have not been able to interpret it perfectly I believe I have the essence of it all, and it is somewhat astonishing to say the least. To me Kerran it appears that your part in these times has more importance than I at first thought possible, or could have even realized. I now believe in my heart that you were in the forest on that fateful day because you were meant to be there. Now this is the part that I am sure you will find impossible to believe, and yet I do. I believe that you are a direct descendant of Chel-a-Sta. From all your experiences with the Seacrest I now think you must be, and so it seems that you *may* have the power, or perhaps the ability, to unite the Wizards' Bane, which must be the Seacrest. The indefinite word 'may' is undeniable. There is this uncertainty in the translation that cannot be denied. It cannot be translated as 'will unite' or even 'can unite'. So Kerran, strange as it may seem you are to my mind undoubtedly descended from wizards, and you have been chosen by your bloodline to be the catalyst of change, the one who may bring about the recreation of Ma-Zurin-Bidar. Though I find it most difficult to believe I know in mind and heart that it cannot be otherwise."

Kerran sat in stunned silence staring at his friend and mentor. Tolth mused for a few moments, looking at the sky with his palms together, lightly touching his bearded lips.

"Rishtan-Sta was a high and most powerful wizard," he continued after a time. "He must have known that some day the Seacrest was to be broken. How this might be I cannot say. I can see a mixed and confused future, whereas he must have seen clearly what was to be. But why Chel-a-Sta I wonder, an unknown who is not recorded anywhere but in these few puzzling words?"

Tolth pondered for a few moments. "I have decided to simplify the name for us," Tolth continued. "The full Chel-a-Sta is a bit of an effort to say, and Chelasta is probably closer to how it was said in those ancient times. He, or indeed she, for there were female wizards in those times, must have been a much lesser wizard than most, if not all others. The history of the wizards is mostly lost in the ancient past, even their names have been almost forgotten, yet most are remembered in some details somewhere. This book was written well after their time, and so I must say that I do not know how much real truth there is in it."

"Then how do you know that I am of the Chelasta line?" asked Kerran of his old friend, feeling that all of this could not be possible. "Shalastar seems to me a quite different name, and there may be no connection at all."

"In truth that may be so," replied Tolth nodding. "But I do not think so; I feel it in my bones."

He reached into the pouch at his waist and drew forth the two pieces of the Seacrest. He looked at them with a puzzled frown. "Yes, it may be that there is no connection at all," he agreed with a smile. "Except for your apparent ability to draw something from the talisman that others have not, and the similarity in names, there is little else except a great many small interconnecting pieces of a much larger puzzle. The Maradass family still holds the most powerful piece of all, and have had two thousand years to draw forth its magic. You have held, for only a short time, what is probably the weakest of the four, and yet it came to your aid. No, I cannot believe that there is nothing but blind coincidence working here. Is there anything that you can tell me of your family and ancestors that may help us Kerran? Something you remember that your parents may have told you of your lineage?"

Kerran cast his mind back to the time before his father's accident. "There is little to tell," he said. "I have never met any relations. My father never spoke of his own father and mother or any other relations. I felt at the time that he wanted to tell me of our family, but all I remember of this is him saying that I was too young, and that he would tell me when I got older. There is one thing he said that I have often wondered about. He said that my birth had been an unexpected miracle. What is it that you seek, Tolth? Is it not just hope that you see in this? I surely do not feel like a descendant of wizards."

"Your family will go back many years," said the old Amitarl. "Yet in all the histories of the land, the only mentions of Chelasta or variations on that name are in the two old volumes I had with me last evening. This is unusual, as most of the ancient families managed to keep a history of their ancestors, even the poorest of families seems to have had at least one scholar in their midst. Chelasta or Shalastar do not fit into the histories as the others do. It is as if they have remained purposefully hidden for these many centuries. It cannot be denied that in my mind you are in some way connected. There are indeed no accidents. It may be that you will play an important part in the times to come, but I am still confused a little, Kerran, and need to think and study this for a time. The Library is the best place for me now." Toth began to rise.

"Before you go there is something that now puzzles me," said Kerran and Tolth sat back down. "From my readings I know that a wizard was almost immortal, so how is it that my father died by accident if he was a true wizard?" he asked.

"A question I have also begun to ask myself," replied Tolth. "Being one of the Lesser Wizards perhaps the near immortal nature of wizards did only apply to the High Wizards after all. This is something that many have pondered over the years; but there is another possibility that troubles me. Maradass has been able to warp the death empowered fragment of the Seacrest to his own ends, and with dark magic he may have been able to kill your father. You speak of your own birth as being a miracle; perhaps it was so unexpected that Maradass has no idea of your existence. I think it best to hope that this remains so."

Tolth gave Kerran a thoughtful look and then stood and left, the old books held carefully in his hands.

"Stranger than strange," said Kerran to himself, and then

foolishly tried to conjure up one of his mother's sweet cakes. It did not work.

Kerran saw little of Tolth over the following days, closeted in the Library; his old friend took his meals there. One day he was walking in the parklands near the Amitarl home when there were cries from the quay side, people were running and Kerran watched as a man sprinted towards him.

"Where is Tolth?" called the runner urgently.

"At the library," Kerran called back. "What is it? What has happened?"

"The sea has turned red!" the man cried over his shoulder as he sped on his way towards the place of records.

Kerran remembered a dream he had of a dark blood red ocean. He and Rark made their way to the docks where many people were gathering. Kerran stood on the quay and looked at the ocean's deep muddy red water that lapped at the stonework. Some sense in Kerran told him that it was deadly. There were people on the lower steps and in boats. Kerran saw one man run his hand through the tide; a child splashed her feet in the red murk.

"It is not safe!" Kerran called to those around him.

He was listened to, the words 'young hero' whispered through the crowd.

The news travelled quickly through the city and soon thousands of people began to line the sea front. Kerran saw Tolth arrive further along the quay and he watched as the old Amitarl carefully collected a sample of the water, using a long handled ladle. Word had spread that it should not be touched until it was shown to be harmless, Kerran returned through the crowd to his room and lay back on his bed. He closed his eyes and walked in dreams.

The ocean spread out before him, sparkling blue-green. A breeze stirred his hair and gulls flew above. He stood on the sands and watched the small waves rushing up the beach, it seemed that he was only there for a short time, but the sun fell rapidly towards the horizon, and then it was gone. Stars twinkled into the night sky, the breeze died and the sound of the waves was stilled. Kerran watched, as from the distant water a glow began to flicker and radiate across the surface, the light did not come from above, but from the depths. It approached the shore and Kerran saw first the head and then the shoulders of a man with flowing hair and beard emerge from the ocean. He came further out of the water and Kerran could see that the glow came from an object that the man carried in his hand. Kerran knew it to be the Seacrest. Rishtan-Sta walked from the sea to the beach, though not a drop of water fell from his clothing. He turned then to Kerran and smiled.

"It is done friend Chel-a-Sta," the wizard's voice came as gentle rain. "We will now have peace in the lands."

The ancient wizard turned and began to walk into the forest that lay close by the ocean. Kerran followed, the dream taking him with it without struggle. Light glowed from the hand of Rishtan-Sta that held the Seacrest, illuminating every leaf and blade of grass. They walked until Kerran could see the now familiar western mountains of Zeta looming above them. Kerran recognised the forest clearing and the rock face. Here Rishtan-Sta passed his hand over the surface of the solid rock and the lines of the lost doorway appeared slowly. Beyond the door they began to mount the steps, spiralling higher inside the mountainside. Daylight flowed down from above and they eventually emerged into sunshine onto the high stone ledge.

"Now is the time of our alliance," said Rishtan-Sta, but he was not looking at Kerran, instead he looked into a dark corner beneath a rock ledge.

There was movement in the shadows and then a figure emerged and straightened, the familiar face of Manzanee grinned at him.

"Well Chel-a-Sta," said the Black Wizard almost laughing now. "Some questions are best left unanswered, but not this one."

The Black Wizard walked to the large stone that stood at the edge of the smooth rock shelf. Rishtan-Sta stood on the other side and reached out to hold the still glowing Seacrest above the stone. He began to chant words that Kerran could not understand and yet were very familiar to him. The High Wizard's voice was joined by a deep song-like intonation from

Manzanee, their songs intertwining and flowing over each other, flowing over the stone between them. Kerran saw lines beginning to form on the flat surface of the stone. Shimmering blue, they formed the outline of an eight pointed star.

Rishtan-Sta, without ceasing the chant, took the Seacrest and placed it solemnly and with great care onto the centre of the stone. The light grew brighter from the talisman and then Manzanee raised a hand and gently placed it on the Seacrest. For a moment his song rose high and reached into a clear unheard sound, then his voice ceased and he slowly removed his hand. Rishtan-Sta reached forward and carefully lifted Ma-Zurin-Bidar from the stone and held it at his breast.

"Farewell Chel-a-Sta," he said to Kerran. "Keep this time sharp in your children's memories, for you will be called upon again."

A transformation took place before Kerran's eyes, Rishtan-Sta shrank and spread his arms wide as they turned to feathered wings, and then with a cry the white hawk that had been Rishtan-Sta flew from the ledge, the Seacrest held in his talons.

Manzanee then turned to Kerran. "In the Past and the Future, in Life and in Death, we will meet again Chel-a-Sta," the Black Wizard said solemnly. "Look for me in your dreams when the time ripens to bare its dark bittersweet fruit."

With that, and a final gleeful laugh the Black Wizard vanished from the ledge. In the last fleeting moment Kerran thought he saw a dark coloured beetle scuttle into hiding beneath the central square stone, then his vision blurred and Kerran slipped into a deep unbroken sleep until morning. He woke early and as usual Nup was there with his breakfast.

"Terrible happenings," said the boy as he laid the tray beside the bed. "People with strong fever what touched the water. Tis an evil thing this red ocean."

Later in the day Kerran found Tolth in his study, buried in work, vials of the red sea water stood in rows; yet when Tolth heard of Kerran's dream he was most excited. They took a long walk together in the parklands and for a time stood with others beside the poisoned ocean. When Kerran had told Tolth all that he remembered of the dream, the old man shook his head in wonder and told Kerran his thoughts.

"Whatever part you have to play in these times it is certain that it was by no accident or chance that you were in the forest that day," said his old friend. "And it is certainly no accident that you found your way here to Zeta. Everything points to you being the ancestral son of the Lesser Wizard Chelasta, who must certainly have been one chosen by Rishtan-Sta and Manzanee to survive that most tragic but necessary of judgements. Rishtan-Sta must have charged your ancestor with passing on the history of those events to his children, and their children's children, so that one day a descendant of Chelasta would come to reunite the Seacrest. How you are to do that when two pieces are elsewhere I do not know. Perhaps it is not even you but one of your descendants that is meant by this. I look to the future and see but shadows of what may be. I see meetings between Maradass and Amitarl. None that I have seen turn out well."

"What of the red ocean?" asked Kerran with concern, looking at the vile murky tide. "Nup told me there is fever?"

"Yes, it is as I feared," Tolth replied sadly. "Maradass has poisoned the oceans, the fishing fleets will not sail and we must rely on our other foods. There is no shortage, though in time we could have problems. It is certain that Maradass has sent this evil to delay the departure of our army, this is something that we must overcome."

He looked at the red sea water before them. "There is nothing I can do with it," he said. "The intensity of the poison means that a mere drop on bare skin will cause sickness, and I fear eventual death. Verardian is doing all he can with the other healers, but I despair for those who have touched the water and it now engulfs all of the Isles I am told. There are boats that have not returned, and somewhere on the ocean between here and the Far Isles is the fleet carrying our first armed force to Andrian."

"I have seen the Far Isles on the map," said Kerran. "They are a very bleak place Flindas once told me about. Will the army be safe there?"

"Yes," said Tolth. "They have always been uninhabited, as the currents and tides are very dangerous. The coastline is treacherous and many wrecks lie on the ocean floor. Before the Amitarl Family left the Regions Darna prepared a safe harbour there, hidden from any passing fisherman who may be foolish enough to sail close. There is only one day of the moon that it is possible to sail a ship between the islands and into that harbour and so far our place there remains a secret. Maradass is not far from testing his strength I think and there are already some thousands of our warriors there, prepared to meet his army. They live a hard life in a desolate landscape and there is no contact with the mainland. If the poison reaches them then they too will be trapped, just as we are, and fish has always been their mainstay."

Tolth talked for a while longer then he returned to his study of the water, while Kerran made his way into the parklands away from the dreadful ocean. He was about to return to Tolth's home for the midday meal when from the sky, with a flurried beating of wings, Storm arrived and alighted on the grass. It was three moons since Kerran had last seen his companion. Storm strutted about as if to show that he was sound and strong, yet Kerran could see that he was not in good condition, but he was alive and Kerran was most happy to see him. A number of feathers were broken at odd angles and his plumage was ruffled and dirty, Rark made a loud sound in his throat as if welcoming an old friend.

"Where have you been?" Kerran asked excitedly, as though he expected a reply.

He walked to the hawk and sat on the grass beside him, and Storm allowed him to do what he could to straighten the feathers.

"I think what you need most is a long rest," Kerran said to the bird.

He continued to gently smooth Storm's plumage then stood again and the three of them made their way back to the Amitarl home where Nup was all too happy to supply Storm's needs, being a basket, a blanket, food and water.

"There will be no fish by tomorrow," Nup said. "Does he

like bread?"

"He will eat bread," replied Kerran. "But I think he will hunt for mice and lizards when he gets hungry."

"Yet another invalid to find a bed for," said Nup with a smile and went to get the basket.

Storm stayed in Kerran's room until the following day then flew from the window, Kerran watched him circle high above the city and then fly to the west into the mountains. Nup was not himself when he brought Kerran his breakfast, tears glistening at the edge of his eyes.

"The news is bad," he said quietly. "All those who touched the red water have died. Verardian could not save them."

Nup turned and left the room. There was no skip in his step that day. In the evening Tolth made a rare appearance and during the meal he told Kerran of how Storm had made at least part of his journey back to Zeta. One of the many small fishing boats had been well north of the Isles when a gale that lasted for three days had blown them far to the west. The tempest had barely died to a rolling sea when Storm had arrived on board, exhausted and hungry. He was recognised as the white hawk that had arrived with Kerran on Zeta, and he was fed and given a comfortable corner to rest in. For several days the small boat had made little headway against the fresh south-easterly, until the wind had eventually turned more to the north. They were able to reach Zeta just as the red tide had begun to lap at the western shores of the Magical Isles.

Across the Flats

The way to the west was slow and arduous. Leana remained within the spell of Maradass and she did not speak, nor seemed to hear. On most of the difficult climbs Flindas carried her on his back. The last of their food was soon gone. Rains came and they forced themselves to go on. Flindas kept to a western route as much as possible and he hoped to come out of the mountains within four or five days. It took them twelve. They were attacked often in the night by the strange hair covered creatures which Duragor had called Dreedow, each night the travellers had to find a place high up where the beasts would have difficulty reaching them. Exhausted and hungry they finally found the outer rim of the mountains, and the Flats lay before them. Beyond was the almost welcome sanctuary of the Broken Lands.

The last few days had been like a dream to Flindas. He had done what was necessary and had not thought much further than reaching the Flats. Now he saw that the barren plains were guarded. Horse troops patrolled the vast wasteland and marauders, many of them, roamed the land freely, searching for a scent. Fires burned constantly on the plains below and Flindas watched in troubled silence as the day grew longer;

burnt higher as the horsemen and dogs hunted into the night.

Hunger kept Tris awake. The weakness she had felt over the last few days was not something she had known before. Her father had always seen that she was never hungry, and when he had died, she already knew the art of keeping alive and fed. Now she was hungry like she had never been before. During the day they had made their way to a wide shelf of rock far down the last cliff face, from here a short rope climb and a narrow ravine would lead them to the plains. She waited until Flindas was asleep then quietly left their camp with the rope over her shoulder From amongst the smoke that had wafted to them from the plains had come the smell of meat cooking.

Flindas woke in the early light and Tris was not there, nor was their rope. He felt angry and concerned at the same time. He could not leave Leana and he knew that there was but one direction Tris would have gone. If she or her scent were discovered it would be impossible to cross the flat lands to the cliffs beyond. Flindas spent the day watching those on the plains. He saw little hope that he and Leana could cross undetected, except quickly and on horseback. His stomach growled and told him of its need as he waited and watched, concern for Tris growing as the day came to golden dusk.

We must move tonight, he thought to himself. Perhaps they would make it if they were lucky and not discovered too soon, or by too many. Flindas did not like having to rely on good fortune, but the alternative was slow starvation in these barren mountains. He thought of Duragor and wished that he could find even a few insects and mosses to eat. He prepared to leave but it would not be easy with Leana and no rope.

"Where is Tris?" he asked himself, almost cursing.

At that moment he heard a familiar whistle from below. The moon was rising above the mountains and Flindas saw her as she climbed the cliff. Slowly she made her way to the ledge. The confusion of anger and gladness that he felt kept his tongue silent and he smelt the meat before Tris had reached him. She peered at him in the moonlight. He looked like stone.

"Eat," she said, and from inside her jacket she passed him a partly eaten leg of cooked goat's meat.

Flindas ate in silence and felt his stomach rejoice. He could no longer be angry.

"Tell me," he said.

"Got to the cooking fire without being smelt out," she began. "They never saw the meat go." She grinned mischievously. "Perhaps they blame a dog," she said, then added with a smile. "I stole a horse."

"Stole a horse!" exclaimed Flindas.

"Got it in a deep gully on the mountainside below," she said. "Safe, maybe." Flindas was stunned. He knew already that he should never underestimate her, but she continued to surprise him.

"Marauders keep out on the Flats," she continued. "Too many gullies and broken rock close in. Best we go tonight." She sat beside him chewing at the bone.

"Yes," said Flindas in agreement. "We cannot delay."

Leana did not eat, she sat silently. The residue of the spells that had cured her and bound her were still within her body and mind. Flindas continued to carry the Seacrest fragment around his neck for she was not ready to receive it, there had been no visions or power from the blue metal and he had looked at it often, wondering at its secrets. It was time to go and climbing down the last cliff they made their way northward, staying amongst the confusion of rocks near the base of the mountains. Flindas realised after a time why it had taken Tris a full night and day to steal the horse and food. They travelled a long way and the moon was nearly set when Tris led them into the deep gully where she had left the horse.

There had been no sign of marauders or troops this close to the mountains, the enemy waited beyond the confusion of fallen rock, confident that none could pass undetected. The bottom of the gully was in darkness.

"I will go and look," said Tris. "Stay here."

She was gone into the black gulf as Flindas watched the sinking moon. There were many fires on the plains and he feared the light they gave, then he heard Tris whistle from below. Helping Leana down the slope they made their way to the floor of the gully.

"Here," came Tris's call and Flindas heard the sound of shod hooves on stone, the horse came close and they gently lifted Leana into the saddle.

"If we are discovered you must ride on without me," said Flindas to Tris. "If I am not with you, get her to Aster's Camp. He will know what can be done."

Tris did not reply. They left the gully and made their way towards the plains and the lights of the distant fires.

The marauder found them well before they reached the fires, there was now little light, the moon having set, and the beast was only a few strides from them when Flindas saw the creature. The animal had not howled to his companions, the familiar smell of the horse had perhaps confused the beast, now it laid back its head and began its cry. The large knife which caught the marauder in the throat cut off all sound and life from the animal; Flindas retrieved his blade quickly. He had managed to retain his bow and had eight arrows left, he notched one of the precious shafts to Aster's gift and they continued as quickly as they could towards the fires.

A troop of horsemen carrying torches rode across the plains ahead of them. From the mountains the fires had shown as a broken line of small lights. Now that they were getting closer the flames were large and quite far apart, the spaces between invitingly dark. There was nothing for it but to go on. If they were seen they would have to run. If they could not run fast enough they would certainly die.

Flindas made for a space between two fires which seemed a little wider than the others. The night was still, the stars shimmering against the deep blue velvet sky. Two marauders passed between them and the nearest fire and Flindas expected discovery at any moment. If a dog or soldier saw them against the firelight the chase would begin. They were now between the two fires and they could see men around the distant flames. Horses stood about as the soldiers warmed themselves, their laughter just reaching to Flindas across the darkness. They were soon past the line of fires and as yet undetected, but ahead they knew there were many marauders and patrols of horsemen. In silence they moved forward, every sense alert for the ones who hunted them. The fires were behind and the darkness almost complete when a marauder got their scent, from behind them came the black dog's howl.

"We must fly!" called Flindas, the ugly cry of the beast tingling through his body like fire.

Tris leapt up behind Leana as the dog howled again. Flindas sighted on the sound without being able to see the creature and let his arrow fly. There was a scream from the marauder, the howl becoming a whimper of pain. Flindas held to the saddle and Tris forced the horse into a run as they heard the baying of more marauders. There came the sound of a horn blast, answered by others as troops of horsemen began galloping toward the continued cries of the injured marauder. Torches flared and the riders held them aloft, though soon the chase would surely extinguish them. Another marauder had the scent, and with an excited barking he began to lead the first of the horsemen towards their quarry. Flindas could see other troops of horsemen, their torches flaring behind them as they rode toward the sounds. To the right and left distant lights flickered and spluttered in the hands of more riders. Tris kept the horse hard pushed but Flindas was tiring, his arms ached as his legs took huge strides to stay with the creature. From the darkness behind came the thundering of hooves as the fugitives approached a small rise in the land.

"They are gaining! You must ride on! I will take a horse if I can," he cried to Tris. With his free hand he tore the Seacrest from around his neck and thrust it into her pouch. "Save them," he called to her and was gone, rolling into the darkness.

Two marauders came on, silhouetted against the starlight. Flindas kept low and the first animal died quickly, then the second arrow struck and the other marauder fell. He saw the riders. There were two patrols; one came from close behind while the other was moving fast from the north. The first riders mounted the slight rise in the ground and Flindas took two from their saddles before the others knew they were under attack, then a third fell and the horses reared back in fear and the remaining three horsemen retreated quickly.

Flindas was now running. One of the horses had not bolted like the others. Its dark shape paused against the night sky. The horse sensed him coming and did not know this man. Flindas now came slowly, gently talking to the fearful animal. With soothing words he had almost assured the horse that he posed no danger, then the second patrol was nearly upon him and there were voices calling from the remaining soldiers of the first group. The horse suddenly lifted its head in fear. Flindas leapt for the reins, his outstretched hand clasping on air as the horse reared back, and ran. The patrol was almost upon him, their dark shapes mounting the rise. Flindas was no longer in such a good position and his first arrow did not find its mark as the dark riders came on. He spent his last two arrows, the men crying out as they fell.

Flindas was hurled to the ground, and he felt a searing pain in his shoulder as the marauder's teeth sank into the muscles near his neck, the hot animal breath stinking in his nostrils. Flindas ripped a knife from his belt, twisted his body and sank the blade deep into the animal's side; it howled and leapt away, no longer part of the fight. Flindas struggled to his feet, the pain in his shoulder fierce and burning. Riders were coming at him and he saw the glint of their spears as they charged. One was foremost, outdistancing the others. Flindas thought about luck and smiled grimly through his pain.

"One last chance," he said to himself.

The lead horseman was upon him and Flindas stood out against the sky, showing himself clearly to the oncoming riders. He did not draw his sword. There was no weapon that could help him now against so many. As he had hoped, the horseman charged, his spear thrust forward and Flindas stood his ground until the last moment. The spear point had almost reached its mark when he moved quickly inside the thrust and his right hand reached out grasping the saddle. With the horse's momentum, Flindas leapt, his legs lifting high. With a practiced turn of his body he was behind the rider. At the same moment, with all the strength he could gather in his injured shoulder, he smashed his elbow into the side of the man's head. The metal helmet fell and rang amongst the rock and Flindas grasped the reins. Dazed, the rider still clung to his mount. He was hit again and fell senseless from the dashing horse as Flindas struggled forward into the saddle.

The others were almost upon him as he urged the startled horse into a gallop. The animal responded, plunging forward into the darkness. There were cries from close behind and the thunder of hooves. Flindas did not look back. He rode hard, for somewhere ahead of them all were Leana and Tris. The horse was strong and fast and he began to gain a little on those who pursued him. Ahead he could see torches burning. A patrol waited ahead. They were not moving and seemed to be formed into a circle, and then Flindas understood why.

As he galloped closer he could see into the circle of fire. Tris and Leana, still mounted, were surrounded by the riders. Flindas rode forward. His pace never slackened as he came closer. Horsemen looked to see who came galloping their way, and then the patrol behind let out a cry as they saw their prey in the light of the other's torches. Flindas drew his sword and rode hard into the patrol that held his companions. His charge took the riders by surprise, his sword afire in the torchlight. A man screamed and fell. Another lost his stirrup as his mount reared, throwing the rider to the ground.

"Ride!" cried out Flindas slashing as the point of a spear thrust toward him. With the pommel of his sword he sent another from his saddle, and then Tris and Leana were gone into the darkness. Torches flickered in the sand as Flindas galloped after them. In the confusion they had a small lead, and Flindas gained on the horse ahead.

Dawn's first light began to touch the sky behind them. The stars dimmed and vanished as they rode. The cliffs ahead looked like a lifetime away. Flindas glanced back. He could see the horsemen as they gained on the overburdened mount. His sword was back in its scabbard now and he drew a throwing blade from behind his back. The horsemen were close, and they could not be outrun. Flindas turned in the saddle and cast his blade into the chest of the foremost rider, the force of the throw taking the horseman from his mount.

Flindas threw again and another rider fell to the earth, then there was the cold ring of steel as Flindas drew his sword. He pulled sharply on the reins and his horse was forced into a tight circle. He charged directly into the oncoming horsemen. The ferocity of the attack put fear into the riders. Flindas avoided the spears and was suddenly amongst them, his blade stabbing and swinging at them in a blur of steel. Horsemen fell and mounts shied and threw their riders. Flindas bludgeoned another man from his horse then spurred away again in pursuit of his companions.

Three riders had given chase to Tris and Leana. Flindas gained on them slowly, and there was still some distance between them when Flindas stood tall in the saddle and with all his strength cast another throwing knife. A rider fell, the blade buried in his back. The two remaining riders looked back in terror as Flindas drew another knife. They did not wish to die. Both horsemen, as if they had practised it, pulled their horses away, one going far out to either side as Flindas galloped through the space between them, a glance behind showed that the riders were again in pursuit, but at a distance. The pain in his shoulder was intense and he felt himself weakening, the horsemen of Maradass came on, but they seemed reluctant now to come within the range of his knives.

"We may beat them yet!" called Flindas as he caught Tris, and they galloped side by side, making for a low point in the surrounding cliff walls.

"Half a league at most," called Flindas, lying forward in the saddle, trying to ease the pain of his shoulder that throbbed with every pounding hoof beat.

The cliff face was close but he could see another patrol riding hard along the southern wall, ahead the ground became broken, crumbling ramparts of the Broken Lands that had fallen to the plains below. Flindas felt his mount stumble in exhaustion and then regain its footing. The chase slowed, the horses now picking their way across the boulders and loose rock.

In the cliff face to their right he could see a narrow cleft that ran deep into the rock face, there was no other choice, there would be no time to climb the wall before they must turn at bay. The horsemen from the south had now reached the broken ground and with them came marauders, the dogs howled as they sighted their prey, and with a bound the creatures leapt ahead of the riders.

"We must leave the horses," called Flindas. "It is quicker now on foot."

Tris quickly dismounted and helped Leana from the saddle. They pushed her to run towards the cleft, almost dragging her in their haste to survive, and then they were stumbling into the narrow space. The rock strewn floor ran back into the shaded darkness, rising sharply as it went.

"Get her as far up as you can go," Flindas said.

They had not climbed far when the first dogs entered the cleft. The creatures came warily, eyeing the group as they moved higher into the rock walled cleft. With a sudden bound the dogs came on, leaping across boulders and rushing up the slope at them, their eyes gleaming with blue fire. Flindas stood ready, he had the higher ground and the cleft was so narrow that he could touch both walls with his arms outstretched. In either hand he held his two long stabbing knives. His left arm was growing numb and he flexed his fingers on the hilt of the knife as the first marauder came at him. The fight was deadly and one sided, the evil dogs falling quickly to his blades. He was a highly trained warrior and they came at him with jaws and teeth as their only weapons.

The rest of the pack slunk back from his wrath as horsemen began dismounting outside. Tris led Leana higher into the narrow place where it became steeper, the light of day beginning to filter in from above. The marauders crept in behind them, waiting for Flindas to drop his guard as soldiers began clambering up the slope below. Tris pushed Leana to climb higher. The way was becoming very steep, the boulders loose under their hands. The weary travellers had climbed to a point where they looked almost directly down upon the men clambering towards them up the slope. Flindas loosened a large boulder and sent it crashing down upon the luckless men, it smashed through them like a ball in a child's game. Another fall of rock and the soldiers retreated to save their lives.

"For now we are safe," said Flindas as he sank to the ground and leaned against the cliff wall.

"Is your wound bad?" asked Tris, a tender concern in her voice which Flindas had not heard before.

She had hardly spoken through the terrible ride, her whole concern taken with keeping Leana and herself alive. The fear when they had been run down and surrounded she did not wish to think of.

"It needs tending. I have had worse," replied Flindas almost smiling.

He reached into his pouch for a small jar containing a grey ointment and a long roll of bandage. He stripped off his shirt and the leather strapping which had held many of his knives. It was useless now with the weapons gone on their deadly errands. He cast it aside as Tris carefully began to clean his wounds.

The marauder's teeth had sunk deep. The flesh was badly torn where the beast had ripped savagely at the shoulder muscle. Tris used water from her bottle and then spread the ointment. Flindas told her to force it into the wounds and grunted with pain as she massaged the grey mixture into his punctured skin. Then she bandaged him as best she could and Flindas leaned back. The pain eased somewhat, though he knew that he was in for much more when they began to climb. Tris handed him a bone with a good amount of meat and gristle attached. He thanked her and ate it slowly with a tiredness in his body that he had never felt before. He wanted to rest but knew they could not.

"We must find a way out of here if there is one," he said as he pulled himself to his feet.

Tris took the fragment of the Seacrest from her pouch and handed it back to him. "The magic did not work for me any better than for you," she joked and began to coax Leana to her feet.

Leana wavered for a moment and then suddenly her eyes became clear and she looked at Flindas. Her arm rose from her side until she held her hand out before her, palm upward. She spoke not a word but Flindas understood and he laid the Seacrest fragment in her white slender hand. Leana stood transfixed, staring at the small piece of blue metal in her palm. Slowly she drew it to her breast, a look of pain contorted her face for a long moment, her eyes closed and with tears streaming down her cheeks she clutched the Seacrest tightly. Tris and Flindas stood and watched in silence as Leana recovered in silence, then took the cord and placed it around her neck.

"Leana can you hear me?" asked Tris.

She stood beside the Amitarl woman, on her face a look of questioning wonder, but she received no reply. Leana's eyes opened again and they could see that she had returned to her other world where the spell of Maradass still held sway.

They moved further into the deep cleft and there were no sounds from behind. For the moment they had made the soldiers of Maradass fear their higher ground. The way became less steep for a time, it was easier to proceed, but now they must surely be followed. Flindas continued to look back, expecting at any moment to see the black dogs appear behind them. The way became even less steep, almost level, and the chance of attack from behind kept them glancing back as they hurried across the clutter of broken rock. The cleft became smaller, yet they could see daylight beyond. They had to squeeze through the last narrow gap and suddenly found themselves in a small valley, which sloped upward, to be dwarfed by the towering escarpments above.

"We must climb," said Flindas as he quickly sought a feasible route.

For a man, fit and unburdened, it would not have been difficult. He knew that he must carry Leana now and the pain throbbed heavily through his shoulder and arm. Tris again tied Leana to his back and she held on, her arms around his neck. The climb began easily though Flindas chose the left side of the valley, its walls the most difficult for a marauder to follow. His thoughts raced across the leagues to Rark on the Isles of Zeta. A mountain dog could climb here, he thought, as he began the ascent while Tris went ahead, seeking the easiest route.

They had not climbed very high when the marauders plunged through the narrow gap and into the valley. Their sense of smell took them to where their prey had begun the climb and they howled as they saw their prize escaping. The dogs scrambled against the cliff face but their feet were unable to gain purchase on the loose and crumbling stone. The cry became more intense and Flindas looked back as soldiers began to enter the valley. They were too high now for a spearman to throw, and only a longbow shot would catch them. Amongst the horse soldiers of Maradass there were few bowmen, the steel tipped spear and the sword being their chosen weapons.

The climb was not long and they reached the ridge of the valley. They began to move along its rim, struggling over the shattered rocks and narrow fissures, which fell deep into the bones of the earth. Flindas knew that the soldiers would be making for the head of the valley. The climb there was easiest and they would hope to cut their quarry off before they reached the higher cliffs. To their left as they ran and stumbled through the rock Flindas saw what looked like the climb he wanted. The dogs would not be able to follow and they could make the top with the use of their rope. The marauders were fast but they would not cut them off, he thought.

Flindas took them left, angling across a small gully and along another narrow ridge, the cliff on the other side falling away to a deep chasm. They heard the marauders before they could see them, a small cliff cutting off their line of sight. The dogs howled as they came. The change of direction fooled the beasts for a time and where they had expected to find a scent there was none. The beasts ranged the cliffs above the valley until the scent was found again. Flindas forced his companions on. Tris was exhausted and stumbled. It was the last dash that they must not lose, now that escape was in sight. The dogs were gaining on them, running low to the ground, a dreadful howl flowing through them as one. The marauders sighted the group as they ran toward the last rock face, their cries increased and they leapt forward, covering the ground at a flat run.

The beginning of the climb was not difficult. The cliffs sloped more gently and there were ledges and easy access to the slopes of the upper escarpments, but the dogs ran quickly and there was no time to begin the climb. Flindas turned at bay as the pack came at them. Tris pushed Leana against a boulder and faced the dogs with her knife clutched in her hand. The marauders came at them in a rush. They had not yet learned that this was a mistake against the man they faced. Two died as they leapt at Flindas. The others backed away and spread wide.

There were perhaps ten or twelve dogs in the pack. They stood amongst the rocks in a semi-circle, all eyes centred on the group. The creatures ceased their howling after a time and stood motionless, their lips curling, and then as a single beast with one mind, they attacked. The very last of his throwing knives left the hand of Flindas and buried itself in the chest of the nearest dog. The two longer knives were now in his hands as the Marauders came from all sides. He lashed out and one of the creatures screamed in pain, then another fell, its skull crushed.

Tris buried her knife into a black hairy body as another knocked her to the ground. In a split moment she saw the terrible jaws descend towards her throat. She screamed and the marauder howled as Flindas struck. The beasts continued their ferocious attack and Flindas almost fell as the dogs pushed in for the kill. Tris was on her feet again. Her slashing blade opened the side of another dog as it lunged at her. Flindas was almost done. A blow went wide of the mark and he fell to his knees. Suddenly a marauder had him by his left arm and pain coursed through him, and then something else seemed to pour through his veins. Screaming in hatred and rage Flindas rose to his full height and plunged his knife into the dog's heart. With an infuriated screaming cry Flindas lunged again, and finally the remaining dogs could not withstand his wrath. He leapt forward as one possessed, the cry in his throat more animal than the beasts before him. The nearest dog felt his blade and the rest slunk back defeated.

"To the cliffs," cried Flindas, his rage sustaining him as they ran to the beginning of the slow climb.

He looked back once and knew the dogs would not follow. He could see them slinking amongst the rocks, sniffing at their fallen kin and howling dismally at the loss of their prey.

The three climbers struggled on the slope and eventually conquered the final cliff face, the last part had been the most difficult and Flindas had again carried Leana, until they finally reached a high point where they could rest and look down onto the plains. Near the cliffs below they saw many horsemen, pulled to this point by the hunt. Flindas lay back, he did not care now, they were safe for a time and he could rest. Soldiers would be sent to hunt, soldiers who could climb and who would carry bows, but that was not now. All Flindas wished to do at this time was to rest. Tris cleaned and bandaged his fresh arm wound, and then he lay back and fell into a deep exhausted sleep.

The Place of Puzzles

Flindas looked down upon the chasm and the stretch of dusty road where a troop of black horse soldiers stirred the powdered earth into a fine cloud, which drifted on a soft, tantalising breeze. It was hot. The sun beat down upon his back as he lay flat against the rock and watched the soldiers finally ride from sight. It was almost a full turn of the moon since he had last seen the Black Army of Maradass. It had been a time of hardship and much struggle through the Broken Lands, but at last they had won their battle over those ancient shattered lands and had once again reached the Border Road.

After the first few days of their escape across the Flats, there had been no sign of pursuit and they had survived on lizards, snakes, and the occasional rabbit, forcing themselves to travel as fast as the terrain would allow. After a time Flindas had known that they would not be overtaken. The land was vast and even the power of Maradass could not find them. Though he had been in much pain from the mauling by the dogs, with the help of the salve he still carried, his wounds had healed quickly without infection.

They had always tried for a southern route but ravines and impossible chasms had forced them ever to the west. It was a direction Flindas knew would be least expected by Maradass and so he had allowed the terrain to dictate their direction. Tris did not recognise the stretch of road below, but she knew they must be far to the west of Shish-Tan-Vara. She chewed on a cold piece of half cooked rabbit meat as she lay beside him, watching the dust settle below.

"Looks like Maradass also owns the west road," she said through her mouthful.

Flindas sat up and squinted into the distance. Though it was but springtime in the south the sun beat down mercilessly in these northern lands. It had not rained for some days and the water in the pools and streams was becoming brackish and undrinkable. Flindas looked at his other companion, Leana sat as she always did, silent, with her eyes fixed on the air before her. There had been no sign of change in the fair Amitarl woman, nothing since she had reached out for the Seacrest those many days before.

Flindas had often found that in his choice of route he would take the easier though longer way, rather than make a climb where he must carry Leana. He was tired, his body ached from overworked muscles, and his hands were split and raw from the climbing. Tris too was exhausted, though she managed to hide it much of the time. Flindas had seen her slip earlier that day on a simple climb, and she had barely had the strength to save herself. He had called to her but she had not responded, ignoring him and climbing on. Of the three, Leana was the least distressed, though she ate nothing at all and did not sleep. The power or spell which sustained her continued to give her strength. Her clothes were tattered and dirty like their own but she had no scratches or marks of any kind on her body. It seemed that she was impervious to the harshness of the land. Flindas had little to thank Maradass for, but he did thank him for the spell, which had helped Leana to survive.

They watched the road for the remainder of the day and there was much movement below. Many horse troops and the occasional foot soldiers marched by before the sun set, and without pause continued on into the night. Rows of torches lit the roadway, while at times a single rider might gallop by in the pale moonlight. Marauders came, moving slowly, searching. Flindas had noticed during the day that most of the troops had marched to the west.

"Maradass moves an army," he said to Tris, as yet another large troop of horsemen rode by. "He is searching the road as he does so he has not given up the hunt I think."

"I see no way south," said Tris looking into the distance. "You have not travelled there but some have. My father told me that it is not possible to pass through those lands."

Flindas also knew this to be true, anyone he had met who knew the Broken Lands had agreed that the land south of the road was more treacherous than to the north if that were possible. It lay shattered beyond imagination they had said. There too were a great many of the most dangerous places poisoned by the ancient Wizards' Wars so to the west seemed their only possible road. To reach the northern tip of Dreardim and to lose themselves in the forest seemed to be their only hope of reaching the Regions, Maradass would certainly be camped on the northern plains of Rianodar and there would be no place to hide or to run.

Flindas turned to Tris. "You need come no further," he said to her, though he knew that the road would be all that much harder without her strength and companionship. "The Broken Lands are your home. You can make your way here, even if the lands are at war. There is only more danger on the road which I must take."

"And what is that road?" she asked, a muted angry tone in her voice. "You cannot go to Andrian or the City Amitarl. You are the outlaw son of the Governor and would be hanged. Would you find a boat and sail to Zeta?"

"If need be," said Flindas, surprised at the sudden bitterness in her voice.

"Then I will come too," she said, a finality in her words which he knew he could not change. Deep inside he was glad.

"But why go further?" he asked. "What is it you seek?"

"I look for something that I do not yet know," she said mysteriously and shrugged away any further talk on the matter.

They travelled on to the west at dawn the next day. The

way was not so difficult, a flat plateau, broken in places by deep ravines stretched out to the west and north. The road, after cutting back several times, reached these flat lands above. They could see the road as it wound its way amongst broken rock and low shattered hills to the distant horizon. The day was clear and not a cloud marred the distant sky. Far along the road they could see a troop of horsemen riding towards them. They watched from amongst broken rock as the riders moved slowly by.

"The road is clear ahead for a long way," said Flindas. "We will stay beside it, far enough away that marauders cannot catch our scent. The walking will be easier."

"I think I know this place," said Tris as they made ready to move on. "It is years since I came this far west, only once it was, when my father took me to see the Wizard's Castle. If I am right we are further west than I would have thought. There is a long bridge across a ravine, and then I will know. We will have to use the bridge. There is no other way to the west."

They had travelled a league or more when Tris pointed out the bridge still far ahead of them. "There," she said pointing. "We have indeed come a very long way to the west."

Tris squatted on a high point amongst the rocks, her eyes searching for movement on the road. Dust stirred behind them, a lone troop of soldiers marched in the sun's aching heat.

"We are not at all far from the Wizard's Castle," she said. "Two, perhaps three days."

She had mentioned her adventure to the west of Shish-Tan-Vara before. Her father had always wished to go and see the ruined relic of a time gone by, and so when she had been old enough they had left their home and gone to see the castle. Warnings from many had stopped them from entering the ruin, and the circle of huge stones which surrounded it. Tris described them, saying that they looked as if they had been placed there by the children of giants in an old forgotten game.

"Tis an eerie place," said Tris, her memory reaching back to the time. "Those huge stones, big as castles themselves; all lined up in a circle around the broken fortress. Only one tower left standing and a pile of rock where two others had once

69

stood. I shiver just remembering it."

"I have heard of this place, but what of the road?" asked Flindas. "You said that it ends at the ruins."

"That is as I remember it, though it is no road as we see here, more a track really," she replied. "Nothing out beyond the old castle, only desert and more Broken Lands to the south and north. No way to the south except by going west into the desert, then south and east to gain the way back into the Regions. Tis what my father told me."

"We must find the Desert Pass, for that is what it is called," said Flindas. "I am done with these Broken Lands. These soldiers that follow are marching somewhere, perhaps they will show us."

They left the shelter of rocks and moved towards the bridge, keeping far from the road. The troop of soldiers reached the ancient stone structure and marched across. They were all natural men. Flindas had not seen the ones known as Krags amongst the soldiers on the road west. These were ordinary foot soldiers who slumped as they marched, weary of the heat and dust.

"We must cross the bridge and leave no trail," said Flindas. "If marauders find our scent we will be forced north and the hunt will begin again."

Far to the west they could see a small mounted troop coming their way. They waited hidden in the rocks as the group of six horsemen and marauders crossed the bridge, the dogs with their muzzles to the ground, searching the bridge carefully. Then they were gone and soon no dust cloud could be seen, except for the larger troop marching westward ahead of them. Tris quickly led Leana across the bridge as Flindas came behind covering their trail, the nose of a marauder would quickly find their scent but the next passing of soldiers would hopefully take with them any fear of detection. Flindas just hoped that marauders would not be the next to cross.

They moved to the south of the road and continued on into the evening, food was no longer a problem. Rabbits were plentiful here, feeding on the tough grasses which grew in this bleak landscape. In some of the gullies a tree or two could be seen growing along a dry watercourse, firewood was not such a rarity now and as night fell they made camp far from the road, and the sensitive noses of marauders.

The small fire cooked a number of rabbits that Tris had been able to bring down, while beside the fire was a pile of small nuts, taken from a large bush which she had recognised well before they came to it. She had eaten the nuts raw, greedily, but then said they were best roasted after Flindas had gasped at the sudden throat burning taste.

"Go well with rabbit," Tris had said, and laughed at his discomfort, eating yet another of the bitter nuts.

By the fire that evening they talked of the road they had come and the way that they must go. Leana was a constant worry.

"What do you think?" asked Tris as they spoke of her. "Will the spell ever lift? I reckon Maradass has still got more of a hold on her than we do."

"The spell may never be lifted," said Flindas, looking at the wan and beautiful face of Leana, her features motionless as though carved in stone. "I must get her to Tolth," he said. "Her father may be the only one who can undo this sorcery. Until then she is my charge. There is much at stake here. Leana and that which she carries will play no small part in the times to come."

The next day dawned clear and warm and they followed the road as it crossed the vast plateau to the west. Troops of soldiers and horsemen continued to pass during the day, and long into the night. Tris had told Flindas that she thought the road had changed. It was much improved this far to the west she told him. It was a wide road now, where before it had been but a narrow trail. Day passed into evening and once again they ceased their long march to eat and sleep beneath the broad sweep of stars.

It was on the following day that they came in sight of the ancient castle called Murin-Ma-Zarn, the Place of Puzzles. Flindas, in his travels, had seen many sights, but the likes of this he had seen nowhere else before. It was not the ruined towers which astounded him. It was the huge rocks which ran in a perfect curve around the ancient relic, no more than a long bowshot from the castle's crumbling walls. Gaps between the rocks would allow a person to walk through, but little more. At some distance from the ruin they climbed to a high vantage point from where they could see the full ring of stones, and the castle which lay in a depression within the circle. Though the sun shone clearly, the castle had a sense of gloom and decay about it and the very air seemed to darken within the circle of stones.

"The road now goes beyond the castle," said Tris with surprise as she pointed to where it made a turn very near the wall of huge stones, and then began to wind its way down into a deep gorge running to the south.

"That was not there before," she said, and marvelled at the precarious road. "Maradass must have built it for his armies," she continued, and watched as yet another troop of soldiers marched along the road and into the gorge.

"It must be that there is a more direct way now to the Desert Pass," said Flindas as he studied the road. "We must either join the road, or go west into the desert. I have had enough of these Broken Lands."

Tris could see the frustration in her companion's face, he was worn and very tired. He needed rest and there was none to be had.

"We will watch," he said and sat in silence, leaning against a rock, his hat pulled low over his eyes.

Tris saw them first, running not on the road, but along the invisible trail of scent which they had left behind. They were less than half a league off and coming fast.

"Marauders!" she cried suddenly and leapt to her feet.

Flindas stood beside her and then he too could see the distant black group as dust stirred beneath their running feet. He cursed in anger. "We must take the road now!" he said.

They were quickly gone, running as fast as they could push Leana and themselves towards the road. They reached it and the marauders were no longer in view.

"Once we are sighted there will be little time," called Flindas.

"I will delay them. You and Leana must take your chances with the road."

"No!" cried back Tris. "I will not go."

Flindas turned and glared at her. "You must go. There will be little chance otherwise," he growled.

"She is your charge. You are bound to protect her," cried Tris. "I could not get her to Andrian alone. We must stay together."

Flindas ran on in silence, and watched the looming wall of giant stones as they drew closer. From far behind came the sound they had dreaded. The sudden howl of a marauder as it spied its prey, then a shrill blast on a horn. The dogs no longer needed to follow the scent and leapt ahead of their masters. Flindas ran hard, knowing they could never outrun the dogs of Maradass now. He could see little hope of escape. Nowhere was there a climb where they could evade the dogs, the flat plateau offered no possibilities, while at the edge of the roadway the cliff fell sheer and unbroken for many rope lengths into unknown depths. The horn was blown again and there were now horsemen on the road behind, moving fast. Marauders howled continuously, leading the deadly hunt, and then Flindas thought he heard a horn blast from ahead of them, further into the depths of the gorge. They ran on and then he heard it again.

"There are soldiers ahead!" he called to Tris. "We have no choice. We must try to escape through the ruins. It is our only hope."

He looked at the fear in the young woman's face. It was the fear of a child whose nightmares have begun to come to life. Far ahead, on a turning in the road, they saw a troop of foot soldiers, running in time, climbing the road quickly to answer the call from above. Behind them the sound of hooves drummed upon the earth and the dogs howled their delight. The rocks of the circle loomed above the three travellers as Flindas left the road and ran towards the nearest giant stone where they stopped and took a moment's breath. Tris looked with dread at the small walking space between the rocks.

"It is our only hope," said Flindas again as he began to lead

Leana between the huge boulders.

Tris stood for a moment transfixed. She could hear the approaching soldiers and dogs. "No choice," she whispered to herself and then followed her companions into the stone circle of Murin-Ma-Zarn, somehow knowing that her life would never again be the same.

The first thing they noticed was the silence, the sound of pursuit vanished as they reached the inner circle. They looked back as they ran down a sharp grade towards the ruins, expecting at any moment to see marauders leaping through the gaps between the rocks, but they did not come. Flindas began to slow his pace; the dogs should have been at them by now. The single tower and its ruined fortifications hung above then, silent and forbidding.

"There is something here that keeps them at bay," he said to Tris as they slowed.

"There is no sound of them either," Tris said, a note of optimism in her voice. They continued to walk, this time to the far side of the circle. There was still no sound from beyond the stones and Flindas was about to pass through the narrow space between two of the stones when suddenly there was no earth beneath his feet. He called out in fear as he began to slide into a dark hole, his right hand grasping for a hold, his fingertips clinging to rock. Tris leapt to his aid, holding tightly to his wrist as Flindas was able to pull himself from the edge of the dark empty pit. A feeling of horror held him as he sat and looked into the hole, which remained for a time, and then slowly filled, to once again become solid earth. Tris touched it with her fingertips to be sure that it was real.

"There is still old sorcery here," she said, rolling fine sand between her thumb and fingers.

Flindas leaned back against the rock. Sweat stood out on his brow, a look of tired frustration on his face, then he rose slowly and made his way to the next space between the towering boulders. Tris followed, and watched as he tentatively placed a foot between the rocks. Nothing happened.

"I will go through on the rope," said Tris and Flindas agreed.

She carefully tied the rope around her waist then began to

enter the opening. Flindas fed the rope to her as she made her way further through the opening, then Tris reached the other side and Flindas could see her standing in the sunlight beyond the rocks.

"What do you see?" he called to her.

Tris remained silent, standing there for a few moments longer, and then returned; she reached him with a look of great puzzlement on her face.

"Tis the same as it is here," she said, which to Flindas made no sense at all.

"What is the same?" he asked.

"The other side," she replied. "Tis the same as here, out there are the castle and the circle of stones."

Flindas peered into the opening, a sceptical look on his face. "I must see," he said and walked carefully into the space, watching his feet for any change in the sandy floor.

He reached the sunlight beyond and looked in amazement at the ruined castle and ring of stones before him. In every detail it was the same as the place he had just been, and he now stood at the same point where first they had entered the ring of stones. He cast his eye to the far wall and after a moment he could see a familiar dark figure against the rock.

"Wave your arm in the air," he called to Tris.

"What?" she called back to him, thinking she had misheard.

"Wave your arm in the air," he called again and after a moments pause the dark figure across the stone circle before him began to move its arm.

He stood for a moment in wonder, and then turned to go. A movement caught his eye near the castle. In the shadow of the tower he saw Leana walking towards the ruins. He was confused for a moment. Which castle should he run to? He turned quickly and returned through the narrow gap.

"Leana is gone!" he called as he emerged.

"No she is not," called Tris.

Flindas dashed past her and then came to a dust stirring halt. There indeed was Leana, sitting against a boulder, silent and unmoving as ever. Flindas breathed deeply. He knew that he must not allow his bewilderment to cloud his judgement.

He told Tris what he had seen. Tris shrugged with a look on her face which told of confusion mixed with wonder. She looked up at Flindas.

"We had best try another gap," she said, a tired smile on her lips.

They walked together past the face of the huge boulder which stood like the wall of a castle above them and soon came to the next gap. Tris again went through, Flindas playing out the rope to her, and she came very carefully into the open, the smell of marauders was on the air.

The plateau spread towards the desert and there were troops of horsemen and foot soldiers not far off. Marauders roamed amongst the soldiers, though they seemed afraid to come closer to the rocks. All eyes looked towards the circle of stones where Tris remained in the shadows, watching for a time before she returned to Flindas.

"That one I believe," she said. "Soldiers and marauders, and the desert beyond."

"There is a wizard's sorcery here," he said to her. "Though you describe what I would expect to see, I will not believe it until I see it myself." He paused. "Then I may still not believe it," he smiled and entered the gap.

When he reached the other side he was not very surprised to find that what Tris had seen was no longer there. The plateau stretched towards the far desert but there were no troops or marauders. He walked slowly into the open, looking either way for hidden attackers, but there were none. The rope remained tied around his waist and he was soon at the end of its length. He untied it and let it fall to the earth. Two things happened in the same instant. The rope vanished as though it had melted into the ground, and suddenly he could see the troops and dogs. Worse still they could see him.

With a cry they began to charge, the dogs outstripping the soldiers. Flindas turned and ran. He seemed to be much further from the rock wall than he had thought, much further than the rope could ever have reached. He raced towards the stone circle and could hear the dogs almost upon him. He knew that he would never reach the wall. He turned at bay as the marauders bore down on him. Riders with lances held forward in the charge were close behind.

In that split moment Flindas knew that he must now die. There was no other outcome possible. He drew his heavy knives for his last defence, and then gaped in amazement as the dogs and soldiers seemed to run into a cloud of fine mist, and then vanished before his eyes. He stood for a moment in astonishment. His body gave a long trembling sigh and he turned to find himself standing within an arms length of the high stone wall. He was not near a gap and he did not know which one he had come through, though something told him

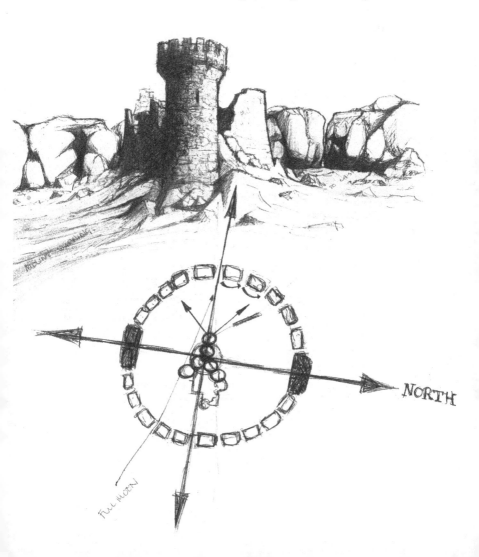

that he must enter the same way as he had come. Then he saw the rope lying amongst the dust and stone, he returned to find Tris looking anxious and worried.

"You were gone so long," she said surprised. "I called but the rope went slack."

"It was not very long," he said, his chest still heaving from the run.

Then he looked toward the sun and realised that even time was not a constant in this circle of puzzles. The sun now lay well towards the west, when it had been no later than noon when he had entered the gap.

"There is much here that cannot be understood," he said as he slumped down against a boulder. "At least for now it seems we are safe, they will not enter."

They ate a little and drank sparingly from their one water bottle, for they had seen no sign of water within the circle. Flindas had for some time been watching the sun until he was sure.

"The sun does not set," he said. "Though it has dropped from the zenith, it no longer moves to the horizon. It becomes stranger than strange," he added quietly, almost to himself.

There seemed nothing else for it but to enter another gap and attempt to discover a way beyond the ring of stones. The next opening in the rock was almost due north of the castle; Tris entered slowly, again with the rope tied around her waist. The way seemed almost closed and Tris had to crawl through the last narrow space. She could see little until she was again able to stand. Before her lay the plateau, and to the west the brown red desert. There was no sign of soldiers or marauders. She tugged on the rope and Flindas left Leana sitting against the rock face and made his way to the other side. He stood beside Tris and saw what she saw and they moved away from the rocks a little.

"It seems too simple," said Flindas suspiciously.

Nothing disturbed the land that stretched before them, and Flindas noticed that the sun had sunk a little lower in the sky.

"It looks like our best chance," he said.

Tris returned through the gap to bring Leana, and then

there was an urgent tugging at the rope. Flindas leapt to the opening and crawling quickly he was soon through to the other side.

"Leana has gone," said Tris as she saw him emerge.

Flindas looked around. He could see Leana nowhere in the curved basin which lay between them and the castle.

"Keep looking!" he called to Tris. "She may have gone to the ruins. Remember which stones we just passed through."

Flindas was away, leaping down the slope towards the castle, the ancient tower looming above him.

Flindas reached the broken walls and after a short climb was amongst the crumbling stonework, but there was no sign of Leana. He climbed one of the two crumbled towers of the castle that formed a triangle with the one tower that remained standing. Then he looked down into what had once been the central courtyard, now but a pile of stones fallen from the broken towers. He caught a glimpse of movement in a gap between two broken walls close to the undamaged tower, a flash of golden hair. Flindas climbed down to the chaos of stone and rubble below. Leaping from stone to stone he quickly crossed to the tower. He was just in time to see Leana step through a low archway built into the side of the high stone wall. Flindas leapt for the opening but came up hard against cold solid stone.

The archway was gone. There was no sign of it in the solid unbroken lines of the tower. He looked up at the ancient stonework. In places the mortar between the stones had crumbled; leaving hand holds which looked easy to climb. He placed his hands in the first small cleft and there was a tingling sensation in his fingertips, his fingers would not grasp the stone and quickly grew numb and lifeless. Flindas pulled his hands away from the wall then tried again, but still the numbness made it impossible to climb, he stood back from the tower bewildered.

"There must be a way in!" he said aloud.

Climbing back up to the broken tower, he placed his fingers to his lips and a high sharp whistle told Tris that he had found Leana. He waved from the broken wall and Tris soon joined him, carrying their pack and sword. They studied the tower for a time. There seemed to be no way in if they were unable to climb. The two companions were standing before the stone wall where the door had been when before their unbelieving eyes the stonework shimmered and the arched entrance appeared before them. Flindas drew his sword, though steel against such magic would be of little use he thought. The doorway was dark and no light came from the interior of the tower. Flindas stood for a moment, and then moved forward under the archway, Tris at his shoulder.

The floor beneath their feet was smooth and undamaged, and Flindas kept a hand brushing against the clean stonework of the wall as they moved further into the darkness. The little light which penetrated into the gloom from the doorway was suddenly gone as the entrance vanished and the darkness became complete. They waited in the cold silence. their ears alert for any sound, then a speck of light began to glow in the darkness. It grew slowly, small flames licking and waving amongst dry fuel in a large stone fireplace. Leana stood by the fire, her face an expressionless mask as the flames grew brighter, to reveal a large circular room. There was no furniture to be seen, but on the floor before the fireplace was a thick, intricately woven carpet of marvellous design, while on the walls hung rich tapestries, depicting many scenes of beautiful country and lofty awe inspiring cities. Strange creatures cavorted amongst the happy folk depicted there, while in the woven skies were wonderful exotic birds, or starry nights, the patterns of stars unrecognisable to Flindas or Tris.

Flindas looked about the room as he moved to Leana's side. She seemed undisturbed, standing as though for warmth beside the blaze, the light flickering on her lovely face. There was a soft sound as though a curtain had been drawn and then standing near them, rubbing his hands together over the fire and looking warmly into the flames was a small white haired old man, no taller than Tris.

"I do like a fire in the winter," said the little man, suddenly smiling at them.

Trontar the Follower

"Yes indeed, I do like a fire in the winter," repeated the little man. His voice was a dry crackle, almost mimicking the sounds from the fire, humour sparkling within his words. His eyes came gleaming from beneath his bushy white eyebrows and he looked at the three who stood in the firelight.

"But tis not winter," said Tris quietly through her astonishment.

"Ah! Of course not, no," said the little man. "It is somewhere though."

"What is somewhere?" asked Tris, and wondered at her own words.

"Winter," he replied, a small frown creasing his brow.

Tris was confused but her fear was suddenly much abated. Flindas too lowered his sword to his side.

"I am glad that you could join me," said the man smiling. "Now that you are all here I can introduce myself. I am the Wizard." He chuckled deep in his throat. "I was once called Della-Ma-Sta or Yellow Star, but I have since discovered it was no star, just another lump of rock like this one."

Flindas had no idea what the wizard was talking about but could not interrupt as the old man continued.

"I was also called the Follower or Trontar in the old tongue, but now Wizard will suffice. And what of you? Who have I as guests in my home tonight?" He spread his arms wide and looked at them expectantly.

"I am Flindas Demsharl, and we mean no harm here."

"Oh, I know you mean no harm," the Wizard laughed to himself. "There is indeed no harm that you could do to me anyway, of that I am sure." He smiled a knowing smile through his beard and tapped the side of his nose with a long finger. "Let me tell you a secret," he said coming forward, whispering as though the walls held ears which could hear. "I cannot die," he said, and his expression became a little worried and thoughtful. "I have yet to find out what happens to me when the earth finally disintegrates." His words were even more than puzzling. "What happens then, eh?" he looked at them questioningly. "Do I end up floating in space watching comets go by for ever and beyond? Or perhaps leap out to the nearest star of the Six Wizards and spend my time trying to adjust to the new complexities of angles and time? And who would be there for me to talk to? No one is my best guess... though I could be wrong." He shook his head and sighed heavily as though the problem was a great weight upon his mind, then went back to warming himself by the fire, finally adding. "At least I have time to think about it. Tis not likely to happen for an aeon or two." He chuckled and gave them a wink.

Flindas could not help but like this strange and intriguing person, his colourful clothing and amusing manner beguiled them both. Tris felt warmth for this old man that she found hard to explain to herself.

"I am Tris," she said, and took a small step forward.

He looked gently into her eyes, then he leaned forward and his hand reached out and softly touched the scars on her face. She did not retreat as she normally would have.

"I can take those away if you want," he said, his compassionate eyes looking deep into her own. "But not now," he said abruptly, straightening to his full height. "Your third companion I know and I know what she carries. Perhaps I can repair what ails her too, but not yet. Firstly you must consider this. The way to leave Murin-Ma-Zarn is not difficult if you wish to continue your journey, though you have but one chance to discover it, and by sundown you must decipher my wonderful poetical riddle."

Before he could speak further Flindas interrupted him. "Tis surely passed sunset now?" he said. Then he remembered that the sun had hung motionless in the sky before they had entered the castle.

"Indeed the sun is still high," said the Wizard. "It will remain unmoving until you leave this tower."

Flindas was startled, had the Wizard read his thoughts?

"Only the important parts," said the Wizard and his joyful scratching laugh filled the room. "Oh it is good to have interesting people to talk to," he said. "Perhaps this will reassure you."

He looked at Flindas with an artful smile, and then raised his hand towards a tapestry which hung low on the western wall. The old wizard's arm became still, the hand palm outward, fingers pointing upward, and then he spoke a simple phrase quietly into his beard. Through the tapestry and through the stone wall beyond, a window appeared, sunlight slanting in at an angle. Flindas and Tris went quickly and looked out upon the circle of stones, and higher, to where the sun remained in the clear sky, its heat no illusion. Tris ran her fingers along the edge of the tapestry. It was as if the sharpest blade had cut through it cleanly, leaving not a loose thread, and yet it did not hang limp as it should. They returned slowly to the fire.

"If you like the window I can leave it," said the Wizard. "It may be reassuring." He looked deeply into their puzzled faces. "So, this is what you must decipher to escape this most dangerous place," he chuckled. "This must be solved before you can leave, and should you manage to leave, you must all go together and never return."

He gave a wide smile. His long moustache seemed to turn up at the ends and increased his look of humorous benevolence. "I made this up myself, before I lost the Tower of Art," he told them. "I think it quite lyrical." He cleared his throat and spoke in a voice that was not quite his own:

The summer solstice comes dawning
On twenty-two doors and one day
The tower looks east in the morning
To admire the sun's early rays
The tower will see the day turning
To the west an eye it doth lay
The eyes will see the day's ending
The sunlight at last cannot stay
To the west the sun it goes falling
The last ray of light shows the way
Full moon will see and give warning
That the Wizard has joined in the play.

I can write it down for you if you wish," he smiled, seeming pleased at his recitation. "I once knew five hundred and seventy-three languages," he said as if to himself, frowning a little and shaking his head. He reached into the air before him and plucked a scroll of parchment from the empty air. "Here," he said. "This may help."

Flindas took the scroll, on which the twelve lines were already carefully and artfully written in a bold confident hand.

"We have until sundown," said Flindas. "Yet the sun does not set. Tell me, Wizard, how can the sun's last light show us the way when there will be no last light?"

"A good question," said the Wizard beaming. "Yes, a good question, but easily resolved. The sun will continue to set when you again leave this tower and choose your way. You may leave by the window if you wish but most prefer the door." At these words the door reappeared for a moment then vanished once again. "When you have the answer and decide to leave, the doorway will return," he told them. "You have but to tell me. Study the scroll carefully. In simplicity you may find great difficulty. I made it up so long ago that it is not worth recalling the number of years." His voice had become quiet, musing, as though he talked to himself in this way often. "I almost forget why," he said, and shuffled on the hearth until his back was to the fire.

Flindas was not clear on the matter of time. Did they have forever to solve the mystery, he wondered?

"That is indeed it," said the Wizard smiling at him. "You have forever, or almost forever."

"But what of the outside world?" said Flindas, again surprised that the Wizard had known his thoughts. "What is happening beyond the stone circle?"

"Nothing," said the Wizard smiling. "Outside the circle there is nothing. There is no time, and yet everything will lie there just as it was before you entered, whenever you decide to return to it. Within this tower time is only relevant to the tower itself. The outside world need not exist until you want it to." He became amused at their puzzlement. "Take your time," he said. "There is no need to hurry. Whatever you have left outside will remain there exactly as you left it until you return."

He turned to go and then stopped. "I almost forgot," he said. "Should you solve the riddle, and there are some who have not, then there is a reward. There are many who have never even tried to leave. They wish to go nowhere else. Oh, there is much here that you could never even guess at until you try. All of your dreams may be fulfilled, all that you want and more can be yours. There is time here, and yet you will not age while you are within the tower. All that you could wish for is here as I say, except for your life in the other world beyond the stones. If you succeed in returning there then you will have one desire fulfilled. I am not all powerful, that was the domain of the High Wizards, but be it in my power I will grant you your one desire. Consider that also."

He stepped from the hearth as if to go. There were many things which Tris suddenly wanted to ask him, but one came foremost into her mind.

"We can have all that we could wish for," she repeated the Wizard's words. "Does that include food?"

The Wizard turned to her smiling. "Oh yes," he said. "It includes food."

He held out his hand palm downward and spoke words in a strange tongue. Instantly a long table lay set in the centre of the round room, and the tantalising smell had Tris leaping for the food. She touched it first as though it may not be real.

"Eat," said the Wizard. "It is the finest food that time can provide."

He smiled as Tris took a leg of some large bird and bit off a bite, then without swallowing she bit into a large juicy unknown fruit. Flindas joined her and began to eat a piece of the same bird.

"Furniture, I think," said the Wizard, and slowly the room became furnished with seats and large exquisitely carved beds. More rugs appeared on the floor. "And for your later comfort," said the smiling wizard, and he waved a slow hand at a section of wall. A screen appeared, inlaid with coloured shell and gold, and from beyond it rose the wafting steam of hot water. "You will wish to wash some of the dust from you and your clothes. All is provided," said Trontar the Wizard and gave a small bow. "I will return when you are refreshed. Take your time. There is all the time that you need, and then there is more again if you want it."

He turned and was gone as though he had never been. Tris did not see him vanish, so intent was she upon the food. Flindas ate with great pleasure and drank from a tumbler of rich deep red wine. He thought he had never tasted any drink so fine. He still did not truly believe all that the Wizard had said and kept going to the window and observing the sun. Then he turned to look at Leana who had remained motionless by the fire, and Flindas remembered the Wizard's words. He had said that he could perhaps heal what ailed her. It had seemed to go by so quickly their meeting with the Wizard, and now there were many things that he wished to ask.

Time went by and the sun did not set, after eating their fill they lay in hot steaming tubs which did not seem to cool, nor the water grow dirty, just as the fire burned but did not consume the fuel. For the first time since Aster's camp Flindas shaved the dark beard from his face, while Tris stayed soaking in the luxury of the hot soapy water until her fingers and toes had begun to wrinkle. After another quick bite from the still laden table, she helped Leana to bathe. There were three robes laid out for them and after washing the dust from their clothes they hung them from the screens to dry. Lying back in the soft chairs was like being on a cloud, and as they relaxed into the comfort, their hurts and pains seemed to flow from their bodies and be absorbed by the chairs. The fire burned on as weariness caught Flindas and wrestled him gently into sleep.

He woke with a start and looked about quickly. He did not expect the room to be the same, but it was, except that now Tris stood by the window and Leana was seated in one of the luxurious chairs. Tris held the scroll in her hand and was looking out towards the wall of stones. Flindas stood and he felt strong. The weariness of the long journey had fallen from his body completely. There was vigour in him that caused a smile of delight to come to his lips.

"Feels good," said Tris from where she stood in the shaft of sunlight. She stretched and shook herself in sheer enjoyment. "Twenty-two doors," she said holding out the scroll. "I can see ten stones. If I lean right out I can just see another. Tis half the circle. The twenty-two doors must be the openings between the rocks." She was pleased with her observation and deduction. "Not sure about the rest, though," and she went back to the table for more food. "The meat stays hot," she said but without any great surprise in her voice. "I could get used to staying here."

She returned with a tumbler of wine to the window where Flindas stood studying the scroll. "What be a summer solstice?" she asked him, the words slipping in a peculiar way off her tongue which made her laugh. The wine was quite potent.

Flindas lifted an eyebrow in amused concern. "The Summer Solstice is the day of the longest sunlight and is considered the first day of summer," he told her. "Some of this rhyme is becoming clear to me. I keep count of the days when I travel, today is the Summer Solstice or one day off as near as I can tell." He looked at Tris in puzzlement. "How could it be that we arrive on this particular day just to correspond with the Wizard's poem I cannot say," he said. "Perhaps it is always the Solstice here, I would not be surprised. Also there should be no full moon this evening but I think I will expect one all the same." He smiled. "That is of course if evening should ever come," he said, somewhat bemused at the strangeness of it all. "I cannot truly understand, and then it gets stranger." He read the second line: "*There are twenty-two doors and one day.*"

"The doors we have," and Tris smiled. "The 'one day' I am not sure of."

"If we are given one day to find our way out then we will not have much time when we leave the tower," Flindas said. He looked at the angle of the sun, judging time and direction, though the window looked more towards the south than west, he read on, going through the poem once again. "There is something about the angle of the sun I believe," he said. "The last light shining on a particular door perhaps, and now I begin to make a little more sense of the rest perhaps."

"What warning?" said Tris. "What warning could the moon give?"

"Perhaps warning us that we have chosen the wrong door," he replied. "What warning would we heed? Only one that told us we had the wrong door. The moon will be full and coming up in the east. At least I hope it is so in this strange place. It may mean that the door we must choose is to the east, though much points to the west. The sun when setting will shed little light within the wall of stone. The last light must shine in through one of the western doorways." He stopped a moment and shook his head. "That seems too easy," he said and smiled in bemused puzzlement. "The last line confirms that we may not understand it at all. *The Wizard has joined in the play.*"

He read the poem over several times, and though it was not cold he sat by the fire and puzzled over the words.

"What about the Wizard?" said Tris as she joined him. In one hand she held a bone from which she was slowly devouring the meat and in her other she held a fruit not quite like any Flindas had seen in the lands. Tris said it was like soft sweet vegetable egg.

"His power is stronger than any I could imagine," said Flindas. "Just the window and this furniture, the food!" He waved a hand towards Tris as she chewed off another large bite. "It is only a small portion of what he can do I think. He has read my thoughts and has obviously lived here for thousands of years." Flindas paused. "Yet why the puzzle and the game?" he mused. "We still do not know what happens if we choose the wrong door."

"I like him," said Tris, a small defensive note in her voice. "He cooks well," she added as Flindas rose smiling and made his way to the table of food.

He looked at it and realised that it appeared exactly as they had first seen it. Not a piece seemed to have been touched. Each dish lay there complete. Flindas took a plate of small pastries and a tumbler of wine back to his chair. The pastries were warm and delicious, each one different and a surprise.

"I do not know anything of him nor have I heard anyone speak of him," he said. "This place has always been the ruined wizard's castle, which I meant to see one day but never did."

"I heard stories," said Tris. "From my father mostly. Old stories. People returning with riches and dying poor. Others going and never being seen again. No good stories I ever heard, haunted stories to keep you awake nights. No one said a thing about food and hot water." She snuggled into her thick robe, luxuriating in its fresh clean warmth.

"You wish to ask me some questions?" said the Wizard, who was by the fire warming his hands.

Tris dropped the piece of cheese that she had been nibbling and Flindas came upright in his chair. Though he sensed no danger from the old wizard, he felt suddenly naked with no weapons within reach.

"Forget them," said the Wizard. "They are of no use at all inside these walls. You have questions which I think I can answer. Come, I enjoy talking about myself." He waited for their words until Flindas spoke. "The riddle you set will take much thought, but I wonder why you invent such a puzzle. You seem a reasonable man, so why set unreasonable tasks."

"You talk of reason," said the Wizard gruffly, an annoyed look on his face. "That was the second tower," he spoke again as if to himself. "Yes," he said. "I am a reasonable man, and that is why I have made it so much easier for you to go. The rhyme is not made to trick you. It is there to aid you as much as I can." He looked at them sternly. "To tell you why you must solve this riddle you must learn something of my past and why I am here." Then he smiled suddenly. "And because I am such a reasonable man," his eyes twinkled with mirth, "I will tell you, and since we all have as much time as we wish I think I will sit."

A chair materialised beneath him as he sat down close by the fire, then he began to tell them of a history that had been forgotten by most in the lands. "Where the wizards originally came from is not important to this story," he began. "We sailed in tall ships from a land that was poisoned and dying. We came with high ideals and great power. Thousands of people left the torn lands in the distant north, and with them, leading them, were the twenty wizards. There were fourteen Lesser Wizards, of which I was one, and then there were six High Wizards, being the most powerful and strong. There are many tales from those old times. Some you will have heard, and many you could never comprehend. There are few now in the lands who know even the least of these stories." He indicated Leana who sat quietly in one of the large ornate chairs. "Her father may be the highest authority of the old times now living in the lands, excluding myself of course."

Smiling he made a small bow then grew serious again. "We arrived on the shores of this great southern continent and here we found a black skinned people living scattered over much of the lands. They had their own powers and magicians, and after a time of mistrust they came to know us, and realised we meant only good for all people. Amongst them was one known as Manzanee, whose powers were unequalled, except perhaps by the six High Wizards themselves. He became a close ally of Rishtan-Sta, the White Wizard, and was invited to join our Council. When the time came that destroyed the wizards, he did not die with the others, but is no longer in the time that you call reality, or now.

"You will have noticed I think that there are twenty-two stones in the circle out there," he smiled as Tris nodded wisely. "There is one for each of the wizards who came from the north, then one more for the Black Wizard who was always here. Then there is one for the wizard who is still to come, of him only Rishtan-Sta, who saw the future, could truly know.

I was never told and do not know his story, or her story," he corrected himself. "Wizardry was never the domain of males alone.

"All peoples, white and black, lived in harmony and peace until the High Wizards began to fall out with one another as the centuries passed. They began to use their High Magic, seeking to disrupt and even destroy the other's powers. They formed alliances amongst themselves and eventually made war upon each other, using humans to do their violent bidding. Rishtan-Sta tried to avert the wars but could not stand against them alone. With Manzanee he did what he could to ease the suffering of the peoples. The lands were poisoned by this violent magic, black skinned and white fought side by side against their brothers and sisters, forced to do battle to the most bitter of ends by the High Magic of the wizards.

"Wizards are not immortal but they cannot die easily. A wizard is the only one who can take the life of another wizard, but that wizard, to do so, must also die. It is a bond which was made to hold us, and tie us together. Because he saw that the wars would eventually lead to the end of humanity, Rishtan-Sta, with the aid of Manzanee, made Ma-Zurin-Bidar, the Wizards' Bane, known to you as the Seacrest. With it he took the lives of almost all of the wizards, including his own. Manzanee survived by escaping into time and I was left alone in a bleak, uncertain land. Rishtan-Sta chose me as the one to remain, as a memory of what had once been."

The Wizard paused, a painful remembrance passing across his thoughtful brow. "Rishtan-Sta had chosen me as the one who would survive," Trontar repeated. "And he showed me how it could be done. I had taken no joy in the Wizard Wars but had been bound into them as though by chains. I had watched the slaughter and saw it to be cruel. The people could not fight the all powerful High Wizards, bound as they were by oaths and spells which could not be broken. Finally Rishtan-Sta ended the wars as I have said, and with my Scribe I began to build my protection, and to keep a true history of those ancient times.

"I built this castle with its three towers, and the circle of stones which surrounds it. I made many spells of protection using a great amount of my powers to keep away any possible danger. I was young still, and unwise, for I feared retribution of some kind for my part in the devastation, but it did not come. I feared the power of the High Wizards who had died, but I should have feared time even more. Wizards could reach across time and space, so why not from beyond death. I had never heard of a wizard dying before and I built my retreat, my fortress, and wound it about with magic and visions, and powerful spells.

"There was little I had not learned as one of the fourteen, and finally I felt protected and secure. I put into the three towers the works and collections of my long lifetime. In one I put music, art and poetry, all the memories, melodies and melodramas which I had loved so well. It made my heart sing to enter that tower."

He paused, a sad smile on his lips. "In the second tower I put Reason," he continued. "All the great works of Philosophy ever written stood in beautifully sculptured bookcases which curved around the stone walls. The highest thoughts of all wizardry and human existence I had gathered there. I would speak with my scribe for days, nay moons, on the delicacies of one philosophical thought. I revelled in knowledge and wisdom, as did he.

"The third tower is this one," he said and raised his arms from his sides, looking up at the ceiling. "It I dedicated to Science, and the analytical mind. Here is where I got my greatest joy, and so when my powers began to diminish and I found I had not the strength to keep the castle from crumbling about me, I let the first tower fall into ruin, and my spirit cried as it fell.

"Time passed, centuries and more, until I found that I could no longer keep the second tower from falling. My scribe had died. I had not expected that. He was almost as old as I was and I thought him protected. I had no one left to reason with, no one to throw great thoughts at and see if they bounced. I gave up the Tower of Reason with great sadness, and I now remain here, engulfed in my science. With the changing of my powers and the passing of time I can no longer govern many of the spells which I bound myself with. The poem is part of that. I cannot give you the answer, as spells of silence bind me as well, but the clues are there and can be easily read." The Wizard pointed to the scroll that Flindas held in his hand. He paused a moment, then said. "You have other questions I think." He looked thoughtfully at Flindas.

"What happens if we do not escape?" Flindas asked the Wizard. "You mention rewards, but what are the penalties?"

"The penalty is not so harsh," said the Wizard leaning forward and looking into the fire. "If you do not choose your path correctly you must stay within these walls forever. A choice that is not so bad, trapped within time but with all the benefits that time can bring. Just as you are now, so it can remain. Only the outside world would be locked from you forever."

"Where are the others you spoke of?" asked Tris. "Where are the ones who have not found the right door, or not wanted to?"

"They are all around you," said the Wizard mysteriously, raising his hands and waving them towards the room. "They arrived here at a different time and so they remain locked into that time. The tower seems but an empty vessel to the ones who have not looked deeply into the shadows. There is nothing you cannot have if you choose to remain. There is almost nothing you cannot have if you fail to leave. There is little to lose, do you not think?" He smiled a benevolent smile. "I would not have had it thus had I been wiser with my powers," he said. "For I too am locked in here. I cannot leave the tower. It is my last refuge and my prison."

Flindas looked at the Wizard as he sat in his chair by the fire, beneath the old man's warm exterior Flindas felt a knot of anger, but the anger was for no one but the Wizard himself.

"You spoke of rewards," said Tris. "A wish to be granted?"

"Yes," said the Wizard. "If you leave the circle you will each be granted a Wizard's Favour. Do not tell me yet what may be your heart's desire. Think carefully, for here is a double edged sword. Used wisely it will take you to where you want to go, and perhaps give you much. Used unwisely and you may find death or worse awaits you beyond these walls. There is much time, ease yourselves, rest and eat, for that is what you truly need."

The Wizard rose from his chair and went to stand before Leana who sat still and lifeless, her eyes seemingly fixed on the fire. "You need more than rest and food," he said to her and laid a gentle hand on her head, Leana stirred for a moment and then was still once more. "She needs to be free of this spell," he said turning to the others. "I can do it, but that will take time. Time in this reality not your other one out there," he smiled thoughtfully. "I would like to take her to another part of the tower. I have a place where it will be more comfortable for her, and there I will release her slowly from that which holds her. Her recovery will not be fast, for my powers will be much taxed by even this simple spell of Maradass. If you like I can show you where she will be, and then I will take you to the observatory."

"What is the observatory?" asked Tris, never having heard the strange word before.

"I will show you," said the Wizard and tapped the side of his nose. "But first let me see to your companion. If you will stand I will take you to the laboratory." Here again was a word that Tris did not know, but she did not ask its meaning. She stood as did Flindas, expecting to be shown the stairs to the upper rooms. The Wizard encouraged Leana to stand, and when she was upright the old man brought his palms together before him and spoke a soft word. There was no sense of movement, only a slight dimming of the light around them, and then they were no longer in the chamber with the fire.

Their eyes adjusted to the new white light which seemed to emanate from the walls of the laboratory. The room was a maze of tables and benches, covered with strange and wonderful things. There was a long table where a tall construction of glass tubing and bottles of coloured liquids bubbled over a number of flames that seemed to have no source, as though the air itself was on fire.

A great mountain of books threatened to crush the shelves and tables which held them. On the walls were diagrams and charts, each one masterly drawn, the writing in a bold hand, precise and clear. A large segment of the curved wall was taken up by a number of tall glass fronted cupboards. Inside there were bones and skulls of many animals, some human, some almost human.

"Welcome to my laboratory," said the Wizard as he began to guide Leana to a bed which had been placed in an alcove against the wall. "Firstly, I will allow her to sleep."

The Wizard helped Leana to lie down, soothing unknown words coming softly to his lips as he covered her with a rug, though the room was neither cold nor hot. Leana lay still, her eyes open and staring at the ceiling. The Wizard reached out and laid a hand lightly over her eyes. He spoke more of the ancient words, deep and powerful, yet said most gently with a caring heart. When he removed his hand Leana's eyes were closed and her face seemed relaxed and at peace. The look of stone had gone from her and she slept soundly, her breast rising and falling gently beneath the rug.

"She will sleep now," said the Wizard. "She has not slept for many moons and now she must dream, her sleep visions will allow her mind to open again, to heal."

Flindas felt his concern for Leana much eased. His own body had been healed of its pain and weariness. Now he felt his mind loosen as the responsibility for Leana was taken from him. "Do you know all of history and that which happens in the lands now?" he asked the wizard.

"There is much that happens that I can see if I wish to," replied the Wizard, leaving his patient and moving to a bench laden with pieces of metal and tools. There were a number of mirrors on the bench, Tris picked one up and looked into it but was surprised to find that she could see nothing but a wavering blur.

"In here it is always now," he said. "So all I see is from the past, I see it but I cannot interfere. The Amitarl Family I have observed since they first made the pact with Maradass, and that which was made by Rishtan-Sta was broken. It should never have been found again, but it was and so it is as it must." A concerned look came into his old face. "It would have been best for it to have lain on the ocean floor forever. I know much of recent history, as well as the old times, I cannot interfere in these dreadful times but I can tell a story or two."

The Wizard smiled broadly. "Since the time of the Dividing I have watched Amitarl and Maradass closely, and many other happenings in the land. Your name is Demsharl," he said looking into the eyes of Flindas. "I have seen far into the Regions since they were formed. The name Demsharl, Governor of the City Amitarl, I have not missed."

Flindas said nothing and returned the inquiring gaze.

The Wizard smiled and nodded knowingly."My means of gathering this information is in part collected by these," continued the Wizard, coming up close to Tris and pointing to the mirror which she held before her.

"They reflect," said Tris. "But much bigger,"

"Yes indeed," said the Wizard picking up one of the small round mirrors and studying its edge. "They are more than mirrors, but I will show you. I will now take you to the observatory, unless you have plans of going elsewhere."

He smiled at the two travellers who both felt enchanted by the small man's humorous gaze. The Wizard placed his palms together, spoke a single word, and the room faded to darkness.

The Wizard's Riddle

"Forgive me," came the words of the Wizard from the darkness. "It is usually night time in the observatory, and I often forget that it will be dark here."

As he said this the walls began to shimmer, then they glowed softly, filling the chamber with a gentle white light. All else in the room was forgotten as Tris and Flindas looked upon the huge dome of dark glass that was slowly rising from a circular cavity in the floor of the chamber. When it was fully raised it was almost a man's height and twice that across. The dark half sphere dominated the upper chamber of the tower. The Wizard stood by it and seemed to be talking to it. He then turned to his guests.

"This is my observatory," he said and gave them a bow of welcome. "It is from here that I have learned to see much, and I learn much from that which I see. It is my life and my true joy. I cannot go beyond these walls, but there is much that is out there which I can bring in here and observe."

He pointed to the ceiling. They looked up to see the high, solid stone roof begin to fade until above them hung the night sky, stars shimmering with crystal like clarity. There were many hundreds of the round mirrors set into the upper walls and more on moveable frames which allowed for an infinite number of complex variations. A light frame of silver wires hung suspended across where the ceiling had been, and at their centre, directly above the dome, there floated a sphere of the same dark glass. Much smaller than the dome itself, it did not touch the wires but seemed to be cradled by them. The ball revolved slowly, reflecting back the light which glowed softly from the walls.

"This is my magic," said the Wizard, pleased at the look of awe on their faces.

Tris walked forward slowly, gazing above her. "Will you show us?" she said turning to the Wizard, her eyes sparkling with wonder.

"Show you what?" asked the Wizard, his voice lifting with hidden amusement.

"Anything," said Tris, excitement overflowed into her voice. "What can you show?"

The Wizard, his amusement and enthusiasm no longer restrained, came to her side quickly, his eyes gleaming. "I can show you many things," he said. "I can show you stars and the moon. I can show you the lands from here to beyond. I can show you dark hearts and great wonders of the past. What would you see my young dear. What would you look upon?"

Tris thought a few moments. So many things came to mind that she kept rejecting one for the next. "I would see the City Amitarl," she suddenly blurted out. She had heard of the city all of her life, and had often dreamed of going there.

"The City Amitarl," said the Wizard gently touching her arm. "Come with me and I will show you the city."

He led her to the black dome. Flindas too wished to see the city he had once called home and came to stand at their backs. The Wizard passed his hand over the dark glass, his fingertips not quite touching the surface. A spray of fine light followed his hand, colouring the glass with a slowly fading yellow glow. He passed his other hand over the surface and a blue light seemed to trickle from his palm and disappear, then he stood back and looked at Tris expectantly. On the surface of the glass before her eyes came a picture, slowly clearing. High on a cliff top stood the castle of Celisor, and below it was spread the City Amitarl. Dark clouds threatened rain and Flindas stared in amazement. It was not just a picture of the city, for he could see people moving about the streets and its walls. The road that came to its high gate was full of wagons going to and away from the place he had once called home. It was like nothing that Tris had ever seen, the city more beautiful than she had thought possible, with its tall high peaked towers and ornate buildings. The picture was so real that she felt she could walk into it.

"Would you care to see closer," said the Wizard, his smile widening.

"Yes," was all that Tris could say.

The Wizard appeared to do nothing, but the vision changed. The walled city began to come closer, its edges fading around the side of the dome. The angle of vision changed also. It was as though they floated above the ground and slowly moved over the top of the outer walls and towers. The picture held still for a time and they looked down into the main square and marketplace. Tris could do little but gaze in amazement. She had never seen such wonderful colourful crowds. There were jugglers, and a man who breathed fire. There were the well dressed rich and the ragged poor moving about together amongst the many stalls. All manner of things were being bought and sold. There were many children at play, and so much more. Tris saw a minstrel singing for coins, though no sound of his words could be heard. No sound at all came from the busy bustle of the city square.

"I would see the castle," said Flindas.

The vision changed and the fortress slowly came into view, drawing closer until it filled the complete side of the dome.

"How much can you see?" asked Flindas.

"I can see a great distance," smiled the Wizard in reply. "Or the smallest bug on the wall, should you wish it."

The castle began to move closer until their vision passed through a high window in the wall. They moved through high stone corridors until at the centre of their vision stood the tall, arched doorway into the Halls of Law, where Flindas knew his father held court. The doorway stood open and slowly grew larger, then vanished around the sides of the dome as they entered. Here they saw the three High Seats of the court, then the picture became still.

"Your father I believe," said the Wizard as he took a closer look at the man on the central throne.

Flindas could see that his father had aged much in the time since they had last been together, his hair was now grey and his face loose jowled and mottled. His girth had grown still larger, and his hands flashed with a great many precious and rare stones. The chair to the Governor's right was empty, while that to his left held his wife, the mother of Flindas, a small woman whose face was pale and grey with illness. She did not seem as if she cared to be there. A bored look tinged with a great sadness clouded her features. Flindas suddenly turned and walked from the picture and the Wizard shifted, and watched him as the vision slowly faded.

"Is there something else that you would care to see, Flindas?" he asked. "Someone perhaps that you wish to know of."

Flindas returned to the now darkened glass. "There is much that I would know," he said. "It is difficult to choose." He thought for a moment. "I would see the Green City of Zeta," he said finally. "I would also like to know of my young friend Kerran and if he remains on the Magic Isles. Will your vision reach so far?"

"Yes," replied the Wizard. "I have looked that way many times over the years." He moved from his place and walked around to a different part of the dome. "Here," he said and began to pass his hands over the glass, causing a rain of fine sparkling green to shimmer across the surface. "From here we look to the east, and Zeta," he said, and spoke a word in the unknown language.

Indeed they faced east, for Flindas had noticed the two windows in the stone walls of the tower, one to the east and the other to the west. Above he could see the stars, but the view from the two windows was darkened where the great stones loomed above the castle. He turned to the dome as colours began to merge on the surface, and deep within the sphere a picture swirled, then began to emerge. It did not take Flindas long to realise that the colours were not as they should be and he suddenly knew why. In the evening light the city lay spread before them. He could see the ships in the port, and around their hulls lay the red poison which had once been the living ocean.

"The fleet has not sailed," he said bitterly. "The evil of Maradass holds them captive."

The picture shifted and moved closer to the docks, and then the Wizard spoke to Flindas. "This young friend that you wish to find, you must picture him in your mind."

Flindas tried to imagine Kerran as he had last seen him, standing with Rark at the door of the Amitarl home. He was waving as Flindas had climbed aboard the wagon which eventually took him to the docks, and the ill-fated ship which awaited him. The image changed and their line of vision began to move above the parklands close by the shore, then it slowed and closed in on two figures sitting beneath a tree. One was a huge dog. Flindas smiled to see Rark asleep on the grass. There too sat Kerran, reading from a small red covered book, though the sun was about to set. Rark lifted his head and looked directly at those who watched. The huge dog barked without a sound. Kerran stirred from his book with a puzzled look on his brow.

"So this is the one who saved the Seacrest fragment from Maradass," said the Wizard as he looked into the dome. He was silent for a time, studying the features of the young man before him. "He reminds me of someone I knew long ago," he finally said. "Though my memory is possibly the finest on this planet, I cannot remember who he looks like, tis so long ago."

He seemed distracted suddenly and left the dome. The picture slowly faded and was gone. "Excuse me," he said, his voice came to them as from a great distance. He seemed troubled and perhaps confused. "You must return now to your chamber. Care not for Leana. She will heal in time. I will visit you again shortly, but for now I must study something long forgotten."

The light dimmed and they found themselves once again

standing before the fire which did not consume, in the chamber where sunlight lay as a constant patch on the stone floor, where a table of food lay fresh and unspoiled.

Again Flindas spent much time puzzling over the scroll, the last two lines making him aware that it was more difficult than it first appeared. Tris could not be still. She walked about the room, continually interrupting Flindas with her thoughts. She marvelled at what they had seen in the observatory. She wanted to go there again, and had been greatly disappointed when the Wizard had abruptly said they must return to their chamber.

"What do you think caused him to change?" she asked Flindas who had also wondered at the Wizard's sudden strangeness.

It had happened when he had seen Kerran but he could not think why. Flindas went to the window and studied the angle of the sun. He was sure he could see the door which the sun's last ray would shine upon, though the window faced more to the south than the west. Also he knew now the eyes of the tower. The two windows facing east and west could be the only answer, but they left him with no clue as to the danger.

> Full moon will see and give warning
> That the Wizard has joined in the play

How could the Wizard affect the sun? he thought to himself. But he knew instantly that the Wizard could change north to south and east to west if he wished them to believe it to be so. The Wizard did not wish to fool them. It was the ancient spells, sometimes regretted it seemed, which caused the Wizard his disquiet and held them all in this magical embrace. The answer was in the scroll. He just had to learn to read it correctly. They ate and slept, and when they woke the sun still shone upon the same patch of floor. It was strange to know that in the outside world time had moved forward not one moment since they had entered the castle. Tris was moving around the chamber feeling restless when the Wizard again appeared by the fire, his manner was jovial as he greeted them and no sign of his earlier annoyance remained.

"I see you are admiring my poetical talents," he said to Flindas with a small chuckle. "As I have said you have all the time there is, but you are wise to wish for the answer quickly if your true desire is to leave this place. There are some who have come here, and though at first they found a great need to leave, they still remain and now wish for no more. Many of them have had hard times, and my hospitality is much better than their lives outside, and so they have remained.

"I come to bring you news of your companion," he continued. "She remains asleep and the spell will take much time to lift itself from her mind, and it may leave her with some unseen scars. This new Maradass has very quickly learned much of the old wizardry, gained through his possession of the one Seacrest fragment. His dark intent has been growing for centuries, and now he is finally in power, which he has coveted for so long. Leana is strong and will fight. She battles with Maradass even now, in her dreams. I will lead her from the labyrinth of his spell, but I must do this slowly and it will take more time. So I thought perhaps you would like to visit the observatory again, I am studying the sixth planet, and thought you may be interested."

Tris leapt at the chance, the intriguing and wonderful observatory with its black dome held her spellbound. She wanted to see and know much more, everything. "What is a planet?" she asked as the light grew dim.

In the next moment they were in the observatory. Its lights were soft, and the sky dark with night. A multitude of stars shone back at them from above, and also from the depths of the dome.

"You asked me what is a planet?" said the Wizard, and drew them forward to stand beside the black glass. "That is a planet," he said and pointed to a small glowing point far inside the depths of the dome. "That is the ringed planet Rishtan-Sta, from which the White Wizard took his name, though it is not a star after all. In the modern tongue you would call it White Winged Star. It is a ball of ice and rock floating in space."

Tris spoke to the Wizard though her eyes never left the starlit glass dome. "You said earlier that we are on a planet too," she said. ""How can this place where we stand be a planet? The world is big and flat."

The Wizard looked at Tris and stroked his long white beard."There are people in the lands, scholars even, who still argue that this is so," he said, "The land appears flat and so it must be so, yet indeed it is not so."

Tris turned to him. "The world is round?" she said with astonished wonder in her voice.

"Yes," he said nodding and smiling. "The world is indeed round. And this," he said pointing again to the glowing ball. "This is yet another planet. It is much further from the sun than our world and is a very different place. It will take some time before we can observe it closely." Here," he said going to a round cabinet. "Here is the sixth planet," and he pointed into a maze of small round balls, suspended on nothing but air.

Tris noticed the ring which circled that one ball, and when the Wizard placed his hand on a larger central sphere the balls began moving, spinning slowly and tracing near circles around the central one. None travelled at the same speed, and it was a bewilderment of slow movement.

"This is a model of our sun's planets," he said to Tris, who gazed at the moving balls in delight. "Truly I cannot build it to the correct scale," the Wizard continued. He indicated the central ball which was of a size that would fit comfortably into a small hand. "If indeed the sun was this size, then the planet on which we stand would be but the smallest of pebbles far out beyond these stone walls, and the furthest planets would be even beyond my great stone circle out yonder. Space is vast, and confounds even my mind."

"What is the ring around the sixth planet?" Tris asked.

"It is rock and ice," replied the Wizard. "Held there by the same force which holds us to this planet. Come, the time is getting closer for a much better view."

He led her back to the dome where deep within the black glass lay the beautiful planet, its soft yellow-blue rings showed clear in an elegant curve around the huge sphere. Tris somehow knew that it was immense. A sense told her that the distance between her and the planet was still great. She watched as the picture slowly grew. She could see several small spheres, and one larger one near to the planet.

"They are moons," said the Wizard.

They were silent for a long time, watching the planet grow before them, until finally it filled the dome with its soft light. The image remained still and the Wizard became occupied with some measurements and writing for a time, while Tris remained gazing at the planet called Rishtan-Sta. She found that when she walked around the dome she could view the planet from all sides, a perfect visual replica within the dark glass.

"Why is it always night time in this room?" asked Flindas as the Wizard paused in his work. The wrinkles around the old man's eyes creased into a smile as he turned to Flindas.

"For viewing the Universe, the night is best," he said, and then chuckled. "Also I cannot make the puzzle too easy to solve." He looked at Flindas for a moment, penetrating to his core, and then chuckled again. "You will find your way," he said nodding and returned to his writing.

"What is the Universe?" asked Tris and the Wizard answered her, seeming to be inclined more towards her questions than the writing he had been doing.

"There is much in time and space that I do not know of," he said turning from his desk and looking happily at this most inquisitive young woman. "The Universe is all of the known and the unknown. It is all that there is. Ever changing, it is beyond even a Wizard's mind to comprehend. I dream of going beyond the known planets and stars. I want to learn about how it began and how it might end, for though much seems stable and lasting, there is nothing that is not impermanent. All things will end one day. In the meantime there is much to know and learn." He looked at Tris, his eyes alive with sheer delight. "No human in one lifetime could ever learn what I know now, and yet all that I know is but a grain of sand compared to the vastness of the Western Deserts."

Tris was having trouble with comprehending a space with no end. Her puzzled frown was answered by the Wizard's wonderful laugh.

"Do not even try," he said, gently laying a hand on her shoulder. "I have spent a great many lifetimes with these questions and yet they still remain but questions."

Much later, though time seemed irrelevant in the Wizard's tower, he took them to see Leana. She remained asleep, though all behind her eyelids was not still; she seemed to do battle within her dreams. Once she cried out softly, though the words were lost.

"She comes nearer to waking," said the Wizard, his hand resting on Leana's brow. "The hardest fight is yet to come I think. It is the length of time which concerns me. She has been under the spell for so long that it will be a hard battle. She is strong and she will win but at what cost I do not know."

Time did not pass, yet it seemed to. They slept and ate and slept again. Their wounds and bruises had healed completely and all trace of weariness had dropped from them both. When the Wizard came to talk or invite them to the observatory, it was always Tris who asked questions and sought to understand all that the Wizard was imparting to her. She became more and more fascinated with the observatory. Though she had lived the life of a thief, her father had taught her to read in the basic tongue. Most of the books in the observatory were beyond her comprehension, yet here and there she began to learn, and it spurred her to crave yet more knowledge and understanding of the world, and the universe in which it floated.

Flindas meanwhile would sometimes stay in their own chamber, alone with the Wizard's scroll. They had been in the tower for six or perhaps seven sleeps, this being the only way Flindas could think of time in this chamber without night. He was puzzling over the poem, sitting by the window lit by the bright motionless orb in the clear pale blue sky. Over and over he had read the words until he could recite them without the aid of the scroll. He did so out loud, looking for something in the words which he may be missing. When he got to the seventh line, he paused. There was something here that did not quite make sense. The line ran: *The eyes will see the days ending*. And he asked himself the question, *How could it be that the eyes of the tower, one which faced east and another which faced west, both see the days ending?*

Then it fell into place. In his mind's eye he pictured the tower and its high glassless windows, the deep sunken bowl in which the castle lay and the twenty-two huge boulders placed around it. He saw the final ray of light as it must shine through one last gap between the stones, and then he knew that he had the answer. He stood quickly and peered from the window, calculating angles of the sun and the ruined castle. It would not be until he could leave the tower that he would be able to tell for certain which the correct door was, but he knew now in which direction it lay.

Much later he told Tris of his discovery after she had returned from the Wizard's observatory. She seemed sceptical for a time but when Flindas drew a diagram on the hearth with a piece of charcoal she understood, and laughed then at the Wizard's play. When next the Wizard joined them it was to say that Leana had woken and to take them to her.

"It is hard for me to know what permanent damage there may be," he told them. "Only time can answer that." He then noticed the drawing on the hearth and looked at Flindas with a smiling curiosity. "You will be wanting to leave soon I think," he said to the tall warrior. "Be sure that you are correct in your choice. I have told Leana of your part in her escape and also of her brother's death and she wishes to meet you. She has no memory of all that has passed since she faced Zard in Dreardim Forest."

When they joined her, Leana was resting. Her eyes were closed and she looked pale and worn. Her eyes opened as they approached the bed and she gave them an exhausted smile.

"Hello, Wizard," she said, her voice coming soft and unsteady.

"This is Flindas and Tris," said the Wizard. "They are the ones I told you of."

"I have no words of thanks great enough," said Leana, looking at them both with her pale green eyes.

"It had to be done," said Flindas. "I am but sorry that it cost so much."

Leana closed her eyes for a moment. "I would learn much

more of your adventures," she said. "The Wizard has told me little. He says I will tire myself. He is worse than the healers on Zeta."

"You may talk for a time, though I doubt you will remain awake for long," said the Wizard smiling. "Your healing from the spell is not complete. There will be time to learn all things soon enough."

Briefly Flindas and Tris began to tell Leana of their journey. Flindas told her first of Kerran and how they had met on the Old Coast Road.

"He is a brave young man," said Leana. "I knew he was there by no accident, and the white hawk too was a great omen. Even as I felt myself dying I was sure that he would reach Zeta." Then her soft voice spoke wondrously. "Yet I did not die," she said.

When Flindas told of Landin's part she wished to know everything, though it grieved her much to hear it. Her eyes flared with hatred when she heard of Luista's part, but she did not speak, as if she had already known of it. When it came to the dark tunnel by the red poisoned river she wept as she heard of her brother's sacrifice.

"He saw it as the only way," said Flindas. "He was too weak to carry on, and he used the last of his strength to save the rest of us, and the Seacrest."

Leana's hand went to her breast where hung the Seacrest fragment.

"Did you put it around my neck?" she asked, holding the piece in a light grasp.

"No," said Flindas. "You held out your hand and I gave it to you."

"That is well," she said with a sigh. "I do not understand this piece as I did the other, but I know that it must be given freely for the power to remain within it. It can be lost or given, but never taken."

After a time Leana became tired and the Wizard returned Flindas and Tris to their chamber below, he remained with them a while, warming his hands by the fire though it was not at all cold. He spoke, looking into the flames.

"She will recover quickly now," he said. "There are good powers within her. I told her of the Wizard's favour should you eventually manage to leave my Place of Puzzles. Leana has told me her desire. I cannot give her all that she wishes, just as I may not be able to grant yours. It is no longer within my power to do all things. I have given her what I could, and I think it is now time for you to tell me of your own desires. Flindas, what would you have to aid you in your quest? Many ask for treasure and such but I do not think that riches are what you care for."

Often Flindas had pondered on this question during their time in the Wizard's tower, what he had wished for most when he first thought on it was simply to replace his weapons. Then he had realised that even if they left the ring of stones, they would still be within the claws of Maradass. There must surely be many soldiers and dogs beyond the perimeter of stones, just as when they had entered. There was little chance that they could break through and escape, for Maradass would want to be sure that they did not slip his net again.

"We need protection from the soldiers and marauders," he said finally. "Can you help us to get beyond their grasp?"

"I can help you only to this extent," said the Wizard after thinking for a time. "For three days I can protect you all from the eyes, ears and noses of your foe. None will see you, nor sense you in any way, except by touch. Three days only," he said, as if he wished it were more.

"That will suffice," said Flindas, hoping that the Wizard could truly protect them beyond the walls of his ancient domain.

"And you Tris?" said the Wizard, turning a benevolent smile upon her. "What would you have that you most desire? I have said already that I could remove your old wounds if you wished. It would not take long."

Tris touched the scars which crossed her left cheek and shook her head slightly. "No," she said, her dark gaze finding the Wizard's own expectant look. "Even if their healing was my greatest desire I would still not lose them. They remind me of much that I would not forget, and perhaps it seems strange but they are now part of who I am. My father's memory lies in each one. No, they are mine and I would not lose them."

The Wizard smiled, for he had known that her answer would be this way. There was something in Tris which he admired, a strength which came from a noble heart, and a youthful inquisitiveness which he found wonderfully refreshing. In a strange way she reminded him of his old scribe who had always been excited over his new inventions, or would sit for days talking at length on the mysteries of the universe. The Wizard stood waiting for Tris to speak.

She knew what she most wished for but could find no words to explain why. She spoke suddenly, her words defensive. "I want to come back," she said, a look both of pleading and defiance coming into her eyes. "I know you said that there was no returning, but I must go, and I also want to stay."

The Wizard murmured a few words under his breath. He stroked his beard and gazed for a long time into the fire. Finally he spoke. "There have been some, usually those who craved riches, who wished to return when their gold was spent," he told her. "They could not return because my old spells, and indeed my own desires forbid it. Most that come here do not choose to leave after a time, and therefore do not have their Wizard's favour granted. To them the tower is a home in paradise, but to you Tris it is different, I see this clearly. I do not think that you desire the comforts of a life produced by my magic. Mostly I see only lust and greed amongst those who remain here and it is rare that I am in their company. Your desire is something else. I can see that unmistakably. So tell me, what is your heart's greatest wish. Tell me truly why you would return?"

He faced her now, his back to the fire, as she stood silently looking at the rug beneath her bare feet, tracing a small pattern with her toes.

"I want to understand all the things that you do," she told him. "I want to help you make things, to do real things." The words began to tumble out. "All my life I have wanted to learn things," she said, tears brimming in her dark eyes. "My father and the Broken Lands have taught me much, but now I see that there is so much more. I want to return when Maradass is finished and dead so I can learn more, to be your helper in all things."

It was the Wizard's turn to be silent. He paced the stone hearth as he thought it through. "Yes," he said finally. "This I can grant you, you may return as you wish, but you will never be able to leave again; it can work no other way."

He was secretly very glad. Since his Scribe had died so many years before he had hoped that one day a person would come, a person who was not caught up in decadence like most of the others who remained within his ancient spells.

"If you manage to leave, then you may return,' he said. "But be sure of this, for as soon as you return and pass back through the stones you must be here forever, or at least for as long as I can hold my last tower together." He joked then and smiled amiably, his heart felt more joyful than it had for a great many centuries. "So now you have but to wait for Leana to recover," he told them. "It will not be so long."

"What was Leana's wish?" asked Tris abruptly, and the Wizard looked at her.

"She asked that I give her the strength to unravel the secrets of the piece which she now carries," the old wizard said. "I will give her what I can, though it may be very little. There is much in the piece which is beyond my control. It was made by one much higher than I. She may learn how to control it, but it will take time. Then again she may never be able to release the powers within it. When you all leave, should you succeed in that attempt, you will remember most of what you have seen and done here, but there are some things which you will not. You will forget the entire poem and the correct door to freedom. There will be no trace of a memory. You will have lost it forever."

His voice had become almost a chant, slow and melodic. For a moment he looked at them, then he turned from the fire and was gone.

Time slipped by in that timeless place. When next they visited Leana she seemed to have regained a great deal of her strength.

"I will soon be able to travel," she said with a soft smile. "The

Wizard tells me that you think you have found the meaning of the poem. I will trust to your judgement. When next we are together I will be ready to travel, though I will miss our host."

"Me too," whispered Tris.

The Wizard took Tris and Flindas for one last visit to the observatory. "Choose what you would see," he said to Flindas as he led them to the black dome. "It may aid you in your future choices, that is of course if you first choose the right door."

"I would like to see the Desert Pass," said Flindas. "I would see how it may be guarded."

"Very well, it is not so far away," said the Wizard, and after passing his hand across the dark glass a picture began to form.

Slowly the darkness faded from within, and there before them lay the road and the narrow pass between the northern mountains of the Bittering and the southern cliffs of the Broken Lands. It was immediately obvious that the pass was held by a large force, their encampment spreading far into the northern plains of Rianodar. Many campfires burned where the foot soldiers of Maradass lay at rest, while a great many troops of Krags could be seen either standing on their silent ranks, or marching towards the east. To Flindas the thought of taking this road into the Regions seemed impossible.

"Three days," said Flindas to himself as he studied the army of Maradass.

Finally he turned from the dome, his brow creased in thought. Tris now stood before the dark glass, knowing that this may be her last chance to see into the wondrous dome. She could think of no one place that she would like to see most of all.

"Is there no one from your past that you would like to find?" asked the Wizard standing at her shoulder. "Someone who you wonder about? Given time I think I can find anyone."

"No," she replied. "I had few who called me friend after my father died, and they are all now lost to me." She paused a moment in thought. "I would see Duragor!" she suddenly declared, her eyes alight at the thought of seeing her lost friend. "Can you find him?" she asked with a hopeful note in her voice.

"I can try," replied the Wizard and turned back to the dark sphere. "You must focus on your friend. See him as clearly as you can."

Trontar passed his hands over the glass face several times, murmuring deeply into his white beard. Flindas returned to the glass dome, also hopeful that he might see his friend again, and know that he still lived. For a long time Tris concentrated, the black man was deeply engrained in her memory and she smiled at the picture she created. The old wizard murmured beneath his breath for a time and then he stood back a little, his brow now furrowed.

"This may not be successful," he said and turned to Tris. "I can observe but a small portion of the Broken Lands at a time. Your friend I think is probably moving, and may even have travelled as far as the Western Desert by now. Indeed he may be anywhere, if he still lives. To look properly would take much time, time that we do not have, as I think you will wish to leave here soon."

The image on the dome focused on high escarpments and deep ravines. It seemed that they flew as the land slipped by beneath them.

"We go to the north and east," said the Wizard. "From your description of Duragor I think he would be going home."

For quite some time the vision within the dome continued to change. The land from above seemed even harsher than when they had travelled through this bitter landscape. The Wizard continued the search, changing direction and viewing to the south.

"If you place your hand on my shoulder it will make my picture of Duragor clearer," he told Tris.

Without thinking it a strange request Tris put her hand on the old Wizard's shoulder. There was a light tremor which suddenly ran through her body. From her toes it rushed through to her head, and at the same moment a light tingling sensation flickered at her fingertips and was gone.

"I hope that did not startle you?" said the Wizard as he patted her hand where it remained lightly on his shoulder. "I have borrowed a memory from you," he continued. "In your mind there are many memories of your friend. I have taken a small piece of one. It will help us search for him if he is still within the Broken Lands. The chance is not high, so do not be disappointed if we do not find him."

Within the dome the lands continued to fall away beneath them, the horizon showing a narrow curve of blue sky. Finally after much time had passed the Wizard turned to Tris.

"It is an almost impossible search," he finally said apologetically. "He could be a few leagues in any direction and we could still miss him." The light within the dome faded slowly. "I get no sense of him, and as I say he may not even be in the Broken Lands," said the Wizard.

"I would guess that is true," said Flindas as he saw the disappointment on his young companions face. He too had been hopeful of seeing his friend again. "He is probably already making his way back to the deserts," Flindas continued. "He was alone and unencumbered, and also a survivor like no other. Think of him as being safely home with his people. That is the best way."

Sadly Tris agreed to end the search.

The Wizard returned them to their chamber and before he left he said to them. "When you next wake, Leana will be with me and prepared to leave," he said. "Then the choice will be yours." He gave a slight bow and was gone.

"You are sorry to be leaving here," said Flindas as he walked to the window and the warm shaft of light.

Tris was silent for a time. "I will come back," she finally said, a determined note in her voice. She went to the table where the food was always fresh and warm.

"You need not come," said Flindas. "We must all leave together but you can return immediately if this truly is your heart's desire. What is it that you would do here?"

"I would learn," she replied and smiled at him, chewing on a roughly cut piece of meat. "There is nowhere, not even the City Amitarl that I would rather be. It is all I ever wanted, and yet did not even know existed."

"Then why do you continue with this quest?" Flindas moved from the window to the table of food. "Your part has been more than played. Remain here in safety. The Wizard seems most happy to have you stay."

"No," she said, a determined edge to her words. "Just as you could never explain your true part in this journey, it is the same with me. I will see an end to it, then I will return." A smile suddenly lit her face. "Besides, you may find you need me," she said with a mischievous smile. Tris laughed and took another bite.

They had rested and slept and there was little preparation needed. They had been told that the food and all else that the Wizard had offered them could not be taken from the tower. Their few weapons were keenly sharpened, and their clothes a little tattered but repaired. When the Wizard came, Leana was at his side, she seemed strong, and a glow of wellbeing came with her into the chamber.

"Well my friends, it is time for us to part," said the Wizard. "I warn you again that if you have not chosen the right door you must remain here. Also, when the light strikes the correct doorway you have but a few moments to leave the ring of stones. Your wizard's protection will begin as you step outside of this tower, if you find your way out you will have exactly three days to escape Maradass. Though the outside world is to me a thing that seems most unreal, I wish you well in it."

"Can you not join us?" asked Tris suddenly. "Are you truly trapped here? The land could use your help."

"No," he replied. "There is nothing now that I could do outside of these walls, and I do not believe I would interfere even if I could. The people must find their own way now. The time of the wizards is almost gone. It is now the final days of Ma-Zurin-Bidar and it is the last act in a very long play. The outcome hangs in the balance. I will watch with great interest the times that now approach. Go now for your time is set."

The doorway appeared in the southern wall as it had when they first entered.

"Farewell," said Flindas to the old wizard. "I hope that you prove to be as good an architect as you are a poet."

The Wizard laughed. "Farewell to you, Flindas Demsharl. Not all they say about you is true." He bowed slightly.

Leana now came and stood before him. They looked into each others eyes but said not a word. Finally the Wizard spoke a muttered phrase in a strange tongue and held Leana's hand for a moment.

Tris was almost in tears when she came to say goodbye. "I will come back," was all she could say.

"Come if you will," said the Wizard, a serious note in his voice. "But be sure why you do so." Then his face wrinkled into a smile and he held her hands in his. "Go now and take care along your way," he told her. "And practice with your sling, you may need it."

Tris looked at Trontar with a question on her lips, but the old wizard shook his head.

"Go now," he said suddenly. "Your time begins to move once again."

Tris saw that Flindas had stepped from the archway into the sunlight beyond. Leana too was passing beneath the stonework.

"Goodbye, Wizard," Tris said to him, and with one last look into his ancient eyes she turned and left the tower.

Tris joined Flindas and Leana in the sunlight. A tear escaped her dark eyes and glistened on her cheek until she impatiently brushed it away.

"Wait here a moment," said Flindas. "There is something I must see."

He left them and ran to the western side of the tower and looked up for a time at the stone wall. Then he ran further to the west up the side of the hollow basin. After looking for a while at the angles of sunlight he returned to the others, and then led them to the eastern side of the circle. They climbed the low slope until Flindas stood before an opening between two of the towering stones.

"This is the one," he said and peered into the slowly darkening gap.

The sun had lowered and was just beginning to disappear beyond the stone circle to the west. Flindas sat and looked at the tower, he could just make out the narrow window slit in the gathering darkness. He thought for a time that he could be wrong. The last line in the poem might be interpreted differently. The Wizard may not have lowered his dome. And then he knew that he need not worry, the Wizard had wanted them to escape. He would not try to hinder them any more than he must. Flindas stood now with the others and waited for the last ray of light.

Beyond the western wall of tall stones the sun was sinking unseen to the horizon, and as it began to set a small ray of light burst through one of the western openings. A shaft of sunlight shone across the distant space and touched the far wall of the tower. A smaller beam then shone through both windows of the tower and uninterrupted, it lit the opening where they stood. Flindas smiled. The light flickered briefly as though inside the tower a hand had been waved, then he made his way quickly into the passage between the stones. The others followed closely, it was a narrow gap and the final struggle was on hands and knees. Flindas came from the opening and crouched, looking at the troops of Maradass spread across the stone ledge until his companions joined him.

"I will test the Wizard's powers," said Flindas. "Wait here until I see how invisible we really are."

He walked from the dark space between the rocks and stood in full view of those before him, not a soldier or dog took any notice. He called out, and still the enemy remained totally unaware of his presence, then he waved for the others to join him. The moon was rising large and full from the eastern darkness, though Flindas knew that this should not be so. He had accepted it, knowing that the old wizard's power had indeed changed time. He spoke to his companions.

"It is as the Wizard said," he told them. "If we do not touch them we are safe. I propose we take the road to the pass. It may be that we will not get there in three days, but we must try. If we can gain the pass then we can become lost to them in the edge of the forest and make our way south into the Regions."

Carefully picking their way between the troops of Maradass, they reached the road and began to walk quickly down its southward slope. After a short while Flindas noticed a change in the light, as though a black cloud had suddenly obscured the silver moon. He looked up and then smiled, the moon was no longer hanging in the sky to the east. It had gone and Flindas understood that they had now returned to the time that had existed before they had entered the Place of Puzzles.

The three companions ran now at a speed which they could keep constant, though Leana took a long time to find her pace. The power which had supported her before they had reached the Wizard's Castle was gone, though now a new and more subtle strength seemed to flow through her. A grim look of determination creased her sweating brow as the leagues fell away beneath their feet. For most of the night they ran, pausing at times to rest. In the dark of the morning they slept, and then they were running again along the steep and winding road that they hoped would take them to the Desert Pass.

The Desert Pass

The horse soldiers and foot soldiers of Maradass had almost ceased to travel the new road. Only occasionally did a troop of horsemen or a single rider pass the three travellers as they made their way south. Each time, the companions would flatten themselves against the rock face to avoid being trampled, and marvelled at the Wizard's power which still kept them from the eyes of the enemy.

They pushed themselves hard as the days slipped away, until the last day of their protection dawned. By sundown they must be hidden and beyond the reach of Maradass. The road continued south, for a time running flat across the top of a plateau, then climbing down into a dark ravine, twisting its way across the cliff face until reaching the sandy floor of the valley below. It was almost noon when they began a long and arduous climb back up a stretch of roadway that hugged a sheer north facing cliff. The escarpment seemed to loom higher above them than those they had so far encountered, though they were all weary of the run there was little time for rest. The afternoon sun beat down mercilessly as they forced themselves up the long incline.

Resting a while beside a small trickle of water which fell

from above, Tris filled their water bottle, and then slumped against the rock. Flindas too felt exhaustion creeping up on him again, and after dousing his face with water he lay prone on the roadway, resting every muscle. Only Leana remained standing as she looked out upon the land below. They were now much higher than most of the escarpments and plateaus of the Broken Lands, and far away she could see two riders on the road, they were not coming fast and would take some time to reach them.

"Riders," she said and pointed.

Flindas sat up and watched the riders' slow approach. He thought of their horses but rejected the idea. The Wizard's protection probably didn't include horses. The sun was but half way to the west and there was still time to reach the Desert Pass, if the road did not take a wandering path to reach the summit. Flindas knew now where he was. Years before he had once stood at the pass and looked upon the Broken Lands from above. He was much younger then and it had been an adventure into the desert, with the added influence of escaping his father's men for a time. Somewhere, not far above was the narrow way, between precipitous drop and the northern mountains of the Bittering.

"Let us keep ahead of them," he said to the others. "We may need their horses."

Taking one more look at the distant riders they began to move quickly up the dusty road. The heat of the sun lingered into the late afternoon as the horsemen slowly gained on them, until they were almost upon the three companions. Again Flindas felt amazement at the power of the Wizard's spell. He could see the riders clearly, yet they in turn were blind to his own presence. The two riders had slowed their pace from a slow canter to a fast walk. Flindas could hear their voices drifting to him on the light breeze as they rode up the slope from behind.

"I would hear their words," Flindas said to his companions and they waited for the horsemen to draw near, their voices becoming more distinct.

"And thems cooks," came an angry little voice. "They cooks

old boots and serves em pretty, like it no matter so longs it taste awful. Never seens such fare."

The second voice answered, gruff and bitter. "Not get no better," he said. "Go south and what we gets, oats and grabbits, an naught else I minds. Rather stays here. Not need alls us to takes blighted Southlands. Easy liftings. Takes it on our backs. Fraid of Amitarls that what." He made a harsh grunting sound in his throat and Flindas realised it was laughter.

"The lands south be empty. I likes our foods up here," the first voice broke in on his grunted laughter.

"We go, thats be it," grumbled the other. "No choice. No matters what we likes, old Maradass has us sure."

The three companions allowed the horsemen to pass by then kept pace behind them. Much of the talk was of their troops marching orders which they now carried to their commander. It seemed they were to ride south, and Flindas remembered the vision in the Wizard's black dome. The army gathered in the north west of Rianodar was about to march, but these horsemen were in no hurry to deliver their orders. The gruff one spoke of the future with dread, not of the enemy, but of the discomforts of a life in camp.

"Still not sees how we needs so many," he said. "The city not holds out, or we starves out. Nowhere else can hold. Monstry be nothin. Amitarl not come, you see. We camp for moons and nothin, you see. Who gets specials huh? Who gets em? Not us. captains and ups gets em. We cooks or freeze, little fire, cook grabbit and cursed oats for moons, just waiting. You see."

"Maybe," said the other horseman. "To me sounds like Cripple messed up for Maradass somehows. Flooded lower levels with poison waters. Road blocked and flood rising. Nothing gets through to poison oceans. Maybe Amitarl comes sooner."

Flindas smiled at this and looked to Leana whose eyes lit up at the words.

"Maybe," the gruff voice agreed. "Not survives us reckon. Dumb Krags be no good but so many. They crush Amitarls like grabbits on rocks."

"There be strong magics there though," said the smaller

man. "They say tough magics, Zeta, Magics Isles".

"Maradass has all magics he needs,"said his companion. "Zard is comes soon. Not hold him, no green magic. Master Lord Maradass no fear nothing."

"Maybe, maybe," his friend said, though he was not convinced, and they rode on in silence for a time.

"I wants free, no more Maradass," said the first voice.

"Sssh!" hissed the other. "Maradass listening. We cannots be free no more. Wants it, yes, needs it, yes, yes, but haves it? Oh, no, no, no. Not no more brother. We's all Maradass now. Old wizard magics got us sure. No more free brother. We's fight and die if he says so."

The three companions remained behind while Flindas walked very close to the two riders, hoping to hear more that may help them reach the Southlands. The riders were content to move slowly up the steep grade and they began to speak again.

"Thems back at the Stones reckons they gots em locked up," said the gruff voice. "Reckon not a ones gots any idea where them be. People not come back from them stones. Maradass wants em bad I reckon. They got away with his prize and he burns to squeeze em bad."

"Well I says leave em," said his partner. "Leave em and they not come out again. Reckon that be why we get orders and march. They no mores than warrior an two womens. Though reckon theres be magic too. They carry somethings Maradass want bad, I reckon. Piece of the old power maybe, but they stay in the rocks and not never comes out. The ways of it that is. March south, no choice. Grabbit and oats and not a swallow of something goods to warm ours belly. Captains and ups get em all." He cursed and spat into the roadway.

The gruff voice lurched into a grunting laugh. "Maybe we can grabbit like any, like times before, and hides it and eats it and drinks it if we gets out away. Eyes open on the ready. Maybe not bad if grabbins be good. Find place aways and tight. Go grabbin an hidin and storin it by away for after wars done. Catch on to food wagons and gets by. We smart, good partners. Make somethings of it. Beat em captains and ups in their own games."

His friend laughed now. "Make the best," he said, and reaching across he hit his friend on the shoulder. "Maybe little gold," his eyes gleamed as he looked at his partner. "Slip away when fightings be on. Not missed. Finds our way. Robs rich houses and thens all ours! Gold and gems!"

He shouted to the valley below, the echo scattering itself through the rocky canyons. They both laughed a little and continued to ride up the sloping road cut deep into the side of the cliff.

"Hush now brother, whisper words," said the quieter voice sadly. "Maradass listens. Dreamses be our only now times. No possibles now. True now. Maradass has us proper. Dreams, not be anythings. Wishes, not fishes, not dishes, all spit and hail Lords Maradass. All gones now... forevers. Old times, gone, gone forevers."

The horsemen began to speak more of their dreams of plunder in the war to come, even though both of them knew that they were now in servitude to the Evil One forever. Flindas had heard enough and led his companions past the pair, keeping hard against the rock face until they were in front of the riders. Flindas wished to be far from the eyes of Maradass before the sun set, though his hopes of reaching the Desert Pass began to fade when he saw that the road again fell sharply into a long, deep and darkened valley. It would take much time to cross, and the Pass had to be up the opposite cliff face and could not be reached by sundown.

The road took them deep into the valley and then began to climb steadily, until it finally reached a place where the cliff beside them dwindled to nothing. They stood at last on a level road and had left the Broken Lands behind. To the east and south loomed the mountains of the Bittering, and to the west lay the red desert, an occasional scrubby tree breaking the vast expanse.

"We must go through quickly if we are to go at all," said Flindas to the others. "We are still some leagues west of the pass and will not be through by sundown. Though we have little choice I think. To become lost in the Bittering and in battle with the wild dogs up there is not an option I would care to choose."

Though dreadfully tired they all began a hard steady run to the east, towards the narrow place between mountain and cliffs' edge. The heat was now gone from the sun as it sank further to the west, and they eventually reached the narrow way that was the Desert Pass. Flindas had expected at least a small guard at this western end of the pass but there was none. The narrow trail that was barely wide enough for two horses was open to them. They rushed on. The sun now touching the horizon was cut from view as they rounded a corner. They were not yet through the narrow place when they all felt a light shiver pass through their bodies and they paused for a moment.

"The sun is down," said Leana breathing heavily as the gloom of night began to gather about them. "The Wizard's spell has ended."

"We must pass and then find a safe place in the mountains," said Flindas, still with hope in his voice, then he continued in a whisper as he realised he could now be overheard. "Come, there is no time," he said.

They ran on into the darkness, the stars giving little light, and the moon was not to rise for some time. Far ahead they saw a flickering glow, there were fires burning, and as they drew closer they could see it was almost impossible to get by, even had they been invisible. The narrow pass here widened a little and in this flat open place several troops of soldiers and horsemen were camped, the fires lighting the roadway, not a rabbit or a bug could pass by undetected.

"We are too late," whispered Flindas in bitter disappointment as they retreated a little from the fires. "A little more time and we could have perhaps been through, but I see no way now. We must return beyond the pass and tomorrow we will look to the hills. The Bittering is a most inhospitable place, but perhaps there are other possibilities than facing the dog packs. We shall see in the morning."

They returned the way they had come, almost reaching the wide dry plain when the moon began to rise. It lit the open roadway and the three running figures. At the same moment that Flindas saw the two riders, he knew that they too had been seen. The leading horseman checked his cantering mount as both men drew their lances from the long leather pouches attached to their saddles. In the moonlight they could see clearly the warrior and two women, and knew who they were. The horsemen began to charge. One came on well in advance of the other.

"We must take them!" Flindas called and ran ahead of Tris and Leana, directly at the leading spear.

He feinted to his left, and as the point of the charging spear swung outward, he leapt high inside the lunging shaft. His forearm smashed the rider from his saddle and the man came down heavily on his back. In the same movement Flindas grasped the lance and turned it against the second charging horseman. The man's terror caused his horse to swerve and rear. He threw his spear in the direction of Flindas and then galloped back along the way he had come. There was no time for the heavy knife which Flindas drew but did not throw, and they heard the sound of hooves disappear quickly into the moonlit night. The other mount had broken through and was now bolting riderless towards the fire lit encampment. Flindas thought of luck and cursed in frustration.

"We have to move quickly," he told the others. "They will be on us soon."

The three travellers took to the road again, running until the land opened out and they were able to leave the narrow track. They made their way as fast as they could into the foothills of the distant snow clouded peaks. Here a narrow valley made its way high into the hills. It was not steep and marauders would not take long to find them. There was little chance of eluding the beasts in such terrain; their only hope was to go higher, though the way was tumbled with rock and loose stone, making it difficult to move quickly.

They heard the pursuit before they saw it, the thunder of many hooves and the howl of marauders on the scent. On the roadway below a horse troop came to a slow halt as the black dogs found the place where the three travellers had left the road. In the moonlight Flindas saw the quick dark shadows that were the dogs. There seemed to be only two of them and their masters did not allow them to continue the pursuit, howling in frustration the dogs obeyed the commands. The three companions paused and watched the happenings below, where soon a fire was set near the roadway.

"If they choose not to follow all the better," said Flindas. "Let us put much distance between us and them."

They moved further into the foothills, travelling eastward and south. The moon was riding high above when they heard the first howls from no great distance.

"Not marauders," said Tris as she tried to see the nearest dog.

Another howl came from far to the west, and then others began to join in from the hills around them. The terrible cry put fear into each of the travellers. Above them and in the valleys below the cry became as one voice. It was impossible to know how many dogs there could be but the number was great, and the sounds were coming closer.

"I see why the troops did not follow," said Tris.

"Yes," said Flindas. "No need to come for us when the dogs will drive us back onto their spears, or finish us where we stand."

They retreated down the hillside but the howls of the dogs began to spread and surround them, and amongst the rocks Flindas caught the occasional glimpse of a moving shadow. He drew his sword and in the same movement passed one of his long stabbing knives to Leana who took it without a word. As the days had passed Flindas had noticed that his charge was becoming more silent in her ways, barely a word had passed her lips since dawn of the previous day and he hoped that the spell of Maradass was not returning to take a hold on her.

"They come now," said Tris as the first dogs moved in for the attack.

It was a short and bitter encounter. The dogs were not huge beasts like Rark or even the marauders. They were mostly short strong creatures with wiry coats and vicious, snapping mouths. Flindas did what he had to do to remain alive; a large number of the dogs fell before the others slunk away in fear of his blade. As the companions moved away from the carnage they watched in horror as the uninjured dogs turned on their dead and dying. A howling blood lust took hold of the animals, and few of the dogs seemed to remember the travellers as they slipped away to the north.

For a time they travelled eastward again but the dogs returned, driving them to the west. A pack led by a large thick set beast attacked them suddenly from all sides. Back to back the three companions fought, and when the leading dog fell mortally wounded the fight seemed to leave the remainder of the creatures, they moved back into the darkness until the travellers had left the battleground.

"These hills must be the home of all dogs," said Tris, a smear of blood across her cheek and down one arm. She saw the look of concern from Flindas. "Not mine," she said and wiped her cheek.

After a time the dogs pressed them again, yet held back from a frontal attack. Flindas again attempted to travel into the east but soon came upon dogs who had not met his ferocity, and the battles commenced anew. Before the moon set the three companions found a small hollow in the side of a steep bank where they need not fear for their backs, the dogs stood away as they too waited on the dawn.

The sun burned hot and friendless upon the three travellers as they were finally driven from the hills the next afternoon. It had been a vicious fight and all showed signs of the struggle. They left the hills to the west of the road, the dogs forcing them far out onto the open plain. When Flindas killed a large dog that ran at their head the rest of the pack finally lost heart. Though a hundred dogs or more had come out onto the parched flatlands, they seemed to understand all at once that they would not win, then they had turned as one and returned with a skulking lope back to the foothills.

Leana fell to her knees exhausted. In the fighting she had surprised Flindas. Though Leana was tall, she was slender, and he had not guessed that she had such strength and skill. She had fought quickly and as one who had been trained well in the art of blades. Flindas looked at her as she rested on her knees, her golden hair streaked with blood. Whatever protection the spell of Maradass had given her was now gone. Flindas found that he wanted to reach out and comfort her. Then he saw the distant troop of horsemen galloping towards them.

"Riders," he said.

Leana and Tris were on their feet quickly, though both were in desperate need of rest and sleep. The horse troop came from the north and east. They did not come directly at the group, but rode to cut them off from any chance of retreat back into the hills. There was now no choice. The large troop of horsemen slowed when they had reached a point between the travellers and any possible escape. Spreading out and riding at a canter, they forced Flindas and his companions further into the desert. There was nowhere now to hide, small ravines and gullies slowed the riders, but only in darkness would the three companions find rest, and night still seemed very far away.

As they ran, high in the east there appeared a moving speck of white which caused Flindas to peer up into the vast blue sky. Hanging on a breeze, high above, flew a white hawk. Tris and Leana ran ahead steadily as Flindas came behind, often looking up to watch the hawk suspended above them. Then after a time Flindas looked up and the hawk was gone. He wondered at it and thought of Kerran far away on Zeta.

The horse troops of Maradass slowly gained on the travellers. Flindas would often change direction to put an obstacle between them and the riders, and a steep and narrow gully slowed them for some time. A little water had lain in the hollow and again their bottle was full, their thirst quenched for a time. Finally, as the sun set Flindas knew that they had won the race for at least this day. The troop of horsemen was at least half a league's distance when twilight turned to dark, and there were no marauders to hunt for them into the night.

They were hungry, having eaten little since leaving the Wizard's tower. Tris fantasised about the laden table as Flindas took them in a wide circuit to the north and east. There must still be a way to reach the lands beyond the pass he thought. The alternative seemed to be a slow death here on the edge of the vast Outlands. There was little food and only an occasional puddle of water to slake their thirst, and they could not expect further rain to fall.

When the moon rose they rested, not wishing to be seen moving against the starkness of the dry barren land. At dawn they lay on a slightly higher piece of ground and studied the land around them, and as yet could see no horsemen. By daylight they made their way back to the east, keeping in gullies and small ravines until they once again came in sight of the road where it emerged from the Broken Lands. A large troop of horsemen guarded the way and Flindas could see four or five marauders with these troops. He was surprised that they had encountered so few of the beasts since leaving the Wizard's Castle. Perhaps they had all gone with the black army into the Regions.

To the south he could see two more troops of horsemen guarding the open lands between road and hills. There was no way that the three travellers could pass undetected. They pulled back, well away from the troops. In a gully where lay a little water they made a small fire and cooked the handful of lizards they had caught. The creatures had lain unsuspecting, basking on rocks in the morning sun.

Flindas kept a wary eye on the flat lands around them as he chewed on the slightly bitter meat. He was now out of ideas. He could think of no way to get beyond the pass. The forest had been his one hope but now there seemed little chance of ever reaching it. His thoughts were distracted by a movement of dust far to the south, a troop of horsemen rode along the edge of the foothills, and back towards the road. Another troop appeared, this one was perhaps two leagues off and came towards them, the dust billowing high into the hot windless air.

"They force our hand," said Flindas to the others.

They were made to run again for they could not hide and hope that the riders would miss them. The distance they could keep between themselves and the horsemen was their best means of avoiding capture or death. Tris pushed the few remaining scraps of food into her mouth and joined the others. They began to run along the bottom of the small gully, the direction of which took them to the south and west for a time. Eventually they could no longer remain hidden, the gully slowly disappearing into the sand and rock. Flindas pointed to a third cloud of moving dust far to the west.

"They search in earnest," he said as the others followed his gaze.

There was now no chance of concealment. Running north and westward they eventually heard the distant blast of a horn. The hunt was about to quicken. The three companions walked and ran, and by noon they were far out into the desert. A deep ravine cutting across their path had slowed them for a time, but for horses it had not been possible. The troop riding furthest to the west had remained there and was the first to find themselves cut off from their prey. The travellers watched as many of the horse troops rode east and west along the edge of the ravine, looking for a way across. There was time now to rest. Flindas searched for one single idea to save them, but there was none. Cut off completely from the Regions, their fate seemed sealed.

"We are trapped out here," he said in frustration. "We cannot even return to the Broken Lands."

He took a small sip from the water bottle which Tris passed to him. To the south and east he could see several more dust clouds. Maradass had many troops to spare it seemed and the prize was within his grasp, Flindas could do nothing other than to move westward, further out into the desert. Later, when they had lost the ones who hunted them, perhaps they could return in stealth and somehow slip by; Flindas knew that this was to hope for a miracle.

The red sandy earth rose in small clouds around their feet as they walked. The occasional stunted tree spread tentacled roots wide about its twisted trunk in search of water. Lizards scuttled away as the companions pushed themselves to the west as the sun fell before them to the horizon. Again a ravine had slowed the horse troops and Flindas knew they were now safe for a time from the riders. In the sun's last light he watched the distant clouds of dust, and then pushed his companions further towards the sunset.

The land was flat now, unbroken by gully or ravine. The

trees dwindled until there was nothing ahead of them to break the long sweeping horizon. They slowed their walk but kept moving until well into the night, when they baked their small lizards by a fire, well hidden from any searching eyes. Leana was having problems with eating the strong meat, she ate slowly, forcing down every bite; water was their greatest problem. There were no more gullies for it to have collected in, and any streams that left the far mountains were soon swallowed up by the desert. Flindas was too tired now to think, and the three companions laid themselves down and slept.

The fiery sun crept into the sky from the lands to the east. Even at this early part of the day its heat struck them hard. Flindas studied the horizon. He had hoped not to see the trails of dust curling into the air from the mounted troops, but they were there, and now there seemed to be many more. Flindas could make out little except the wafting clouds which slowly crept towards them on the breeze.

During the morning the three companions travelled west and south, trying to get beyond the most distant of the horse troops, but to no avail. The way the riders were spread it was impossible to get by them without being seen. By nightfall the three had again out distanced the horse troops, who seemed intent on little more than pushing them westward, and depriving them of water. Exhaustion and thirst caused Flindas' mind to wander at times. He was desperate, and knew of no way that they could reach safety. He spoke that evening with Leana and Tris, and they agreed to try and pass through the horse soldiers' lines in the darkness before moonrise.

Under cover of night they slipped back the way they had come. The Outlands lay silent around them, and after walking a league or more Flindas knew that they must be nearing the encamped horse soldiers. If they did not come directly upon a troop it may be easy to slip by, unless there were marauders. No campfires showed and not a sound broke the eerie desert night. In silence the three companions moved across the sands, lit by the vast sweeping cloud of stars.

Time slipped by, and when the moon rose Flindas knew

that they must have passed beyond the first troops, though he did not know how many more may be scattered across the land between them and the pass. They returned to more broken land where they could keep hidden at times. In each gully or ravine they searched for water, but the sun's heat seemed to have dried up every puddle. They had yet to see any sign of soldiers or dogs, when from not far away they heard the dreaded howl of a marauder. They could not see the animal, but its voice caused others to answer from further away.

"Quickly!" called Flindas and they ran.

They headed north into even more broken country, while the marauder did not take up the chase but continued to howl.

"There will be more with him soon, and then they will hunt us," said Flindas as they ran.

They came to a wide gully which would slow any pursuit by horsemen. There was no time to use the rope as they tumbled down the steep slope into darkness. Far away they could hear the call of the black dogs and the distant thunder of hooves. The bottom of the gully was filled with deep loose sand and their legs ached as they pushed themselves further to the north. A lone horseman galloped above along the edge of the gully but saw nothing of the three figures crouched in the darkness below.

From further away came a horn blast and the distant sounds of the hunt as Flindas led them up the western bank of the gully. As they scrambled up the sandy slope they were in time to see a large troop of horsemen gallop by on the other side. There was a cry as one of the riders saw them. Flindas had noticed earlier that many riders in the hunt now carried bows, and the three companions were almost out of bow shot when a number of arrows fell around them. They ran into the gloom and for the remainder of the night managed to avoid their hunters.

By dawn they were again well to the west, out of immediate danger but tired and desperately thirsty. They drank the last drops of their precious water and then rested. During the day the horse troops did not advance to the west, seemingly content to still keep the travellers trapped in the desert, knowing there quarry could not last much longer. At nightfall they again tried to find a way through to the foothills of the mountains. Flindas could see that it was their only chance. If it meant fighting dogs all the way to the forest then so be it, though he knew they would probably die in the attempt.

They were parched and weary beyond endurance when they began to move eastward again at dusk, the lack of water almost sapping the last of their strength. The moon had not yet risen when the first marauder caught their scent and again the hunt began. Forced westward during the night, by dawn they were again beyond the reach of the horse soldiers, yet Flindas knew that any hope of passing through to the Regions was now gone. His body ached and his mind was becoming confused, wandering in strange dark thoughts.

He sucked on a small pebble to keep moisture in his mouth but it was no substitute for the water he craved. He looked at his two companions, Leana seemed almost asleep on her feet, and Tris, though strong and resilient, suffered much from lack of water. Flindas determined that the following night he would go alone in search of that life giving liquid, there was nothing left without it but death.

They spoke little during the day, Leana not saying a word as the heat of the sun dragged the remaining strength from their bodies. They found scant shelter beneath a twisted and long dead tree and Flindas leaned against it, his hat pulled low over his eyes. He looked into the distance at the clouds of dust stirred from the desert by the horsemen, and then his head nodded forward. He did not want to sleep, the fear of being caught unawares uppermost in his mind. He looked at the others stretched out beside him, then his eyes closed and his head fell forward onto his chest.

Flindas woke with a start. His eyes narrowed to slits against the sunlight, but he saw nothing moving nearby. The desert was still. Slowly his head fell forward again. Flindas slept as the day grew long, and when he did wake he knew immediately that something had changed. He lay in shadow and he lifted his head quickly to find that the sun was blocked out by the dark silhouette of a man standing above him. He was pushing himself to his feet to defend himself and the others, when the man spoke. He knew the voice immediately, and the wide flashing smile. Flindas collapsed back to the earth.

"Greetings, Flindas," said the black man. "I am glad to see you again."

Flindas smiled through cracked lips as the wiry frame of Duragor squatted down beside him.

Glimpses of Power

Time passed on the Magic Isles and the ocean remained red with the poison of Maradass. During the last days of spring Piata came to the Green City and stayed with her aunt for a few days.

"The men have gone into the fields," she told Kerran. "They hope to increase the harvest this year; we will need it I think. I did not realise how much I liked eating fish until now."

They read together, long passages from history and myth, tales of sorcery and the lives of the ancient wizards. During the long warm afternoons they sat in the park talking, and often wondering at the mystery surrounding Kerran and his ancestry. The days passed too quickly for Kerran and he watched her depart with a heavy heart.

Kerran spent much time studying and learning, and he began a journal to write his thoughts in, and to practice his letters. In his mind he imagined his mother reading it and he smiled at the thought, though his heart often ached for her warm presence and true friendship. One evening he was sitting in the park looking at the first stars when Tolth joined him. The air was warm and the night clear. It was the summer solstice. Tolth was worried over a great many things.

"The ocean is our life's blood here on Zeta," he told his young friend. "There is no news from the Regions and we cannot sail there and expect to survive. I sometimes see the evil face of Maradass gloating over our plight. There is much struggle to come and I hope we have the strength to fight it, I must join the army with the remainder of our forces if we are to make a defence of the lands."

He paused and looked searchingly at Kerran for a moment. "Would you hold the Seacrest for me again?" he said. "I would not ask you except that the times are desperate, and I cannot hope for a miracle. You may be able to find answers where I cannot."

"I will help if I possibly can," said Kerran, then he paused before taking the offered piece. "I had a vision not long before sunset," he told Tolth who raised an eyebrow, remaining silent as Kerran searched for an explanation. "It was strange," he said. "Not like anything that has happened before. I felt as though I was being watched."

"By Maradass?" queried Tolth, a worried look coming into his eyes.

"No," replied Kerran, a small frown creasing his brow. "It may seem strange but I felt as though Flindas were near by. It seemed that he was right here with me, watching me. Rark felt it too I think. He looked up suddenly and barked for a moment, and then he seemed puzzled. It was strange, and may mean nothing. Perhaps I was dozing and it was but a daydream."

Far away, in a wizard's tower on the edge of the Outlands, Flindas and Tris had just been introduced to the wonders of a magical dome.

Kerran lay back on the grass with the Seacrest fragment in his hand and Tolth took him into sleep, where he again walked in the welcoming soft mist.

"I am here Kerran," said the voice into his mind. "What is it that you wish to ask?"

"The oceans are poisoned," said Kerran. "There is no news of Maradass or from Landin. I do not know what to ask, except for help."

"I cannot aid you in this," replied the voice. "I am memory. I am the past. If you can dream now, perhaps what you seek will be shown to you."

Kerran's mind drifted and slipped into true sleep and dream.

He stood on the sands by the stormy wind tossed sea. Red waves crashed on the shoreline, the foam turning to an insipid pink as it rushed up the beach, the water reaching his feet. Kerran sensed no fear as he felt the dampness sink into his boots, then the next wave rushed in and came almost to his knees. Wave after wave rolled in, higher each time, until Kerran felt the water pass over his head, and he was standing on the sandy floor beneath the sea. Still he felt no concern as the ocean engulfed him, and then his mind changed and he felt his spirit being drawn from him. Suddenly he felt fear like he had never known before, a creeping horror lay in the darkness just beyond his sight. He wanted to cry out, to run, to swim away, but he could not. He stood frozen in the inky purple darkness and waited for the thing that stalked him. The redness before his eyes began to shift and swirl. There were sparks of blue light, and within it he could make out a shape slowly forming in the waters before him.

An evil face, old and savagely wrinkled began to float before his eyes. Lank dark hair wafted on the slight currents, and a leering smile bent the aged lips. A cracked malevolent voice entered Kerran's mind, though the face only smiled.

"So you are the one," it said. "I have been waiting for you, looking for you, and now I see you. Not a creature for me to fear I think. There is little within you of true wizardry. Yes, I am Maradass, the one who will end the line of Amitarl. The land will wither and die, and then there will be only Maradass, forever and ever."

The voice, which had been cold and softly evil, now broke into terrible cruel laughter. "Very soon I will come for you and what you hold, pretender to wizardry. You need fear me boy, for you are powerless against me. I will come soon and I look forward to meeting you again. Nothing will save you, not even that fool Amitarl or his benighted family. So farewell for now young Chelasta, your death will come soon and I will delight in it greatly."

The face of Maradass sneered at him, eyes dark and gloating, and then it slowly faded away. Then from the dark waters came a distant soft light, which grew until it glowed brightly before him. The ocean shimmered, and then in a moment it was gone and Kerran found himself standing on a plain that stretched as far as his eyes could see, dry grass blowing and waving in the breeze. He felt relief as he looked above, somehow expecting to see Storm flying high above him, but it was not so. He looked to the distant horizon and suddenly he saw movement far off. Lines of soldiers were marching towards him. Troop upon troop of dark foot soldiers spread across the plains, all carrying long shining spears. Horsemen rode ahead, while black dogs ran at their heels. Banners flew in the breeze that bore a white dog's skull on a red circle surrounded by a black field. The armies of Maradass were marching to war.

Kerran stood and watched them pass as though he were not there. The army was vast, rank upon rank of strange stony faced men causing the dust to rise and swirl about on a light breeze. Kerran knew that what he was seeing was happening in the present time, in the real world outside of his dream. He wanted to wake and tell Tolth but he could not. The vast army finally passed and Kerran watched their backs as they marched across the plains to the south, flocks of scavenger birds flying above the dust cloud. Further above, so high that Kerran felt rather than saw it flew a white hawk. The instant he recognised it his mind leapt across the distance and he then flew within the hawk, and he looked below with the eyes of a bird of prey. A road met another far to the north, and a dull red line showed to the east. It was the ocean. Villages and towns were aflame on the coast and out on the plains. Inside the body of the hawk Kerran was taken to the west and the destruction was left far behind. Through the next few nights and days the creature took him ever westward. One early dawn he saw mountains on the western horizon. The land to the north was broken by ravines and cliffs, while tall mountains marched to meet the shattered lands from the south. A pass led between the two different lands and beyond it Kerran could see a dry and barren red desert. He flew on and eventually saw troops of horsemen riding hard as they pursued a group of running figures across broken country on the edge of the desert. There looked to be little hope of escape for those who ran.

Kerran knew without yet seeing him that here was his friend Flindas. The hawk took Kerran into a slow downward glide and he was able to discern the features of the runners below. Flindas was behind, looking back at the still distant horsemen, while ahead ran two others, the dark figure of a small woman, and beside her a taller woman, blonde hair flowing out behind her. A sudden confusion clouded his mind and the hawk began an uncontrolled plummet to the earth. He fell, the land rushing up to meet him. With a deep almost painful shudder Kerran woke abruptly.

A dim light shone through a doorway. Kerran felt around himself and found that he lay in his bedroom in the Amitarl household. He sat up slowly, feeling weak and very thirsty. He was about to leave the bed when Nup came to the doorway.

"Kerran!" he exclaimed, rushing to the bed. "You have woken. I must tell Tolth."

And the boy bolted from the room only to return within moments. "I forget myself," he said. "Can I get you something Kerran? You have been asleep for such a long time."

"How long?' asked Kerran as he lay back on the pillow exhausted.

"Three days," replied Nup. "Tolth has been ever so worried."

"I would trouble you for water," said Kerran. "Then I would very much like to see Tolth. I have important things to tell him."

His patient's thirst administered to, Nup ran from the house and returned in no great time with the old Amitarl.

"I am so pleased you have woken, Kerran," said Tolth with a concerned smile. "I feared for you when Verardian could not reach your mind and bring you back." Tolth turned to Nup who stood in the doorway. "Food, please, Nup," he said, and the boy disappeared into the kitchen below. "Nup tells me you have important news."

Kerran looked up at his old friend. "I do not know what it

may mean," he said. "Though it was a dream, I feel the truth in it. I believe that your daughter Leana is still alive, and is with Flindas and one other. They are being pursued into the desert."

Tolth sat down on the chair beside the bed, his eyes a sharp question. "Tell me," he said in a quiet voice.

Kerran told of what he had seen. He remembered it all and left nothing out. The telling took some time. Tolth did not interrupt and when Kerran had finished he sat quietly in his seat, fingertips together at his lips. Finally the old Amitarl spoke.

"Verardian has always felt that his sister was not dead," he said. "They were so close that he could not fully believe it, even after you had told us of her certain death. This is news that I must ponder upon. Thank you, Kerran." Tolth rose, he seemed greatly distracted. "I must see Verardian," were his last words as he left the room.

Kerran ate and then rested, though he had just woken from three days of sleep.

The following day a meeting of the Council took place and Kerran was asked to attend. The only real discussion centred on the need for Tolth and the Seacrest to go to Andrian and the City Amitarl.

"War has begun in the north," he told those seated at the round table. "Maradass now marches through Mendan-Var and Rianodar."

"From a dream you get this!" it was Davin who abruptly spoke. Kerran remembered him from his first Council meeting. Davin had spoken against the protection of the Regions. "From a dream," continued Davin, "And you will risk all by attempting to sail to Andrian against this deadly sea. First this boy says Leana is dead and now that she is alive. If we put our faith in such dreams we will be lost. Listen not to these dreams, for they are not part of reality. Those are my thoughts."

Davin sat, though he seemed most agitated and stared at Kerran for a long time. Orlandi, the woman who had chaired the earlier meeting also spoke against any attempt at sailing to the Regions.

"We cannot risk the defence of Zeta," she said. "If Tolth and the Seacrest are lost to this red horror that surrounds us then both the Regions and Zeta will perish."

"And what of our army on the Far Isles?" asked a man who Kerran had not seen before. He had introduced himself as Mantris. "Our army, our friends, our brothers and sisters, do we abandon them? No, I say everything must be done to reach them and then to protect the Regions."

"The army there is not at full strength," said Davin impatiently. "Unless you plan to risk more of our friends and brothers in the poisoned sea then I say we can yet do little for those on the Far Isles. They alone are too few to defend the Regions, and if Commander Torian has any sense he will remain where he is until this poison leaves the ocean and we can rescue them and bring them home."

"The red horror may never leave," said Tolth. "Not unless Maradass is destroyed. Also, with the army on the Far Isles unable to fish, they will not have a food supply for much longer. They can last one moon, perhaps a little more if the poison has reached that far already. Commander Torian will take his troops across to Andrian rather than have them starve, and I must join him before that time. If he marches into Andrian without me, without the family Amitarl, he may find himself at war with the Governor instead of Maradass. Remember that the city has not been home to Amitarl for centuries. They remember the legend that Amitarl will return when the need is greatest, but to most it is a tale from the past, and my father Darna is but a myth. No, the Governor will not believe any except me I think, for I have the means to show him that I truly am Amitarl and heir to the City."

"What of Landin?" said Davin rising from his chair quickly. "What of the third piece of the Seacrest? If you were even to reach Andrian, you would still have less than half of our army with you, and only the power in the two weakest pieces. You hold them now and are still unable to undo the sorcery of Maradass. Look at the sea. Can you change it back to how it should be? No! Maradass and Landin hold the true power. The future and the past, what good are they to us? It is now that we must live and die, and decide. I say we can do nothing for the Regions. We must defend ourselves on Zeta and remain here. Send no more soldiers to certain death. Those are my thoughts."

He sat slowly. He seemed exhausted from his tirade and slumped in his chair, then he held his hands to his face, sweat on his brow.

"Brother Davin," said Verardian, concerned. "Can I help you?"

"No, I am well," he replied, a bitter note in his voice. "I am as well as can be," he added mysteriously and said no more.

There was much discussion on the possibility of building a single ship that could sail the poisoned sea, but when the meeting came to an end little had been decided. Tolth remained adamant that he and the Seacrest must go to the Regions, while others were not so sure. At dinner that evening the subject of the ship was much talked about.

"When I sail," said Tolth to Kerran "I ask that you go with me."

"I had no doubt that I would come," replied Kerran. "If I have a further part to play, then it is in the Regions and not on Zeta that I must be."

Tolth nodded and smiled. Then an eerie monotone voice came from the back of the room.

"I will go," it said.

All at the table turned in surprise and looked at Mindis, who instead of sitting in his usual seat, was now walking with slow deliberate steps toward the table. Both Tolth and Verardian stood quickly but did not move towards Mindis, who now looked directly at Tolth and spoke again.

"Father, I will go with you. I must go with you."

He had now reached the table and stood behind an empty chair, his arms hanging limp at his side.

Tolth found his voice. "Why must you come with me?" he asked with a tremor in his words.

"Mother tells me," was the reply.

"Luista!" Tolth exclaimed. "Mindis tell me! Where is your mother?"

"She is inside my head," said the dull empty voice. His eyes were vacant and looked into space.

"What does she say?" Tolth said quickly.

"Mother says I must go, so I will go." Mindis now turned, and his eyes came to life as they looked at Kerran. "This one should not go," he said bluntly. "He has no right. I am Amitarl. I must bear the Seacrest, and I must go."

The voice of the dark Amitarl son showed almost no emotion, yet Kerran saw anger in his eyes. They glared with intense hatred from his thin sallow face for just a moment, and then became dull and lustreless once again.

"What else does your mother tell you?" asked Tolth.

He was trying to coax more from his silent son, but Mindis said no more and eventually Verardian led him back to his chair. Tolth sank slowly to his seat at the table and sat for a time looking at Mindis across the room.

"This I do not understand," he said finally, and it was Verardian who turned to Kerran and spoke.

"No one has ever heard Mindis say more than a short sentence or two at any one time," said the healer. "He has been closed to us for all of his short life." Verardian then turned to his father. "Luista," he said softly, and Tolth met his eyes with a look that was both sad and worried.

"I do not know what this means," he said looking at his dear son. "Why does he speak of his mother, and why does he wish to join us? These times become more perplexing and I cannot guess at the answers."

He remained silent for the remainder of the meal, often looking across at his youngest son.

That night Kerran slept, only to find Manzanee looking at him thoughtfully from across the embers of the fire.

"You have learned much young Chel-a-Sta," he used the ancient wizard's name carefully, pronouncing the separate syllables. "Time slips by in the lands, and you will soon need all of your knowledge and memory to play out your part in the time shattering events to come. Remember who you are. There are those who would destroy you if they could. Beware of sounds in the night. Beware the Dark Shadows."

"Who must I fear?" asked Kerran, his voice seeming to offend the silence of the cave.

Manzanee looked at him closely. "That is not a question that you can ask," he said finally. "A warning is all I will give. Think carefully young Chel-a-Sta. There is a question which you wish answered. Think carefully before you ask."

Then the face of Manzanee disappeared from the light of the glowing embers. The fire began to die until one last red glowing point flickered and was extinguished. Kerran could think of many questions, but discarded each one as being trivial or unanswerable under the conditions that Manzanee placed on them. Slowly his mind became quiet and he felt that he floated. A peacefulness came gently into his mind, and the only sound was that of his heart beating softly. Kerran felt himself lift from the floor of the cave and pass without interruption through the rock above, and into a cloud covered sky. Lightning flashed above distant hills, and thunder rolled across the land. He flew toward the hills and into the storm.

He had no sense of body, nor did he fly on the wings of a hawk. It was as if a shadow of him passed across the lands. His mind and many thoughts flew alone within that shadow. Into the eye of the storm he sped, to a place where lightning crashed. In a state of awe he watched the tempest as he truly became the dark clouds and lashing rain. Here was power. Here was High Magic. Within his thoughts he threw bolts of lightning across the sky. Thunder cracked and rolled from his mind. He was filled with power and wonder as night came, and still the storm raged. Kerran's exhilaration increased with the darkness. He took no time for thought or self. He was the storm and the storm was he, bursting across the roof of the forest, and crashing against the mountain sides. Now he knew the question he would ask Manzanee. As it formed in his mind the scene before him wavered slowly and then was gone. He found himself once again sitting across the fire from the Black Wizard, his fiery shadow but an exhilarating memory.

"I hope you have found your question Kerran," said Manzanee. "It would be a pity to lose the chance to learn something." He chuckled. "Come now, come! What is your question?"

"I know now that I must be a descendant of Chel-a-Sta, one of the Lesser Wizards," he said. "And so my question is this. Do I hold unknown powers?"

The Black Wizard smiled at the question. "Only a direct descendant of a wizard, and only the first born, will inherit true powers of wizardry," said Manzanee.

"Am I a direct descendant and firstborn?" Kerran asked abruptly and Manzanee broke into laughter.

"That is another question," he said. "Am I to answer both, or none at all? Impatience is a thing only the young can afford." He was silent for a time then continued. "I will answer your second question Star of the Morning," said Manzanee. "And this answer will of course answer your first question, which I will allow to pass unanswered."

The Black Wizard laughed quietly to himself before continuing. "Yes," he said staring at Kerran with deep interest. "Yes, young Chel-a-Sta, you are indeed a firstborn direct descendant of wizards, and therefore you have powers within you that lie dormant, but a warning to you now. Do not look for powers where you might expect to find them, for they will not be found there. Try looking in another place. You may not be able to move mountains, but you may be able to move small stones... ah, I have said too much."

The Black Wizard laughed gleefully as the fire flared to the ceiling of the cave, and then, just on the edge of hearing Kerran heard his final words. "Beware of sounds in the night. Beware the Dark Shadows."

Light blazed before Kerran's eyes. He blinked and then blinked again. He saw light flooding in through his bedroom window, dazzling. He rolled over and saw Tolth sitting beside the bed.

"You have slept for two days and nights," Tolth said, with a worried frown on his brow. "You have been dreaming I think."

Nup entered carrying food and drink. "Must be hungry Kerran," the boy said with a smile and left the tray beside the bed.

"I asked Manzanee another question," said Kerran as he

reached for the glass of goat's milk.

"And what was the question?" Tolth asked.

Kerran took a long swallow of the delicious liquid. "I asked if I had wizard's powers and Manzanee said 'yes,'" replied Kerran. "But then he said that I should not look for them where I would expect to find them. Again the question is answered but confused. He also said that I might be able to move small stones which meant nothing at all to me."

"That is the way of Manzanee," said Tolth. "I too cannot think what you might be able to do with small stones. He is beyond us, and will not be made to give more than he will."

"He told me to beware of dark shadows," Kerran continued.

Tolth wondered that his young friend was perhaps in danger and he asked closely about what Manzanee had said. "Beware of sounds in the night," Tolth said quietly to himself, repeating the words. "I cannot think that danger threatens you here on Zeta, Kerran. Manzanee must mean when you go to the Regions. There can be no enemies here on the Magic Isles. The power of the Seacrest and the ancient wizard's spells would not allow it, though it puzzles me all the same that Manzanee should tell you this now."

Kerran finished the telling of his dream and Tolth thought for a time.

"There are ways of testing for mental powers, Kerran," he said stroking his beard. "If you feel strong enough perhaps you would come to my workroom and we could conduct some experiments."

"I am not unwell," said Kerran. "In fact I feel in wonderful health." As if to prove it he hungrily ate much of the food before him.

"Do not rush to join me," said Tolth standing. "I will be in the workroom all day."

Kerran bathed and dressed and was just leaving the house when Storm fell from the sky and landed on the grass by the path. He seemed intent on being with Kerran, and both soon joined Tolth in his workroom.

"I am glad that Storm is with you," said Tolth as they entered. "He may be able to answer a few questions also. Please sit down

Kerran," and he indicated a chair across the desk from him.

"What I would like to do first is test your reception to another's thoughts, namely mine. Relax yourself Kerran, close your eyes, and let your mind wander where it will. When I say the word 'now' you will tell me exactly what is in your mind. I will do this a number of times."

Tolth's voice was soft and mesmerising as Kerran's mind began to float from one thought to another.

"Now," said Tolth.

"A white horse in a green field that I saw on my way to Felstrar," Kerran said, remembering his short journey. There was silence for a time.

"Now," said Tolth again.

"Davin at the Council meeting," he replied.

Again: "Now," and again "Now."

This went on for some time until Tolth broke off. "There is nothing of significance that I can see here," he said looking at the paper on which he had been writing. "Let us try something else," he said. "I will write a word and then you will try to picture what I have written."

They began to investigate and for some time Kerran would say what he thought Tolth had written. The old Amitarl ceased after ten words.

"Not even close," he said smiling. "Unless we say that fish and ocean is a match, no, the wrong track I fear. Another test of the same type can be done with drawing. You are accomplished with a drawing block, and perhaps we may get a result that way."

Tolth took from a drawer two charcoal sticks and handed one to Kerran. "I will draw a picture, and then you will attempt to draw the same image," he said and added. "In all my long years I have never more than dabbled in artistry, so my own drawings will be somewhat primitive."

He bent over his paper and drew slowly and with great deliberation. When he had finished Kerran concentrated, and then drew quickly a picture of a small sailboat on a calm sea. He handed his drawing to Tolth, who looked at it but did not speak.

"Another," he said, and once again began to draw.

When Kerran completed his own drawing and passed it across the desk Tolth looked at him closely, and then showed his own drawing. Both had drawn a small house nestled at the foot of a tall mountain. Tolth then showed his first drawing and there unmistakably was a small boat under sail upon a calm sea.

"A little more than coincidence," remarked Tolth with a broad smile. "A small step in a promising direction I would say. Now, let us see what happens if we reverse the procedure. You draw something and I will attempt to reproduce it."

Kerran drew a tall tree with two birds flying above.

"Try to project the image into my mind," said Tolth, and after a moment he began to draw.

He completed the work and they compared the two drawings, Tolth had drawn a lofty tower, above which he had placed a quarter moon and a radiating sun; the symmetry if not the subject of the drawings was unmistakable.

"Again," said Tolth, eager to delve deeper.

Kerran drew a resemblance of Flindas with Rark walking beside him. Tolth drew a woman holding the hand of a child as they walked.

"Wonderful!" said Tolth as they compared them. "It is nearer the mark than any experiments with others." He mused over the drawings for some time. "Let us try something else," he said abruptly, and almost leapt from his chair as he went to a set of shelves against the wall.

He returned holding what Kerran took to be a ball of gold. Perfectly spherical, it was no bigger than his smallest fingernail. Tolth brushed the papers from the centre of his desk and placed the ball on the polished wooden surface.

"Now," he said sitting back in his chair. "Make it move."

Kerran, after a moment's confused hesitation, reached over and flicked it with his finger.

"No! No!" said Tolth in mock anger. "With your mind, move it with your mind."

Kerran looked at the ball and concentrated his thoughts. He willed the ball to move, but it remained still. Some time passed until with a sigh of defeat Kerran leaned back in his chair. The ball suddenly rolled across the desk and into a pile of papers.

"Again," said Tolth with great intensity in his voice, moving the gold sphere back to the centre of the desk.

Try as he might Kerran could not move the ball, and this time it remained stationary when he abandoned the effort.

"One more time please Kerran," said Tolth. "This time not so concentrated, let the energy that is outside of you flow through you and into the ball."

Kerran looked at the gold ball once again and what happened next brought both Tolth and Kerran to their feet. The golden sphere had not just moved, it had vanished before their eyes. It was there, and then it was gone. Into the midst of their exclamations came the amused voice of Manzanee floating on the air.

"Thank you young Chel-a-Sta. A most pleasing gift, I will treasure it." The Black Wizard's voice broke into laughter and was gone.

Astounded, Tolth sat down slowly, a look of wonder on his face. "You sent the gold ball into time," his voice was hushed in reverence. "Be careful with this power, Kerran. It may work on much larger objects than a golden ball." He looked around the room, his eyes alighting on an old broken chair which leaned against the wall. "That chair has been there for more years than I know," he said. "It was a gift, and when it broke I was loathe to discard it. In the name of experimental magic and science I will be pleased to see it disappear. Perhaps Manzanee can repair it!" He said the last words loudly to the room, but there was no reply. Tolth then placed the chair in the middle of the floor. "Now Kerran, just as before."

Kerran sat and brought his mind into a state of relaxed concentration. It seemed easier this time but when the chair did not vanish he felt disappointed. Tolth reassured him.

"There may be no end to your powers, Kerran, but we must not be hasty," he said. "Perhaps I am meant to keep the chair after all." He smiled and placed the broken piece of furniture against the wall, and then a thought came to him. "I will be gone but a moment," he said and left the room, returning a short time later, his hands cupped together.

"We will try a live experiment," he said, and put a small dark beetle into a shallow metal dish, which he placed at the centre of the desk. The small beetle scurried around the dish looking for an escape as Kerran concentrated. When the metal dish suddenly vanished from beneath it, the creature accepted the occurrence and quickly scuttled across the desk to a hiding place amongst Tolth's papers. Both Kerran and Tolth sat in silence and looked at the vacant space on the desk top.

"Stranger than strange," Tolth muttered, and shuffling through his papers he found the beetle and released it out the window to the gardens below.

They continued the tests for most of the day, and Kerran felt drained by the time they had finished, although little more had been uncovered of Kerran's abilities. He could reproduce another's drawings, and he could send small metal objects into another time and place. One other thing they had discovered towards the end of the afternoon. With one or both pieces of the Seacrest in his hand Kerran's powers did not increase, instead they seemed to disappear altogether.

The following day they began again.

"This is something that I thought of last night," Tolth told Kerran, and produced an ancient and tattered book.

Kerran could see that many pages were missing. Others were torn and faded, the words smeared and lost. Tolth gently placed the book on the desk.

"These are surely the oldest pages ever discovered," he said, placing a reverent hand on its cover. "Maradass the Philosopher, knowing that it was from the time of the wizards, gave it as a gift to my ancestor Celisor the First, who was a scholar of words and symbols. Celisor discovered little except that he believed it to be a book of magical symbols and spells, while also being something of a history of the wizards. I have looked at it a number of times over the years, but not a word nor figure can I understand. If it is a book of magic, then I am hoping that you will find some meaning in it that all others have not."

Slowly Tolth began to gently leaf through the book, and

then passed it across to Kerran. "You choose," he told his young friend. "Perhaps your intuition will find some clue amongst these pages that is lost to me."

Kerran began to look through the book which was full of strange writings and many diagrams. He came to a page near the end that was complete. There were only a few symbols on the page and the characters were large and well defined. Although Kerran could now read and write slowly in the language of the lands, the symbols on this page before him seemed even more familiar to him than those of his lessons.

"I know this," he said looking up at Tolth. "I cannot read it, but somewhere in my memory I have seen this before." He returned his gaze to the book, studying each character and figure carefully, and then he sat back again and shook his head. "It is as familiar as the palm of my own hand," he said. "Yet it tells me nothing."

"I have an idea," said Tolth, and again turned the book back to himself. "As I draw one of the characters I want you to concentrate and tell me what you might see in your mind."

Tolth took a piece of charcoal and carefully drew one of the more simple characters from the book, it was a circle intersected by an elliptical curve.

"Moon," said Kerran immediately from behind closed eyes.

"Good," said Tolth and drew another. This time an inverted triangle with two long diagonal lines running through it.

"It is..." Kerran began and then paused. "I see darkness," he finally said. "All is black. Perhaps 'black' is the meaning. Tis hard to say."

So began a long afternoon of translating word by word, character by character, what might be the meaning of the page before them. Many times Kerran could not make sense of what Tolth had drawn, and it soon became clear that he could more easily decipher those characters which related to some physical object in the real world, also words such as fear, strength and power came to him. He felt the emotion or sensation rather than seeing the meaning. Kerran was positive in his identification of many of the symbols, but no connecting words came to him that could help make sense of the whole. They finally stopped in frustration and returned to the Amitarl home for the evening meal. Over the dinner table they discussed their progress. Tolth held the list of characters and words before him and began to read them out in the order that they appeared in the book:

> Night black moon high wizard free
> Ma-zurin-bidar ocean deep
> Peace people lands
> Night black moon ancient ones speak
> Hear understand gift history truth.
> Night black moon choose path ruin truth.
> night black moon choose

"Some of it almost makes sense, almost," said Tolth, his brow creased in thought while his meal remained untouched at his elbow.

"*Black moon*," he muttered quietly to himself. "The *high wizard* may be Rishtan-Sta, then again perhaps not. He then sets free *ma-zurin-bidar* to the *ocean deep*. That makes little sense. All of the old known histories tells us that he actually formed it in the ocean. At some later time he took it to a high place above the other wizards to destroy them. Who are the *ancient ones* I wonder? The other wizards? And who is it that will *choose* a *path* to *ruin* if that is what is actually meant? Confound it!"

Tolth forgot his meal altogether, and without a word to the others at the table he left the house and was not seen by them again that night. When they met for breakfast Tolth was weary and had made little progress with the translation.

"*Black moon* may be an eclipse," he told Kerran.

After he had eaten Tolth seemed to regain much of his energy and they left the house to return to his workrooms and the ancient book. Tolth continued from the point where they had left off the day before. It remained a time consuming exercise and there was much that baffled him. When the day was done they had managed to decipher the major words on the complete page. On one of the earlier pages which had been partly destroyed, Kerran had studied for a time, a diagram that he recognised as being the eight pointed star which he knew now was part of the design on the Seacrest. The diagram meant little to him, smudged and crumbling as it was. To translate the entire book into something that read sensibly would take a very long time if it were at all possible. Kerran felt exhausted and excused himself, while Tolth remained poring over the old and tattered pages. Now that he had symbols and characters to work with, the Old Amitarl was able to translate more from the pages without Kerran's help. It was not until the next morning that Tolth emerged from his workroom and returned to the Amitarl home. He was both excited and distracted. There was much that remained unclear.

"I believe the book to have been scribed by a wizard of some power, and yet it was surely written some time after the destruction that Rishtan-Sta wrought. It has been believed until now that all of the High Wizards and their lesser allies were destroyed by Rishtan-Sta. You are no doubt the ancestral son of Chel-a-Sta, and your ancestral family chose to remain hidden for all this time, and so in your case history must be rewritten... Perhaps others survived those times also."

Kerran had read and learned very little of the true history of the wizards and so he asked Tolth to tell him more of their story. Tolth was happy for the distraction.

"The first true wizards in these southern lands were black men and women," he said. "Their magic had subtle power and little is known of it. It is said that much of their power still remains in the earth, hidden from those who would discover it. When the white people first arrived in these lands, with them came the twenty wizards, if that indeed was the true number.

"Much is forgotten, and perhaps the truth of those times may never be fully known," he continued. "At least the names of the six High Wizards are remembered well. Of them, Rishtan-Sta, the White Wizard, was most powerful. Then there was Cranda-Sta, translated as Dark Fire Star, the Red Wizard, and Ma-dran-Thara the Brown Wizard, whose name, with difficulty, becomes Mountains of Night. Among the High Wizards were two sisters. There was Drinda-mira-Sta, the

Evening Star, whose colour was blue, and Orlandi, the Yellow Wizard, who took her name from the moon. The last of the six was the Green Wizard, Lardan-Mor, whose name becomes Ocean's Dark Light in the modern tongue.

"Of the Lesser Wizards not so much is known. There were fourteen of them tis said. There is of course much written concerning wizards, but how much is true can only be guessed at now. Much of course is speculation in many of the histories, and I believe most are truly fantasy. Over the great many years since their passing I believe only a little of their true history has ever been discovered.

"When they arrived in the lands from the north they wished to live quietly and in peace. All was well. Even the black people learned to accept them. For many centuries they lived in harmony, the wizards using their powers for the good of the people, and all were content it seems. No one has discovered how it came about, but there was discord amongst the High Six. Rishtan-Sta attempted to make peace, but when two of the Lesser Wizards were killed it turned into a violent war. Many so called scholars have written varying accounts of how and why the two wizards were killed. I think that no one can now truly know the truth in this. None of the six could die except by the life sacrifice of the one who killed them. This I am quite sure is the truth for in all histories it is told that way, and it is something that rings true to me. It is speculated by many scholars that this applied to the Lesser Wizards also, but the truth of this is unknown.

"War raged through the lands. The black people who could escape the wild wizardry left for the deserts, while most of the white men and women, enthralled by the power of the High Wizards, fought centuries of war that slaughtered them in great numbers. Rishtan-Sta called for a truce, and after a long time he was able to bring the High Wizards together to discuss peace. A union was struck between the six and Rishtan-Sta was content.

"Years passed, many centuries perhaps, and then Rishtan-Sta heard once again that there was war amongst the wizards. He again found a terrible destruction being wrought upon the peoples of the land. The earth itself was being destroyed. The Broken Lands are surely a legacy of that time. Rishtan-Sta searched for the other High Wizards and eventually found them together, and not now as enemies. To them it had become a game. They had learned to enjoy the killing and humanity, along with the many fell beasts that they had created. All creatures were now but playthings, an amusement, a horrifying game. It is thought that Rishtan-Sta came here to Zeta, and with help from Manzanee he formed the Seacrest. From your dreams you probably know the rest I think.

"The White Wizard stood on a mountain and drew down a great destruction on all of the wizards. Tis said the cataclysm he wrought destroyed far more than he could have guessed it would, and the lands suffered for it. The six and the fourteen were said to be totally destroyed, though we now know that at least Chel-a-Sta survived. Perhaps Chel-a-Sta himself wrote the book we now work on."

"No," said Kerran and surprised even himself. "For some reason I cannot explain, I know that my ancestor did not write of himself, or the history of those times. He left no personal history except perhaps an unwritten one. He wished to remain hidden. I am sure of it."

Tolth looked at his young friend but did not question Kerran on this. The young man was no longer a raggedy boy from a distant corner of the Regions. He was the descendant of wizards and his words should be relied on as truth.

"From the little we have now translated of this book I sense that it was written after the Destruction," said Tolth. "If not Chelasta, then perhaps there is another wizard, or even more than one, who survived the destruction of Rishtan-Sta."

"Except of course for Manzanee," smiled Kerran, and looked about the room as if expecting a response. There was none.

Beware the Dark Shadows

Over the following days Kerran worked with Tolth on the translation. Many passages were left undeciphered, while others were so faded and torn that they would be illegible forever. Kerran heard Tolth name three of the Lesser Wizards. They were Valdaris, Dinismar and Pelan. The names hung in Kerran's mind like an old memory. His mind drifted away from Tolth and the ancient book. He began to see faces swimming before his eyes. He seemed to know them as well as he knew himself. His eyes remained focused on the book though he saw nothing of the pages. Kerran saw these faces. Powerful eyes stared at him from the air before him, and he knew them to be the eyes of the almost immortal men and women who were known as the Lesser Wizards.

A last face came before him, and of all the others this one seemed most alive. He knew it then to be the face of Trontar, the one who was called the Follower. A light flickered within the Wizard's eyes as though a storm raged within his head, and then the face changed. Kerran could not tear his mind away as the evil smile and hateful eyes of Maradass held his own. Words full of malice and warning came into Kerran's mind.

"Do not call on Ma-Zurin-Bidar," said the voice with a wicked snarl. "It will not aid you, for you do not have the strength to hold it. Even Rishtan-Sta could not govern it in the final end." The old wizard's name came like a curse, spat out in bitterness. "You know nothing of this," hissed Maradass. "Go no further in this search for the knowledge of wizards, which you will never understand and it will finally destroy you. In your ignorance you will bring down a final destruction upon the land that you will never live to see. Be gone from this game in which you hold no power. Do not think you can play and win, for even now dark shadows hold your doom in their grasp."

The eyes glared into Kerran's. A sneer of bitterness came to the lips of Maradass as he faded slowly and was gone. Kerran collapsed across the book before him as Tolth gave a startled cry and leapt to his feet. Kerran's eyes were closed and there was no response when Tolth tried to rouse him. Gently he laid Kerran on a low couch beneath the window. His young friend appeared to be in a deep sleep and Tolth sent Nup in search of Verardian. In his workroom Tolth sat beside Kerran and looked with distress at the young face. He could see that dreams were passing behind Kerran's closed eyes.

Darkness covered Chelasta's vision for a long time as he floated, totally conscious, but with no power to change the situation. Then he saw that a light burned far below. He began to descend and found that the red glow came from fire, the blaze coming from the mouth of a tall mountain which belched smoke and ash. A river of molten rock flowed down the steep sides to the valleys below as Kerran felt his shadow descend. From the fires he sensed no heat although the flames flickered around him violently. On the very edge of the fiery pit he came to rest. Smoke billowed up from below. The air shimmered and moved with the heat. A voice, deep and fiery, came from the depths.

"What do you seek, young one?"

"I seek knowledge," said Kerran, the words coming from his mind before he thought them.

"Some things can be dangerous in the hands of those who do not understand," said the crackling voice. "What is the knowledge that you seek?"

Kerran did not reply. He could not reply until the words of Maradass came back into his mind. *In your ignorance you will bring down a final destruction upon the land.*

"I seek to avoid the destruction of the land," he said finally.

There was a silence, except for the sound of fire.

"You ask much for one so young and new to the knowledge of these so called wizards," said the voice from the depths. "If I name a way for you to save the land it may lead you far from your true path, and your true path is your only way ahead to reach your final goal. The destruction or deliverance of the lands lies not only in your hands. When you seek for knowledge you may not find it, or you may not understand it when you hold it. Remember this and little else. Wisdom may come without knowledge. So young wizardling, follow your path to where it may lead. That is all that need be done... Go now!"

A blast of heat caused Kerran to fly from the fire, and his shadow burnt. Kerran's body burnt in fever for a long time, and when he finally opened his eyes he saw Verardian's concerned face looking down into his own.

"Welcome back, Kerran," the healer said softly, unable to hide the worry in his voice. "You have slept again and had a terrible fever until just a short time past. Now it is gone. Four days you slept this time. How do you feel?"

"I am hungry," said Kerran, realising that his body ached for food.

He felt weak and there was a strong pain in his head. Verardian eased Kerran's pains and went to the kitchen to prepare food. He returned with a tray and set it beside the bed.

"Tolth wished to know immediately when you awoke," said Verardian. "I have sent Nup to tell him."

Tolth arrived soon after, pleased to see Kerran awake and in such little discomfort. Then Kerran told of his dream of fire and the words of the strange voice.

"This dream was so different," he told Tolth. "It was a voice like no other, so much older than the wizards. It sounded a little like Manzanee but with such power and a great understanding. I cannot explain it. I wanted to remain in that fire but I was sent away."

"I am afraid for you Kerran," Tolth said, sitting beside the bed. "These dreams lengthen, and sap your energy. You say that you wished to remain in the fire, but to linger may have harmed you deeply. These words that have come to you now are important for they say that you should not search for answers yet, so I think you should avoid for a while this old man's obsession with knowledge. For myself I cannot cease my delving into the mysteries of the past and I will continue, but you should rest. Perhaps a visit to Felstrar is what is needed."

"Yes," said Verardian. "A restful time in good company."

The trip was arranged, once Kerran had recovered enough to travel, and he was warmly welcomed by Piata's family. After a few days Kerran's strength returned and he and Piata climbed again to the ruins above the town. Rark and the other dogs enjoyed the adventure. The view was very different now. The red water spread before them in the bay, and to the far horizon beyond the harbour mouth.

It was during the fourth day of his visit that some people of the town began to notice a difference in the poisoned tide. It was as if the redness was becoming diluted and thinning out. Occasionally a patch of the sea would take on a tinge of green. It was a slow change but by the following morning unmistakable, the colour of the ocean was returning to its natural blue-green. News was rushed to Nariss where the sea still retained its poisonous colour. People rejoiced in the town, though none would yet touch the water. Three children of Felstrar had died in agony when the poison had at first surrounded the isles. Kerran and Piata stood by the bay and looked across the water.

"I must return to the Green City," said Kerran sadly. "If the poison is really going then we will sail for the Regions very soon." He held Piata's hands and looked into her eyes. "I will come back," he said, a certainty in his voice.

"I know," she said, with equal certainty.

Kerran returned to the city and arrived in the early evening. He found Verardian and Nup preparing dinner.

"Hello, Kerran," called Nup as he entered the house.

Verardian looked around the kitchen door. "Welcome home," he said. "We did not expect you until the morning. I will put on some more vegetables to cook."

Kerran relaxed into a soft armchair and continued to read the history book that he had carried to Felstrar with him. The book did not concern the time of the wizards and nothing troublesome had disturbed his time in Felstrar. He had been reading for some time when he felt that he was being observed, looking up he found the strange dark eyes of Mindis staring at him intently from his usual corner. Kerran held the gaze for some moments, and then in his slow and deliberate voice Mindis began to speak.

"You do not belong here," he said quietly. "Nothing you can do will prevent the devastation to come."

Verardian came to the doorway of the kitchen. He stood intently watching Mindis who said no more and had returned to his inner world. When Tolth arrived for dinner, Verardian told of the words that Mindis had spoken.

"Well, Kerran," remarked Tolth. "If you do not belong here then there is no need for you to remain for much longer. Already the poison has lost almost all of its potency. The fleet will sail on the evening tide the day after tomorrow. We cannot delay any further. We sail to the aid of the Regions."

Tolth was excited and as happy as Kerran had seen him for moons. The weight of his missing offspring seemed to lift from his mind. Soon he would be sailing to Andrian, his ancestral home. Leana and Landin would know he was there and join him. His conversation at dinner was lively and bounced around many different subjects.

"Time is short," Tolth said. "Maradass has been on the march for many days. He will have reached the Crossroads by now, and his first goal I believe will be Mendan-Maradass. His ancestral home will pull him to the old Philosopher's city and there will be little resistance. The Council will capitulate. They have no army, only bands of rogues who do their dirty work. Will we get to the south in time?" Tolth asked the night air. "Will there be anything to save?"

"Yes, father," said Verardian. "We will be there in time."

Tolth turned and looked at his son. "You are no warrior Verardian," he spoke tenderly. "You should remain here on

Zeta."

"No, I cannot," Verardian replied. "There will be much need of me in the lands. Blood will be spilt. Much healing will be needed, and I cannot stay here when my family are gone."

"I am glad," replied his father. "You sustain me more than you know. Yes I am glad that you sail with us." Tolth turned slightly and looked at Mindis. "He too seems determined to come," he said. "So for good or ill, all of the Amitarl family will return to the Regions."

Kerran was tired from his travels and retired early. He laid his head on the soft pillow and fell into a deep sleep where he dreamed.

Kerran walked the familiar cliff top, bush clad and moist, the air heavy with mist. The deep valley below lay enshrouded in a soft whiteness. He came to the waterfall and the narrow path which led its winding way down to the cave of Manzanee. Kerran was about to begin his descent when he saw something in the path before him. A large black snake lay coiled and waiting. Its tongue flicked, sensing Kerran's presence. Kerran knew he must pass and slowly walked forward.

The fear he felt was no less in his dream than it would be in reality. He moved closer until the snake lay close to his feet. Still moving slowly, without sudden movements, Kerran gently stepped over the snake. He took another step and then another. Two more steps and he looked back. The snake was no longer there, instead he saw Manzanee crouched where the snake had been, a broad grin upon his face. Then in an instant the Black Wizard vanished and a small dark beetle scuttled beneath a large rock.

Kerran turned and resumed his descent. He saw a small black bird swoop to the depths below, soon to be lost in the fine mist. Icicles hung from the stone ledge where the waterfall fell against the rock. Ferns and mosses were frozen in place and the path slippery with ice. Kerran was aware of his body and felt the cold biting deeper as he continued down the path. He came to the cave and within he saw the welcoming fire. Kerran entered and sat before the low flames, feeling the warmth seep into his body. From the darkness at the back of the cave Kerran heard a slight movement, and then Manzanee came from the shadows.

"Welcome young Chel-a-Sta," he said as he sat down opposite Kerran. He juggled a small object in his hand. "Tolth may like to see this again." He reached across the fire and dropped the small golden ball into the palm of Kerran's outstretched hand. "You increase your powers, and yet much is still hidden, for this is as it should be," said the Black Wizard. "There is much danger that will come upon you soon. Beware of the dark shadows."

Kerran found his voice. "What is this danger?" he asked sharply. "Who is it that threatens me?"

"There is much that threatens you," replied the Black Wizard. "Every soldier of Maradass is a part of that threat, for you can still die by any hand, but that is not what I speak of. The enemy is close and is coming soon. Believe this for I can say no more. Instead I will sing you a song. It is the first song that was sung when man first found his voice. It is a long song and it never ends."

Manzanee was quiet for a time, his eyes closed. At first Kerran only thought he heard the sound which came from the depths of Manzanee's being, a low note filled the cave and the walls seemed to resonate in harmony. The note changed, deepening further as the fire burnt low. The black magician's voice began to chant words, and time retreated deep into the past. The words had no meaning for Kerran yet he sensed their significance. The song told of times long passed and peoples long forgotten, except that they were remembered in this ancient song. A new scene began to appear before Kerran. A red desert stretched to a far distant mountain range. He stood on a hilltop and watched as far away a line of dark figures walked across the barren inhospitable land. They were black people who carried spears, and into Kerran's mind came memories that were not his own.

Long before the white man and the wizards had reached this place the black people had walked across these vast dry lands, moving with the game and the climate and their nomadic inclinations. Kerran continued to hear Manzanee's song, and then realised that some of those who walked the red desert were singing the same song. The unknown words of Manzanee mingled with those of the people and became one. Kerran began to find meaning in the words. They spoke of the sun and stars, of the beauty in the dry lands, of ancestors who had walked this way for thousands of years. Their song spoke of much that later Kerran was unable to find words for.

The sun blazed down upon the almost naked bodies as the black people continued their march. Kerran somehow knew that their destination was many hundreds of leagues away. They were going to a place across the mountains where others would gather. They would sing and dance and tell tales of their own journey, and of the lands which they called home. A joyous cry went through the long straggling line of people. All voices as one sang joyously of their gratitude and indebtedness to the earth, the mother. Kerran heard their call and wanted to follow but could not. He stood rooted to the spot and watched for a long time as the sun sank gradually to the horizon. The black people had passed far to the north, disappearing into the gathering darkness when the sun dipped below the far mountains and was gone.

All was silent and Kerran stood alone and unmoving on the hilltop. There was much now that he understood, though he would never find the words to explain it. He felt humbled and awed by the wonder that he now sensed, and he spoke into the night.

"I will follow," he said. "I will come, but now is not the time."

"No," said Manzanee, who was standing beside him now. "It is indeed not the time to go with them. Now is the time for understanding. You have discovered much young Chel-a-Sta. I see it in your eyes. Go back now! Awake! There are fearful omens about you. Awake and beware the dark shadows! Awake!"

Blackness descended upon the scene before him and Kerran found himself waking in the semi-darkness of his room. He felt the small golden ball in his hand and smiled. The light of the full moon slanted in through the open window and Kerran did not remember leaving it open so wide. Then he felt that he was not alone in the room. In the corner, near the foot of his bed, he sensed rather than saw someone lurking in the shadows. A darker shape emerged slowly and came towards the bed. He saw a raised arm and the glint of a blade as the darkened figure approached.

Kerran cried out in fear and leapt from the bed as the knife descended viciously, tearing into the bedclothes. In fear Kerran called out again and grasped for a small wooden chair that stood near the window. The silent attacker came toward him. He was a tall well built man whose face could not yet be seen, and Kerran held out little hope of overpowering him. He heard Verardian and Tolth call out to him as they reached his door, but they could not open it. Whoever it was that wished him dead had locked it before making his attack. The man came on slowly, sure of his quarry. Kerran could hear Rark below his window, barking wildly.

Kerran feinted to the right, and then swung the chair with all of his strength. He caught the man hard on the wrist of the hand that held the knife. With a cry of pain the knife clattered to the floor and was instantly lost somewhere in the darkness. Kerran could hear Verardian and Tolth hammering at the door with what must have been a heavy piece of furniture. With an angry shriek the man came at him, lunging and missing as Kerran leapt across the bed and rushed for the door, but the key was missing. The dark figure came at him again, a tall relentless shadow silhouetted against the moonlight. He was about to trap Kerran in a corner when the door splintered and broke. The figure hesitated, snarling in defeat as light shone through the gaping crack, then he turned and leapt to the window sill.

Kerran was never able to say for sure if he jumped or fell, but without a sound the man disappeared from the window sill and plunged the two floors to the stone pathway below. Rark ceased his barking and gave out an unearthly howl as Kerran's knees went from beneath him and he collapsed to the floor. Fear had sapped him of the strength to stand. With a final crash the door swung open, pieces of wood falling into the room. Tolth came swiftly through the doorway, a short sword clasped before him. Verardian entered behind his father carrying a lamp; they saw no attacker and rushed to Kerran's side.

"Kerran are you hurt?" said Tolth urgently, deep concern in his voice.

"No," replied Kerran looking up into the old man's face. "He went out the window. I think he fell."

Tolth went to the window and looked down, while Verardian assisted Kerran to his feet. In the moonlight Tolth could make out a dark figure sprawled on the pathway below, Rark stood over him, snuffling at the still body. Several people attracted by the noise stood by, not knowing what to do. Tolth rushed from the room and made his way to the parkland below while Verardian helped Kerran to a chair. It was some time before Tolth returned a worried and mystified look on his face. He sat on the edge of the bed and gazed at Kerran.

"It was Davin of the Council," he said. "He is dead."

"Davin!" exclaimed Verardian. "Why would he do this thing?"

"I do not know," replied Tolth. "He was dressed as an assassin, all in black and hooded. I cannot understand what this means." He shook his head and was silent.

"There is a knife," said Kerran peering about the room. "There," he pointed to the blade which lay hard against the wall, lit now by the lamp.

Verardian retrieved it and held the knife close to the light. It was an ornate weapon and the pommel was carved into the likeness of a dog's skull, its wicked blade long and curved. Tolth took it silently from Verardian and studied it carefully.

"I dreamt," said Kerran remembering. "Manzanee told me to wake up, to beware of dark shadows. He warned me, Tolth. If he had not I would be dead now." Kerran shuddered and could not look at the blade which had so nearly ended his life. Nup came sleepily to the broken opening and looked in astonishment at the shattered remains of the door, Verardian asked him to warm milk for Kerran and he scuttled below to the kitchen.

"I must attend to Davin," said Tolth. "There are people below who will help." He rose and left the room, carrying the knife with him. Verardian took Kerran to another spare room to spend the remainder of the night, and Nup soon arrived with warm goat's milk which Kerran drank, its goodness stealing slowly through his body. With a sigh he lowered his head to the pillow. Much of the terror had left him, though for a time he found his limbs trembling with the memory. Verardian sat with him and Kerran fell into a restless sleep, waking often with a start. Verardian was always there to lay a gentle hand on his arm, reassuring his young friend. Dawn came slowly, a grey mist threatening rain. Kerran remained in bed for most of the morning, the terror of the night still haunting him, leaving him weak and exhausted. At noon he was in the large sitting room below when Tolth entered carrying with him the knife wrapped in a cloth.

"I am glad to see you are recovered," he said, sitting in a chair opposite Kerran. He unwrapped the knife and placed it on the table between them. "This weapon comes from Maradass. There is little doubt," he said. "I still do not know why Davin attacked you, nor how he came by such a thing. It is evil and is wreathed with a spell that I cannot decipher. No one must touch it. I will lock it away and keep it safe."

Tolth became silent for a few moments in thought. "Ever since Davin came to sit on the Council he argued in favour of remaining on Zeta and not returning to the aid of the Regions," said Tolth. "Although he always bowed to the vote of the others. To attempt such a murderous thing as last night's deed he must surely have been under the power of Maradass. How, I do not know. I fear that if Maradass has been able to reach into the mind of Davin, there may be others on Zeta who are corrupted by his power. I think that Rark should sleep in your room tonight. Tomorrow evening we sail for Andrian."

During the day Kerran watched as hundreds of men and women, armed in many various ways, arrived in the parklands and made camp there. Fires burned and the people of the city joined those who would sail on the morrow. There were no great celebrations. The people were subdued, knowing that they may be seeing friends and loved ones for the last time. The rain that had threatened during the day began to fall in drenching sheets upon the many tents pitched on the grass.

Thunder rolled amongst the far mountains and the wind grew until it began to rake at the encampment. Kerran watched from the shelter of the Amitarl home as several tents were flattened by a powerful gust. People scrambled out from beneath their collapsed shelters, rushing to replace tent poles and ropes. Soaked, they crawled back beneath their temporary homes, or were invited into nearby buildings to shelter for the night.

"There are much harsher times to come for them," said Tolth as he came to stand beside Kerran. "They will face the might of the Maradass army very soon. May they remain brave and true to their task. And you, Kerran, who knows what may eventually be asked of you? With all that we have learned since you arrived on Zeta we are still no closer to answering many of the riddles that surround your ancestry and your purpose in these coming times."

The following day was again heavy with rain and ominous dark clouds hung above the city of Nariss. Many ships that could find no berth at the docks lay at anchor, as men in smaller craft rowed the troops out to their allotted vessels. It was in the late afternoon that Tolth returned from a day with the Council. It had been the last time that they would all meet together for a long time, and much had been decided for the defence of Zeta should Maradass ever find and attack the Magical Isles. Tolth looked around the living room of his home, and thought that it may be the last time he would ever enjoy the comforts he had felt within its warm walls.

"It is time to go," he said to Kerran.

He laid a gentle hand on Nup's shoulder. The young boy had held back his tears all day, but now could not stop them flowing.

"The ships are in readiness," continued Tolth. "They wait only for us before setting sail."

There were a great many people lining the docks when the Amitarl family arrived amongst them, there was just one ship remaining there, tied to the wooden piles and rolling gently on the tide. The ship was smaller than most, but was known to be the fastest in the fleet.

"It is called Moonchaser," said Tolth as he stood beside the hardwood planking of its hull and looked up the ramp which would take them aboard.

The people at the dock were quiet and as sombre as the weather, and there were many sad goodbyes before Kerran, Rark, and the Amitarl family climbed to the deck of Moonchaser. Captain Ronsarl, a man of many years experience with the sea, gave the orders to cast off from the dock. With the help of strong men in three smaller boats, they were rowed out into the stream. Captain Ronsarl called to his crew to set their sails and the craft turned to join the other twenty-eight ships which comprised the fleet of Zeta. Kerran watched the Green City recede, while high on the ocean breeze he saw the distant spread wings of Storm, following them towards the open sea. Nup stood at the dock waving frantically in goodbye, tears flowing down his cheeks.

Moonchaser was soon sailing among the other ships and Kerran remained at the rail, Rark by his side. As the sun set in the darkness of the west Kerran thought again of Piata and his heart ached. He did not know when, or even if he would ever return to Zeta. The future lay before him as a vast expanse of unknown dangers. The lights of the Green City finally dwindled and were gone as the fleet turned to the south, sailing beyond the hills which shielded the city from the easterly winds. Rark gave out a soft whine.

"You should be happy," said Kerran. "With fortune on our side you may soon rejoin Flindas."

Kerran thought again of his friend as he had many times since Flindas had left Zeta, and he wondered where he might be. A strong southerly wind pushed the fleet deep into the night, occasionally Kerran could see lights from other ships spread across the ocean's surface, and then rain would return and wipe all from his vision. He had no desire to go to his berth below, and after a time he joined Rark in the dry corner provided for the mountain dog and curled up against the warm hairy body. Tolth found him asleep there much later.

"Come Kerran, the wind freshens and whips the sea," said Tolth in a kindly voice to his young friend. "I am sure that Rark is accustomed to such weather, but you will be warmer and more comfortable below."

Kerran rose and found that his body would not follow his commands. He almost fell and Tolth assisted him. He was soon in his bunk in a cabin which he was to share with three of the ship's crew. He could not sleep, and for a long time he listened to the creaking and pounding as Moonchaser forged onward through the heavy seas.

It was early dawn when he awoke to a soft light filtering in through the small window of the cabin. The other bunks were empty, the three crewmen having been allotted the midnight to dawn watch. Kerran stretched and found that his limbs and the rest of his body felt as they should. The stiffness and disconnected sensation seemed to have passed. A pleasant feeling of hunger stirred in his stomach and he dressed quickly. Once he had left the cabin he had no problem in following the smell of food to the galley. The large jovial cook was very happy to serve the young hero. He spooned him out a big helping of oats and honey, and with a large mug of tea in hand Kerran found his way up on deck. The ship rolled continuously and his tea slopped about in the mug. The sun pushed its light through the grey mist around the ship, and not far off he could see other ships of the fleet pounding through the heavy seas. He joined Rark who raised himself into a full stretch. A large empty bowl showed that the dog's needs had not been forgotten by the cook.

"A little more comfortable than our trip to Zeta," said Kerran to Rark as he scratched him behind the ears.

The mountain dog gave a contented sound from the back of his throat and settled back into his corner. Kerran ate his oatmeal and was sipping on his tea when he was joined by Tolth.

"How are you this morning?" Tolth asked.

"I am well," replied Kerran. "I do not feel the strangeness of yesterday."

"That is good; it may have been the residue of your fever, or perhaps a little seasickness," said Tolth. "For myself I did not sleep, I had many visions and warnings last night as I lay in my bunk. Manzanee came to me for the first time in moons, but he spoke no words. I felt that he wished to warn me, and yet could not interfere further." Tolth rose again and stood at the ship's rail gazing into the gloom. "The captain believes that the weather will deteriorate. The wind has already changed," he said quietly, as if to himself. "A storm is brewing and advances from the north and west. It does not portent well for our journey."

As if to verify Tolth's misgivings a larger than usual wave crashed against the ship, sending a shudder through Moonchaser's hull. Fine spray swirled about them and touched Kerran's face. His tongue tasted the salty tang on his lips.

By mid afternoon the storm was upon them and Kerran was forced to return to his cabin. Rark too went below to lie amongst the many boxes and parcels lashed in the hold. A message had been sent from ship to ship. To avoid collision the fleet was to spread out across the turbulent ocean. Wind and rain tore at the stout sails and waves crashed upon the decks, Kerran lay on his bunk able to do little more than hold onto the wooden sides and prevent himself from being pounded against the cabin wall. The closeness of the space and the constant rolling of the ship caused him to become ill. He could not eat and took no more than a little water during the remainder of the day. Verardian came to his cabin in the darkness of night and with his gentle touch was able to ease Kerran into a deep sleep.

For the next two days and nights the storm raged, then on the morning of the third the wind began to die. Kerran woke, feeling weak. His head ached, and when he stood he was forced to support himself as he made his way up on deck. Food was far from his mind, but Verardian joined him and insisted that he eat.

"You will be of no use to anyone if you cannot regain your strength," he said, passing Kerran a bowl of oats.

After a few spoonfuls Kerran began to feel a little better. The hot sweet tea also did much to revive him and for the rest of the day he remained on deck with Rark, watching as the fleet slowly began to regroup. He saw their tall white sails catching the sunlight that filtered through the clouds, as patches of blue sky began to appear. Kerran was gazing into the soft light when Storm plummeted from above and with a cry alighted on the deck, Kerran was pleased to see him and Rark gave out a friendly bark. The fleet continued on its journey as all of the ships had now regained the company of the others. The wind remained constant, pushing from the northwest as they sailed into the gathering darkness.

Kerran ate his evening meal on deck. The closeness of the cabin below brought back the memory of his illness over the past days. Taking blankets aloft he wrapped himself well and sat beside Rark, the great dog's warmth helping to keep out the chill night air. He was sipping at his tea when Tolth came out and sat by the ship's rail, oil burning lanterns shedding light on the deck.

"Your health returns," Tolth said, studying Kerran's face closely in the dim light. "It is well. We will all need to be strong if we are to survive these coming times." Tolth paused and looked at Kerran thoughtfully for a time before he spoke again. "There is something that I have wanted to ask you since we left Zeta," he said. "The confusion generated within the two fragments of the Seacrest is making it difficult for me to channel my thoughts, and to see things that were once clear to me. What I would ask is that you again carry Leana's piece of the Seacrest. Within you there is something of your ancestral wizardry that seems able to harness it to your needs. Will you bear it for me until Leana's return, if that should ever be?"

Kerran did not hesitate. "Yes," he said looking at his old friend. "If it will help; it has never harmed me."

Tolth removed the piece from his pouch and Kerran saw that it was once again attached by the silver clasp to the strong cord. He took it from Tolth's hand and slipped it over his head. A feeling coursed through his body as if warm hands touched his head, and then flowed downward, all the way to his toes. It was pleasant and he described it to Tolth.

"I can feel every part of myself all at once," he said. "My skin tingles, and even my hair has feelings."

He laughed in pleasure and Tolth smiled. He could indeed see a healthy glow beginning to radiate from Kerran's face. He clapped his young friend on the back and was about to rise when harshly spoken words suddenly disturbed them.

"He must not have it!" said the voice of Mindis as he stepped slowly from behind a pile of stores. "I am Amitarl," he continued, his words slow and deliberate. "It is mine." He came forward, his attitude threatening. "It is mine," he repeated, his hands coming out before him, fingers curved like claws.

Tolth slipped quickly between them, and with little effort he held his youngest son's wrists. Motionless for a few moments Mindis looked with hate into his father's eyes, then his hate filled look turned towards Kerran. Their eyes remained locked together, and then slowly the face of Mindis lost its expression. His hands became limp and Tolth allowed them to lower, as Mindis again gazed blankly at nothing, his mind receding into the dark place where it dwelt. Without further words Tolth led him below deck. Some time passed before Tolth returned, a concerned look creasing his brow.

"I am worried for Mindis," he said sitting beside Kerran. "Something drives him. The disappearance of Luista is a mystery that only he may know the answer to." A wistful look came into the old man's eyes. "I hope one day that I too will know the answer," he said quietly, as if to himself.

Tolth sat for a time in thought and then went below, returning to his books. Kerran remained on deck well into the evening where many others sat around in groups. Soldiers, men and women, tended to their equipment, polishing and oiling the light armour and chain mail that was the standard livery for many of the warriors of Zeta. A grindstone turned by a foot pedal was in constant use. Sparks flew as swords and daggers were sharpened. Thick oil was rubbed into goatskin straps and thongs to prevent mould and rot, occasionally a soldier would strike up a conversation with Kerran who they continued to call, 'the young hero,' much to his embarrassment.

Often the soldiers played a complicated game using several small, many sided pieces of hardwood, marked with a variety of symbols and numbers. It took Kerran a long time to finally grasp all the intricacies of the absorbing game which they called Swords and Wands. Much humour was involved as pieces were either tossed into the centre or retrieved with a groan. Only once, during that first evening was Kerran able to free his hand of all pieces, this being the object of the game. He was roundly applauded and clapped heartily on the back.

A light-heartedness which he had not felt for a long time entered Kerran as he laughed and joked with his friendly companions, all worries and care lifting from him for a time. His heart warmed to these natural and honest people who played games in the face of oncoming war. Many remained on deck that night, preferring it to the closeness of their berths below.

Various musical instruments of strings and wind were produced. Many voices joined in song and as Kerran had learned the words of several of them during his stay on Zeta, his voice at times joined with the others. They sang of ancient times and adventures long past. There were songs of the Amitarl family and the wars with Maradass, songs of heroism and treachery amongst the smoke of war. Kerran heard the words and felt a stirring within. There was one song which ended in a rousing battle chant.

"We fight for peace and the lands beyond.
With our mortal bodies we war on those,
Who would smite our children, and our life long friends.
We will die for their freedom and the lands beyond."

During the early morning, the wind rose, blowing hard from the south, and all those who were not required on deck were ordered below again. Kerran heard the sailors talking of a southerly gale. There was apprehension in their voices as they went about the ship preparing Moonchaser for the oncoming storm. The fleet spread out again. Though the possibility of collision in the darkness was not great, the various captains were taking no chances. If any ship was disabled, or separated from the others, the captain was to make his way as best he could to the coast of Andrian. There would be no time to wait, or to search for any ship which may be blown off course, or worse.

All hatches and ports were now closed and Kerran sat with

Tolth and Verardian in their small cabin. Mindis lay prone on his bunk, eyes open and unseeing. The ship lurched and pounded against the waves as Moonchaser fought to make headway to the southwest. Captain Ronsarl joined them briefly.

"The storm strengthens," he told them. "I have sailed through these southerly gales before, and I know that it will not be an easy time. They can last for several days." He stood silently for a moment, his brow knitted into a frown. "Moonchaser is a fine ship and I have no doubt that we will come through without danger," he said. "But others of the fleet I am not so sure of. If the storm is overly strong I fear that there are some that may not make it through to Andrian."

After Captain Ronsarl had left them Tolth sat silent and thoughtful for some time. The ship lurched and rolled through the high seas, and a mug of tea which Kerran had been drinking slid from the table and clattered to the floor. Tolth became engrossed in one of the many books that he had carried on board and Verardian took himself to his bed. Kerran tried to read but the continued rolling of the ship made it impossible for him to concentrate. He went below and sat for a time with Rark, who seemed to enjoy the company. The great mountain dog laid his head in Kerran's lap, accepting the kindly hand that scratched him. Kerran's thoughts went to Storm, for he had seen little of the hawk since they had sailed from Zeta. If the sky were clear he would often see, far aloft, the spread white wings as the hawk followed the fleet. In the evenings Storm had taken to resting amongst the wooden boxes and barrels which were tightly lashed on the upper deck. The cooks, though very busy feeding the crew and soldiers, still found time to provide for the two animals, both of whom had become quite used to fish as a staple in their diets.

With a last ruffle of his wiry hair, Kerran left Rark and retired to his cabin. Though he still experienced the strength and vitality which had not left him since once again wearing the Seacrest, he now felt a strong need for rest. He climbed into his bunk and with the fragment of the Seacrest held in his hand he fell into a pleasant untroubled sleep. He was awakened by a violent lurch of the ship sometime in the early morning. Rubbing his elbow where it had hit the woodwork of the bunk, Kerran realised that the gale had strengthened and was now tossing Moonchaser about like a twig in a rain barrel. The wind could be heard whistling through the rigging, the ship creaking loudly in protest against the storm. Kerran could sleep no more and in total darkness he managed to dress and make his way along the dimly lit corridor to the Amitarl cabin. A light shone from beneath the door and Tolth was awake, his grey head bent low over one of the several books that lay about the cabin.

"Ah Kerran," he said as the door swung open. "Another who could not sleep I take it."

"It is hard to sleep when half the time one is not in contact with the bed," replied Kerran with a rueful smile. "What is it that you read?" he asked, steadying himself against the table and looking over Tolth's shoulder at the indecipherable markings on the old yellowed paper.

"It is a book that comes from the time of Maradass the Philosopher," replied Tolth. "It was not written in the common language of the time, though it tells much of the doings of that period. Partly it tells of the bond between Zard and his father. The arrangements they made which they hoped would give them immortality. You know that Zard can only die in combat against a single opponent, which is just one key to this most interesting and intricate of magical arrangements. The Philosopher loved his eldest son most dearly, and with the power of the Seacrest he forged the alliance which he hoped would hold the family beyond the grasp of Death. This book tells something of the devising of this arrangement."

Tolth knew that Kerran already new much of this but he could see that his young friend wished to hear more, and so he continued. "Some of this story you already know," said the old Amitarl. "Maradass the Philosopher would live forever so long as Zard did not die in combat and Zard was the most beneficial of rulers and made few enemies. He was skilled in arms though he would always use diplomacy rather than fight. He was a most peaceful man. Without enemies, and with peace in the land, there was little chance that he would ever be challenged.

As long as there was no strife in the Regions the two families had no need or desire for war, or to capture further lands, and the borders were well held against any who might come from the outside. Darss the younger twin was also bound into this web of immortality. Yet he wanted more, and eventually it drove him to cunning, then madness, and finally murder. It seems that Darss felt resentment towards his entire family for a great length of time. It may have been a plan long in the hatching that finally culminated in the death of Zard and the shattering wars that followed. There is something that perhaps you do not know, which also points to a deep resentment on the part of Darss. Though his father the Philosopher and Zard his brother did not age from the time of the Dividing, Darss was not so fortunate. When the oath was made just before the dividing of the Seacrest it was an omission on the part of his father it seems. The aging came slowly, but it continued..."

Tolth was about to say more when a mighty vibration shuddered through the ship. An audible groan came from Moonchaser as yet another huge wave crashed against its hull. They had been talking quite loudly to overcome the sounds from beyond their small haven but now, as the wind and sea combined in an effort to crush the small fleet, they had to almost shout to be heard.

"No more study for a while!" called Tolth with a regretful smile.

Kerran could see that, though on the surface his old friend made light of the storm, beneath his calm there lay a worried mind. Worry for the fleet and the many men and women in his charge. Tolth and Kerran remained seated, all furniture being well anchored to the floor or walls. Verardian woke and lay upon his bunk, having to grasp for a hand hold as wave upon wave crashed about the ship. Somewhere above a hatch must have opened for a strong wind suddenly blew through the cabin. The lamp flickered and was extinguished. Lamps in the corridor had also been blown out and now those who occupied the cabin sat or lay in total darkness. Not a spark of light could be seen.

For a time they remained in the dense blackness and Tolth

was just about to relight the wick, when all in the room noticed a faint glow emanating from Kerran's breast. The Seacrest fragment which he carried there felt warm against his skin and he brought it forth, holding it in the palm of his hand. The light was an eerie white-yellow and he could see the faces of his companions as they stared at the glowing piece. Kerran felt the heat begin to flow down his arm, and pulse through the rest of his body. His very toes tingled with a pleasant burning sensation.

Just for a moment he felt his mind turn to sleep, and then he was walking again through the familiar welcoming mist.

"I am here Kerran," said the voice of the past through the gentle mist. "I cannot remain with you for long, and I cannot guide you any further on your path. Follow those who you trust. You will need other guides in the times to come. You tread a narrow edge between many dangers; perilous are the possibilities."

Kerran found his silent voice. "You speak of possibilities," he said. "Can you now tell me of the future also?"

"No," replied the voice. "Your power has strengthened and there is much use to be had from such powers, that is if you can find them and harness them. If anything is to be learned from the past it is that nothing is constant. There is only change. The past has caught up with the present now and my work is done. This is a time of great change for you and all of the future that is to come. This moment has opened the doors to many possibilities and has closed others behind you. Find your powers, for time is short. This journey is perilous. Dangers you cannot yet see threaten you, but I cannot say what they may be. Maradass is sliding and crawling into the very hearts of those you wish to deliver from his darkness. The storm you feel is but a trifle. The threat comes from all around you, and you will have to learn how to lead as well as to follow if peace is to prevail. That is all that I can say, for many things change, and so it is with me. I am no more, but will be with you always, for I am part of you. Find your powers Kerran, time is always now." The voice, which had become a whisper, was gone and would never return.

Kerran opened his eyes and found that he was still sitting in darkness, the fragment of the Seacrest held in his uplifted palm. Instantly he realised that the dream state had taken no time at all in his physical world. The darkness was unbroken, as the glow from his palm slowly faded.

"Can you tell us what has happened?" asked Tolth softly.

Kerran spoke thoughtfully. "There is much that I do not yet understand," he said. "And sometimes I wonder if I ever will. What is it that makes me who I am? I am told that I am descended from wizards and that I have powers. I can taste them, but they are so distant and unknown. It is wearisome at times, and just now I have lost the voice from the past that has comforted me so, and even saved my life at times. I feel hunted and yet cannot face my enemy. There is a horror that haunts me that lies just beyond thought. An evil that haunts me so very softly."

He felt a strange and sudden anger burning in him, while something else deep inside told him that a power other than his own was reaching out to engulf him. In fear he stood and took a step backward, then his strength failed and he found himself falling. Kerran's head hit the edge of the table and in pain he crashed to the wooden planking, and then for a time he knew no more.

The Shores of Andrian

Kerran lay in total darkness. He felt trapped, his body bound. His mind wandered in evil dreams for what seemed an eternity, but eventually he stirred with a searing pain behind his eyes, and only slowly did it ease to a dull ache further back in his head. He lay on his bunk and felt the ship continue to lurch and plunge to the whim of the storm, his waking was slow and painful. He had no idea how long he had been unconscious, and he lay still for a long time with his eyes barely open. He moved his body a little, easing the numbness in his limbs, and felt the soft bandage on his head; he then became aware that Verardian sat beside him, silent and watchful.

"How long?" croaked Kerran, his throat dry and constricted.

"You have been away for three nights," said Verardian softly. "We have all been worried that you could not return."

Kerran lay silent for a long time, eventually asking for water. Then he lay back, looking into the darkened light behind his closed eyes.

"Are you still here Kerran?" asked Verardian, his voice calm.

"Still here," said Kerran softly.

The smell of hot soup woke his stomach and he was able to

sit and take the nourishing broth. Tolth came and Kerran told them what he could remember of his dreams, though there was nothing in them that could be relied on, only drifting pain and dark dreadful clouds. He learned that the storm had passed through its most intense stage the previous day and they did not know yet if all twenty-nine ships were still with them. The storm abated slowly and it was two days later that land was sighted on the distant grey horizon. Sixteen ships stood off from the land until it was determined that they must sail south. The rugged north coast of Andrian stood tall and inaccessible to them. To the south lay the Far Isles and the safe anchorage that the fleet sought, more ships joined them as they followed the coast, yet four remained missing. Kerran was sitting with Tolth when Captain Ronsarl joined them for a time.

"We will reach the safe harbour by morning, but our passage has taken too long," he told them. "The tide will not allow us to pass through the narrow heads. We must either wait out the moon, or land on the South Coast of Andrian."

Tolth thought for a while before speaking. "Is there a way to get a small craft into the safe harbour?" he asked, looking hopefully at the captain. "We must know where Commander Torian and his troops are."

"It has been done before with stout oarsmen and a fair wind," replied the captain. "It is a treacherous stretch of water, but I have no doubt you will have many volunteers."

"Thank you, captain," said Tolth as Ronsarl left the cabin. "I fear the South Coast." Tolth turned to Kerran. "It is wide and exposed, and there are many eyes there. If the Maradass armies have marched south and were to meet us on the beaches they would engulf us. I do not pretend that our force, though skilled as they are, could overcome such superior numbers. I would that I knew where the Black Armies now march."

That night Kerran saw the answer to the old Amitarl's question as he flew swiftly within his shadow in his dream world. He soared above a wide sweeping plain and below lay a long ribbon of road. Traffic on the road was heavy yet it was no army that marched. People were fleeing to the south with wagons loaded high. The refugees swept by beneath him as

Kerran flew at great speed to the north. He knew that he must be flying along the City Highroad, and this was confirmed when ahead of him he recognised the hillock that marked the Crossroads. Here lay confusion. People streamed into the old ruins from the north and many came along the Philosopher's Road, to be joined by others coming down Narinda's Road. Some had stopped to rest amongst a great clutter of goods and animals near the ancient ruins. Most left by the City Highroad, but others were making their way down the South Road into Glandrin, and a few on foot chose the Old Coast Road which Kerran remembered so well.

He flew onward and the river Glandrin-dar passed below him. Northward across the plains he sped until he saw a darkness that did not belong there. He flew closer and found that an army lay in camp upon the plains. Cooking fires sent smoke curling upward from the army which spread as far as his keen eyes could see. Kerran could see that the army was a strange one. There were horse and foot soldiers, and yet the greater part of the army were the strange stone like soldier that he had seen before. There was no advance. The mighty army lay at its ease. Structures were being built as though for a long stay, and there seemed to be little hurry amongst the dark horde. He flew westward to the edge of the forest, here troops of black horsemen fought an uneven battle against a small number of men on foot. Kerran turned then to the east. He returned to the Crossroads and flew towards Mendan-Var, there was no fatigue and his shadow flew with great speed now, and knew where it wished to go, and what it wanted to see. A large army lay in camp around the old city and the ruined castle, there was no doubt that Maradass now controlled the two Northern Regions, but strangely was not preparing to march further to the south it seemed. Kerran watched the gathered troops for a time, and then he was able to return to the ship's cabin. It was a slow easy awakening and later he spoke to Tolth of what he had seen.

"I know it is true and that what I saw is happening now," he said to his old friend. "For some reason the Black Army has stopped and made camp north of the Crossroads."

Tolth pondered Kerran's words. "If Maradass waits for us then it can only be to our advantage, and we may have time to prepare," he said. "We cannot meet his force in open battle, but there are many ways to fight a war, it is vital though that we join with Torian and our other troops."

The following morning the fleet stood off from the Far Isles as a small sail boat was lowered with four strong men on board. They sailed across the heavy swell and entered a yawning gap between high cliffs. Gulls swooped above them, crying angrily at their presence.

"They will be some time," said Captain Ronsarl.

They stood by the rail and watched the small craft disappear from view. It was not until the early evening that the small boat limped out from the dark cleft and made its way back to the ship. Its mast was shattered and only two men were able to row, the others lay in the bottom of the boat hurt and bloody, but still alive. The two uninjured men reported to Captain Ronsarl and then one of them came below to the Amitarl cabin where he told their story.

"Going in was no problem," he said. "A nice turn of wind and we were there. The fleet is still at anchor and manned, but the army has gone, they left for the mainland twelve days ago. The sea lost the red poison and Commander Torian took his chance, the army should now be in a hidden camp well to the north of the city."

"I doubt they will remain hidden for long," said Tolth looking at Captain Ronsarl who nodded. "We will join them by sailing for the South Coast."

Early the following morning Kerran went aloft, enjoying the freshness of the breeze. Rark was already on deck, kindly souls amongst the crew having seen to his needs. Storm flew amongst the sea birds, causing panic as he swooped through a cloud of gulls, and Kerran watched as tall forbidding cliffs passed by the ship. They had caught a fair wind and the fleet sailed from the Far Isles towards the beaches and towns of the South Coast. Kerran stood by the ship's rail and watched the waves breaking against the bow, there was wonder and fear in his thoughts. It was but three seasons since he had stood in the forest and watched two knights fight to the death. From the person he was then, to where he stood now, seemed like a lifetime and more had passed.

"Who am I really?" he spoke the words softly and paused, but no answer came except the sound of the waves.

He decided to experiment with his powers to see if he could unravel any further secrets. So far the most impressive thing he seemed to have done was send metal objects into another time. He held a small knife, designed so that the blade retracted into the steel hilt, and he concentrated. It took only moments to connect with the inner unknown part of himself. The knife vanished. Then he looked to the distant cliffs slipping away behind them. Silently he willed Storm to come to him, but the bird seemed more interested in the gull's nests on the high places. Kerran thought of Tolth sitting below in study, his mind went to the books there and he decided to see if he could move them. In his mind he saw the table cluttered with a number of volumes, he picked one up in his thoughts and turned it over. He imagined two more floating, doing slow circles above the table, then he felt foolish and replaced them. Though even this felt absurd as he did not think that it could have worked. It was only moments before Tolth was on deck. He walked to where Kerran was standing, a quizzical smile on his face.

"Have you been playing with my library?" he asked, coming to stand beside his young friend.

"It worked," smiled Kerran, surprised. "I did not expect it to."

"What else have you been moving about and levitating?" asked the old Amitarl.

"Nothing except a small knife that Manzanee will probably find some time soon in his cave," replied Kerran.

Tolth chuckled and inhaled deeply of the salt sea air. "Your powers unravel, but there is no textbook on how to be a wizard," he said.

"Do you truly think I am a wizard?" asked Kerran.

A descendant of Chelasta he was certain of, but the thought had never actually entered his mind that he may be a wizard. Yes, he was convinced of his ancestry, but to be called a Wizard was a very strange thing to him.

"From Chelasta you have inherited the wizard's line," replied Tolth gazing into the blue distance. "Somehow it was preserved and nurtured until this time. You are young, Kerran, and by wizard's standards you are barely an apprentice. The problem is that there are no teachers to show you the path."

Tolth thought for a time. "Your dreams are a part of your power," he said. "Your dreams and visions have shed light on a stage which was dark. Do not push yourself, for I feel that time will eventually reveal all of the answers. Follow your intuition. It is a most important friend. Take your time but do not hesitate, that is my advice, young Chelasta." They stood together for a time in silence then Tolth returned to his studies. "I do not expect to find books doing acrobatic turns when I get there," he called back from the hatchway.

Kerran watched the sails as they curved gracefully with the wind. Crewmen were at their work and a number of the green and brown clad soldiers were also on deck. Several were grouped together playing a game of dice, and a small stringed instrument was being tuned somewhere aft. The day became warmer, the happenings on deck more boisterous with laughter. Those on board did not disturb him with questions, for they knew that he had been unwell. Kerran listened to the songs, the words conjuring up places and people that he had never seen. When a particularly sad and mellow story was told in song he thought of Piata, then a powerful ballad took him into a world of strife and war, a time when the Mad One held sway in three regions, and Celisor, the castle builder, fought against him on the Central Plains.

Kerran sat with Rark, warm and comfortable together, listening to the tales. The next day would be midsummer's day and his thoughts went to his mother, each year on this day there was a fair in the town of Westerval. Indeed the festival was held in many parts of the Four Regions. His mother would sell the weaving which she had done during the previous year, but she never had time she had often said, to do enough. A pang of loneliness invaded his heart and mind. Rark lifted his great head and laid it on Kerran's lap as if knowing of his sadness.

The fleet sailed on across the placid sea, and Tolth had explained that they would not enter the port of the City Amitarl. He did not wish to disturb the people with fears of an invasion. Nothing had been heard of the Amitarl family for centuries and to most the stories had become myth, told to the young ones before bed. When Darna Amitarl had sailed from the lands he had left no more than the history of Amitarl behind, and the people who remained in the Regions had no time to remember those who had gone. Darna had departed in the hope that all would be well. The Governor he had left had been an honest and caring man, but Darna would have been disappointed had he known that the situation in the Regions had not improved at all over the centuries. Governor had replaced Governor, and corruption had replaced hope, heavy taxes had been levied on the country people, the farmers who supplied the cities. The Highroads were not safe from thieves and wild dogs, while most villages and towns stood behind walls of packed earth and logs. The decadence in the cities was renowned. In Mendan-Var it was a Council that ruled, while the Governor alone held court in the City Amitarl.

"I expect problems with the Governor," Tolth said as they discussed the situation that night.

They had been joined from another ship by a man who Kerran remembered from the Council on Zeta. He was Mantris, a slim dark man who was the commander of this second force, which now sailed to Andrian.

"We must be careful not to have the city fear us," said Commander Mantris. "After all, we will probably appear to be an invading army. We must have their assistance not their opposition. Food and horses we will need, the second most quickly. The Elbrand must be mounted, for we cannot compete on foot."

Kerran then learned from Commander Mantris what some of their strategy would be should they find the Southlands still open to them. As soon as some of the Elbrand were mounted they would ride north, gathering news of the enemy. If they came upon small numbers of the enemy troops they were to attack, but only to win horses. From Kerran's description of the Maradass armies Tolth knew that perhaps one in twenty of the real men rode horseback. It was not yet known what the stone faced army was, but none had been seen to mount a horse. To even up the numbers of horse troops a little would be vital in the battles to come, and no one knew how well the strange stone soldiers would fight. A network of scouts and runners would be quickly set up to gather further information from all parts of the Southlands. Dreardim Forest was an enigma, full of ancient stories of terror and danger, but also of possible advantage to the troops of Zeta. Only in the north, in the Region of Rianodar, had people and their dwellings penetrated any distance into the forest.

"The Central Plains are broken with bogs and marshlands," said Mantris. "It is not the battleground of old, but will serve us much better I think. We have trained for living in such land. There is much to eat there, and many ways to fight and hide in such country. The people of the Regions fly south and food will soon be a problem. We can feed ourselves for a time, but supplies must be found if the war is not won quickly, and except by magic I doubt that it can. The ships now at anchor at the Far Isles will return to Zeta on the next favourable tide and replenish our stores as well as bringing further troops, but they will not return for a full moon or more, and by then we could be blockaded within the city itself, or driven far from the coast."

"I do not wish to occupy the city," said Tolth. "It must defend itself or the Governor invites us in."

"The mountains to the south are also a place of refuge," continued the commander. "It is now high summer and game will not be scarce, though our troops will take some time in getting used to eating wild goat and rabbit."

The meeting ended and Kerran went to his cabin to find that his other bunk mates were there. Two of them slept while the third deftly stitched a hole in his heavy sea jacket.

"What be the nod?" he asked Kerran as he entered.

"The nod be that the times are not easy, even though the war is not yet begun," replied Kerran. "I fear for those who take arms against Maradass."

"Ah! Do not fear for us of Zeta," replied the man confidently. "Though we have not fought in battle for hundreds of years we are a strong people, and can endure much. We have trained for this time, knowing that some day Maradass would march to war. Do not fear. He will run skulking when the Elbrand have chewed on his army for a while."

He chuckled at the imagery and continued his careful stitching. Kerran lay back. He felt tired and was soon lost in dreams.

Kerran sat again before the low burning fire, facing the darkness at the back of Manzanee's cave. The firelight illuminated the face of the old dark skinned wizard, and there was a quizzical look in his eyes and silence for a long while.

"The time approaches," said Manzanee finally. "A time when your powers will truly be tested." Smiling he handed Kerran the small knife across the fire. "There is little you can yet do to affect the flow of the game," he said. "There are many forces gathering and not all are yet in play. Take care, young Chel-a-Sta. The future is not set in stone, and the possibilities are magnified by the numbers who play."

Manzanee grew silent and thoughtful as Kerran searched his mind for a question. "No," said the Black Wizard abruptly. "There is much that I would have you know, but do not ask, for time has changed and you may no longer learn these things from me, except at your great peril. You are alone young Chel-a-Sta, and my words can do as much harm as they might do good. I will watch for you. Look for me in dark shadows."

Manzanee held Kerran's gaze for several moments, his wide staring eyes attempting to will an understanding into Kerran's mind, and then the cave went dark as the fire crumbled into ashes and was gone. Kerran woke in the darkness of his cabin, the small knife held in his hand, he lay awake until dawn glimmered through the porthole, then he made his way on deck, the cloudless blue sky a welcome sailing companion.

To the north was Andrian, Kerran knew, though the captain sailed far from the coast as they did not wish Maradass to hear of their arrival just yet. Once they had landed it would not be long before their presence was known to his black armies. Tolth sought to delay that time for as long as possible, and their arrival was not expected to be until sometime the following afternoon. The bell from the galley sounded at the same moment as his stomach told him it would appreciate some food.

The day remained clear with the afternoon sun beating down upon the bare backs of the sailors as they went about their duties. It seemed that all of the soldiers from below had come on deck to enjoy the perfect day. It was not easy for the crew but they managed with a smile. The voyage was almost over and their friends and kin were soon to go to war. There would be few easy days such as this in the long campaign to come.

The warm day turned to a clear star clustered evening, and there was no moon to detract from the marvel of the bejewelled sky. Above the south-eastern horizon, rising into the night sky, hung the constellation of the Six Sorcerers as if it were an omen; though for good or ill none dared predict. The night seemed to last forever and Kerran woke several times to the darkness of his cabin. Once he felt the ship change course, a slow creaking of the hull, as they moved to a more westerly tack. Dawn came and Kerran rose and took his breakfast on deck. Tolth soon joined him and they spoke of the times to come.

"I will go to the city and request a council with the Governor," said Tolth. "I would like you to come with me. I am sure that the Governor will not refuse us. He will want to know as much about us as he can. I do not wish to threaten him. I wish to bargain. If he is at all a reasonable man he will listen, for he could not hold out against Maradass alone. If he has an army, they will be but a gang of villains by the descriptions we had from Flindas. He told me once that Dantas could make little way in teaching them anything, their lack of discipline being inherited over the centuries. No enemy could be imagined I suppose. Maradass had left the lands and Amitarl had sailed to the east. Mendan-Var had been crushed and the castle in ruins. There was no threat from any quarter, so the Governor and his favoured friends of the court grew rich and fat and indolent. Flindas did not expect much from the City Amitarl if it ever came to war."

"Why do you think Maradass has not yet taken the city?" asked Kerran.

"I do not know," replied Tolth. "No matter what the reason it has given us time that is precious, and we must not waste it."

Tolth remained on deck for much of the day. He was restless now that they were so near to Andrian and his ancestral home. The sun had not yet reached its zenith when there was a call from aloft. They were again in sight of the coast.

The fleet sailed directly to the west now and in the distance they began to make out the nature of the coastline and inland terrain. By mid afternoon they were close to the shore, where rocky headlands led into small sandy bays, dotted with houses and small villages. There were fishermen out in small boats who sat aghast as the fleet sailed by. A large open bay was soon found where the ships could all lie safely at anchor. Kerran stood at the rail as he watched the sails being furled, anchors dropping into the clear depths of the bay.

"Would you care to be one of the first ashore?" asked Tolth as he came from below deck. "The long boats are being lowered. Come, let us feel some earth beneath our feet. Ocean travel is hard on a body and I would stretch my legs on the shores of Andrian."

They made their way down the ship's side and into one of the boats. Kerran was joined by Rark who seemed unperturbed as he was lowered by rope and harness onto the boat. Several Elbrand warriors sat with them and they were rowed to the pebbly beach. They had been seen by a number of people on shore, a fishing village stood to the northern end of the beach and now a great many people had begun to gather. There was much pointing and cries of wonder from the fisher folk. Some approached down the beach but would not come very close.

The longboats began to arrive, crunching on the pebbles and sand as they reached the shore. Together Kerran and Rark leapt from the boat and waded to the beach. Standing on the shoreline Kerran felt his body continue to move and sway with the ship that was no longer there. He suddenly felt light hearted, as though an unknown depression had lain on him aboard the ship. He wished to run along the beach, or climb amongst the low hills that lay near the coast. Rark gambolled about as if he was a puppy and Kerran laughed. The smell of the land was euphoric, and pockets of bushland and forest grew down close to the ocean. Kerran wished to walk in their shadows and hear the familiar birdcalls of his home. He walked a little further up the beach.

"Do not go far," called Tolth. "We do not yet know the situation here."

He joined Kerran and watched as a group of people came down towards them from the village, they stopped at some distance. Many held large dogs on tight leashes and Rark eyed them watchfully.

"What do you here?" one called across the space between them.

"I am Tolth Amitarl," he called back. "We come in peace and to defend the people and lands from Maradass."

The people murmured, casting looks of dismay at those who had landed, and at the tall ships in the bay. A smaller group of three men came forward, slowly.

"Amitarl you say," called a rotund man who wore more refined clothes than the two burly fishermen beside him. "Amitarl is a city and you are not from Amitarl I think. Where do you come from?" His arrogance was just managing to quell the fear he felt as many well armed soldiers continued to land on the beach.

"We come from the Isles of Zeta," replied Tolth, which caused the fat officious man to break into convulsive laughter.

"You are from a place of children's fables," he called back. "You say you come to save us. What would you save us from pray tell?"

The look on Tolth's face told of his astonishment. "Do you not know that Maradass has massed armies on the northern borders of Andrian?" he asked incredulous.

"Oh that!" exclaimed the man. "That is all over. Maradass is making peace with the Governor. Maradass only wanted his

old city back, and the North Regions. He is welcome to them
as far as I care. Infested rat holes so I hear. No! Whoever you
are and wherever you come from, you had best return the way
you came."

Tolth wanted to discover more of this pact between Maradass
and the Governor. "What of Rianodar?" he asked, walking a
little further up the beach. "Has the Governor conceded all to
Maradass?"

"Yes," was the reply. "No use anyway, too far to collect real
taxes. People up there live wild mostly. Maradass can have
them."

"The armies of Maradass are vast," spoke Tolth. "Why do
you think he does not take all of the Regions?"

"He has enough maybe," the man replied. "He saw the south
country rising against him and thought better of it."

It was now Tolth's turn to smile. "You put great faith in your
ability to repel the vast army of Maradass," he said. "He will
not stop at the Crossroads for long. As for us, we will not leave
these lands until we have spoken with the Governor, and then
it will be to march north, not to sail away. We will not disturb
your village, and if you have horses for sale we will pay in gold."

At the word 'gold' the spokesman's eyes lit up. "Gold is it?"
he smiled. "Horses? Yes, we have horses, fine animals."

"Bring them to us in the morning," said Tolth. "Then we will
bargain."

The fat man looked once more at the soldiers and stores
that were beginning to clutter the beach. His greed could not
be disguised. "I am Maldara, I am an official of the Governor,"
he spoke importantly. "You will deal with me in this matter,
no one else." He turned and walked back towards the crowd of
villagers.

"Not the welcome I had hoped for," said Tolth, an amused
tone in his voice, then his manner became most serious. "Why
indeed has Maradass not yet taken the Southern Regions?" he
said. "There is nothing here to stop him."

"Perhaps he wishes to have all the players in the game
before he brings it to total war," said Kerran. "When Manzanee
spoke to me he said there were other forces gathering."

"Yes," said Tolth. "Your dream vision of Leana alive, and the whereabouts of Landin may be part of the reason behind his delay. Another reason may be that he now waits for Zard to come. It is now high summer. In no more than two moons the Maradass sons will be born. One moon later Zard will be able to join the black army. This may be what has caused his troops to delay their march south. It is of great advantage to us no matter what the cause, and we will make use of it."

Tolth paused for a moment in thought, and then he chuckled at the thought. "Perhaps there is something else to our advantage in his delay," he told Kerran with a strange smile. "Maradass will never be a wizard, yet I think he may want to follow them in thought and action. The wizards played games with their forces, matching one against the other. This war may be just a game to Maradass. He may be playing with us like a cat with a mouse. He is so sure of his victory that he will take his time, but there is an unknown factor that he has not yet seen and cannot yet comprehend, something that he has not included in his plans."

Kerran looked at his old friend with a questioning look and Tolth smiled knowingly.

"Maradass has yet to see how well our small green army can fight," he said, still smiling.

The ships continued to unload soldiers and cargo onto the beach. Kerran helped carry sacks and boxes of food from the pebbly sands to a low hill a little further inland. It would be their base camp for some days. Pack horses would also be sought to transport the food and other supplies. The hillock overlooked the gardens of the small village which were securely fenced against the invasion of the many goats and pigs which lived around them. The place itself was spread along a stream which flowed through the valley.

A great many people now stood and watched as the army arrived. Dogs would howl at the sight of Rark as he followed Kerran from beach to hill. On his third trip Kerran noticed two small children peering through the fence at the unusual happenings before them. They were no older than six or seven years and showed no great fear when Kerran and Rark approached them.

"Hello," called Kerran.

"He may be big but he is friendly," he said as he saw the children eyeing the great hairy beast beside him. "Would you like to meet him?"

The pair of roughly dressed children leapt to their feet and came forward as Rark sat and greeted them by letting them stroke and pat his back and shoulders.

"Do you really come from Zeta?" said the boy, his face a smear of dirt and large teeth.

"Yes, we come from Zeta, but I was born in Glandrin," replied Kerran. "You know where that is, do you not?"

Both children pointed to the west.

'The sun comes up in Andrian and Glandrin sees it set', they chanted from an old children's rhyme.

"Why have you come?" asked the equally grubby girl. "My sister said you come to fight Maradass. He has magic. He will win, and then you be dead. My sister says the Gov'nor promised to protect us. She says you better go home now because Maradass gets angry and make war if you stay."

"Tell your sister that Maradass will make war on Andrian even if we had not come," said Kerran. "He is evil and wants all the land."

The children looked frightened.

"I not want to be in a war," said the little girl. She seemed about to cry.

Kerran knelt beside her. "Do not worry," he said. "We will not let Maradass win, and we have some magic too."

"What magic? What magic?" they called out, their eyes alive, excited.

"Different magic," said Kerran. "Secret magic. You will see that Maradass will not have it all his own way."

He left the children and returned to the beach where the unloading continued for the remainder of the day, and into the evening. Cooking fires were lit and there was warmth and company for those camped there on a foreign shore. Kerran was glad to have returned to the lands of his birth, and he slept by a fire on the hillock amongst the soldiers of Zeta. The camp was well astir the next morning when Maldara, the Governor's official arrived, riding a tall and beautiful stallion. In his train came a line of horses led by a number of men from the village. The soldiers of Zeta came closer to inspect their marvellous fortune. Here truly were excellent steeds. None could fault them except their number; no more than ten animals were being made available to them.

"The purest quality," said the fat official disdaining to leave his saddle. "I will not quibble with you, one hundred gold pieces for each horse; that is my price."

Tolth mused for a moment before speaking. "On Zeta we do not use money, but we have gold," he said. "Show me if you will a gold piece, so that I can judge its weight."

Maldara laughed aloud. "No money indeed," he smirked. "You surely must come from the Nursery Tales."

He reached into his pouch and cast a small coin to the ground; Kerran retrieved it and passed it to Tolth.

"Bit young for a warrior," said the official with amusement.

Tolth weighed the coin in his hand. "Yes," he said "I will not argue the price."

In the same moment he cast the coin back towards the official. The arc of the throw was graceful and the coin landed unexpectedly upon the man's protruding stomach. Maldara clasped it before it could fall. He looked suddenly perplexed and unsure. Tolth brought forth the gold in small even bars.

"Five gold bars," he said to the official. "More than you ask."

The man sat, eyeing the gold, his greed taking over all other thought.

"We will need wagons and horses to draw them," said Tolth. "These mounts are not made as draught animals."

"That is not possible," said Maldara, and he was truly sorry that he could not provide more.

He saw that these fools from Zeta did not know the value of gold, and seemed to have much to give away. He thought too of the amazing luck that had come his way so recently, firstly his sudden rise to the post of village official with the demise of his superior; then the horses had come. The horses, that belonged to the Governor, had been taken in the night from closed and guarded pastures by clever thieves, and then sold through a chain of hands to his brother, a dealer in what was known as 'Unofficial Business.' Then had come this old man and his bars of gold. Maldara smiled. He was now a wealthy man, and he felt all important and secure astride his tall mount.

"There are no other horses in the village," he said. "It is fortunate for you that my own private stable could supply these. You have made a good bargain." Then he laughed openly, enjoying his joke immensely, as his men transferred the gold to his saddlebags. "We must do business again," he said, and rode away still laughing, his men following behind.

"That was much gold," said Kerran, his memory returning to a time when his father had let him hold a single gold piece in his hands. *We will not see many of these in our lives*, his father had said. Kerran also remembered when Flindas had bought a small seaworthy boat for a tenth of the cost of one horse.

"Yes, it was a high price, but gold is of little use to us," replied Tolth. "There is much gold still on Zeta, though it was heavily mined many centuries ago. It can buy us what we need in these lands and that is the important thing. Now we have the means to reach the city quickly. We are perhaps twenty or thirty leagues away and can be there by nightfall or camp and arrive at dawn. Prepare to leave, Kerran. I have matters to attend to before we go."

Kerran collected his small pack and bedroll. He would not carry a sword. At his belt he wore his hunting knife, and in his pocket he carried his sling and a few select stones. He was dressed as usual in stout boots, breeches, a strong woven shirt and a warm tunic. Tolth had asked if he would like to take on the light armour of the Elbrand but he had declined. He would survive best he thought, not dressed as a fighter, which he surely was not. His tunic was brown and green as was all the clothing worn by the soldiers, for travelling undetected would play a crucial part in the times to come.

Saddles and bridles were brought from the stores of Zeta and the horses were made ready. Soon Tolth joined him and those others who were to ride. They mounted and prepared to depart. Seven would go to the City Amitarl. With Tolth and

Kerran rode Mantris, the army commander and four of the elite Elbrand. Tolth consented to have Rark join them and they were soon on their way, they clattered over the bridge which crossed the stream and followed the dry, dusty road that led them by the village. People gaped as they rode by, while some hid behind doorways and curtains, afraid of the strange army from a land long forgotten.

They left the village behind, moving at a canter along the narrow dirt road which would eventually lead them to the City Highroad and then to the city itself. There were few other travellers on the road. Occasionally a wagon of produce would slow their ride, or tired refugees from the north would leap from the road as if they expected to be trampled by the horsemen. A ragged man who travelled towards the coast told them that many people had been forced from the north and were travelling into Andrian. Most, like him, had lost all that they had owned. He travelled now to the coast, hoping to find a place amongst the fisher folk.

Late in the day they reached the Highroad. It was not as congested as Kerran had seen in his dream. They joined the road and began to move more slowly towards the City Amitarl. They would camp before dark and reach the city the following morning, entering a strange place by night did not seem wise, even with the Elbrand to guard them. A group of trees in a small valley gave them a concealed place for the night beneath the stars, and Kerran slept soundly for the first time since leaving Zeta.

The City Amitarl

Another day of bright sunshine and blue skies greeted Kerran as they returned to the Highroad, and travelled the last few leagues to the City Amitarl. The number of villages and small towns began to increase and they were noticed and pointed out as they rode past, Rark causing many a wondrous and fearful look as he loped by. Soon they were caught up in the daily traffic outside the city walls. Tolth admired the stonework of his ancestors, which remained as strong now as it had those hundreds of years before. He looked above the city to where, on a high rocky buttress sat Celisor Castle, its pale stone glaring in the sunlight.

Kerran looked in awe upon the castle which appeared to hang suspended in the sky above the city. The only way to ascend to its iron gates was by a narrow roadway carved into the side of the rocky plateau. The castle was beautiful thought Kerran and on Zeta he had not seen anything to compare, the outer walls towered above the rock face and above these were yet more walls. Higher still and seeming to pierce the clouds were three towers. Kerran sensed that this castle could never be taken by force. only surrender or starvation could end a siege of such an impregnable fortress.

They were now amongst the many that were entering the city that day. The road was congested with people and horse drawn wagons with families coming to sell their wares in the city markets. The gate was not unguarded, six large men, heavily clad in leather, armour and chain mail, were lounging upon a low wall beside the gate. More intent upon talking to the young women in the crowd than watching for anything suspicious, they made an exception of Tolth and his following. The group stood out from those around them: the old man, the boy, the dog, and the five well armed men riding horses from their Governor's own stables. Suddenly the guards were on their feet, barring the gateway with their spears.

"Hold there!" one demanded of them, a captain it seemed. "What do you here old man with your stolen horses? Speak quickly, or receive the sentence of all horse thieves." He brandished his spear threateningly.

"I am Tolth Amitarl," said the old man. "I come to speak with the Governor."

"With the Governor you would speak is it?" replied the man, a haughty sneer in his words. "Do you have an appointment? The Governor does not speak to just anyone."

His fellows at the gate smiled at their captain's jesting manner.

"I bring him news to his advantage," spoke Tolth calmly.

"News to his advantage," mused the man, his men laughed now, their captain was good at such banter. "Would that be the news that you have come here to save the lands from the dreaded Maradass." He leered knowingly. "Oh yes, we have been expecting you," the captain continued. "But you have wasted your time old man. Maradass has what he wants and the Governor is busy today."

"What!" cried Tolth, his anger flashing across the space between them. "You tell me that the Governor is busy when your lives are in the greatest jeopardy? When all these lands are under dire threat from an army you could never hope to conquer? I am tired of your words. I will see the Governor."

Tolth's hand reached out before him, a pointed finger stabbing at the captain who dropped his weapon and cowered back in fear. Tolth's commanding voice caused the other guards to stand quickly, though they did not seem to know what they should do.

"You will go to the Governor and tell him that I am here," Tolth told them impatiently. "You will say that I am Tolth Amitarl, and that I have with me gold and gems as a gift of friendship. Tell him, and then return with his answer. We will wait here at the gate."

The man seemed stricken, and left his comrades standing foolishly as he ran quickly into the city. The group dismounted and left the roadway. A rocky shelf nearby the gate gave them a place to stand apart from those entering and leaving the city.

"What did you do to that man?" asked Kerran, still surprised at the change which had come over the guard, and indeed the change that had also come over his old friend.

"I merely showed him something that changed his mind," said Tolth, smiling mysteriously.

Kerran was silent, for if Tolth wished to tell him more Kerran knew that he would.

"I showed him his fear," said Tolth, finally. "Whatever his real fear may be, I conjured it from his inner mind to his conscious thoughts. He felt or saw that which he fears most." Tolth paused for a moment. "There are few who do not have fear," he told Kerran. "There are even fewer who can bring it forth in another's mind. It is a power I have that is inherited, and does not come from the Seacrest. My mother was, as you know, not of natural birth. She came from the ocean, from the Elveren, and she remained with my father unto her death. Some of her powers passed to me, but they do not come without cost. To use them is to sap my own human strengths for it weakens my body and my ability to hold a clear mind. That was a small thing that I made happen at the gate. I have not had to use these powers on Zeta, and in reality I do not yet know their true strengths."

He became silent and thoughtful and Kerran left him, going to stand nearer the gate so as to watch those who passed. He stood with Rark against the stone wall and watched the procession of people. He did not notice the two Elbrand move away from the others and come to stand where they could watch Kerran, and ensure no harm came to him. The people entering the city seemed to be growers of vegetables and makers of other foods. Bread and cheese was in abundance. Occasionally three or four wagons would trundle through, taking loads of hay to the city stables. Chickens and ducks arrived in cages stacked high on wagons, while goats and pigs were herded by to meet the butcher's knife. Those who left the castle at this time of day were few. Kerran watched as a horse and open carriage came from the gate and passed by. Seated within the polished and luxurious vehicle sat four stiff faced men. Their attire was of the most expensive kind, and they carried with them a look of the greatest self importance. They neither looked to the side nor acknowledged any in their way. People scattered as the carriage rushed through the gateway and travelled down the road.

Others who came from the gates were not so well attired. A man in rags stumbled from the gate and fell into the dirt. None helped him, and he lay still as the people moved around him, uncaring. Kerran saw one of the guards move toward the prone figure and for a moment he thought the guard would help the man on his way, but no, the guard stood over the ragged creature and screamed at him. When the man still did not move the guard kicked him viciously, and then dragged him from the road to lie against the wall. After a time the ragged man began to move, crawling along the very side of the road he made his way slowly towards the place where Kerran sat. As he came closer Kerran could see that the man's face was heavily scarred from many beatings. Fresh blood could be seen around his mouth, and his left eye was almost closed, a huge bruise covering his cheek and forehead. Pity shook Kerran to his core when he saw that the man crawled down the road on just one hand. The other had been lost at the wrist, the stump gnarled and scarred. Kerran waited as the man came nearer, his tortured breath panting with the strain of moving. When the man saw Kerran he was no more than a few paces away. He stopped and spoke, his words coming fitfully from a broken mouth.

"Would you have a crust for an old man?" he asked.

"I would," replied Kerran and quickly returned to his horse.

From the saddlebag he took a small loaf, a piece of cheese and his water bottle back to the man.

"Here," said Kerran. "Sit and eat."

The man took the cheese as though it was a most precious gift. "Thank you, young master," he said with great humility. "This is the kindest deed that has come my way for a very long time."

His mouth became full as he swallowed the food in a hurry for it to reach his shrunken belly. He drank water from the bottle, washing each mouthful down. He ate it all to the very last crumbs which had fallen upon his clothing.

"Life does not treat you well," said Kerran, and then felt foolish at his words. The man heard nothing wrong in what Kerran had said and leaned his back against the wall, the day a little easier now that his hunger had been satisfied.

"Life is not expected to be easy for one such as me," he said, and held up his tortured arm.

"How did you lose it?" asked Kerran, though he seemed to know the answer before he asked.

"I was a thief," the man said. "Not much, just food and a few small things to sell. This here is the punishment." He looked with curiosity at Kerran. "How is it that you do not know what I am?" he asked his young benefactor.

"I do not come from here," said Kerran. "I am from a quiet corner of Glandrin. The city has always been but a distant place to me."

"You see that carriage that came out before me?" said the old man. "The four nobs in their finery? They be the real thieves. They be the ones want lopping off a hand or two. They wring the taxes from the country folk, and then mutilate us for stealing some back."

"Why do you come to the city?" asked Kerran. "What can be here for you?"

"Little," replied the man with a sigh. "There is little here for a hungry thief tis true, but out there be nothing." He waved his arm to indicate the countryside. "The city be the only place where there might be a few scraps left over after the dogs have eaten their fill. The city be rich, and feeds its dogs well." He chuckled, though no real humour sounded in his voice. He then managed to stand and began to make his way past Kerran and into the roadway again. "I thank you again young master," he said. "Retain your kindness through the rest of your life and you will enjoy a kindly death."

The man stumbled once, and then continued to make his way through the heat and dust down the roadway. Kerran could see then that Tolth and the Elbrand were beginning to move.

"The messenger returns!" called Tolth and pointed to the gate.

Indeed the captain had re-emerged, and with him came ten or more of his comrades. They were all large and brutish men, obviously picked for these qualities by the Governor and his court, each bore a sword and a long spear. Tolth moved towards the captain who could be seen to tremble a little at his approach.

"You are to come with us," the captain announced, his voice an attempt at bravery. "Leave your weapons and horses here."

"We will not leave our weapons and horses unguarded," said Tolth. "We will have three of our men stay here and I will come unarmed with three others."

The man was not pleased. "You must all come, those are the orders," he blurted out.

"Then I will not come until the orders are changed," said Tolth, and turned to go.

"It is not your choice," screamed the man, now angry and perplexed.

"I will come on my own terms," said Tolth, turning back to him, his voice carrying a calm threat. "That is my choice. Go back to your Governor and tell him so."

The man trembled now, whether in anger or fear one could not say. "Seize them!" he finally called.

"No!" called Tolth loudly, his finger now pointing at the man.

It was enough to stop the captain as though he were frozen, an expectant look of fear on his face. The other men stopped their advance, not understanding their captain's hesitation.

"No," said Tolth more quietly now, looking intently at the terrified man. "Go back to your Governor and state my requirements, or take me with three others to see him now. It is your choice." Tolth lowered his arm and waited for the man's reply.

"I will take you now," the captain finally managed to say. No longer was there any bravery in his voice. "Leave three men with the horses as you wish," he whispered.

Mantris and another of the Elbrand quickly stripped themselves of their weapons. Bows, swords, and knives were given into the care of the three who would remain behind. Kerran gave over his hunting knife. There was a cursory search which revealed nothing, though the Elbrand still carried several small throwing knives amongst their clothing. Rark remained with those at the gate as Kerran found himself being marched with the others into the City Amitarl.

They walked up a wide road between tall elegantly carved buildings, many were in disrepair but that did not lessen the wonder and admiration which Kerran felt for the craftsmen who had created such works. The roadway was of stone, worn over the years into curved depressions by the innumerable feet and wagons that had walked that way. The people he saw did not match the elegance and style of the buildings. Most were drab and dirty, except for the occasional over dressed merchant or lawyer, who would watch with curious disdain as the group from Zeta was marched by.

Eventually they came to a wide open square where fine sculpture and highly carved buildings looked down on the clutter and mayhem of the city market place. They were looked at from all sides, their garb being most curious, and the accompanying guards showing that something interesting was afoot. Eventually they came to the narrow road which took them to the castle high above. Kerran looked down on the city as it fell away below them. He could see to the south and west the wide harbour, alive with many small fishing boats setting their sails to catch the tide. All had been a great bustle of noise when they passed through the streets but now it was quieter.

Tolth began to tell Kerran of the city's history and founders. The guards did not interrupt, wishing themselves to hear what Tolth had to say.

"Much of this coastal land was old Barthol's domain," said Tolth pointing outwards to the sweep of land where it met the ocean. "He began the early Amitarl Township a few leagues along the coast to the east. The city grew up around the port as trade came here from the South Coast, and from as far away as Mendan Maradass. Some ship owners chanced the Outer Ocean to avoid the ports of Shardis and their taxes. The most fertile land is to the north and east of here, land which Amitarl caused to be the food supply for much of the Regions. Then came the Mad One, and the city, which had become wondrous over the centuries, was walled in and protected. Celisor built the castle as a final defence, but fortunes changed. Maradass suffered heavy defeats from the Amitarl armies after Zard lost his fearful powers, and the family of Maradass was finally driven from the land." Tolth looked above at the castle which stood towering and strong, overlooking the city and plains. "Perhaps the workmanship of Celisor will be tested now by the Mad One's brother," he said.

The day was hot and still, and Kerran was pleased when the climb ended. They reached a single span wooden bridge which crossed a deep cleft in the road to the opposite cliff face. The bridge could be drawn upward to isolate the castle from attack. Their feet echoed on the hardwood planking as they walked towards the tall elegant gateway. The huge iron doors stood wide. They were led into an inner courtyard where a large stable took up much of the crowded space. Guardsmen sat about playing games of chance, or lay asleep amongst the piles of hay. All stopped what they were doing and looked at the new arrivals.

"So this is them," sneered a dark bearded giant from a seat against the inner castle wall. "Not much like warriors from what I see," he spat on the stone before him.

"They are not to be molested," called the captain as he entered a doorway, leaving Kerran and the others to wait.

Some of the escort drifted away while others sat and

watched the group with no great concern. The large bearded man stood and nudged two of his comrades.

"These are no warriors," he called out, stepping across a sleeping guardsman and coming toward them.

Several of those watching began to smile. It was a familiar game of Marlto's, this prisoner baiting. The large guardsman came and stood before Kerran and Tolth.

"An old man and a boy, what use are you in a fight?" Kerran felt fear of this armoured giant until Tolth laid a hand gently on his shoulder.

"Perhaps no good at all," said Tolth amicably, a small smile flickering at the corners of his mouth.

"Huh!" exclaimed the man. "Just as I thought, useless! And what are you?" he said as he turned to Mantris, his words and manner threatening.

"I am a warrior of Zeta," Mantris said simply.

"I am a warrior of Zeta," the man mimicked the words of Mantris and received hooted laughter from those who watched.

"Go on Marlto," called one from the crowd, pushing his friend to continue his game. "Find out what our warrior can do."

The men laughed as Marlto pushed Mantris in the chest.

"We are here at the Governor's request," said Tolth. "It is not a fight we have come to seek."

"Quiet old man," spat Marlto. "Governor's request," he sneered. "You are prisoners, and we get to have fun with prisoners." He leered and returned to Mantris, pushing much harder this time against the chest of the Elbrand commander.

"Do not do that again," said the Elbrand commander.

'There is a limit to diplomacy,' Mantris thought as with the next violent push of the man's hand, he turned the giant guard aside. With ease he threw the much larger man heavily to the ground, a strangulation hold almost cutting off the air to the guard's lungs.

"Do not struggle," said Mantris calmly. "I could break your neck before you took another breath."

The man went limp. Mantris held him for a moment longer then stood slowly and rejoined the others. There was silence amongst the guards. No one had thrown Marlto for as long as they had known him. They watched in silence as the tall guardsman lifted himself from the ground and stood seething, seeming ready to continue the fight. His intent was interrupted by the return of the captain from the Governor.

"You are to follow me," he said brusquely, unaware of the tension around the courtyard.

He led them through a doorway and up a long flight of broad stairs. Four guardsmen following as they climbed. They passed along wide arched hallways, and were eventually led through a magnificently carved doorway, and then they entered the large hall where the Governor held court. Though the rest of the castle had appeared austere without any great display of adornment, here it was otherwise. Many gay colours crowded in on Kerran's vision. There were long looping drops of the finest cloth draped across highly decorated walls, scenes of hunts and battles covered many of the larger spaces. Gilt mirrors reflected the multitude of coloured lamps which lit the nearly windowless hall. Many people sat about on chairs, or lay upon low divans, drinking and eating from the laden tables before them. There were guardsmen scattered amongst the expensively clothed people from the city, enjoying a life of decadent luxury. Young women poured wine and ale, much of their soft white flesh exposed for the pleasure of the court.

The men of Zeta were led the length of the hall as people on both sides pointed and began to take notice of something other than the delicacies before them. There was laughter and much talking amongst those who watched. Kerran could see ahead a dais on which stood three tall and elaborate thrones. On the central seat sat a large aging man who wore the finery of a king. Much gold and silver adorned his colourful elegant clothes and he wore a strange blue wig, as did many others in the court. Kerran almost laughed at the ridiculousness of it. Each fat finger held large gems set in silver or gold, and around the Governor's neck hung a large sparkling green gem set in clusters of lesser stones. To his right the seat lay empty, and to his left sat a small and frail woman, her luxuriant gown doing little to disguise her great sadness. She sat forlorn and did not seem to care or notice the happenings within the hall. Guards sat about on the steps below, tankards of wine within easy reach. They watched with surly arrogance as the procession made its way to the foot of the dais.

Tolth spoke out loudly. "Greetings to you Governor Demsharl of the city Amitarl," he said. "I am Tolth Amitarl, and I ask that you hear my words."

The Governor leaned forward. "Speak," he said, a look of scornful triumph on his soft florid face.

"I believe you have made a pact with Maradass," continued Tolth. "He will not keep it, of this I am sure. He has the forces to crush the Southern Regions at will. I bring an army for the defence of the lands. I ask that you invite us into your city and castle for the protection of all."

"Invite you into the castle I certainly will," said the Governor. His voice, though soft and low, reached to all ears in the room.

With bated breath the onlookers made not a sound lest they miss one point of the delicious game. The Governor was at his best when the balance of the argument was tipped so firmly in his favour.

"To the castle tower I will invite you!" he bellowed the words. "Locked in chains as a horse thief." Then his voice softened and he added with a sickly smile. "But there are other crimes that are not such simple matters," he said. "Invasion by a military force, perhaps even treason since you claim to be Amitarl."

"The crimes you level at me are serious ones," spoke Tolth. "Yet this is no invasion of your country. We come for your defence, and there is no treason. As for the horses, I bought them from one of your own officials when our ships landed on the coast."

"Do you have a bill of ownership?" smirked the Governor, enjoying himself immensely, well aware that all eyes in the hall were fastened on the scene before them.

"No," replied Tolth.

"As I thought," said the Governor before Tolth could say more. "Your guilt is proven by the laws of the court." The Governor spoke loudly for all to hear. "Clearly you are horse thieves and will go to the tower unless...?" he paused for affect.

"There was some mention of gold and jewels I believe, a gift was spoken of." His slippery voice caused Kerran to shudder.

"We have much gold on board our ships," said Tolth. "We come to buy horses, not steal them. Our purpose here is to rid the Regions of Maradass and his armies. That is all."

"So you say," spoke the Governor leaning still further forward. "Tell me how much gold you would give to set you and your comrades free?" He leaned back and waited confidently. The price would have to be large.

"The price I would give is nothing," said Tolth, looking into the eyes of the Governor.

The Governor jerked forward, his game taking an unexpected turn. "Nothing!" he cried. "What do you mean, nothing?"

Tolth spoke calmly, his eyes never leaving the Governor's face. "I will give no gold to set us free for I do not believe that we are yet held captive," he said.

A murmur of surprise carried around the hall.

"What?" exclaimed the Governor, though now a broad smile began to spread across his face. "You do not believe that you are held captive," he laughed aloud now, his audience totally won. "You are unarmed and surrounded by my guards," he sneered. "In your situation I would consider myself to be in dire need of a miracle."

One of those amongst the watchers could not restrain himself and applauded the Governor's wit.

"Do not pride yourself on knowing all things," spoke Tolth, his voice quietening the amused laughter. "I will not be taken as your prisoner. If you wish to bargain for horses, or reconsider your position, we will talk. Otherwise I will leave and make war on Maradass without your assistance."

"I do not understand you old man," spoke the Governor genuinely perplexed. "You are not wanted here. I have made peace with Maradass. His armies will not come beyond the Crossroads. We are comfortable here. Why do you come and try to cause trouble?"

"The trouble comes from the north," said Tolth. "If you knew the black heart of Maradass you would know why I am here."

"If Maradass wishes to conquer the Southern Regions why has he not done so?" asked the Governor. "His army lies in camp north of the Crossroads. If he is so sure of success, and if that is his desire, why has he not taken the Southlands and slaughtered us all? No old man, we are safe here. There is no threat from Maradass. You are the threat. Perhaps Maradass would pay me well for your head. There must be some way of making a profit from this."

The audience burst into laughter, clapping and stamping their feet at the Governor's jest.

Tolth spoke, his voice in dire earnest. "Before you could take my head I would take your mind into the realms of madness and then leave it there," he said for all to hear. Tolth raised his hand, his forefinger pointing. "Believe me in this," continued Tolth. "Your sanity hangs at my command."

The Governor was taken aback. He saw in the old man's eyes a certainty that he suddenly feared. A power flowed through Tolth, the force of which was immediately obvious to the hesitant Governor.

"No!" he called a little too loudly. "We will not have any of your childish witchery here. You are now free to go."

The crowd were upset at the turn in the game, but they had not seen the deadly intent in Tolth's eyes, though still the Governor played.

"You will be taxed of course," he said, a subdued but cunning look on his face. "For each of your soldiers who set foot upon Andrian soil you must pay ten gold pieces."

It was a ruse and Tolth knew it, a way for both to part without violence. Tolth also knew that at the bottom of all of the Governor's high words was his lust for wealth.

"Agreed," said Tolth. "We have no way of delivering it, so if you would kindly send a wagon." Tolth left the rest unsaid.

"And you will leave these Southlands," continued the Governor. "Go and fight Maradass if that is your desire but expect no allies here. You trespass where you do not belong and should you return to this city you will find the gates shut to you."

"We will go," said Tolth simply. "We will meet Maradass in the north."

They turned and left the hall escorted by the same four guards. The Elbrand were wary, expecting a trick, but the group were not molested and were eventually returned to their comrades at the gate.

"That was not as I would have hoped," said Tolth as they made ready to ride.

"We were somehow fortunate to get away with it at all," said Mantris, somewhat surprised as he looked back at the guards who stood around the city gate.

They rode until they recognised their turning from the Highroad just on dark, and after travelling a short way they camped in a small wood. Here they lit a fire and enjoyed a more pleasant meal than the previous night. Other fires burned amongst the valleys and hills around the Highroad, refugees from Maradass finding a place where they could rest. They had eaten and were readying themselves for sleep when there was a call from beyond the firelight.

"Would you have a bite for a hungry old woman?" said a high pitched voice from the darkness.

"Come forward," called Tolth.

Into the firelight shuffled an old and ragged woman. The hood of a tattered cloak covered her head and her shoes were worn, though they still had some life in them. She pulled back the hood to reveal matted grey hair and curling eyebrows which grew wildly above her strange eyes. One of which bulged and did not seem to have any vision.

"You are welcome to what we have," said Tolth. "It is simple fare."

"It will do me well," said the woman as she sat and scooped the remaining food from the small pot.

She ate some bread and a piece of cheese, and though eating no great amount she did not speak until apparently satisfied.

"You are not from Andrian," she said finally, her accent sharp and unusual.

"No," replied Tolth. "We came a great distance to speak with the Governor, but he gave us no help with our task."

"And what is that pray?" asked the old woman, her good eye catching the firelight.

"You ask many questions for a guest at one's fireside," replied Tolth. "It is a curious thing but I almost feel I know you."

The old woman chuckled. "Yes, Tolth Amitarl," said the old woman. "You know me, but from another time and another guise."

Tolth peered deeply into the face before him. Though the features had grown older and the hair turned grey, Tolth recognised the face of an old friend.

"Dantas!" he exclaimed.

"Yes Tolth," the old man replied with a laugh and drew some of the cleverly made disguise from his face. "It has been a long time, though time treats you much fairer than I."

"How do you come here?" Tolth asked, still amazed at the old Elbrand commander's sudden appearance, and the excellence of his disguise. "On a night of many fires it is not chance which brought you to ours."

"No," replied Dantas. "My powers of perception were never as good as yours." He laughed, the strange accent now gone. "I followed you from the city," he continued, "I am a lot older now, but I have led a fortunate life. I am still strong."

"Is your life so fortunate that you dress in rags," said Tolth.

"Tis but a disguise, just as the eye and accent were," said Dantas. "I am not a popular man in many circles, and the Governor wishes for my head."

"I heard that you were in the Governor's employ," said Tolth.

"I was," said Dantas. "That was a long time past, though I would ask how you heard such a thing on Zeta?"

"From one who was once your pupil," replied Tolth. "His name is Flindas."

"Flindas!" exclaimed Dantas. "What news have you of him? I have not seen him for many years."

"He lived when I saw him last," said Tolth. "He has taken on a most dangerous mission and I do not now know where he may be."

"Flindas," said Dantas again, speaking the name softly and

with great fondness. "I would know more of him, but firstly I am here to speak to you on matters which concern your mission. Since falling from favour with the Governor I have remained in Andrian, but in different guises, and I enter and leave the city at will. There are many in the city and country around us who despise and distrust the Governor and his court. The pact with Maradass is a farce of course. I do not know why Maradass remains at the Crossroads unless it was to wait for you. There is a movement amongst the people and a market in many goods which do not come under the eyes of the Governor's taxmen, and there are those who speak of full rebellion against the Governor and his court. You will find allies throughout Andrian, though some may not trust your motives any more than the Governor's. All fear Maradass, only the Governor and his cronies are foolish enough to trust him. The rewards for their compliance cloud their greedy minds."

Dantas became silent for a moment, his eyes fixed on his old friend. "I would hear more of Flindas but it must wait for another time," said the old warrior suddenly standing. "There are many ways I may be of help to your quest here in the Regions," he said. "I will send messengers to you. They are talented and trustworthy and will carry your news to me in the city. If you need food it can be organised."

"We need horses," said Tolth. "If at all possible," he added.

"Anything is possible," Dantas chuckled and was gone into the darkness.

They arrived back at the coast a little before noon of the following day, the army that now lay on the hillock was somewhat reduced from the four thousand who had come ashore from the fleet.

"They have gone to the west and north," said Mantris when Kerran wondered about them. "There will be forward patrols and scouts far out into the lands by now. Some are making their way towards the Crossroads, and unless Maradass has advanced to the south, I would not expect to hear from our runners for some days. Others will be seeking places of refuge on the edge of the forest and in the wetlands of the Central Plains."

Soon after they had arrived in camp they were greeted by the news that their troops to the east under Commander Torian had been contacted. Torian had kept his army hidden in a forested coastal strip near the Far Islands. He had scouts along the coastline as lookouts for ships from Zeta, and the fleet had been seen as they sailed near the Far Isles towards the South Coast.

"Good," said Mantris. "Torian will be marching to meet us. It will surprise the Governor to find an army marching from the east, and going by his front door," he paused.

"This man Dantas," he said to Tolth, as though he could no longer hold his words. "He is the one who betrayed his fellow Elbrand and left them to die by Zard's sword. How can you trust a man who has done such a thing?"

"I have known Dantas since he was a child, and I already an old man," replied Tolth. "He did not betray his comrades. He turned in the face of his own death and fled, brand him a coward perhaps, but not a traitor. Do any of us know what we would do in the face of the black son of Maradass?"

Mantris kept his own thoughts unspoken and gave orders for the army to march. Each man and woman carried a large pack of food along with their bedroll and weapons. One hundred would stay behind to protect the fleet and the remaining stores. The ships lay at anchor with a full crew aboard each, and Tolth spoke one last time with Captain Ronsarl, then the army of Zeta began its march. Kerran rode together with Tolth and Mantris, while behind them rode Verardian and Mindis, though Tolth's youngest son remained in his strange other world he would not be denied going. In an unusual fit of rage he had screamed that he would not remain behind with the ships, his silence now in great contrast to his recent fury.

They rode into the evening and made camp in the forested hills far from the Highroad. The army would not travel on the paved ways unless their need was greater than their need for stealth and surprise. They had crossed the Highroad late that evening and lay in the hills to the north, the night was warm and the cooking fires kept low as they lay at rest and ate their simple meal. The army had passed through villages and towns as they had made their way westward that day, and many curious onlookers had followed them, even now several children played near the camp.

"The Highroad and country to the north and west becomes wild and less populated," said Mantris who had heard from his forward scouts. "We will meet with Torian in the hills north of the meeting place of the two Highroads. An old ruined watch tower stands there on a hilltop. It will be the place to join our forces. We can be there in two days. Torian will not arrive for perhaps seven or eight. When the scouts begin to return we will understand more of the enemy."

The army arrived in sight of the ancient tower during the afternoon of the second day. It stood like a finger high atop a tall conical hill which overlooked the road. The green and brown army made its camp in a valley to the north of the tower. Information began to come in from scouts who had run to the coast of Shardis, and the south of the Central Plains. No signs of Maradass could be seen. Relays of runners were being spread further north. Soon they would bring almost daily word on what transpired in many parts of the land. On the south coast of the Sea of Shardis life seemed to be going on as usual. The fishing ports and towns were busy and unaffected by the threat from the north. The townsfolk and officials alike seemed ill informed of the threat. An interesting piece of information had come from this direction. For some reason the poison of Maradass had not affected the Sea of Shardis, and fishing had gone on there as usual.

From the Central Plains the first runner returned. He brought the news that the swamp lands were an ideal place of refuge, and the leader of the man's troop was preparing a camp deep in the boggy terrain. From Glandrin and the forest came the news that no enemy was to be seen, the army under Commander Torian was sighted the same day that word came from the Crossroads of the Maradass Army, Kerran was with Tolth and Mantris when the woman made her report.

"We came up the Old Coast Road as far as we could," she told them. "Marauders were everywhere, just loose and roaming the land, sniffing. We could see the Crossroads and the Black Army, their command seems to be centred in the old castle there. The old curse that lay on the Crossroads does not seem to affect the soldiers of Maradass. It may be that the curse was really brought about by Maradass in the first place. We travelled west, staying well to the south of them. It is six leagues from the Crossroads to the forest, and the army of Maradass is large enough to spread across it. Horsemen and marauders cover the spaces between troops. We estimate there are perhaps up to a hundred thousand foot soldiers, mostly these strange stone soldiers we have heard of; and then there may be eight thousand horsemen, it is difficult to assess." She paused, looking for words. "There is indeed something very strange about those foot soldiers" she said thoughtfully. "As though they are not really human at all."

"How do you mean?" asked Tolth, though he had heard from Kerran of these strange troops, his curiosity sought for the truth of them.

"They are much different from the other soldiers and horsemen," replied the scout. "Moved differently, whenever they moved at all. Hard to tell from a distance but it seems that they all held their ranks, standing tall, while the other soldiers just sat or walked about. They were all spearmen these strange ones, troops and troops of them. That was another thing that was peculiar about them, they all seemed similar. Height, build, they looked like they came from the same seed pod."

Tolth was fascinated and wanted to know more but the scout could tell them little. They had not been able to get close enough without detection.

"The armies are in camp and do not look as though they intend moving," she said finally.

The troops under Commander Torian arrived as the scout had finished her report, and they began to mix with those more recently from home. There was much boisterous laughter amongst the troops, stories were told and news from Zeta spread to those who had been in camp on the Far Isles. Torian joined Tolth and the others by their low cooking fire. They welcomed him as the old friend that he was, seeking news of the lands east of the city and the condition of his soldiers.

"The land is empty of Maradass's troops," said the powerfully built Torian, a strong contrast to Mantris, his fellow commander. "As for our troops, they have grown lazy resting out there on the Isles. This little walk will have done them good." He laughed through his red beard and began to investigate the pots around the fire. As they ate they talked of their future plans. All agreed that the edge of the forest was their best place of defence. Few had ever ventured into the heart of Dreardim. Since before the time of Maradass and Amitarl it had been a forbidding reminder of a time that was lost. Creatures, unknown and unnamed, were said to roam its dark centre; it was a place where even the dead lay uneasy. It had been reported by scouts that there were many hiding places amongst the rocky outcrops, and numerous small rivers which fed the swamps of the Central Plains, without having to enter the heart of the forest.

The following morning the army of Zeta began its march to the west. It would take them at least ten days or more to reach the forest. More horses had been bought but still they numbered no more than thirty. Kerran rode beside Tolth for much of the day and eventually the army crossed the Highroad again, much to the surprise of the few travellers there. Horses were of crucial importance and in disguise a number of men were sent to the old ruined city of Crysta-Sha with gold, to see if any could be bought.

Kerran shaded his eyes against the sun and gazed aloft to where Storm soared on the wind. He thought of the days ahead and what they may bring, then he wondered where Flindas might be in the vastness of the lands.

To Blackman's Pass

Flindas leaned back and smiled as Duragor reached out and passed him a small water bottle, it was no more than half full and he drank sparingly.

"It is very good to see you my friend," he said to the black man.

Tris stirred within her sleep, then in a moment was on her feet, her senses telling her that things had changed. A sudden look of wondrous recognition came over her face. She gave a cry of joy and threw herself at Duragor, flinging her arms around him.

"Whoa!" he cried to her. "Take care to treat an old man with respect."

Tris could not help but punch Duragor in the shoulder. He let out a cry of false pain. Leana woke and watched the scuffle, smiling.

"Water, water!" Tris cried out, and though she could have drunk every drop she took a small sip and passed the bottle to Leana.

"You seem to have stirred up a nest of stinging flies," said Duragor, indicating the distant horsemen. "The way is closed to you I think."

"Yes," agreed Flindas. "The foothills of the Bittering are overrun and alive with dogs, it would be an endless battle to go that way. We must attempt a return to the Broken Lands I fear, and then try to reach the coast. It will not be easy."

"That is a long and dangerous road," said Duragor. He paused and trailed his hand through the sand thoughtfully. "There is another way into the Southlands," he said mysteriously. "Also a long walk, but not so dangerous."

"What is that?" asked Flindas, ready to hear of any possible road. "I know of no trails through the mountains."

"There is one, if the old stories be true," said Duragor, and a broad smile flashed across his face. "Have you not heard of Blackman's Pass?"

"I have only heard tales of that place," said Flindas. "Do you know how to find it? Does it really exist?"

"I too have only heard the tales," said Duragor. "But they are true Blackman's stories, and so I believe they will lead us to the pass, and how to walk it." He paused. "If it is still there," he added with a smile. "We will just have to go and see." He turned then and spoke to Leana. "Greetings and well met, Leana Amitarl," he said. "I am Duragor, and while I am your guide I will aid you in any way I can against the dark forces you face. My home is to the west, but my heart is with all lands, and I would not see them destroyed by the ones you call enemy."

Leana smiled at the black man. "And to you Duragor I too say greetings," her voice came softly. "Your part in this tale I have heard from the others. Your friendship with my brother is something I would hear more of."

"I heard of his death," said Duragor sadly. "Soldiers boast. I was sorry to hear it."

Leana bowed her head slightly and said no more.

"Drink the water," said Duragor. "I will go and find more."

"Where do you find water out here?" asked Tris as she took another swallow from the bottle. "Do you sing it like rabbits?"

Duragor laughed and the sound warmed them deeply. "Water cannot be sung," he said with mock seriousness. "But there are places to look, and things to look for."

He stood and began to walk into the desert.

The sun was lowering to the far red horizon when Duragor returned. Both water bottles were now full and they all drank deeply of the delicious liquid. From around his shoulders the black man took a long dark bag made from a tattered cloak which had once been part of a Maradass captain's uniform. He reached in and brought forth a thick root of a plant which he proceeded to scrape with his knife, when he had a handful of soft white pulp he passed it to Tris.

"Do not swallow the fibre," he said. "Suck the juice from it and spit the rest out."

Tris took the doubtful looking mush and put some in her mouth, the delicate sweetness was a surprise, and the juice in the pulp was like a salve to her throat. It seemed even more thirst quenching than water, if such a thing could be.

"Oh!" was all she could say at the delightful effect.

"It is called mishlee," said Duragor. "It will not only quench your thirst but nourish your body too."

He passed some to the others. As the liquid coursed down his throat Flindas felt as though the mishlee root had more than water and nourishment to give them. There was an almost immediate feeling of well-being. The sun, as it cast its last rays across the land seemed benevolent, where earlier that day it had seemed their worst enemy.

"It has more to it than meets the stomach," said Flindas as the feeling of lightness coursed through him.

"Yes," smiled Duragor. "It wears off quickly but the sustenance it gives can keep you alive when all else fails. I will show you how to find it, and other things as we walk south."

Dawn came and they began the long march to the south and west. They kept far from the foothills of the Bittering, though in the distance, within that harsh land, they could see tall snow capped peaks catching the sunlight. There was no sign of Maradass horsemen after their first day's march and the relief they felt made the journey almost pleasant. The mishlee was difficult for Tris and the others to find, only a mound of fine red sand would show where Duragor told them they should dig. Lizards and snakes they found in abundance.

For many days their way led south and west, until the

foothills slowly dwindled and they turned further towards the south. When the moon allowed they would travel by night, attempting to avoid the harshness of the afternoon sun. Occasionally they crossed a small flowing stream, but water that flowed to the west from the Bittering did not last long in the dry lands. At night, when the moon was high, the distant howling of dog packs could be heard from the hills. Once a pack came down to investigate their presence. The creatures were beaten off by the four companions, who were determined to stay further from the hills after that night.

A full moon slipped by and then another on their long march. The days stretched behind them like their footprints in the red, dusty sand. Food became more plentiful as they travelled, and rabbits abounded in the tufted grasses and many low lying bushes. It was a day of hot dry winds when Duragor called to them and pointed ahead to where a lean dog, with a short light brown coat was eyeing them carefully from a distance.

"Dog pack," said Tris looking around for the others.

"No," said Duragor. "Not this one. I know this dog, or I know his grandfather."

He moved forward slowly, indicating for them to stay where they were. Duragor approached the dog and he sang as he went. The dog stood his ground, ears alert, watching the approach of the black man. Duragor reached the dog and held out his hand for the animal to sniff. He leant down and appeared to speak quietly to the creature which listened for a time then moved away slowly towards the west.

"Come," said Duragor. "There are friends nearby."

The others could barely believe that in all the vast empty lands they had passed through, they should come upon people who Duragor called friends. They followed the dog as it loped ahead of them, often looking back to be sure that they followed. The first sign they had of a camp was the smell of meat roasting on a fire. Ahead, through the low scattered scrub, they could make out a group of people around a smouldering fire. They were black people, dressed in scraps of clothing, if at all. A number of children played and fought in the dirt.

As the dog entered the camp those at the fire looked up to see the approaching figures. From beside the fire a lean but powerful man rose and came towards them walking quickly, a ferocious look on his face. Duragor, who had walked a little ahead of the others, stood his ground and Flindas reached for the hilt of his sword. Then the charging man came to a dusty halt in front of Duragor. He spoke in a loud tumbling language. They seemed to be very angry words full of reproach. Then he threw his arms around Duragor who did the same, bursting into laughter. Many of those around the fire had come to their feet. A low chanting song began from many voices. There was a rhythm of movement as the black people came forward and welcomed Duragor into their midst.

There were many hands reaching out to touch him, to assure them that he was real. Children ran towards the three other dusty travellers, and then at the last moment stopped. With many a snigger the gleeful children examined the strangers. Several dogs and puppies also came to investigate the newcomers as they walked slowly into the camp; the singing had died now to an undercurrent of humming melodious sounds. The man who had first greeted Duragor was talking with him at the fire, and the people's voices faded away as Duragor told his story in the same rolling tongue.

There were many questions from those in the camp, Flindas and his companions sat around the fire and were passed pieces of meat and various small, sometimes unidentifiable foods. The children had become bolder and were beginning to pull and pry into the traveller's belongings; a gruff word from an old woman sent them scampering away. The day grew longer as the story was told, and the three companions had said not a word, until to their surprise the man who had spoken with Duragor turned to them, and spoke in their own tongue.

"I greet you, Flindas, Leana, Tris," he said. "My language of yours is not good. I am Mardeed. Welcome to our home." He paused as he searched for words. "Duragor, brother," he said. "Duragor gone long. Come home well good."

He smiled at them now and it seemed as though everyone around the fire turned and finally accepted their presence.

It was as if a wall between them had fallen, talk broke out amongst the people and several now stood and left the fire for a last short hunt before nightfall.

Duragor now told the others much of what had been said between him and Mardeed. Duragor did not seem at all surprised to find his people at this place. Indeed it seemed that somehow Mardeed was expecting them, and had known that he should travel the many leagues just to be in this place at this time. Duragor could explain it only as something his people understood, and that the white people did not.

"It is like the songs we sing," he tried to explain. "Every newborn will know every song and understand it."

"And the dog," asked Leana. "Does it too have this gift? It appeared to be waiting to lead us to this camp."

Duragor smiled. "He is a wise dog," he said. "Yes, he has eyes and ears and more."

"What are those?" asked Tris.

She pointed to a number of rabbit skin bundles which had been handed to Duragor at the end of his talk with Mardeed. Duragor picked one up and spread it.

"They are warm cloaks," he said. "There are four of them. Mardeed brought them with him because he knew they would be needed." Duragor looked then towards the east. "It will be cold in the mountains," he said.

That night, by the light of the fire, there was a dance in celebration of Duragor's return. His companions learned from Mardeed of the importance of Duragor to the people. He was a Rememberer, they learned, one who knew their stories and ancient tales in all their details, but the stories were only part of his far greater knowledge and memory. Duragor had told Mardeed that nothing was lost. Everything he had ever known remained stored within his memory, despite the evil times which had passed. The dance began in earnest, the night was cool but soon all who participated felt nothing but heat. Heat too came from the thick syrupy drink made from the mishlee root. The pounding rhythm and the mishlee were enough for Tris to be coaxed into the dance of drumming feet.

For the first time in so long, Flindas felt his whole being

relax. He looked across to where Leana sat against a large boulder. Many children were gathered around her, awed by her golden hair and fair skinned beauty. Whether by nature, or the residue of the Evil One's spell, she had remained quiet and softly aloof from the others during their long southern journey. Flindas watched as Leana took a sip at the strong mishlee drink. Somehow he found his own small cup again at his lips. He had not realised that he had picked it up. The drumming of the dance and the cries of many voices now made talk impossible around the fire. A sudden streak of fire crossed the sky falling to the west. He watched it as it burned and was gone.

"It falls towards my homelands," said Duragor as he joined his friend to look above at the many sparkling gems of the night. "It is told that if you follow the star which you see fall you will gain happiness and peace." His smile flashed in the firelight. "We go the other way tomorrow," he added with a small chuckle.

"You must long for your home," said Flindas, looking at his friend through the darkness.

"Yes," said Duragor. "It is some years since I was with my family. I have two sons; they will be almost grown by now. Perhaps you will find your own home when this is all done, my friend. Everyone should have a place they call home, and those that they call family. If you cannot find it in the east, come to the west and look for me. Anyone you ask will tell you where I am. They may be suspicious of a strange white man, but I am sure that when you say my name they will be willing to help." He looked to the fire where Tris continued to dance wildly amongst others, who cheered and clapped at her pure joy. "Everyman should have brothers," said Duragor. "And sisters."

Duragor placed a warm friendly hand momentarily on his friends shoulder then returned to the dance, while Flindas was handed a gourd of mishlee juice. The old man would not take no for an answer, insisting that Flindas drink of the intoxicating liquid. He felt happy and yet there was an intangible touch of sadness he could not have explained. Mardeed called to a young girl child who sat with her mother. The girl came quickly to Mardeed's side. He spoke rapid tumbling words to her and then to Flindas's surprise the girl spoke to him in the language of the Regions.

"Mardeed say, 'Man without tears is man without heart'." She smiled warmly and held to Mardeed's side.

"Daughter," said Mardeed proudly. "Rememberer."

Flindas woke the next morning to an evil pain which ran through his brain, the mishlee juice had left him weak and dry, and the slightest movement of his head brought a harsh drumming ache. His eyes opened slowly to see Duragor approaching. He had something in his hand. It was not until the black man knelt down beside him and offered the gourd that Flindas realised what his friend carried. He pulled back from the offered mishlee as though it would bite him. Instantly he wished he had remained still, pain exploding in his head as he slowly sat up.

"Drink," said Duragor. "It may be the poison, but it is also the cure. Drink and the pain will go quickly."

Flindas reached for the mishlee and took a large swallow, anything to rid himself of the pain. Within a short time the mishlee began to ease the tightness inside him, and he sighed as the pain fell away. Leana and Tris had already eaten and were sitting by the low smouldering fire surrounded by the children of the camp. Flindas joined them and was offered meat and dough, which, when baked in the fire, came out dark, golden, and heavy with strange flavours. Tris looked across the fire at him and smiled.

"You too must be glad of the cure," she said, then shook her head as she held it between her fingers.

The children laughed at her comical expression and imitated her, giggling and falling about on the dusty ground. A young dog barked at the commotion so early in the morning, which made the children laugh even more. Duragor had gone with Mardeed and it was some time before the two black men rejoined their friends. Others came to the fire. Some carried the rabbit skin cloaks, while others brought bags of food.

It was a song of sorrowful parting which followed the four travellers as they began to walk from the camp. At the last moment the daughter of Mardeed ran to Flindas, her radiant smile spoke more than her words.

"Mardeed say, brother come back one day."

She reached out quickly, touching his hand, and was gone. The song followed them until they could hear it no longer.

"If we have fortune on our side we will be at the head of the pass in six maybe seven days," said Duragor as they walked together through the low scrub and scattered gaunt trees. "I know the way from the old songs," he continued. "None have been on this path for a long long time. It may have changed."

Several days passed and the land began to rise as they travelled further to the east. Each day the ground became rockier as the trees and scrub were left behind, and soon only the strongest of grasses grew where they walked. The sand lost its red colour, becoming a dark grey. The air was cooler and already they had each decided to wear their welcome cloaks. A bitter wind swept at them from the south, cold shafts tearing at them from the distant Icelands. Old discoloured snow lay in sheltered hollows, telling of the winter that had passed, when none, not even the mountain dogs, could survive in such a bleak and inhospitable place. Eventually, even the grasses could no longer survive, and the dust and sand of the Outlands had become grey shattered rock, where nothing could live for long. The travellers sheltered in the lee of a large boulder and ate a cold meal. There was nothing to burn up here on these bitter highlands.

"The signs have all been there," said Duragor when Tris asked if they were close to the pass. "Tomorrow we will make our way between two pointed hills," he told them. "The mountains and snows are beyond. Until I recognise the remembered landmarks I cannot be sure of the way, tomorrow we will know how true the old song is."

"Will you tell us of the pass?" asked Tris. "How was it found?"

Duragor paused and thought for a few moments. "This is the story of the Blackman's Pass," he said looking back the way they had come. "When my people were pushed to the west by the Wizard Wars they joined with some who had always been there in the desert. They were the children of the Old Ones and they knew nothing of the wizards and the armies of white men who had come across the sea from another place. Some from the desert would not be discouraged and went to look at these strange, white men. Some came back through the Desert Pass and shook their heads in dismay, while others did not return at all. If they were caught they were sure to die by white hands. Sometimes they were used in the games, which saw them die all the same. Sometimes they were given the possibility of escaping into the mountains. They were set free and given a time to run, and then the horse soldiers and gangs of white men with their dogs would hunt them. Many died under the hooves, or spears, or were torn apart by the dogs. It is told that some, only a few, did escape, only to die of the cold.

"It was a man named Tarn who alone came across these mountains and told stories of the white man's cruelty," continued Duragor. "But Tarn was not a black man like I am black, and he was not a white man either. He was a very big man and his skin was not so dark, a warm brown colour. He said he came from a land many leagues out into the ocean. He came from a place where brown people were many, like him. They were warriors and there had been many wars in his country. Then the white men had come and attacked his home, and he had been captured. When they came to this land he saw that war followed these white men like a plague.

"Tarn stayed in the desert until he died an old man. During his time with my people, he had retraced his path across the mountains showing my people of the way. In the high summer they had come through the narrow pass up near the snow line to find that before them lay a clear way to the far east lands. It became the knowledge of all black men in the desert and they made a song to remember the way. Though it was found by a brown man it was called Blackman's Pass in your language. It is the humour of my people."

Duragor smiled and paused for a moment. "No white man has ever found it that I have heard of," he continued. "Tarn was not only a bold warrior, he was defiant and proud and angry.

Many times he returned over the mountains alone and became something terrible that would come from the night and kill white men, and then disappear. A horror that slaughtered all it found. Every time he appeared to the white man no one lived to tell of their attacker.

"Every year in summer until he was unable because of his age, he would go beyond the mountains and kill again, and yet again. He said he was avenging the invasion of his home by the white man, and all of their killings. His people are still believed to inhabit many hundreds of islands far to the sunrise. Tarn would speak of his country with longing, but he knew not how to return. He would kill from his summer lair high in the mountains, but to cross all the land beyond the mountains to the sea was impossible. Armies of white men, driven to a type of madness by the wizards, fought many battles in the lands. Tis said that when he died Tarn became one of the Old Ones. He is remembered by my people for his passion and bravery. That is the story of Blackman's Pass." Duragor grew silent then turned over to sleep.

The dawn came bright and fair, a pleasing change which they welcomed. The wind had dropped and the travellers moved on quickly towards the mountains. Soon they could see the two tall cones of ancient volcanoes, a smear of snow still clinging to their dark sides. When they had passed beyond them Duragor took a route towards the lofty snow-covered peaks where a narrow canyon ran steeply to the south and east. A river flowed from above and thundered violently along the valley floor.

Duragor pointed to the mountains beyond. "The pass is there," he said.

The next morning Tris was the first to peer from beneath her cloak and see the soft white flakes as they fell continuously from the sky. Wrapping herself close, she stood and gazed at it in wonder. Never had she seen anything so beautiful. Snow did not fall in the Broken Lands and she had never imagined something so wonderful in its simplicity. Tris held out her hand and let the soft flakes fall on her arm, and she blew them as they gathered on the fur at her shoulders. When Flindas saw the snow he was not pleased. They still had a long walk before they would be across the mountains. They had not yet reached the high pass, and if the cold and snow continued their feet could be frozen before they reached the far side of the mountains. Duragor as always wore no shoes, seeming to be adapted to the cold as well as blistering rock that had been baked beneath the desert sun.

The travellers moved on quickly, and by the end of the day were well up the valley which would lead them to the pass. They trudged through snow up to their knees, the white softness now biting into them as the wind returned. In the lee of a sheer rock they made their camp. Tris was no longer in wondrous awe of the falling snow, and she could see that such a beautiful thing would easily kill the unwary. She dreamed of the harsh sunshine of the Broken Lands as she lay almost warm between the others. When Tris woke there was a weight that held her down. She struggled upward a lump of snow and fell onto the others. Duragor growled and shook himself awake. The snow lay thick on their rabbit skin coverings and it continued to fall gently. The wind had died completely and soft grey light filtered though clouds at the head of the pass.

The push to the top was slow and hard, and Flindas began to forge ahead, creating an easier path for those behind. He finally gained the summit of the ridge and sat looking to the east until the others were able to join him, breathless and exhausted.

Duragor sat in the snow and smiled. "It is all downhill from here," he said, though he knew that more climbing would be required before they could actually leave the mountains.

They rested and looked at the way ahead. Duragor pointed out their next landmark, and they were soon moving downhill, sometimes sitting or lying on their cloaks and skimming across the snow. Tris was once again filled with the joy of it, and came close to crashing into a small gully before she slowed down and kept with the others. The light falling snow ceased, and by day's end they had reached a buttress high above a cavernous valley.

"We must go down," said Duragor. "It is not an easy climb."

Dawn came clear and it seemed that Blackman's Pass would allow them to enter the Regions. The morning passed as they slid and clambered down the steep slopes. Their one rope, which Flindas still carried, was used several times before they reached the valley floor. They passed through a narrow defile and came out above a high frozen landscape that spread as far as they could see.

"The old words do not tell me of this," said Duragor as he looked to the north. "There should be a deep valley here."

He clambered down the slope and made his way onto the ice and packed snow. The others followed their friend onto the broken and sculptured slope.

"The lands grow colder and the southern ice advances," said Leana, speaking more on this day than on any previous one of their journey. "Tolth and others before him have known of this," she continued. "Perhaps in many years the lands themselves will disappear under the ice, and the Regions will be but a memory."

Flindas sensed that Leana was almost free of the spell of Maradass, though not of her grief over her brother.

Two more days passed on the slope before they reached the ice river's end, which fell away in a swiftly flowing stream.

"Ah," said Duragor smiling and looking down on the valley beyond. "Of this the words tell, a valley of four sisters." He pointed to where four similar peaks ranged themselves at the head of a deep valley. "This is the source of the River Glandrindar," he told them. "Though we cannot follow it into the lands we will meet it again beyond the sisters. The way is clear before us now, and the pass remains open."

Two further days passed before, weary and sore, they again stood beside the river which would lead them into Glandrin. High towering mountains still seemed to bar their way but the river was now their guide. Duragor stood on a rock ledge above the river and was glad that he had been able to bring his friends to safety. They were sitting together and resting as he rejoined them.

"Welcome to the Regions," he said, but he knew that his joke had failed.

Tris looked at him with eyes full of sorrow and hurt.

"Yes, my little one," said Duragor. "It is time for me to go home now. Your way is clear ahead to the east and mine must go now to the west."

Tears came to Tris's eyes, and as she went to the black man and they held each other, he keened a soft song into her ear alone and she felt warmed and strengthened by it. They drew apart and Leana came to Duragor, holding his hands in hers.

"I thank you Duragor for all you have done," she said. "The Amitarl hearth will always welcome an old friend, should you wish to visit us in kinder days." Duragor bowed slightly and smiled. "You may be surprised one day to find me on your doorstep, fair lady Amitarl," he said. "Good fortune in the times to come. I will dance for your victory over the darkness."

Flindas looked at his black friend, and he could find no words to say to the man who had become like a brother since they had met. "Take this," he said and passed Duragor the rope. "You may need it on the ice."

"Thank you, my brother," said Duragor. "We will meet again, I know. Come to the west some day and I will show you the ways of the black man." He held out his hand and they clasped, both looking into his brother's eyes. "Depart now!" cried Duragor. "Go with great fortune."

Then he scooped his bundle from the ground and was gone, running up the slope towards the top of the ridge. He turned once and waved, then disappeared from their sight.

Days passed as they followed the river into Glandrin. In the spring and summer melt the way would have been impossible, as the rushing torrent would have barred them from many parts of the path. Summer was gone now and autumn hung as a grey cloud over the lands. Peaks and sheer escarpments began to give over to rocky slopes, until far ahead they could see the forests which grew to the north and east of the mountains. Standing on a high knoll as a storm rumbled amongst the distant snow peaks at their backs, they were glad that it would be their last night in the mountains. Sitting together that night they ate the last of their food, for the following day they would hunt in the forest.

Warriors of Zeta

Under a cool autumn sun the army of Zeta marched across the open plains. They did not move in any order, other than that they advanced in the same direction. The men and women of Zeta spread wide across the open grasslands. A few moved well ahead of the others, using signals to show their comrades the easier road, for bogs and wetlands dotted the vast expanse before them. It was not a welcoming place and few lived out on these windswept flat lands, occasionally the smoke from a small village could be seen further to the south, and sometimes they came upon single dwellings built of wood, or carved from the earth, A small vegetable patch struggling to survive, rabbit pelts hanging from a tumbled down fence, with a goat or a pig, and perhaps a few chickens and ducks.

The few people, who saw the silent army pass, pulled their children indoors and looked with fear through the cracks in the shutters of their homes. Kerran knew these people. In Glandrin and near Westerval there were similar folk who eked out a living from the difficult lands. He often thought of his mother and was very aware that he now rode in the direction of Westerval and his home. Tolth seemed to read his mind.

"You may be able to visit your home," he said turning to

Kerran and smiling. "Let us hope that Maradass will give you time."

That evening Kerran sat with the others in council. Their scouts had reported no movement in the Maradass camp at the Crossroads. For the present Maradass seemed to be keeping his pact with Governor Demsharl and the Southern Regions. The camp in the swamps of the Central Plains had been prepared. It lay no more than thirty leagues south of the Crossroads. Of the elite Elbrand, five hundred would march north to wait there in hiding, while another five hundred would go to join the small band of soldiers who had gone into the forest to the west of the Crossroads. They would make their way north under the cover of Dreardim, and it would be their task to capture as many of the enemy horses as possible. The remainder of the army would continue west until they reached the south of Dreardim, a strong place of defence would be found amongst its many rocky valleys and escarpments, and then more troops would be sent north to harass the enemy.

There was a sudden commotion from beyond the large tent which they used as a place of council and sleep, and a soldier entered. "There is a group come from the City Amitarl," he said. "Horsemen, and well armed. Dantas rides at their head. He wishes council."

"Send him," said Tolth. "I would greet my old friend again."

Orders were called into the darkness and the sound of horses could be heard, then the flap was pulled back and the old wiry frame of Dantas entered. He was not alone. two others entered who caused sudden exclamations from several gathered there. Kerran instantly recognised the large craggy features of Brook, and the small man called Teaker. Tolth was the first to recover; he crossed the space and welcomed them warmly.

"How is it that you are here?" he finally asked. "Have you news of Landin and the others?"

Brook and Teaker quickly recounted their story. When they told that Leana still lived, Tolth looked at Kerran and nodded slowly.

"My head was addled for a time," continued Brook. "I would have been a burden. Teaker would not leave me and so Flindas walked alone into the Broken Lands in search of Landin. I think another went with him but I am not sure."

"The small dark woman," said Kerran suddenly.

"Yes," said Brook, and gave Kerran a most curious look before continuing. "They went west and north, and that is the last I know of them," he said. "We went to the west and managed to escape the Broken Lands. There is a road that now connects the Desert Pass with the Border Road. Maradass has built it for his armies. We came into Rianodar and finally to Mendan Maradass. We stayed in that awful city until it was heard that the Maradass armies were marching south. We had no intention of being caught so we stole a boat and sailed to Andrian. We almost made the mistake of going to the city when Dantas recognised us."

"An Elbrand can never completely hide his training," the old man said. "I knew them for what they are, and also knew that they would wish to join you. I have others with me and some spare horses. In the south there is a stirring amongst the people. Many trust Maradass as little as I do."

"Thank you Dantas," said Tolth to his friend. "Your news is most welcome." Dantas would not stay. He knew that there were many among the army who did not trust him, or care for his presence in their midst. "I will gather news in the south," he said before he left. "Horses too," he added and was gone.

Brook and Teaker told their tale in more detail. One of the most surprising things they were to relate was that Flindas was not just the son of a member of the Governor's Court, he was in fact the Governor's own offspring. Tolth felt that this explained much about Flindas, and his need to prove himself, if only to himself.

The morning came soft with mist upon the Central Plains. Kerran sat eating warm oats and watched the camp stirring to the new day. The sun rose slowly from the east, spreading its warm glow and dispersing the haze. No great sound came from the army of Zeta, they ate silently or spoke in subdued voices, for the practice of silence was also part of a warrior's training. Dantas had brought with him a small number of men from the south. Each rode a strong mount and came well armed.

They would be used as messengers and scouts throughout the Southlands.

The army rose and moved to the west, leaving nothing behind except the crumpled grass. The plains stretched as far as the eye could see in every direction and as the day came to a close they reached a wide shallow river, no deeper than a man's knees. The army crossed and made camp on the western side of the River Lanstra-Dar. Many men and women returned to the river to wash. Though he had ridden all day and was not really hot Kerran dived in. The cold was a sudden shock to his body for the River Lanstra-Dar was mountain fed from the Southern Icelands.

Kerran did not stay in the river for very long but the freshness on his skin had made it worth the cold plunge. He joined Tolth at the small cooking fire and warmed his hands by the dancing flames and embers beneath the pot. Tolth was studying a map which Kerran had looked at himself many times. It was a copy of the map which Darna Amitarl had taken to Zeta when the family left the lands. It showed the Four Regions and the surrounding Borderlands. Kerran peered over the old man's shoulder. He had devaloped a great fascination in maps, and this was such a skilfully drawn diagram of the lands that Kerran had often pored over it. He saw where the village of Westerval stood, though it was much too small a place to be on the map. Other larger towns were shown straddling the connecting Highroads, as was Crysta-Sha, the now ruined city that had been built by the Philosopher's son Zard.

Kerran lay down to sleep that night with the fragment of the Seacrest held in his hand. For a time he lay awake, looking up at the starlit sky. A small streak of fire flashed across the darkness; another, and then another burned and was gone. He smiled as his eyes closed. His mother had once told him a story of two children and the great wonders they had found when they had followed the burning stars. Sleep settled softly on his eyelids and Kerran began to dream.

He had not expected the city of Crysta-Sha to be so beautiful. The towers and spires were tall and elegant. The great many windows and vast curved walls of glass were a wonder. Every stone seemed finely carved and perfect. Kerran moved closer, his shadow floating high above the plains below. It was a large city, greater even than the City Amitarl. Small forests grew, entangling and highlighting the magnificent buildings. Many cultivated gardens lay under vast hollow domes of glass and stone. The central spires of the great palace were so delicate it appeared that a slight wind would be enough to see them topple. Kerran knew that they could not stand alone, a strong magic must be there to support them. People moved about beneath the glass arches and covered walkways, and a wide central square and market was a bustling colourful place. Large sweeping trees gave shelter from the sun to the many who sat in their shadows, drinking tea and watching the ever changing scene in the market place.

There began a stirring amongst the people at the side of the square at an entrance nearest the palace. Cheering was heard and then applause ran through the crowd. Into the square walked a very tall and powerfully built man, his long dark hair and plaited beard hanging to his waist. Zard, their benevolent leader, walked amongst the people, who felt honoured to call him 'Lord.' There was no evil in his face, nor any black armour, but Kerran saw the same man he had seen once before in a sunlit glade of Dreardim Forest. In another age and another time Kerran now saw him again, the revered and beloved son of the Philosopher. Zard moved toward a high dais at the centre of the market place, then climbed the steps alone and stood on the polished surface of the top stone. He raised his arms and the people grew quiet. Their Lord would speak and they cared not to miss one word.

"Today I leave you," Zard called out across the square and the uplifted faces of his people. "I go to visit my father for a time. All is well in your hands while I am gone, this I know. We live in a time of abundance and understanding. The road to prosperity is easier to follow than people had once thought possible. Do not thank me for what you have. Tis not I who has given you these things. Tis your brothers and sisters who support you, all those who now stand beside you and will always reach out if you stumble.

"Thank the earth, for it has a giving and nurturing way. Keep in your hearts a love for one another, and for the world we live in. Respect it, honour it, and you will receive respect and honour in return. You hear my words, and you understand their meaning. I am not here as one who would tell you how to live your lives. You must all find your own way, but all who are here, I call friend, sister and brother. If we are a family to strangers and friends alike, then our time here will be lived well, and that is as much as anyone can ask." Zard paused and smiled down upon his people. "Farewell for this time," he called out across the square, and with a final wave he left the stone dais.

There was not a sound or movement from the people in the square. A silence of deep respect and love followed Zard as he left his people and walked towards the palace. Only when he had gone did they return to the business of the market, chattering and laughing in the sunlight. Kerran's dream condensed into a soft mist until eventually his vision cleared again.

He stood high on a windswept bluff, looking out to the far horizon of the vast ocean. The wind whispered, buffeting him as if trying to push him back from the cliff's edge. The sun was rising in the east and Kerran knew that he looked out on the Sea of Shardis from its southern coast. Far out on the ocean, as distant as his eyes could reach, he thought he saw a small dark patch against the green sea. The pattern began to break up into fragments, small sections becoming separate, more easily defined. Soon Kerran knew what drew nigh the coast of Andrian. Under dark sails and flying the emblem of the dog's skull there came a fleet of small ships from the north. The towns below lay unaware of the approaching danger. Kerran wanted to run and warn them, but found that he could not move.

"Coming," said the voice of Maradass, whispered on the wind.

Kerran shuddered in fear and fell to the ground, and then he felt the pressure of a gentle hand against his forehead. Though he remained in his dream vision Kerran knew that Verardian protected him and gave him strength. The people along the coast could now see the dark fleet,and they stood and gaped. Some could be seen rushing to their homes, gathering family members and friends. Carts were hitched and people began to leave the town. Though some did not go, seeming to have no fear of the fleet. The Governor's pact had many supporters. Just as Kerran knew that what he was seeing was a true vision, he knew also that it was happening at this moment in time. Maradass was invading the inner coast of Andrian.

The Black Fleet, under the northerly breeze, sailed into the large open bay and other small harbours further along the coast. Dark figures began leaping into the water and wading ashore. Ramps fell from the ships and down them marched thousands of the ones known as Krags. The troops of armed men stood on the sands, waiting for their orders until in roughly scattered troops the army of Maradass began to move inland. Kerran watched in horror and disbelief as the men began dragging people from their homes and putting each and every one to the sword or spear. Blood flowed deep in the streets and gutters of the small town below him, and nothing could save them. Kerran saw a woman pleading for the lives of her children with some of the stone soldiers, but there was no mercy. The dark army moved inland, trampling the rich and plentiful fields of Andrian beneath their feet.

"Coming," said the voice on the wind once more, and then with a final soft mocking laugh it was gone.

Kerran collapsed onto the grass, hot tears coursing down his cheeks. He gasped in horror and trembled at what he had seen. Again he felt the presence of Verardian, caring hands easing him of his anguish. In his dream he managed to stand again and look at the terrifying scene before him. The towns were burning, tall spirals of smoke drifting on the air.

Kerran's eyes reached up into the blue sky where high above he saw the slow circling of white wings. Instantly Kerran's mind flew to the bird, and with a sharp hawk's vision he looked down upon the ravaged country beneath him. To the south he could see the Black Army marching inland, then the bird turned to the north and west and the Sea of Shardis began to slip by beneath its wings. The sun was falling to the west when the Crossroads came in sight. There was movement on the south roads and Kerran watched from high on the wind, circling slowly. Most of the remaining stone troops of Maradass were on the march, accompanied by troops of horse soldiers. Others remained in camp around the Crossroads and beyond, but on the roads, tens of thousands had begun a slow march southward. Many turned aside and travelled down the City Highroad, while a similar number marched on the South Road into Glandrin. Kerran saw again the soldiers who did not seem human. Their steps were neat and orderly, the spacing in their ranks precise, as they marched six abreast into the Southlands.

Kerran flew beyond the Crossroads to where the army had lain in camp for the last moon. In places the earth seemed scorched and brown, and large patches of bare earth now stood amongst the grasslands. Nothing like this had happened where the ordinary troops had camped. There the grass had trampled and crushed, but it had not crumbled and turned to dust as it had beneath the feet of this stone army.

In the body of the hawk he now flew south across the Central Plains, above a large mist enshrouded bog, where tall grasses and twisted grey trees stood up above the murk. Much of it was open shallow water, dotted with small islands and banks of reeds. A larger island appeared through the mist and here Kerran could see movement, and slipping by he caught a glimpse of figures dressed in green and brown. Here were those who laboured to prepare a camp for the five hundred Elbrand who now marched north. At times it seemed to Kerran that he could guide his flight, and yet at others, such as now, he was but a passenger carried wherever the bird might fly. Day became night and then darkness gave over to another dawn. A large river wound across the plains and soon he was flying above the main army of Zeta. He could see the tent where Tolth held Council and slept, and a cooking fire burned just outside the entrance.

The hawk carried Kerran down from the sky, plunging quickly to a swooping dive directly at the tent. Just as he thought they would crash, the flap was pulled back by Tolth, who cried out in dismay as the hawk flew by him and gently came to rest on someone who slept beneath a blanket at the back of the tent.

Kerran woke to find Storm standing on his chest. Kerran felt stiff and his mouth was parched. The thought of food suddenly stirred his stomach to life. He moved and stretched as Tolth came quickly to his side.

"You are awake!" the old Amitarl exclaimed as he came to kneel beside Kerran, who stretched again and took a drink from a jug beside him.

Tolth listened with great anxiety as he was told of the invading fleet, and the armies marching south from the Crossroads.

"You have been gone for three days," Tolth said to him after Kerran had told his story. "Verardian sat with you through much of it. He said there were times when you slipped beyond his touch, that you hung suspended between life and death. I fear for you Kerran. I will find Verardian and send him to you. I must see Mantris and Torian. Your news, though terrible, is better to know than not. Maradass is now showing his hand and we are forewarned."

Tolth left the tent and soon Verardian came to Kerran's side, carrying a bowl of hot soup and a large piece of warm bread baked in a camp oven. Kerran was famished and ate hungrily, until every drop and crumb was devoured

A war council was held that evening and Kerran was asked to repeat much of his dream. Mantris voiced the thought that had occurred to Kerran.

"If Maradass has waited this long to come against us, it may be that he knows our movements," said the commander. "How this can be I do not know. Our scouts have seen no one riding to the Crossroads."

"Why do you think he knows our movements?" asked Verardian, who sat in on all of the meetings though he was no soldier or strategist.

"He has timed his advance perfectly," said Torian as he pored over the map of the Southlands. "We cannot return to the city before his soldiers, who sailed to Andrian, surround it, and this also means that our own fleet is under threat. He moves his troops from the Crossroads into the Southlands in time to cut us off from the forest. His troops march down the South Road to meet us on the plains. In open country his superior force and particularly the mounted troops could see our army decimated in the first battle. We must speed our advance to the forest." Torian became silent and continued to study the map, judging distances and time.

"Do we send troops back to Andrian?" asked Mantris as if to himself.

"They will not reach there in time," replied Torian with assurance.

"But the lands will be ravaged by those who have come there," said Mantris. "Are we here to protect a sparsely populated plain, or defend the city and its people?"

"The choices are difficult," said Tolth, stroking his beard as he stood looking over Torian's shoulder at the map. "Our force is so small that to contemplate an open attack against a superior force such as now moves into Andrian from the coast seems most dangerous. If we return to defend Andrian, his troops will close from behind and snap the trap shut. Also, I do not believe that Maradass will burn Andrian yet, if at all. He must feed his troops, at least for now. I think the slaughter that was shown to Kerran was but a ruse to force our hand. The City Amitarl too may fall, but that would not end the war. For now I feel the forest is our safest hope. We need places of refuge as this struggle may go on for a great length of time, perhaps years. We must move quickly but with care. For us to lose one soldier is harder on us than if Maradass were to lose an entire troop."

"We will be receiving reports of their movements within days," said Torian. "Perhaps the horse troops coming from the north will not move so quickly, and they may remain with these stone foot soldiers." He looked up at Mantris.

"No," said his friend. "I do not think we can expect Maradass to move slowly once he has begun. I fear, no matter how quickly we march to the forest, his horse troops will be there before us." He looked across at Kerran before continuing. "We may yet win out," he said. "Without these tidings from our young wizard we could have been facing half of the Black Army in the open, and not just the horse troops. We must hasten to the forest without delay."

It was decided to send out their own horsemen in pursuit of the Elbrand who had marched to the north and west. They were to be told of the movements of the Maradass army, and then both bands were to advance to the forest as quickly as possible. A message would be sent to the Elbrand who prepared the hiding place in the swamps south of the Crossroads. They would be told to remain where they were, unseen. If Marauders were in the lands around them it would be most dangerous for them to move.

The army of Zeta was almost at rest when the word came that they were marching that night. A late moon rose to find the troops of Zeta moving quickly to the west. During the night they passed to the north of a range of tall, rocky pinnacles called the Pillars. Kerran, who had slept for three days, was having trouble staying awake as his horse moved ahead with the others who were mounted. He remembered something in the meeting which had not seemed to be answered. It was Verardian's question on how Maradass could know of their army's movements. They were a small army in a vast land. He queried Tolth on the problem partly to help keep himself awake.

"It does seem that he knows our plans," agreed Tolth. "As Torian said, the timing was well judged. Perhaps it is the Seacrest that betrays our presence." Tolth became silent as though he had thought on this before.

The army marched hard throughout the night. Never in troops or an ordered line, they would rest as they needed but never slipped far behind. Some would run forward for leagues then wait until the others reached them. Kerran had at first been amused by this disorderly advance. His ideas of soldiers and war had always been regimented and strict. This scattered army of many individuals covered the ground before them at a pace much quicker than the fastest army. These men and women took orders because they wanted to, because they were in the Regions to honour their ancestry, and an ancient vow.

Kerran had spent much time studying the Elbrand and soldiers of Zeta. None seemed to be dressed or armed exactly alike. Practically all of them carried a bow and a sword, but the variety of extra equipment was staggering. Some carried multiple knives. Some had spears, or shields and many other individual weapons. Some chose to wear helmets while others did not. There were a few who wore heavy breast plates or light mail, while others wore nothing but thick woven jerkins which may stop the edge of a sword but not a direct thrust. Some wore no protection at all except their normal clothing, and their own ability to survive. Dawn came at their backs, lighting up the vast plains. The land sloped downward imperceptibly to the north and they crossed a muddy river flanked by tall reeds. Those who cooked supplied a hasty breakfast, and then the army marched again into the warmth of the day.

Over the next two days they advanced quickly to the west. The troop of five hundred Elbrand who had gone towards the forest had been contacted and would await their arrival on the edge of the trees. Of the other troops who were marching to the northern hiding place amongst the swamps, there had been no word. They were thought to be travelling through low hills and woodlands to the east of the plains. Scouts returned with tidings from ahead. Maradass's horse troops were already gathered on the road between them and the forest, and by noon of the next day they would be in sight.

All the troops of Zeta tried to rest and sleep that night, but thoughts of the morrow kept many a young soldier awake and nervous, wondering if the next day may be their last. There were five or perhaps six thousand black horse troops spread for leagues along the South Road. Single riders connected larger groups, and there were many hundred marauders roaming the country, watching, waiting, knowing that soon they would smell the blood of battle.

The day dawned ominous with heavy grey clouds gathering in the west. A late summer storm rolled across the sky and by noon the road was in sight. A harsh wind blew with sharp pellets of rain, stinging their faces as they looked towards the dark lines of horsemen. The troops of Maradass stood mounted and waiting, marauders held back behind them, ready to reap the rewards of the horse soldier's first charge. The troops of Zeta began to spread out across the plain in a great arc, almost a league from tip to tip, at their centre a tight knot of Elbrand and horsemen advanced across the plain, the standard of the white hawk waving violently in the wind.

It was a slow, steady march into the biting gale. The sky opened and sheets of driving rain swept across the battlefield. For a time Kerran could see nothing ahead of them, the road obliterated by the downpour, then the squall eased for a time and once again the black troops could be seen much closer this time, the emblem of the dog's skull flying from many standards. Kerran could see the distant horse's breath as it condensed in the air. Individual horsemen began to stand out and he could see one who must be a commander, a tall silver helmet upon his head.

No more than two long bow shots separated the opposing armies when there was a shattering horn blast, and a roar from the black horsemen as they began their charge. As the thundering of hooves bore down upon the army of Zeta foot soldiers, Kerran heard in his mind the words that had been spoken at the war council before they had marched that morning.

"If we spread them wide we can combat their speed and strength," Mantris had said. "If they charge through us we will let them go. If we can unhorse them, then we will take their mounts, and this will be our most important task other than staying alive. They outnumber us, but not by so many, we are on foot and so they will expect us to be overwhelmed by their first charge. They have not yet fought against our troops and are in for a surprise I think. Beware of the dogs. They will attack you from below and behind when you think your enemy is above, our best archers are set to concentrate on them. We do not want this fight so when we break through we will continue towards the forest. Horses are of the most importance as I said, capture enough horses and our army becomes mobile. We will not use arrows against them until we are sure of our marks.

The horses must survive."

The words faded from Kerran's mind as the reality of the thunderous charge shattered his thoughts. The wave of horsemen swept down upon the army of Zeta who ceased their forward march and prepared to absorb the attack. To the south the two opposing lines had already come together, the sudden mixing of Black and Green was savage and violent. A cry went up as steel clashed upon steel, horses reared and thrashed against the press of foot troops. Through the falling rain Kerran saw a lone soldier of Zeta leapt to the back of a riderless horse, and waving his sword he thrust himself and his mount into the thick of the battle. More charging horsemen were dismounted, the Elbrand had perfected their technique and Kerran began to see many leaping into empty saddles. Some of the black horsemen broke through, leaving Elbrand and others lying dead in their wake. The main press of troops around the white hawk standard pushed forward. Lines of black horsemen broke on them like waves upon a rocky shoreline. Kerran saw Torian suddenly leap to an empty saddle, his sword crashing down upon the head of another horseman. He gave a huge battle cry that rose above all others and thrust forward into the fray.

To the north the long arm of green and brown troops stretched beyond the first rush of riders. Those not yet in the fight began to sweep west and south, enveloping many of the horse troops. Bitter fighting took place, hand to hand. Horsemen were toppled to fight upon the ground while marauders rushed in, savaging the wounded of both sides. The knot of Elbrand around Kerran and the Amitarl family was battered by the withering charge. At full gallop the riders of Maradass crashed into the foot soldiers and the dead of both sides began to spread across the battlefield, though most of them wore the black armour of Maradass. The horsemen who had broken through now turned to attack the rear of the marching army, and number of green and brown foot soldiers were cut off by a wedge of charging horsemen. They drew into a tight circle as many of the horse troops thundered down upon this easy prey. There was a loud cry from Mantris as he led a charge of warriors to the rescue. Their weight broke the flank of the circling horsemen. Men fell from their mounts and heavy bladed knives, thrown with great skill, tore through chain mail and flesh.

To the north the horse troops were pulling back, scattered and numbed by the mastery of the soldiers against whom they had just fought. Small groups of Zeta's warriors, mounted and fearless, rode after them for a time, capturing more horses. From their saddles they began to use their bows on the scavenging marauders who foraged amongst those who lay dead and dying upon the open ground. The battle remained bitter and furious around the white hawk of Amitarl. Kerran could see beyond the dense press of soldiers surrounding them to where sword flashed and horses reared and fell. Arrows began to fall amongst the troops of Zeta. In front of his horse a man cried out and fell, a short dark shaft deep in his chest. Flights of blonde wooden shafts arched through the sky from the bowmen of Zeta, and with their extra range and accuracy they pushed the horse troops back beyond their own bow range. To the south many hundreds of horsemen had pulled away, and then charged again. A group of fifty or more of the best Elbrand bowmen, who had been held in reserve behind the main standard, were now sent quickly to their aid. With deadly accuracy the archers began to pick off horsemen one by one. As each fell a green and brown figure would leap to the empty saddle. Many horsemen of the Black Army fell to the deadly shafts before the others retreated. Now only about the central core of the slow advance was the battle still raging.

Torian rallied his troops on from the back of a tall stallion. He parried a lance thrust and his short broad bladed sword ripped into the man's abdomen. Another horseman charged him and met the pommel of the sword against the nose guard of his helmet. The man fell stunned from the saddle. Kerran saw the silver helmet of the horse troops commander. He had sat aloof from the battle, but now, with a wedge of a thousand of his horse troops gathered about him, he thundered down upon the white hawk standard.

Torian saw him coming and like a plough through soft earth he forged his way forward to meet this chief of adversaries. His sword claimed two more horsemen almost in abstraction, his whole being intent on coming together with the silver helmet. Other Elbrand who had mounted now pushed forward to join him. From a distance Kerran recognised the large figure of Brook amongst their number. A battle cry, high and dark, coursed from the red bearded lips of Torian as his sword clashed against that of the horse troop's commander.

Kerran watched the short fierce battle. Both men were highly skilled and their blades slashed and parried in a blur. With a lunge of his free hand the commander battered Torian with a vicious fist to his unprotected head. Torian did not fall as more blows fell fast and shattering. Torian's sword broke and he almost fell from his mount, clutching at the saddle. He was still off balance when the commander aimed a blow which should have taken Torian's head from his shoulders, but it did not. The army commander of Zeta avoided the blow, the sword ringing sharply as it was deflected by his shoulder plate. Torian then slipped quickly beneath his lunging horse and wrenching a sword from a dying hand he thrust upward with all his strength through the chain mail and high into the black commander's body. Kerran heard the man's dying scream across the distance and tumult of battle.

Torian leapt to the empty saddle and charged at the horsemen around him, and his ferocity could not be countered. Horses and men fell back from his charge. A standard bearer was too slow as the hand which held the wooden shaft was severed from its arm. Torian bellowed and charged again, followed now by a number of mounted Elbrand. It was too much for those around them. Their commander lay dead on the ground and the mastery of their enemy had never been realised until now. Horsemen broke away and bolted to the north. Others, finding themselves deserted by their comrades, gave up the fight and galloped from the carnage. The main press of Zeta's army, where Kerran sat upon his horse, had shuddered to a halt against the weight of attack but had not broken. A cheer went up from the army of Zeta as the last of the black horsemen retreated in disarray, and then the green and brown warriors began to move around the battlefield, searching for injured comrades.

Verardian went quickly to do what he could for the wounded. Kerran watched as an older member of the Elbrand dressed a jagged wound in a young soldier's arm. All over the field soldiers were helping the injured, and there were some who found that they must help the dying. Many of the wounded were put on horseback to ease them from their wounds. The forest was still a day's march to the west. Soldiers began the sad task of collecting their fallen. Though the whole might of Maradass should come down upon them, they would not leave their dead to the marauders. A thousand pairs of hands using knives and short swords scooped a deep hollow in the soft earth of the plain. Their dead comrades were laid gently within and buried. Many a tear streaked a battle weary face as friend, brother or sister was covered beneath the dark earth.

The army prepared to march again. Far off could be seen the gathered troops of Maradass horsemen, but they did not again attack the army of Zeta as it moved across the South Road. The horse troops of Maradass had never thought to lose this battle, and now almost half of their number lay dead or dying upon the bloody field. Some black troops stood stunned and bewildered amongst their dead, the wind and rain lashing at their still dark forms until a swirling mist obscured them from view.

Voice on the Wind

The march to the forest did not cease until the army of Zeta had reached the edge of the trees and joined with the Elbrand who waited for them there. The night was dark with the continual threat of rain. Moving back in amongst the trees the troops of Zeta made camp and the injured were attended to. Dry wood was found, enough to heat water and clean their wounds. Guards were set on the edge of the trees, though none expected the horse troops to follow and attack, though marauders may come on the blood scent. Kerran joined Tolth and the others in the dry interior of their tent. Wind buffeted the walls as steady rain continued to fall.

"We lost many good soldiers today," Mantris was saying as Kerran entered. "More than two hundred dead, and as many wounded who will fight no more. It was a victory that we could ill afford, though we gained almost six hundred horses." He smiled now for the first time. "Maradass will surely not miss them, and we will have much need of them in the times to come.

"A scout has arrived from the forest to the north," he continued. "Marauders are scattered through the woods there and hold the way, many hundreds of them the man said. They push slowly south, already they have discovered a high rock shelf which we thought to use as a refuge, there were too few to defend it so they retreated, and there is still no word from the Elbrand who went north to the Crossroads." He did not voice the thought which none wished to hear, what if the Elbrand had been detected by a much greater force and had been attacked? "We have dispatched riders to the South Coast," Mantris told them. "Those from the black fleet which sailed on Andrian could be nigh the city by now. I think their further plan will be to take our ships if they can and leave us stranded here, though I doubt Captain Ronsarl will be taken unawares."

"Have you thought more on the question of how Maradass knows of our movements?" The question came again from Verardian who was resting for a time from his labours with the wounded.

"I have thought on it," replied Mantris. "But I find no solution."

There was a stirring from the corner of the tent. Mindis stood slowly from the cot where he had lain and came forward, shuffling slowly into the light, an arm out before him, an accusing finger pointed at Kerran.

"There," said Mindis, his voice sharp and strained. "There is the one who tells Maradass where we are. It is he who would betray Amitarl. Take it from him!" An insane look swept across his face. "He must not have it," he cried again and suddenly lunged at Kerran.

Tolth and Verardian held him and his attempts to fight free were weak and feeble. Soon he ceased his struggle but remained looking with anger at Kerran.

"You will bring Amitarl to its knees," he hissed across the space between them. "You will destroy us all and the land with us."

"What do you mean?" asked Kerran sharply. The day had taking its toll on him and he was tired. He did not know why Mindis should hate him so much, or why the boy thought as he did. "I mean no harm to anyone here," he said more softly.

The dark eyes looked menacingly at him from under heavy lids.

"My mother has told me all," he said quietly now. "She will come for me when all is done." Mindis's voice was a soft whisper, fading, gone.

The eyes which had looked with such emotion now stared at the space before them, seeing nothing of those around him. Verardian led Mindis back to his bed and laid him gently down.

"What can he mean?" said Kerran to Tolth who stood pondering the same question and did not answer.

Kerran slept late and when he woke the next morning he found that many of the soldiers from Zeta had gone. Tolth saw Kerran as he came from the tent, the sleep still a haze before his eyes.

"You slept well I think," said Tolth as he came smiling to his young friend's side. "It is almost noon."

Kerran looked up through the branches above. The sky was grey and gloomy, the forest dark and unfriendly.

"There has been a place chosen that we move to," said Tolth. "A refuge deeper in the forest. Eat quickly for we ride soon."

Kerran made his way to the small campfire. There was a scraping of cold oats left in a pot and a jug of warm tea sat amongst the embers. A shiver ran through his body. The air was cold and damp, and the trees nearby trailed away into the soft shadows of mist. The word 'Coming' entered Kerran's mind as if it were a sliver of glass. The inside of his skull was suddenly torn by a shattering intensity of pain, and he cried out in anguish. A young man at the water's edge stood aghast as Kerran screamed in pain and fell to the ground. Tolth came running from the tent and others hastened towards the terrible cry. As Kerran slipped into unconsciousness he heard the words of Maradass, like a voice on the wind.

"Coming," it said, "Coming."

Kerran fell into darkness, deeper and deeper into a black endless void.

Tolth reached Kerran as he collapsed and his attempts to revive his young friend were to no avail. Verardian was sent for. He too could do nothing but confirm that Kerran lived, but hovered on the brink and could slip into death at any time. A stretcher was prepared and four soldiers carried it gently as the last troops left the camp and plunged deeper into the woods. The storm which had been threatening broke now in great fury upon the forest. Tolth rode beside Verardian close to the covered stretcher which held Kerran. Rain fell in sheets around them and the horses moved forward slowly, the ground soft underfoot where others had ridden earlier. At several points they passed over wide rock shelves where few trees grew. The forward scouts had led them in this direction to help confuse those who would try to follow their trail. Torian joined Tolth, he had spoken with the scouts who had discovered the refuge. It sounded ideal but they would not reach it until the following day. The majority of the horses were going a different route to a place not far from the main force but further to the south. Scouts could disguise the army's trail but horses left many signs, and the two forces would remain separate but in close contact.

Torian looked up at the skies and smiled. "Even marauders will find it hard to discover us now," he said to Tolth. "There are three hundred bowmen following well behind us. Any marauders or horsemen who wish to follow us will pay dearly."

He looked again at the sky, the raindrops running into his beard. He laughed aloud once more and rode to the rear of the column. The sun's light faded from the cheerless grey sky and darkness came quickly. They camped without fires, eating cold fare and huddling into the shelter of tents or under simple waterproof sheeting. It was an uncomfortable night for many and at first light they were moving again, cold oats and dried fruit eaten as they travelled.

They finally came from the north into a narrow valley which ran sloping to the east. The south side of the gully was lower than the north, where rock outcrops, weathered by time, stood grey and stark against the green of the forest. The north side of the narrow valley towered above them, laced through with caves and overhanging rock. Over the centuries it had been eaten by the rain and wind, forming a natural haven for the army of Zeta. As Tolth rode into the camp he looked around at the soldiers who were gathered along the length of the gully. The rain had ceased for a time, and small fires and the smell of cooking told of the army's hunger.

It was a good refuge that the scouts had found. It gave shelter and a defendable position, while it also allowed them a place to retreat to over the lower side if they were forced to abandon the camp. To the west and south the land fell away to another small valley with a river running swiftly through it. Tolth and Verardian rode to the large dry cave which had been set aside for them. Kerran was laid down gently on the dusty floor where a fire had been set. Food was being cooked by a young man named Taris who had spoken with Kerran the previous day. Rark stretched his great length by the fire and was asleep almost immediately. The mountain dog had played no part in the battle on the South Road, and Tolth had noticed that the dog had remained very aware of Kerran during the battle, as though protecting the young man.

"Wake not?" queried the young soldier as Verardian knelt beside Kerran.

"No," the healer replied. "He sleeps as if dead. His heart is slow and his breath is barely present. I can only hope."

Verardian placed a gentle hand on Kerran's forehead for a time and then joined the others at the fire. He needed a bowl of soup to take the dampness from his heart. Tolth stood beside his son and placed a hand on Verardian's shoulder.

"You do all you can, then you do much more," he told his son. "How much sleep have you had since the battle I wonder?"

Verardian looked into the old man's eyes and gave his father a tired smile. "Perhaps a little more than you father," he said in reply.

Tolth had barely laid his head to sleep since they had fought Maradass on the South Road.

"We must both take rest," said Tolth and sat against a rock near the fire.

He looked into the flames for a time then realised that though they sat in a dry, almost enclosed cave, the smoke did not collect against the high ceiling. He peered upward. There was evidence of many past fires. Black soot had collected on the stone above for what must have been generations. Tolth detected a movement in the smoke rising from the fire. It floated slowly towards the back of the cave where he could see a narrow shaft leading further upward. Light from beyond did not penetrate but Tolth knew that there must be an exit for the smoke high above them. He glanced about the cave and imagined his great ancestors living in such a den for generation upon uncounted generation. He relaxed and felt at peace for the first time in many days. Worry fell from him, and closing his eyes, Tolth slipped into sleep. His last thought was for Kerran, who lay by the fire near him.

Tolth jerked awake at a sudden, clattering sound. There was daylight streaming across the entrance of the cave and the young man Taris was stirring the fire into life, a pot of oats hung above.

"Fine morn," he said smiling at Tolth, and then looked to Kerran shaking his head. "Bad not he eat," he said stirring the oats and adding a little salt. "Eat must," he said almost to himself, looking intently into the pot.

"Indeed, eat must," said Tolth as he knelt beside Kerran.

Nothing had changed during the night. Kerran lay still and almost lifeless. Tolth had seen him in this cold trance-like state before and Kerran had always come back to the living, but Tolth feared that one time he may not. Little sign of life showed on his young friend's pale unmoving face. The old Amitarl rose and went to the entrance of the cave. He gazed at the army which lay camped in the almost treeless valley. Small, almost smokeless fires cooked the troops' morning gruel, while some of the soldiers bathed in the small streams which came together near the centre of the valley. Tolth stood and admired these men and women who had come to this unknown land to fight a war in his family's name. He saw Torian and Mantris coming towards him up the valley side, they greeted him then began to tell of the latest reports from the scouts.

Nothing had been heard of the Elbrand who had gone north. From the City Highroad came the news of the steady advance of the force which now marched into Andrian. The scouts reported that thirty thousand stone soldiers as well as four thousand horse troops travelled south on the road.

"They will besiege Andrian," said Torian. "So many of these

stone soldiers march with them, the scouts are calling them Stone Soldiers because of the way they keep stiff and precise."

"There are another twenty thousand of these soldiers marching down the South Road, no more than six days march from here," continued Mantris. "They are not all Stone Soldiers, the horse troops we met in battle have fallen back to join them, and marauders are everywhere, from the road to well inside the forest."

"What of the city and our ships?" asked Tolth, anxious for some good news.

"There has been no word," said Torian, breathing a heavy sigh into his beard.

"Ronsarl will not lose the fleet," said Mantris. "He will stand off and give Maradass no opportunity. It is the city that I fear for. The Governor would give it up to save his own skin, of this I am sure. The ruffians gathered around him are no more than large brutes, there to lean on the small people. They will not defend the city. The troops of the invading fleet must almost be at the city gates by now. We may return to find Maradass sitting in Celisor Castle, or find the city in flames."

"Our choices were few," said Tolth. "The Governor would not have us enter the city and I would not take it by force. The city must care for itself. We are but a few compared to those who march against us. Our allies are our skills, stealth and the awareness of how few we are. No soldier of Zeta must die needlessly. Maradass will be driven from the land. It may take years and the fall of the city, but it will be done." There was a deep fire in Tolth's voice that stirred the commanders and captains who had gathered around him.

Much of the day was spent in planning their next move. It was decided that an attack on the marauders in the forest should be made. One thousand of their most expert archers would be sent north the following morning. They were to remain in the forest and seek out the dogs. They should not be hard to find as they too sought their prey. Meanwhile scouts would keep the approaching army in sight from the safety of the swamplands on the Central Plains. Marauders were not sent to those wetlands but had been kept to the west of the road. If the Black Army was to leave the road for the forest, the commanders wished to know quickly, and a force would then be sent to confront then at the edge of Dreardim.

During the afternoon a messenger arrived from the city Amitarl. As with many people, he had left there the day before the army of Maradass was to reach it. After the initial slaughter at the coast, the black troops had marched down into Andrian, taking what they wanted but moving quickly towards the city. Villages emptied before them, people ran and hid in the woods and grain fields. The best news that the man had brought to them was that Captain Ronsarl had indeed sailed the fleet from the coast, preferring to weather gales rather than have his ships fall into the hands of Maradass.

Tolth remained amongst the soldiers for much of the day, returning to the cave often to see if Kerran had woken. Taris had taken to sitting with Kerran, and Verardian also spent much time within the cave, now that the wounded in his care no longer needed his attention as they had. Night came and from the entrance of the cave Tolth looked down upon the camp where small glowing points showed at the cooking fires. He reached into his pouch and clasped the fragment of the Seacrest and felt its subdued magic, warm and comforting. All knew that the Seacrest had power, but few had ever seen even a small hint of its magic. None, not even Tolth, had ever brought forth its full potential. He knew that one day he may have to unleash it, if indeed he could, yet he feared the outcome. Though he had lived a long life he knew now that he was truly old. He did not know if he could find the balance between the power of the Seacrest and his own ability to harness and use that power. He looked up at the stars and saw his own sign high in the lofty heavens.

Kerran did not wake until the following evening, but it was the news which reached the camp at noon that crushed the army of Zeta into a painful deathly silence. At first light the one thousand bowmen had moved north as planned, disappearing into the trees like so many shadows. Little had happened during the morning and Tolth was sitting quietly talking with Mantris when a horse carrying two riders entered the valley.

The mount was ridden by one of the men from the Southlands, and behind him clung an Elbrand, her clothes ragged and muddy. Clotted blood showed at her brow and one arm was strapped roughly to her body. Soldiers stood and looked as the horse slowly picked its way through the troops towards Tolth and Mantris. The horseman walked his mount up the small slope and came to a halt before them as the woman slid to the ground, then buckled at the knees, falling into the dirt before anyone could reach her. Tolth called to Verardian as soldiers rushed to pick the woman up and make her comfortable, her arm was broken and she needed attention. It was some time before she could tell her story, and when she did there were few who did not cry openly at the telling.

The woman's name was Imlon and she was one of the Elbrand who had gone north to the Crossroads. She told her tale briefly, her voice numb, emotionless. The five hundred Elbrand had been one day's march from the refuge in the swamp when a single marauder had found their trail, even though they had travelled much through wetlands to avoid the dogs. When they were discovered they did not realise that this one dog was a scout for the vast army of Maradass which marched south on the City Highroad. The Elbrand had been keeping far from the road and it was only the saddest chance which brought the marauder onto their scent. The dog had followed them until he was within sight. Several arrows had almost caught the marauder and he had turned and fled. The Elbrand had pushed on quickly for they did not know how close the Black Army might be.

They had been running for a long time when they saw a great many horse soldiers come into view, far to the east. They had leapt forward, running to save their lives, looking for a large stretch of dense swamp to lose themselves in, but it was not to be. They had run until the horse soldiers were almost upon them and then they stood and fought, their arrows soon spent. Many black horsemen died, but they greatly outnumbered the Elbrand and there was only one possible outcome.

The muddied and battered woman was the only survivor of the battle. She had been clubbed to the ground in one of the early charges and left for dead. When her mind cleared she could see the closing stage of the battle not far away, and could do little but slip further into concealment as night had come to the plains. With the last light she had seen the horse troops of Maradass riding to the east, leaving the bodies of enemy and friend alike strewn across the bloody ground. Amongst the dead were many close friends, brothers, sons and daughters. There was not a soldier who did not grieve that night for someone now lost to them forever.

Kerran returned to the cave slowly. At first he lay still, his mind quietly adjusting to the feelings of his body. The cot on which he lay felt uncomfortably hard against his back. There was stiffness in his neck and shoulders but he did not yet move to ease his discomfort. Sounds began to slowly intrude upon his hearing, the scraping of a spoon against the inside of a pot, the soft bubble of cooking, and the quiet crackle of the fire. From behind his eyelids Kerran could see the light flickering, and smell the nearby food. He stirred, rolling slowly over and looking towards the fire.

The young man Taris was stirring a pot, his back to Kerran, who found that he could not speak, his throat being so dry. Kerran reached out and touched Taris on the arm. The young man leapt in fright, the large spoon falling from his hand into the fire. Taris turned quickly from alarm to concern as he saw that Kerran was awake. He called to the cave entrance where Tolth and Verardian sat in the soft light of dusk. They came quickly to Kerran's side and Verardian helped him to drink a little water. Then Kerran lay back. He was weak but elated. A change had come over him yet he could not place the nature of it. Unlike his previous dreams he remembered little more than floating high above the earth, escaping from cold blue flames, and he had wanted to remain there forever, at peace.

"I feel a new strength in me," said Kerran to Tolth when he had recovered enough to speak. "I cannot explain it, for there is so little to tell. The dream took me to a place where I felt truly at peace and completely safe. There were no thoughts or feelings, other than a sense of tranquillity that I have never felt before. And yet there was something else, an understanding that came that I cannot explain, even to myself. It was so strange. I could almost taste something that seemed to have no flavour, like hearing a song without hearing the words, but knowing the meaning of it all the same."

Kerran paused and gave a wistful sigh, then shook his head. "I feel like someone who is threatened from all sides but feels no fear," he said. "Like one who holds a bow and arrows yet does not know how to use them. I believe now that I must be the son of Chelasta. I know that it cannot be otherwise. I just wish I knew a little more about my powers and how I might use them to help us."

"Do not concern yourself with these things just yet," said Tolth. "All will come in time I am sure. Perhaps it is meant to be that you remain unknowing for now. It will come when it must. Though Rishtan-Sta is now long dead, his influence continues in the Seacrest. Your own powers, though unformed and unknown, are part of a wizard's inheritance. The Seacrest piece that you carry may strengthen those powers, but it will take time."

"We may not have that much time," said Kerran.

"We will not be beaten," said Taris, who passed a bowl of soup to Kerran.

Mantris had come to the fire and now told of reports from scouts and the troops who had gone north into the forest. The archers had met marauders in the woods. Many of the dogs were killed, led into traps by false scents and dead ends. The day had been one skirmish after another against the animals. Few of the troops had been attacked by marauders and none had received serious wounds. The hunt for the dogs continued, though the creatures had become reluctant to attack once they had seen their companions fall under a hail of arrows. From the road came the news that the black troops who had come south were now camped not far from the recent battlefield; there were a great many of the stone soldiers amongst them.

"They will come into the forest after us," said Mantris. "Our allies are our speed and ability to stay hidden. We will dog them, attack unexpectedly, and leave quickly to attack elsewhere. Depending on how many they leave beyond the edge of the forest we may use our horsemen to attack in the open. Horses remain of most importance, and if they bring mounted troops into the forest, then our chances of taking them will improve."

He seemed puzzled and stood looking into the fire for a time. "Word has also reached us from the City Amitarl," he continued. "The troops of Maradass have camped outside the city gate and have not attacked. This seems most strange when they could take the city, and probably the castle, with very little resistance. Maradass plays an unknown game."

"I think Maradass has other plans for the city," said Tolth. "He could be trying to draw our forces into the open to defend it. This gives me hope for those of my family who remain lost in the north. If Maradass had managed to seize Landin's piece of the Seacrest he would have no thoughts of biding his time."

He paused a moment, then smiled. "I am pleased that the city and castle have not been taken and destroyed," he said. "It would be a travesty to see such a place become a ruin. I would still like to know what Maradass has in his plans for the Governor."

"It may be that he would use the Governor to try and turn the Southlands against us," said Mantris. "It would create civil war if the Governor found support enough. Many would follow him to save themselves from Maradass, those with property and wealth, those with much to lose, and those with power over others. Maradass treats this war as a game, I think, like the wizards of old. "

"Ultimately Maradass *will* destroy the lands," said Tolth. "I have no doubt that he wishes death on all those in the Regions. His desire is for a total ending of all those with a free will. He would become as the ancient wizards were, building armies to war against each other. He wishes to live forever and could make it so. He desires the power within the four pieces and would own them all if he could, and this cannot be," Tolth spoke with a fierce look in his eyes. "This will not be," he added darkly.

"Indeed," said Mantris.

The night passed and dawn came softly slanting through the forest, bird calls of many kinds filling the air. Kerran rose early, though he felt a little weak as he made his way into the morning light. The camp was awake and there was much movement of troops. Many would now go to the edge of the forest. It was expected that the army of Maradass waiting at the South Road would soon be marching towards Dreardim. Small bands of Elbrand would harass them as soon as it came within range, then fall back setting traps for any that pursued them.

Taris served Kerran hot oats and tea before bidding him good day as he left with his troop. The valley after a time became almost empty of soldiers, only a few hundred remaining to watch the camp. Tolth continued to receive messengers during the day. The entire army of Maradass had marched towards the forest as expected, and by evening they had camped within sight of the trees. The troops of Zeta waited through the dark and by first light they were astir. There were many bowmen now amongst the black troops. They used the short bows and shafts that were traditional in the lands. They could not reach the range of the longbow, but amongst the trees of the forest distance would not count so much. Accuracy and speed would be the keys. It was later that evening that Kerran heard the full account of the battle.

The army of Maradass had spread wide before entering the forest. They stretched for a league across the plain. The dogs came on first into the edge of Dreardim, scenting the air warily as they slipped beneath the shadows of the outlying trees. Dark troops on foot followed, while a great many of the horse troops did not mount; they watched their army from a small hillock which looked to be their permanent camp; behind them stood troop upon troop of the Stone Soldiers, as yet untested in battle. The marauders had not gone far before they were under attack; many died before they retreated beyond the trees and nothing would make them enter the forest again ahead of the army. Then the soldiers had begun to fall, the long deadly shafts of Zeta piercing their armour and mail. Occasionally a black shaft had found a mark, but they were few compared with the enemy's injured and dead.

During the day the soldiers of Maradass advanced beneath the trees, the troops beginning to split up as gullies and rocky outcrops had to be traversed. The troops of Zeta dropped back slowly, never allowing the soldiers of Maradass to reach them and come into close battle. Sometimes a large number of Elbrand would remain hidden until a troop of soldiers was almost upon them. These attacks were ferocious and over quickly, the Elbrand not allowing themselves to be overwhelmed or surrounded. The battle continued into the afternoon, and by the time the troops of Maradass ceased their pursuit they had lost a great many of their foot soldiers and had come no more than a league into the forest.

The Black Army continued to come under attack from Elbrand as the sky darkened to night, and marauders had been brought forward to guard their encampment. The skill of the forces from Zeta had staggered the black commanders so many of their soldiers had died that day they did not wish to hear the count. The soldiers of Zeta remained in the forest, the sounds from the opposing army within their hearing. Fires were being lit in the enemy's camps until Elbrand marksmen killed a number of those who sat or stood about the flames. The fires were extinguished and the camp became dark. Only cold fare would be had by the Black Army this night. By the light of a hazy moon, many of the soldiers of Zeta began to comb the forest for arrows, so many had been spent that some bowmen found themselves using the dark arrows of the enemy, though they were not suited to the long bow as were the keenly crafted shafts of Zeta. At dawn the scattered battle continued.

The troops of Maradass again pushed deeper into the forest, besieged on all sides by the archers of Zeta, who they could not get within their frustrated grasp. At the same time, on the edge of the forest, five hundred mounted Elbrand suddenly rode from the trees and attacked the unsuspecting camp of sleeping horsemen. Few guards had been set, and perhaps they were asleep, for the Elbrand were almost upon the camp before many of the men had even come to their feet. The Elbrand charged amongst the troops, scattering them, and in the confusion a large number of horses were cut from the lines and led quickly away. The camp was alive with black horsemen running after their mounts or fighting from the ground where they were not used to being. The victory for the Elbrand was crushing. Almost a thousand horses were captured, most without saddles, but the soldiers of Zeta had all learned from their childhood how to ride a horse bare back. During the entire battle the Stone Army had stood silent, seeming to be totally unaware of the conflict.

By day's end the Army of Maradass had ground to a halt. The continual attacks and deadly shafts from the brown and green soldiers had withered the confidence of their commanders. In two days of fighting, fully one third of their force had been killed or injured. They had lost many horses, and it seemed that they had barely seen the enemy, let alone defeat them. In the narrow valley where lay the refuge, Tolth and Kerran watched as the wounded were brought into camp. Verardian and the other healers had little time for rest. The injured lay uncomplaining as the most serious were attended to.

Mantris came with news in the late evening, joining them for a warm meal in the cave. "They fear us," he said as he dunked a wad of bread into his soup. "They begin to avoid the battle, pulling back and hoping others will reach us first. They have no liking for these conditions." He paused a moment then glanced at Kerran, who did not notice the look. "There is something which has become obvious to me over the last few days," continued Mantris. "Though the Black Army is at times scattered, it continues to move in one direction, it comes towards this refuge as though they know where to find us."

Tolth looked at the army commander. "So it continues," Tolth said. "There is a much greater danger for us if Maradass can somehow know where we are. If it is the Seacrest which gives us away then it may be time for me to test my own strengths. I cannot hide in this cave forever."

"You should not expose yourself to the enemy," said Mantris. "Though we have lost many who will be mourned when all is done we have the Black Army at bay. Another day and they will have no heart to pursue us, even if I am wrong they will never reach the refuge before we have time to remove ourselves. The forest is vast and we could be here for years, though we would probably have to learn to eat rabbit more often." He smiled at

Kerran and the memory of the young man's first arrival on Zeta in his rabbit skin coat.

"There is one thing that may force us to make more haste," said Tolth. "There is a full moon in ten days. It is the full moon of Zard's birth, and by the following moon he will be amongst us, again a full grown man."

The words hung heavily on the air as those about the fire pondered the return of the Black Knight.

"Will he be the same?" asked Kerran, the image of the dark giant coming vividly to mind.

"I do not know," said Tolth. "It may be that he will be different, but I cannot say. He was once a man of peace. and then he became the dark spectre of war. Even Maradass cannot know the true nature of his son who is as yet unborn. Though he will try to warp Zard to his ways with spells before Zard can gain his own self. It is said that the Mad One cast such spells to make Zard, the Black Knight, into the monster that he was to become." The old Amitarl paused and looked into the fire. "He will come," said Tolth eventually. "And he will come in war. Of this I have no doubt."

By the end of the following day the army of Maradass had begun their retreat. They had fought against phantoms all day, rarely had they even struck a blow against the green and brown warriors, whereas their own men continued to fall from arrow or blade. The retreat became a rout as the troops of Zeta pursued them. Black soldiers threw down their packs and weapons and ran for their lives. They were thralls to the will of Maradass, yet the threat of imminent death was stronger than any spell. Some would stop for a time, a captain holding his men together, but the troops of Zeta still did not attack the front. Instead they pushed elsewhere along the rear of the retreating army. In this way many bands of black soldiers were cut off and surrounded. Some were able to fight their way back to their lines while others were slaughtered before they could escape. Death flew at them from amongst the trees and the rout became total panic.

As the first of the black soldiers reached the thankful

sunlight beyond the trees a thousand riders of Zeta attacked from the south. The accuracy of their bowmanship, even from a saddle, saw a great many more of the Black Army fall. The army of Maradass ran from the forest and they did not stop running to fight or to help their comrades. They ran for their own lives until they were far out upon the plains, harassed still by the mounted bowmen. The number of black soldiers who died that day would never be counted, the army was decimated, and by the last light of the sun the remnants had been brought to a standstill far out upon the plains, and far to the south of their horse troops and the vast Stone Army. They could run no more and were forced to stand and fight, during the night they broke through the circle of attackers. Arrows were now few, and the last of the Black Army escaped death and ran blindly into the night.

Torian and Mantris stood together amongst the dead and dying. Both bore signs of the battle, some which would be with them until they died. A blade had raked the face of Torian, his blood mixed darkly with his red beard. Mantris, in the last stages of the battle had been struck in the thigh by a Black shaft from the darkness. Fortunately the arrow had lost much of its power before it had reached him and in the frenzy of the fight he had torn it loose and fought on. He now crumpled to the earth, and Torian too bent his knees and eased himself to the ground slowly. He felt a rib twinge violently in his chest. With a grunt of pain he sat heavily. Others around them stood or sat in exhaustion. The battle was over. The day had been won.

Tolth and Kerran heard the sound of returning soldiers from beyond the cave. They went quickly into the soft twilight of the evening as the green and brown warriors began to flood back into camp, carrying their wounded and dead. The thought of marauders had made many a weary man pick up a fallen comrade and carry him, until he could carry him no more. There were always others there to take up the burden.

It took all of the following day before the scattered, battle weary troops had returned to the refuge. There were few sounds of celebration and laughter, though it had been a victory that should be sung of. The soldiers of Zeta grieved for those of their number who would never again return to the Magic Isles. They dug a large grave and buried their friends gently, and a cairn of many thousand stones was raised over the dead. Reports came in from the road and beyond. The remnants of the battered army now moved north towards the Crossroads and riders of the Elbrand had been sent after them to continue the attack. There were no longer any reported movement of troops coming from the Crossroads down the South Road, so for a time there would be peace for many of the weary fighters of Zeta.

Mantris limped into the cave that evening and was welcomed to the fire. There were a number of people in the cave, and a small victory feast was being eaten, though the fare was plain and the company subdued. Kerran thought of Taris who had cooked his meals so often, and had talked as he worked about the fire. The young soldier now lay under the cold stone of the grave mound below their cave. Mantris eased his damaged leg as he sat down beside the fire, while Torian stood talking to a scout who had recently arrived from the City Amitarl.

Kerran sat beside the fire. A deep feeling of concern had descended upon him, for Rark was gone. Sometime during the morning the mountain dog had left the cave and disappeared from the valley. Elbrand scouts to the west had told of seeing him going deeper into the forest. Kerran was looking at the place by the fire that Rark had made his own when, from the entrance of the cave, there was a flurry of wings and a screech as Storm flew into the crowded space. All in the cave became quiet at the sudden entrance of the white hawk, Storm pecked at the Seacrest fragment that hung around Kerran's neck. Kerran looked at Tolth with a curious look as he removed the fragment and held it in the palm of his hand. His eyes were still on Tolth when a blaze of light suddenly filled his vision. He closed his eyes against the glare and felt his body slump onto the cot where he sat. His mind remained aware of all that was around him, though his body now lay as if asleep. He could see it so clearly that he knew he now looked with the eyes of Storm, who then flew swiftly from the cave. To the west the last light of evening was leaving the sky and he flew that way into the night.

Kerran travelled swiftly into the following dawn, the hawk's strength never weakening. Dreardim swept by beneath his wings and then he knew where he was being taken. Finally, with his keen vision, he could make out the river far ahead. The trees of the forest became scattered as he flew out above the valley of Westerval. His eyes sought out his home and he saw it nestled against the forest as he had always known it. He flew towards it and then saw movement amongst the trees to the north of the house, there was the flash of riders amongst the dense foliage, and he saw marauders as they chased a concealed quarry. Kerran sped onward until he could see three running figures as they broke from the trees and sprinted for the river; marauders and horsemen close behind.

Kerran knew the three before he recognised them. Below him he could see the running figures of two women, one tall and fair, the other small and dark. Behind them ran Flindas who turned quickly to strike at a dog which had outrun the others, and then he turned and ran again. The horse soldiers began to close the gap, and Kerran watched in fear as he saw that the three could not reach the river before the horsemen would be upon them. Whether his fear was conveyed to Storm, or the bird chose to attack on its own, Kerran did not know. In a long swooping dive the white hawk flew at the leading rider and the man screamed as flashing talons raked his face. The horse reared violently and the man fell from his saddle. Again the hawk flew at the horsemen, their mounts suddenly baulking against their riders wishes, fear of the white winged attacker slowing their charge. The few moments that the horsemen took to recover were enough for the three runners to finally reach the river and plunge into the swiftly flowing stream. Marauders ran along the riverbank as two horsemen, foolish enough to ride into the current, were swept away.

Kerran watched from far above as the dark specks which were the heads of Flindas and his companions were swept into the narrow gorge where the river met the forest, he then turned slowly to the east, Storm taking him high above the trees and into the morning sun. The light was dazzling, and then it shone suddenly bright with blue fire. Storm veered and began to fall, his wings unable to hold them aloft, the trees rushing up to meet them. At the last moment, darkness came over Kerran's vision and for a long time all stood still.

The River Glandrin-Dar

Flindas now regretted his decision to seek out the home of Kerran's mother in the valley of Westerval. He had wanted news of the Magic Isles and had hoped that if Kerran and the army of Zeta were in the Southlands she would have heard from her son. She had not, and had wept with happiness when he had told her his tale. It was after they had left her that the riders of Maradass had appeared at the forest edge and pursued them to the river, where the magical appearance of the white hawk had surely saved them from being overrun by the horsemen. The river had swept them away quickly and now, still wet, the three travellers sat in the darkness of a small island in the middle of the fast moving river.

Far off in the night they heard a savage growl, Flindas did not know what it may be and cared not to know if it meant fighting the beast. The forest was a lost world to those who lived in the Regions. People did not go to its depths very often and survive. Only tales of death and worse ever came from the heart of Dreardim. The three companions had floated some leagues in the strong current and were now beyond the reach of Maradass for a time. Flindas wanted to know the situation in the Regions. Maradass may already have taken the lands. Kerran's mother had told them of black horsemen who had come to Westerval. If the Regions were in the hands of Maradass already, and the fleet from Zeta had not arrived, what chance had they now of ever reaching the sanctuary of the Magic Isles?

To return up the river was to walk into the hands of Maradass, and to cross the forest would take many days in unknown and very dangerous country. The beast they had heard in the forest would not be the only one, and there would be more than savage beasts in the forest to be afraid of. Flindas remembered Kerran's strange story of the dead hands which had reached to him from the mist. In their discussions together Kerran had showed more fear of the misted valleys than he had of the wild dogs that later had come close to ending his life. There was one other choice which Flindas could see that would take them to the coast. They could build a raft and float down river to the Crossroads, or beyond to the sea. He had no idea of what lay ahead but the alternatives were few, and fraught with danger. The unknown could sometimes be the easiest way he thought to himself as he tried to sleep in the cool night air. Somewhere on the river much of the little they carried had been lost, including the three warm cloaks of rabbit skins.

The three travellers woke to a chill mist that hung upon the forest, bringing with it a death-like silence. The swift flowing river made little sound as it swept by, cut in two by the small island where they had spent the night. Flindas told the others of his plan to build a raft and float to the coast. Tris thought he joked until he pointed out the dangers of their few possible roads.

"The river here is too swift for a raft to survive," he said. "I have seen it far to the north where it is wide and slow moving. It will be another long journey but I see little choice in this." He looked towards the trees for a moment. "I fear the forest most by night. We cannot sleep on the shore. You must have heard the beast in the night. When we have a raft we can sleep on it, but each night until then, we must seek shelter away from the trees. This may be the only island on the river but I think not. Even without a raft I think we will travel faster and with more safety if we go on the river."

He looked to where many broken trees and limbs had been washed against the island by the current. Some had been pushed high during some past flood and had not been in the water for a long time.

"We will swim with the help of a log," said Flindas. "If we come to dangerous rapids or falls we will pass them on foot and return to the river as soon as possible."

It did not take them long to find a large limb that would help to keep them afloat and they dragged it to the shoreline. They were preparing to leave the island when Tris smelt the dogs.

"Marauders," she said urgently.

Quickly they launched the log and slipped into the water. They were far downstream, keeping low behind the floating log, when they heard the howl of the black dog from the island.

"He has found our scent," said Tris. "Not seen us though."

They stayed in the water and saw no sign of marauders on either bank. The black dogs were soon left far behind. They travelled many leagues during the first day, the river Glandrin-dar flowing wide and deep about them. No rapids barred their way and the current pushed them far into Dreardim. Dark brooding trees hung back from the river, leaving a rocky tumbled edge between the water and the forest, and here they rested for a time. The water had been deathly cold and they warmed themselves in the sun which had broken through the mist, driving it from the vast river basin they had entered. The floor of the forest at the edge of the river grew many edible mushrooms and late berries. They easily caught several large lizards that basked on the warm rocks, for they were not afraid of these strange two legged beings.

By nightfall of the following day the River Glandrin-dar had slowed and widened considerably. They found themselves on a small rocky peninsula which jutted out into the river a short way, giving them a safer camp than if they had been within the forest. Maradass must surely know of their presence on the river. So rather than seek a place of hiding, they built a fire with enough wood to keep it burning through the night. There were few wild beasts that would attack a group armed with fire.

Flindas remained awake for much of the night, his eyes and ears open to the sounds from the forest. Nothing disturbed their rest, but in the morning they found traces of a large animal which had stood on the sandy soil of the river bank, and watched them from beyond the firelight. Flindas studied the marks of the large four legged animal, which could stand on its hind legs. He had never seen such tracks anywhere in the lands. Large padded feet with the tell tale scratches of claws, showed on earth and stone.

"Not something I care to meet," said Leana as Flindas had shown her the size of the creature.

"I agree," said Flindas. "Today we will build a raft. There is wood and the river runs deep. I do not expect rapids with the river so wide."

They began to collect wood for the raft as the sun climbed above the distant tree clad hills of the river basin. There were strong vines amongst the thick undergrowth which grew amongst the trees. Not knowing if the night creature hunted by day they kept a wary eye on the forest, and by noon the raft was complete. Four large broken limbs had been brought together at the water's edge, and by tying many smaller lengths across the logs they were able to raise a platform above the water level, if the river continued to flow smoothly. They tied on a layer of brushwood and long grass which grew at the edge of the river bed to make the raft more comfortable, and then they cast off into the river.

The travellers drifted to the north on the strong currents. The long poles they had with them may be needed later, but for now they floated easily with the river. By day's end they had covered a good distance, though the river had now widened considerably, the current slowing to what would be a fast walking pace on land. Their craft had floated much nearer to the eastern bank and the blue haze they saw to the west was the other side of the river, lost in the gathering darkness. Deciding to remain on the water, they drifted on through the night, at times hearing the cry of strange animals in the dark forest as it slipped by.

Five more days passed on the river and nothing had

disturbed their journey except for the beasts that had growled in the night. The current had slowed considerably and they found that they must use the poles to keep the raft moving. By the morning of the following day they reached a vast lake. The western shore now lost from sight. The raft was lying much lower in the water and it was useless now, for the current had been absorbed by the lake. Somewhere at its distant northern end, Flindas knew they would find the outfall where the river continued to the lands beyond the forest, but they would have to walk there. He could see several islands further out on the lake, and by the end of the day he thought it might be necessary to swim to one. The three companions left their raft and began to skirt the eastern shore of the wide forbidding lake.

It felt good to walk again. The cramped raft had not allowed much movement for them and their cooking fires on the riverbank had been few. The way ahead was not difficult and keeping away from the forest they walked across boulders and sometimes small beaches at the edge of the lake shore. Many smaller waterways fed the lake from the eastern hills. The companions were often wet and by the time they reached the shelter of a small island, not far from the lakeshore, they were cold and hungry. The small fire, built on the far side of the island from the forest, was a welcome friend as a heavy mist began to form along the shores of the lake. The sun cast its last light upon the shrouded waters as the full moon rose in the east like a ghostly phantom of itself.

The island was a large tumble of boulders where a few scanty trees and grasses clung to the little soil which had collected there. Tris, who despaired for want of game, had managed to scoop a large fish from a stream which had joined the lake. Her smile of glee, as she had held the fish aloft, had been more than equalled by the smiles of the others when that night they ate the delicious fish. The moon had climbed well into the sky when they laid themselves to rest. Flindas did not like to leave the forest unwatched, even though they could barely see the darker haze through the mist. He sat with his back against a stunted tree and observed the shoreline for much of the night, when he could stay awake no longer he woke Leana, and it was during her watch that the beast came.

Leana had been watching for sometime when in the pale moonlight she saw movement on the opposite shoreline. In the dense mist, though the forest was no great distance from her, she could see little that might tell her the true nature of the animal. It was large and moved on four legs along the lake side from the south, and then a thick bank of mist moved gently across the water between her and the forest. For a time she could not make out the shoreline, and the last she saw of the animal was its dark shadowy shape as it neared the point where they had swum to the small rocky island.

She thought to call the others who slept beside the glowing fire, but chose to be sure of any danger before disturbing them needlessly. There was no further sign of the beast and after a time she began to relax again. The night was still and silent, not a sound coming from lake or forest. It was only in the brief moments before the creature emerged that Leana saw the large dark head gliding silently towards the island. It suddenly gained its footing and sprang from the water. Leana cried out to the others but the beast was almost upon her, then it passed, leaping across the island towards the fire.

Leana came to her feet unhurt, surprised at her good fortune. She rushed quickly towards the firelight, drawing the large knife, which Flindas had to given her. The animal was upon the others before they could rise. Tris was first to her feet as the creature leapt upon Flindas. In the darkness and mist he fought with the wild howling animal. The two women ran to the aid of their warrior friend but slowed in astonishment as they heard amazed laughter from Flindas. The great beast was looming over him as if eating his head from his shoulders and Flindas laughed again. He wrestled with the huge grey dog, dragging him to the ground and rolling away in play.

"It is Rark!" he called to the others who had heard him tell of the large mountain dog.

Rark leapt upon Flindas again, carrying him to the ground, his great tongue licking at his friend's face. Finally the huge mountain dog let Flindas rise without crushing him to the ground again. They both stood panting and looking at each other as if ready to begin again. Flindas reached out and scratched behind the great dog's ears.

"Kerran is in the land," he said. "Tolth and the fleet must have arrived."

"How did he find us?" asked Tris, incredulous at the sudden appearance of the huge dog.

Rark greeted her, and after sniffing briefly at her and Leana, he seemed to accept them as friends of Flindas, and therefore as friends of his own.

"I do not know how he comes here," replied Flindas. "But I am very glad of his company."

He could not stop reaching out and ruffling the mountain dog's huge body. Leana built up the fire, and in its light they now saw the numerous wounds which Rark carried, he had not escaped the dangers of the forest unscathed. There were many signs of dried blood upon his matted coat, at first light Flindas cleaned the dog's injuries at the water's edge. He found a number of smaller wounds but the one which worried him most was a row of deep claw marks which had raked the dog's shoulder viciously. Though almost all else was gone, Flindas had managed to keep his small bag of medicines and ointments in the pouch at his hip. Flindas allowed the wounds to dry and then applied a small amount of salve to the worst of the injuries. Rark accepted all the attention stoically and when it came time to go, Flindas noted that the dog showed no signs of wishing to return the way he had come. The troops of Maradass may no longer be behind them, but Rark, who had often led the way on dangerous roads, was now inclined to follow his friend's choice.

As the mist cleared from the surface of the lake the four companions began to make their way north along the shore, clambering over boulders and walking soft sandy beaches. Tris's shoes had finally fallen apart and she now went barefoot and did not seem to mind the change. The boots that Flindas wore had become so thin in the soles that he had lined the inner with leathery bark from a tree he did not know. There were many trees and birds in the forest which Flindas had never seen before. Often they would startle creatures in the undergrowth which were too quick to be seen or caught. Flindas wondered at the dread which surrounded the name of Dreardim, there were fell beasts in the forest, Rark had met at least one, but Flindas had faced many dangers before, and the walk beside the lake was quite enjoyable compared with many roads he had travelled. Nothing disturbed them that night, and with Rark beside them, they slept soundly, his keen ears picking up any night sounds before their eyes could ever see its source. The next day saw the travellers reach the northern end of the lake, there were now no islands and so they camped on a small beach, their backs to a large log which had become embedded in the sand. They ate the fish that they had caught that day and settled down for the night.

The moon was darkened by approaching storm clouds and Rark did not sense the creature when it came. The mountain dog had moved away from the fire towards the forest, for it was from the trees that they expected danger. The first that Flindas knew of the attack was when he felt something slithering around his ankle, he jerked awake but the thing had him by both legs. He cried out to the others as he reached for his sword which lay beside him, his companions leapt to their feet from beside the low burning fire and in the near darkness they could see Flindas being dragged towards the water's edge as he hacked furiously at something which held him.

All Tris could see was a grey moving tangle, as though a huge snake, or more than one, had come from the lake. With a cry she leapt to the aid of her warrior friend as Rark raced towards the water's edge, his huge jaws attacking the slippery writhing creature. Tris and Leana were side by side, slashing violently at the twisting, living coils, but their knives were turned aside; the skin of the creeping thing was harder than any they had ever known.

Slowly, but inexorably, Flindas was drawn towards the waters of the lake. In the gloom his companions heard the fear in his voice as again and again he slashed with his sword. He could not penetrate the slithering wet thing which held him and then a coil slid up his body and tightened around his chest. The frustrated howling of Rark was joined by the sobbing cries of Leana and Tris as their blades continued to be turned aside. Tris raced to the fire. There was time. Whatever the thing might be, it seemed in no hurry to take Flindas into the depths. She ran back with a glowing brand and thrust it hard against the creature, Flindas roared in pain as the coils suddenly tightened. The wild howls from Rark joining with his friend's anguished cry. The thing then dragged Flindas more rapidly towards the lake. He was at the edge of the water and being drawn deeper, when a coil of the beast looped around Leana's legs. She screamed and stumbled to her knees in the shallow waters, her knife falling from her hand.

Tris continued to attack with her own blade, tears of fear and defeat streaming down her face. Rark had managed to get a hold on the hard sliding coil which held Flindas, but it was of no use. The creature moved swiftly then, dragging Leana and Flindas into deeper water. Tris plunged after them, blinded by her tears.

"Save yourself!" cried Flindas, terror ringing in his voice.

Tris waded deeper, following until the water reached almost to her waist. There was a last cry from Leana as she was pulled below the surface. The sword of Flindas was held high still attacking the beast, and then he too was drawn beneath the waters of the lake.

Tris stood wide-eyed in silent horror as Rark swam in circles, howling and thrusting his head below the surface. He would not cease, and as the moments slipped by the enormity of what had just happened came down upon Tris like a dark and terrifying cloud. It had taken such a long time, and yet she had been able to do nothing to save her friends. Through her dread came the thought that the creature may still be lurking beneath her. She turned and plunged towards the shore, tears blurring her vision.

Tris stumbled from the water and fell. After a moment she turned and looked back in horror at the dark surface of the lake. Rark was still swimming about in confusion, no longer howling, instead a strange whimpering came from the huge dog. Tris stood and called him but he would not come. She remained standing, with tears streaming, and looked to where he swam, and then, further out on the lake, she thought she saw a shimmering light glow briefly on the surface of the water. Tris dashed the tears from her eyes and looked again. She was not mistaken. An eerie red brightness flickered and played across the surface of the lake. Suddenly the water bulged upward, and Rark was swept towards the shore where Tris was met by a violent wave, which caused her to fall, the water rushing over her. She struggled to rise as further waves pounded at her. Then the water began to recede and Tris found that she could stand. Rark was nearby, looking steadily into the gloom beyond the shore.

The light which Tris had seen was no longer there and she waited without hope for it to come again. Rark moved back towards the shoreline, and then paused at the water's edge. Tris's heart leapt in her breast as she saw the mountain dog give a very tentative wag of his tail. She looked far out on the lake as the moon slipped from behind a cloud to brighten the gloom. Rark suddenly barked loudly and leapt into the water. On the edge of hearing, Tris heard a distant splashing, and far out on the lake she could see a small disturbance. She dared not hope until she was sure, and then there could be little doubt, someone was swimming for the shore. Tris cried out in joyous wonder as she finally saw those who swam towards her. Flindas was pulling Leana along in his wake as he struggled to gain the shore.

Tris leapt in, and disregarding any danger she struggled towards her friends. Flindas swam slowly, holding on to Rark until his feet touched the bottom. Tris reached them and helped Leana from the water. Flindas was in some pain but Leana looked as though she was one of the walking dead from the old tales. She stumbled a short way up the beach and then collapsed. Flindas fell to his knees but seemed more concerned for Leana than himself. He said not a word as he helped Leana to a comfortable place near the still glowing fire. Rark stood back as if knowing that he must, while Tris built up the flames until they crackled and warmed her companions.

Leana lay exhausted and unmoving, her eyes closed, as Flindas dressed a wound to the palm of her hand. Tris saw it in the firelight. It looked like a severe burn and was in the unmistakable shape of a quarter circle, the size of the Seacrest fragment that still hung around Leana's neck. It was not until Leana had fallen into an exhausted sleep that Flindas spoke.

"She saved us both," he said to Tris, without lifting his eyes from the pale almost death-like face. "The Seacrest burned the thing and her also. I thought us lost. I was being drawn down. I saw bright red fire and amazingly the creature let go." The words of Flindas came in short exhausted bursts. He looked up to where Tris sat near him, a look of grave concern on her face. "I cannot speak any more," he told her and hung his head, finally lying down and slipping into a fitful, disturbed sleep.

Tris and Rark kept watch for the remainder of the night but nothing came to trouble them from the forest, or from the depths of the silent lake.

For the next two days the travellers remained camped near the shores of the lake. Leana recovered slowly from the ordeal and spoke little with her companions. For a time she again seemed to be under the spell of Maradass, yet during the evening of the second day she came from her quiet solitude and was able to tell them the little she remembered of her struggle with the thing from beneath the surface of the lake. She had been pulled under and felt certain that she would die. The creature was entwined about her and death had seemed the only possibility. Then a vision had come to her. She had seen Landin in the waters beside her. He had called to her but once and then he was gone. Through the dark enveloping waters she had heard his desperate words: *Ma-Zurin-Bidar*.

Leana had clasped the Seacrest fragment and red fire had at once radiated from it, scorching her hand and burning the creature. She remembered being released and sinking, and then she could recall nothing more until sometime the previous day when a dream had come to her. Landin had walked with her beside the lake and they had spoken of death. Leana remembered little of the dream except her brother's final words. *Death is but a continuation of life*, he had told her. *Look for me in your dreams, for that is where you will find me. It may be that we shall never meet again, but know that I am always beside you.* Leana could remember nothing more to tell her companions, and then after she had eaten a little of the fish and berries, which Tris offered, she slept soundly until dawn.

Flindas was eager to continue their journey, for he felt exposed upon the shore of the lake. He now carried a long sharpened staff, though nothing more had been seen of the creature from the water or any beast from the forest. In the shallows he had found the long knife which he had given to Leana, but his sword lay somewhere on the bottom of the lake and nothing would bring him to search for it in those dark waters. The morning had come unusually cold, with a freshening wind from the south. the surface of the lake was whipped by the wind until spray broke free of its hold and flew through the moving air. Waves washed the shore as the travellers made their way north. Rain came and with it a violent storm. Dreardim was torn at and stripped of dead leaves by the powerful winds which battered the forest. The winds became so strong that the travellers were forced to shelter in the lee of a large boulder until the gale eased and would allow them to continue. Not until late that night did the tempest pass by, rumbling across the vast expanse of forest to the north and east, lightning flickered in the distant thunderheads long after the sound and fury had departed.

The Coming of Zard

For a long time there was only darkness. Kerran struggled to overcome it, as in his dream he again saw the three figures as they leapt into the river and eluded the black horsemen of Maradass. Kerran knew now that Flindas and his two companions were alive and had entered the Regions. He wished to wake and tell of his dream vision but he could not. He tried to battle his way out of the darkness which engulfed him but he was trapped. A dread came upon him as he saw a faint blue glow in the darkness. It grew until it overpowered his vision. An evil laughter came into his mind. It filled the air around him.

"I am coming," said the creaking, venomous voice of Maradass. "Fool! You fly in the face of all the power I hold, and yet you do not expect to fall."

Again the laughter echoed within the blue fire and beyond into the darkness, and Kerran felt himself engulfed, smothered. With a violent effort he began to fight back. His mind cleared a little, the voice of Maradass losing some of its control. It seemed that he fought for a very long time, and then it was as though he simply shrugged and the bonds melted from him. His mind felt cleared of an evil spell and he smiled within his shadow. Kerran opened his eyes to find those of Tolth and Verardian looking into his own, deep concern clouding their brows. He tried to speak but found his mouth dry and unable to form the words. Verardian helped him to drink, and then Kerran rested his head back onto the pillow.

"Leana and Flindas are in the lands," he whispered when he could finally manage the words.

The look of sudden wonder on both his friend's faces showed of their need to know more, and Kerran then told of his dream. There could be no doubt. Leana and the others were somewhere in the forest. Perhaps still on the river where Maradass's troops hunted them. Word was sent quickly to Torian who immediately began organising a troop of Elbrand to go through the south of the forest to Westerval. Though Kerran was still weak from his dream he said that he must go with them, and Tolth could not deny him.

Kerran was not fully recovered when he rode from the camp with one hundred Elbrand. They would skirt the valleys of mist and reach Westerval within a few days. As they rode Kerran kept looking above for the familiar spread of white wings but he saw nothing of his companion. He feared for the hawk's safety but could do nothing to ease his worry. Rark too had not reappeared and Kerran hoped that the dog had not met with a sad fate at the hands of black soldiers. The troop moved as fast as they could through the rocky outcrops and sudden deep valleys of the forest, riding hard to the west.

It was almost evening of the third day and the troop's captain was soon expected to call a halt for the night, when from above Kerran heard a familiar cry and Storm fell from the clouds. He swooped through the trees and then disappeared back into the treetops above. In the few moments of flight Kerran had caught a flash of dark red on the white of Storm's feathers. He had been damaged but had seemed to fly in the dangerous manoeuvre to prove to Kerran that he was not harmed. The last rays of sunlight caught the white wings far above as Storm returned to his place high on the wind. By nightfall they had reached the southern end of a misted valley, whether it was the one Kerran remembered or another he could not tell. He shuddered within himself and did not sleep well that night. By first light they were in the saddle again, eating as they rode. Scouts rode well ahead of the main force, for if black horsemen had been in Westerval, then they could still be in the forest. It was late on the following day that the troop finally came to the thinned trees and cut stumps which told that they neared the edge of the forest and inhabited lands.

Kerran looked out from the trees upon the distant village of Westerval where small spirals of smoke drifted from many chimneys as evening meals were being prepared. Nowhere was there sign of black horsemen or marauders. Kerran longed to rush through the forest towards his mother's home but the Elbrand would not allow it. They studied the land for some time before they were sure that no troops of Maradass camped upon the sloping ground leading to the river, or amongst the outer trees of the forest. The sun had slipped beyond the far mountains of the Bittering when Kerran was carefully escorted to the trees near the back door of his silent home. Smoke billowed softly from the chimney and the Elbrand remained motionless for a long time, watching.

From inside the house, which Kerran knew so well, he could see movement just inside the window by the door. A large candle was being lit. He knew the movements so well for it was his mother lighting the evening lamp. She would soon sit by the small fire and finish preparing her solitary meal. Kerran's eyes glanced across the yard to a distant tree. Beneath it he saw the stone marker where his father lay at rest. The Elbrand were eventually satisfied and Kerran was allowed to approach the house. He became cautious himself as he came nearer the dwelling, but not from any fear of Maradass. His mother had not seen him for almost a year and she may presume him dead. His mother was not a superstitious woman but his sudden appearance in the night might cause her great shock. There was nothing else he could do but knock gently on the door. He heard the sound of a pot being stirred. He knocked louder and the stirring ceased. Footsteps came towards the door, slowly, unsure.

"Who is it? What do you want?" called his mother's voice

from behind the door and for a moment Kerran could find no words.

"Mother," he finally said to the door. "It is me, Kerran. I have come home."

Kerran's mother threw back the door and stood looking at the bearded stranger who stood before her. In the dim light his face remained in shadow and his clothes were outlandish to her eyes. She began to close the door quickly, but he called to her.

"No mother, it *is* me!"

She paused and then opened the door wider to allow the light from the lamp to reach his features, and then she came forward, slowly, smiling.

"It *is* you," she said softly as she reached up and touched the unfamiliar light beard that he had not cared to shave. "You have grown my son," she said gently, her eyes brimming with tears.

Kerran crossed the doorstep and held his mother in his arms. They stood like that for a long time. She keened a low soothing song as she patted him gently on the back.

"Come by the fire," she said "I will fetch you some food." She looked up at him, her hands holding his. "You have grown, but there seems little enough meat on your bones," she said patting his arm softly. She wiped away her tears and went to the table to cut several large slices of bread, a stew cooked on the small fire. "You have been to many strange places I hear," she said as she ladled stew into a bowl.

"How is it you know?" asked Kerran surprised. "What have you heard?"

"There was one who was here called Flindas," she said, and then Kerran understood. "He came here to give me news of you," his mother continued. "He was with two very strange women, and at first I would not talk to them. There are evil times in Westerval and any Outlander could mean danger. He finally convinced me and told me of your journey. He hoped that I had word of you and was disappointed when I had not, and now here you are perhaps only half a moon later on the very doorstep where he stood."

She hovered over Kerran as he ate heartily of her delicious rabbit stew. She could not help but reach out often and touch her beloved son. She stroked his hair and shoulders as if to reassure herself that he was real.

"You speak of evil times in Westerval?" he asked through a mouthful. "What is this evil?"

"Black horsemen and dogs," she told him almost in a whisper. "They came two moons passed and terrorised the town and the country about. They killed a few of the men who fought against them, and then robbed much from the people. Poor Master Bandra the cart-maker was one who was killed. He was one of the few people from the town who was ever kind to me after your father died." She stopped speaking for a time, the grief in her life held at bay by the presence of her son. "The horsemen have gone now it seems," she finally said. "There is no sign of them since the day your friend came."

"Did he tell you of his travels?" asked Kerran, eager to hear news of Flindas.

"He told me that they had come a great distance but little more," his mother replied. "They remained only a short time, mostly he sought news of you."

Kerran talked far into the night, telling his mother of his travels. He took the Seacrest from around his neck and placing it in her hand he told her of its meaning. She looked with great wonder into her son's face as the story was unravelled. When the tale was done she stood without speaking and went to a small chest that had always contained her special things. There were a few drawings that his father had done of the land and forest around Westerval, a small delicate vase that had belonged to her own mother, and a few other cherished things. As a child Kerran had always thought of the chest as a place of small magical wonders. He remembered the fascinating glass buttons and beads which had come to his mother from many different places. Though she was poor, this was her treasure. Kerran watched as she began removing things gently from the chest.

"What is it you search for mother?" he asked.

Her only reply was a mysterious smile as she delved further

into the small chest. Finally she found what she wanted and returned to the fire carrying a tiny pouch. She handed it to Kerran without a word and he felt the weight of a small but heavy object through the leather. He drew the tie strings and let the object fall to the palm of his hand. It was an intricately crafted piece of silver. An elegant eight pointed star stood entwined with the limbs and leaves of a finely sculptured tree, circling the star and enmeshed with the tree were three fine rings. The piece was very small in his palm but the clearest of details showed the marvellous skill of the maker's hand. Kerran turned it over and saw carved into the trunk of the tree as if by another hand a letter unknown to him from his recent reading lessons.

"Where did this come from?" he asked his mother, wondering that he had never seen it in his life before.

"Your father left it for you," she said. "He once said that if anything were to happen to him I was to give you this when you became a man. There was much in your father that was secret and hidden but I cared not. He loved us and that was enough. He told me almost nothing of his life before we became husband and wife yet I still wanted him, for I loved him dearly. He told me that one day he would be able to tell all of his story to us. That he and you were of an ancient line he spoke of just once. He wanted you to have this and so it is yours now." She stroked the small silver piece with her fingertips before passing it to Kerran. "Before you left I thought that you were still a boy," she told him. "Now I see that you have become a man."

Their talk continued into the early morning, Kerran's mother unable to rest or sleep now that her son had come home. She knew now that he must return to the forest and the defence of the Regions. She tried to feel glad that he lived and breathed, and yet fear for his future stalked her thoughts. Finally she could remain awake no longer, and he led her sleepily to her bed, then he lay down on his own, falling into untroubled dreams.

As the moonlight spread across the land, the Elbrand who had travelled with Kerran began to scout through the outer forest and towards the river bank, where they hoped to find evidence of the recent chase. By the river they came upon the place where many horsemen had stood above the current, then had followed it to the north. Signs could be seen beneath the trees but only daylight would reveal the true nature of the chase, and perhaps its outcome.

Kerran slept late and it was the smell of his mother's cooking which finally reached through his senses and into his sleeping thoughts. To feel his own bed beneath him and lazily open his eyes to the familiar room was a pleasure he enjoyed slowly. Then he dressed and greeted his mother. She was quiet this morning, reaching out and simply touching him, looking into his eyes as if she sought answers to unknown questions. There came a soft tapping at the door and Kerran rose to speak for some time with the captain of the Elbrand. The signs showed that marauders and twenty or more riders had followed Flindas and the others into the forest, keeping to the river side, while others had left the troop and galloped towards the South Road. A number of the Elbrand had begun to make their own way down the river and would send word back as soon as there was any.

Kerran remained a further two days with his mother, while news slowly filtered back to him from the Elbrand. They had found horses at a point where the river cut sharply into the side of a steep range of hills. Then the Elbrand had picked up the trail of marauders and the riders, now on foot the horsemen had made their way along the riverbank, clambering over rocks and through the dense undergrowth in their search for the three fugitives. The first sign of something strange was when the Elbrand had come upon the mauled bodies of two marauders. A strong animal with claws, or perhaps a man wielding a weapon of many jagged blades had torn the dogs savagely. Another league downstream they had come upon the remains of several of the Maradass horsemen. They too had been attacked by the same creature, unless there was more than one. The Elbrand who first found the bodies had shuddered at the look of terror on the dead men's faces.

Then the Elbrand had moved further along the river, the

dense forest, threatening and dark. They came finally to the place where the remaining soldiers had made a last stand against their attacker. Here a cold fire lay trampled and the partly devoured bodies of man and dog had been scattered about the blood soaked clearing. The Elbrand had returned quickly. They knew now that all the riders were dead and that Leana and the others must be now far beyond their reach, if they had not suffered a similar fate as the soldiers of Maradass. No trace had been found on either side of the river to show that the three had left the water, only on a small island had there been signs that they had escaped, at least for a time.

Kerran and his mother said a sad goodbye in the yard of the house. As he mounted she reached out silently to touch him one more time.

"Goodbye, son, take care to return," she spoke these last words to herself as Kerran and the Elbrand disappeared from view amongst the trees.

Though she could not see them she knew that ten Elbrand now remained to protect her. Should riders of Maradass return, the warriors of Zeta would take her into the forest and safety.

Kerran and the Elbrand travelled quickly and returned to the refuge late at night, pushing through the darkness to be hailed by a far-flung sentry of Zeta. The camp was quiet when he reached the dark cave entrance, and Kerran could see the glow of embers and the sleeping forms of the three Amitarl. Another man lay near the fire, Kerran could not make out who it might be and in the near darkness he lay down, where sleep clasped him and he was carried by it into the late morning. When he woke the cave was empty, but the sound of voices at the entrance told of a conference between Tolth and others. Kerran emerged into the sunlight after eating a little food at the fire. Tolth, Mantris and Torian were there. Kerran then recognised the man Dantas as he stood away from the others, looking down on the army spread about the valley. Dantas turned as he heard Kerran being welcomed by the others. Their words were courteous but their grave voices told Kerran that all was not well.

Tolth began to tell him of the news from Andrian. The

large army of so called Stone Soldiers accompanied by black foot soldiers and horsemen had been observed for many days marching down the distant City Highroad. Scouts had reported their progress each day and nothing seemed more probable than that they would continue on to the city, the last report had them two days march from the junction of the two Highroads. A watch was kept at the meeting of the ways but to the surprise of those who lay hidden there most of the black army did not appear. Only the regular foot soldiers and horsemen had passed by, but not the Stone Army.

Men of the Southlands had scouted the country all over. An army of many thousand men, stone or not, could hardly vanish in such rocky, bare country, but the search had been in vain. The Stone Army had disappeared and left not a trace. There was a look of great concern on all faces at the council meeting.

"The powers of Maradass increase," said Tolth. "We cannot know where that army may be, or what evil deed Maradass has planned for them."

Scouts would be doubled. Nothing would be able to move across the plains or roads that they would not hear of. Tolth was distracted for much of the day and it was not until evening that Kerran showed him the small silver sculpture.

"A truly wonderful thing," said Tolth as he turned the piece over in his hand, then he stopped and looked closely at the tree. He held it near the fire to see better, then exclaimed in astonishment. "Rishtan-Sta!" he said with amazement in his voice, holding the sculpture in awe.

He looked again, almost burning himself on the embers to examine the sculpture more closely by the light of the flames. "Yes," he said finally, the glitter in his eyes telling of his wonder. "The letter carved into the back is the high initial of Rishtan-Sta in the old language. There can be little doubt that this piece was in your father's possession for an age. This is a wondrous thing to possess. See how it has never worn in all that time. There is some old magic in this piece. Keep it well."

He handed it back to Kerran who returned the sculpture to its leather bag which then went into the larger pouch at his hip, that night his sleep was troubled by many dreams but by morning he could remember little of them.

The day passed almost without event. A group of the hardiest Elbrand set out that morning to travel through the outer fringes of the forest to the north. They would take perhaps twelve days to reach a place near the point on the River Glandrin-dar where it emerged from the forest. There they would wait in hope that Leana and the others might emerge that way from the forest. Dreardim had many evil tales to go with its name, but none as fearful as those of the deep craggy valleys through which the river ran. Here it was said the earth itself was of evil intent, and fell creatures stalked the hills. None would give up hope but all knew the dreadful stories of Dreardim.

Kerran went to sleep wondering where Rark might be. Again wild dreams swept through his sleeping world and by morning he felt exhausted, though he remembered nothing of the night. During the day a heavy depression hung on him, he could not explain how he felt, and he became withdrawn from those around him. It was not the disappearance of Rark which affected him, though he did worry much for the dog. No, it was something else that overshadowed his day and made him ache with unknown troubles. He took a short walk late in the day and found himself, as the sunset, at a high point above the cave and valley. He was alone though he knew that Elbrand were amongst the trees and rocky outcrops nearby.

Kerran watched as the sun disappeared beyond the distant marching treetops. He stood there for some time, and then felt eyes boring into his back. He spun around but there was no one there, except that the full moon was rising slowly from the east. Kerran looked at it and for a moment was comforted. He had always felt an affinity with the moon. He began to turn, to retrace his steps back to the camp, when something on the face of the moon caught his eye. At the very centre of the silvery orb, a dark patch began to grow. The moon floated above the trees now, the dark area becoming larger and more distinct. A sinister face began to form but it was not Maradass who now gazed out at him with wicked intent. It was his first born, Zard, who now looked upon Kerran from the face of the moon. The face kept its dark malicious expression, the eyes afire and burning into Kerran's. The mouth suddenly broke into wicked laughter though the eyes never left Kerran's.

"I am coming for you," said the Black One.

The feelings that Kerran had felt during the day suddenly intensified and he fell to the ground. Looking up with difficulty he saw the laughing face of Zard slowly disappear from the moon. An Elbrand was beside him almost immediately.

"Young master are you ill?" came the words from the green and brown soldier.

He helped Kerran to his feet, and when he found that the young man could not walk alone he called a friend, and they carried Kerran back into camp, laying him gently on his bed beside the fire.

"I have seen Zard," Kerran said to Tolth as the old man came to his side.

"I too have felt this," said Tolth. "My nights have been darkened by dreams, and today a strange heaviness has hung on me that I could not throw off. Zard comes and his presence affects us all."

"I fear to sleep," said Kerran.

The confidence he had felt in himself during the last few days had melted as wax before a flame under the cold dark eyes of Zard. Verardian came to sit by Kerran and placed a gentle hand on the young man's brow. A feeling of lightness slowly passed through Kerran, his cramped and fearful thoughts beginning to fade. Kerran eased slowly into sleep, the darkness of his dreams kept at bay by the healing powers of Verardian.

A cool mist lay upon the valley when Kerran emerged from the cave the next morning. There was still no sign of Rark and he worried much, but could do no more than the Elbrand scouts who kept a watch for the dog. Nothing had been seen of him which led them to believe that Rark may have gone far to the west, deeper into the forest. No sign of his body had been found amongst the trees to the east. At noon a war council was held. The scouts reported no movements by the Black Armies. Maradass had paused, as though waiting for the armies of Zeta to move against him. Still, the forest was their safest refuge, for little could go undetected passed the watchful eyes of the Elbrand. Torian argued that the war was to free the lands and that they must soon move against the black forces, while they waited in the forest the Region of Andrian was being pillaged and crushed.

It was finally decided that a large force would be sent north through the forest. Torian with five hundred mounted Elbrand and another thousand mounted soldiers would make their way to a refuge which had been found much earlier and then abandoned as Maradass had moved his troops south. They would be within striking distance of the Crossroads but would not move against the Black Army unless fortune gave them a chance to attack smaller numbers split away from the main force. There were still many thousands of the stone soldiers and troops of horsemen at the Crossroads.

By the following morning the horse troops of Zeta were gone and with them went Verardian, who felt that his powers would be needed more amongst those who would directly confront the Black Army. Both Brook and Teaker had gone too with this force, wishing to strike further blows at the army of Maradass. They would travel the South Road until the danger became too great, scouts and runners along the way would tell them whether the Black Army had moved. The refuge in the north, should it be discovered, would be in peril of being overrun by a far superior force. All care would be taken to ensure marauders did not follow a scent back to the refuge. The black dogs remained an all important target for the bowmen of Zeta.

Summer was long passed. The days became cooler and Kerran often spent his time by the fire, talking with Tolth, who continued to study the ancient tattered book on wizards. They had deciphered much but it had told them little.

"There is mention again of the Wizards Way," Tolth said pointing to the familiar characters on a page, which had survived intact amongst the many that were tattered and scarred. "The Wizards Way seems to have been a game of sorts," Tolth continued. "Or possibly a means of communication, perhaps both."

Clasping the Seacrest in his hand, Kerran, with Tolth, worked for days to find meaning in the lost tongue. From the north came news of skirmishes along the fringes of the forest. The casualties were light, the Elbrand preferring to fight on foot and keep their mounts well hidden deeper in the forest. The marauders now feared the darkness beneath the boughs of Dreardim and would only enter when the black horsemen drove them forward. The Stone Army from the South Road had not been seen, gone as if they had never existed. Now the new moon was upon them and they knew that the mighty warrior Zard would once again don his black armour and soon stalk the lands.

Kerran studied the words on the small scroll where Tolth was writing the translated text. Something about the Wizards Way intrigued him, and they had begun to search the tattered book for further mention of it. By the end of a long day they had come upon what seemed to be a partial description of the game, though it still did not make any sense. Many of the jumbled words were interspersed with symbols they could not decipher. There were references to High Wizards and Lesser Wizards, there was a pattern on one page that Kerran had looked at often since he had first seen the book, but nothing of its meaning had come to light. It depicted what must be an eight pointed star, though much of the page was missing. It intrigued Tolth and Kerran, for the symbol seemed important throughout the old times, yet they still felt as though they stumbled about through a dark maze. There were references to what they had finally decided to call 'Wizard Seats' and 'Wizard Lines.' Within the centre of the star was a pattern of smaller dark circles, scattered in what appeared to be a random manner. Two more of these circles could be seen far out on one arm of the star. There were very small symbols within these circles yet they were hard to interpret, dark and aged as they were. Something about the pattern seemed almost familiar to Kerran, yet he could not say why. The eight pointed star was carved into the face of the Seacrest, and also appeared on the small silver sculpture, and yet Kerran could see no connection that told him of its meaning.

The next morning Kerran made his way to the valley floor and the stream which ran along its bottom. The air was cool and he shuddered as he washed the sleep from his eyes, the warmth of the sun not yet finding its way through the steep tree clad slope to the east. Early songbirds called to each other and welcomed the day as the camp awoke. Small spirals of smoke wafting on the chill air. When the runner came into camp Kerran could see that her news was important. The woman was exhausted but pushed herself up the slope which led to the cave. Kerran finished his wash quickly and made his way upward. He saw that Torian was there already, while Mantris could be seen moving quickly towards them from the other side of the valley. The first word that Kerran heard as he came within hearing was *Zard*.

The message had come from the north. The Black Knight had arrived at the Crossroads, his unmistakable tall dark figure astride a powerful white warhorse. He had been seen by the most daring of scouts, who at times would come within sight of the old castle. By noon another scout raced to the cave to bring the news that Zard was now riding south. The messenger shook his head as though he thought the message relayed to him must be wrong.

"He rides alone," the man told them, looking up at the faces of those who heard his words. "He rides the South Road without horsemen or soldiers."

The news was astonishing. Tolth had been waiting for, and expecting a battle with the Black Army commanded by Zard. To have him coming towards them alone was inexplicable. Was his plan to defeat the army of Zeta on his own? In battle Zard could be defeated only if he fought against one adversary. Zard held much strength and power. Yet it was known that even he could tire. He was not invincible. Yet messages kept coming to say that Zard did not stop or falter in his ride into the Southlands. Days passed until finally the Black One reached the point in the road where the first battle had been fought. Those watching said that he had reined in his horse and removed his dark helmet, standing tall in the saddle and looking about the field. The remains of the Black Army's dead still lay scattered there, picked over by roaming packs of wild dogs and scavenger birds. Zard had then turned west and was now riding across the plains towards the forest in a direct line for the refuge.

"I remind you that he cannot be killed if attacked by many," said Tolth to Mantris as the army began to prepare to meet the Black One. "Remember that only in single combat can he be killed, and though the Elbrand are most skilled, I do not believe that any could stand in his way and live. Let him come if it is his intention. Only the powers which I and Kerran hold could possibly conquer him, or turn him aside. I know that many are prepared to face him and die, but this is not an option that we can ever take."

By nightfall Zard had reached the edge of the forest but he did not enter. Those Elbrand amongst the outer trees watched the tall black figure as he stood by his horse, and moved not once the entire night. He faced the forest, while a thin hazy moon shone down upon him. Nothing moved, the stillness hung in the air around the watching men of Zeta, and there were some who felt true fear for the first time in their lives. At first light Zard mounted his white charger and rode beneath the trees of Dreardim. He was watched continuously but cared not it seemed. He rode tall and upright, his head not turning once as he came further into the forest.

It was well past noon when the final runner came in to report that Zard would ride into their hidden valley within moments. Tolth, Kerran and Mantris stood at the entrance to the cave, when the runner had gone Tolth turned to Kerran.

"I think it wise that Zard not see you," he said. "Though he no longer carries any part of the Seacrest much power is passed to him by his father and remains with him. I would not have him test you."

Kerran could see at the end of the valley the soldiers of Zeta moving back amongst the trees. He caught a glimpse of the dark rider and then moved back and entered the cave. He could remain hidden and yet still hear what may be said beyond the cave's mouth. The only other person in the cave was Mindis, who lay on his bed, oblivious to all around him.

Zard rode without haste to the foot of the small slope, where he paused and looked up at those who stood above, turning for a moment he looked back down the valley and then spurred his mount quickly up the rise. The horse and dark rider came to a lunging halt on the level shelf before the cave. He towered over those who stood there and silence held them all for a time.

Elbrand were everywhere in the trees and rocks above, though none could fight Zard and hope to win there were many who would lay down their lives if the Black One chose to attack. The heavy breathing of the horse and the tinkling of its harness were the only sounds that broke the stillness. Tolth stepped forward and spoke.

"What would you here, black son of Maradass?" he said defiantly.

Tolth was answered by a long deathly silence. Zard sat astride his horse for endless creeping moments before he raised his hands to his helmet and pulled it without haste from his head. His dark impenetrable eyes fell on Tolth like death. "What would I here?" he snarled, hatred dripping from each word. "What would I here? I would have what is mine!" His voice lifted in anger and carried to many who shuddered at the sound. "I have come for what you have, old man," Zard growled. "That which your family stole from my family. I will have it back and I will have it now."

"There is nothing here that is yours," Tolth replied, his hand bringing the fragment of Seacrest from the pouch at his waist. "Go back to your evil father and tell him to be gone from these lands. He is the enemy of all true people, and if he does not go, there will be few remaining to tell the story of his end. Be gone from these lands I say, before death takes you again and all of your black hordes."

Zard laughed and the sound cut deep into the fears of those who heard, then it stopped as abruptly as it had begun; the dark eyes coming to rest once again on Tolth.

"You stand there, old man, as though you think you have power to resist me. You have nothing!" he sneered. "You cannot harm me. None amongst your rabble can stand in my way." He laughed again, the evil merriment hanging in the air, threatening. "Give me what is mine!" he cried. The vicious unguarded hate in his voice came like a heavy shadow that spread wide upon his listeners.

"There is nothing here for you," Tolth repeated. His words had a quiet strength which told those about him that he would die rather than submit. Black hatred cooled as Zard held Tolth's eyes with his own.

"You are a simpleton, Amitarl," spat the Black Knight. "You think you have the power to overthrow Maradass, you and that brat who pretends to wizardry." At these words Zard looked around the gathering. "And where does the whelp hide himself?" he asked, his eyes returning to Tolth.

"Far from here, where none will find him," replied Tolth. "You will never have what you desire. Go now before I call on the ancient powers of wizardry I hold to drive you into blackness and death."

"You are a fool to play me for a fool," said Zard. "You do not have the strength old man. 'No death but by single combat.' These are the words of the Philosopher and cannot be undone. No, old charlatan, there is nothing you can do, and now..." He paused a long moment, smiling and looking towards the sun. "The time is here," he ended simply.

There was silence. Zard sat astride his tall war horse, his sneering smile unnerving even Tolth. Within moments there was a cry of many voices from high above, towards the end of the valley soldiers of Zeta could be seen rushing for their arms, while others ran quickly towards the alarm. A bow string sang. Zard caught the arrow as one would catch a fly, and snapped it between his fingers.

"Still you do not understand," he cried, and cast the pieces aside. "Your death is nigh, old man. Give me what I want and save yourselves. Go back to Zeta before the wrath of Maradass falls upon you like stone."

Tolth held the fragment of the Seacrest aloft. "This was never truly yours," he cried. "Go now, for your time is short."

A soft green glow began to emanate from his uplifted hand. Mantris and the others moved away from the light as it grew and dazzled their eyes. A blast of intense power flew from

Tolth's hand. The warhorse cried out and reared backwards as Zard slipped easily from the saddle to the ground and stood before the light. He laughed viciously and strode forward, and then the green light held him for a moment, a look of pain twisting his dark features. Zard wrestled forward and Tolth was driven back towards the cave entrance. From far down the valley could be heard the sounds of battle.

Mantris stood transfixed, unable to take his eyes from the scene before him. Zard struggled forward through the light as Tolth was forced to retreat further, his back to the cave entrance. Mantris suddenly leapt towards the two figures. If Zard could die then who else but an Elbrand might accomplish such a victory. He laboured forward only to be thrown backwards by the power of the struggle. Again he tried, but the fight was beyond him. He stood back and his eyes quickly took in the valley below. Troops of Maradass were forcing the soldiers of Zeta back into the trees: grey troops, spearmen, many thousands of them.

Soldiers of Zeta suddenly appeared from above, forced down the slopes by vast numbers of Stone Soldiers who were attacking from the east. Zard was almost upon Tolth, and Mantris cried out in frustration and fear. Stone Soldiers began to appear through the forest, Elbrand fought and slew many but their numbers were great and their flesh was hard. Mantris drew his own sword and with a fierce battle cry rushed toward the battle. Tolth was beyond any help that he could give and Mantris was soon amongst the fighting, and did not see the outcome of the struggle at the cave's mouth.

Battles raged about the forested valley for the rest of the day, the troops of Zeta, forced to the north and west, battled from besieged hilltops. The grey army pushed relentlessly into their ranks, spears held forward and large shields covering their bodies. They fought with no great agility, the weight of numbers being their sole advantage. Many lay about the battlefield amongst the green and brown of Zeta. Though the Stone Soldiers were not difficult to strike, they were not easy to kill. The Stone Army fought on with the most vicious of injuries and they did not bleed as ordinary men. Their blood, though red, did not flow from their wounds, but thickened quickly.

By dusk the troops of Zeta had forced a retreat through the engulfing army of Stone Soldiers, they were well to the north when suddenly the grey army ended their advance and simply disappeared back amongst the trees. Many soldiers of Zeta circled wide through the forest, attacking the enemy's flanks, and then pushed on towards the refuge where peace had reigned only that morning. Mantris returned now to the valley, the grey army was gone, even their dead seemed to have melted into the earth. He walked up the slope towards the cave and feared what he might find. Numerous soldiers of Zeta lay dead about the cave entrance. Drawing his sword Mantris stooped and entered slowly. Little could be seen until his eyes grew used to the darkness. The cave looked as though a great wind had rushed through it. Ashes from the fire were spread upon the floor, mixed with the bedding and other possessions that lay scattered or thrown against the walls. Mantris looked about but the cave was empty. Tolth, Kerran and Mindis were gone.

The army of Zeta buried their dead during the night and on into the morning. Many would be sadly grieved for when the news came to Zeta. Without Tolth, Mantris and the army of Zeta felt desolate. Without the two Seacrest fragments, which surely must now be in the hands of Zard, there seemed little hope in a war so inclined towards the enemy. The Stone Army had appeared from the very earth said the scouts who had seen them emerge, and they still shook with the terror of it. They described the sudden moving of the ground beneath their very feet as line upon line of grey, stone faced soldiers had risen slowly from the forest floor, as if grown from some evil magic seed. They must have returned to the earth thought Mantris, for there was no longer any sign of them. The magic in it was beyond anything he had ever imagined or dreamed of. The valley was no longer safe and at dawn he ordered the camp evacuated. By noon none but those beneath the earth and stone mounds were left in the valley to tell of the sombre army that marched to the north through the trees. Torian and his force were still in the forest near the Crossroads, and Mantris could think of nothing better than joining him, though all seemed lost now; nothing he knew could now stand in the way of Maradass and his Black Son.

9 781991 189837